ng author of FIRST
mbo was created. He
erican Literature from the
ate University and taught in the English
tment at the University of Iowa. The co-president of the International Thriller Writers Organization, he is a multiple bestselling author with over eighteen million copies of his books in print, translated into twenty-six languages. His titles include such bestsellers as THE BROTHERHOOD OF THE ROSE, THE FIFTH PROFESSION, EXTREME DENIAL and recently NIGHTSCAPE and CREEPERS. Noted for his research, Morrell is a graduate of the National Outdoor Leadership School for wilderness survival. He is also an honorary lifetime member of the Special Operations Association and an honorary member of the Association of Former Intelligence Officers. With his wife, he lives in Santa Fe, New Mexico.

More praise for David Morrell:

'A gripping story that demands to be read in a single sitting . . . Morrell delivers first-rate, suspenseful storytelling' *Publishers Weekly*

'Morrell, an absolute master of the thriller, plays by his own rules and leave you dazzled' Dean Koontz

'If you're reading Morrell, you're sitting on the edge of your seat' Michael Connelly

Also by David Morrell

Fiction

First Blood (1972)
Testament (1975)
Last Reveille (1977)
The Totem (1979)
Blood Oath (1982)
The Hundred-Year Christmas (1983)
The Brotherhood of the Rose (1984)
The Fraternity of the Stone (1985)
Rambo (First Blood, Part II) (1985)
The League of Night and Fog (1987)
Rambo III (1988)
The Fifth Profession (1990)
The Covenant of the Flame (1991)
Assumed Identity (1993)
Desperate Measures (1994)
The Totem (Complete and Unaltered) (1994)
Extreme Denial (1996)
Double Image (1998)
Black Evening (1999)
Burnt Sienna (2000)
Long Lost (2002)
The Protector (2003)
Nightscape (2004)
Creepers (2005)

Nonfiction

John Barth: An Introduction (1976)
Fireflies: A Father's Tale of Love and Loss (1988)
American Fiction, American Myth (Essays by Philip Young)
edited by David Morrell and Sandra Spanier (2000)
Lessons from a Lifetime of Writing:
A Novelist Looks at His Craft (2002)

DAVID MORRELL

scavenger

headline

Firs
by H

First publi
by H

Cataloguing in Publication Data is available from the British Library

ISBN 978 0 7553 3718 7

Typeset in Times by Avon DataSet Ltd, Bidford-on-Avon, Warwickshire

Printed and bound in Great Britain by Clays Ltd, St Ives plc

Headline's policy is to use papers that are natural, renewable and recyclable products and made from wood grown in sustainable forests. The logging and manufacturing processes are expected to conform to the environmental regulations of the country of origin.

HEADLINE PUBLISHING GROUP
A division of Hachette Livre UK Ltd
338 Euston Road
London NW1 3BH

www.headline.co.uk
www.hodderheadline.com

Acknowledgements

Authors don't work in a vacuum. *Scavenger* wouldn't have been written without support from a lot of people. I'm grateful to the following:

Jane Dystel, Miriam Goderich, Michael Bourret, and the good folks at Dystel Goderich Literary Management.

Roger Cooper, Chris Nakamura, Peter Costanzo, and the rest of the team at Vanguard Press and the Perseus Books Group.

Nanci Kalanta at horrorworld.org.

Eric Gray and Mike Volpe at Jet Aviation, Teterboro Airport.

Sarie Morrell. The last name's the same as mine for a reason. She's my daughter. But she's also my friend and one of the most inventive book publicists I know.

I had monuments made of bronze, lapis lazuli, alabaster and white limestone and inscriptions of baked clay . . . and I deposited them in the foundations and left them for future times.

Esarhaddon, King of Assyria, seventh century BC

I had an assignment the other day. Someone asked me to write a letter for a time capsule that was going to be opened in Los Angeles a hundred years from now . . . It sounded like an easy assignment. They suggested I write something about the problems and issues of the day, and I set out to do so, riding down the coast in an automobile, looking at the blue Pacific out on one side and the Santa Ynez Mountains on the other, and I couldn't help but wonder if it was going to be that beautiful a hundred years from now as it was on that summer day. And then, as I tried to write . . . let your minds turn to that task. You're going to write for people a hundred years from now who know all about us. We know nothing about them. We don't know what kind of world they'll be living in.

Ronald Reagan, from a speech at the 1976
Republican National Convention, after failing to
receive his party's presidential nomination

LEVEL ONE: THE CRYPT OF CIVILIZATION

1

He no longer called her by his dead wife's name, even though the resemblance was strong enough to make his heart ache. Sometimes, when he woke and found her sitting next to his hospital bed, he thought he was hallucinating.

'What's my name?' she asked.

'Amanda,' he was careful to answer.

'Excellent,' a doctor said. The watchful man never mentioned his specialty, but Balenger assumed he was a psychiatrist. 'I think you're ready to be released.'

2

The taxi entered the Park Slope district of Brooklyn. Trying not to stare at Amanda's long blond hair and soft blue eyes that reminded him so much of Diane, Balenger forced himself to peer out the window. He saw a huge stone arch with a statue at the top: a winged woman with flowing robes.

'Grand Army Plaza,' Amanda explained. 'You like history, so you'll appreciate that the arch commemorates the end of the Civil War.'

Even her voice reminded him of Diane.

'All those trees – that's Prospect Park over there,' she continued.

Down a narrow street, the taxi stopped in the middle of a row of four-story brownstones. While Amanda paid the fare, Balenger mustered the effort to get out. He felt the cold bite of a late October wind. His legs and ribs throbbed, as did the abrasions on his hands.

'My apartment's on the third floor.' Amanda pointed. 'The one with the stone railing.'

'I thought you said you worked in a bookstore in Manhattan. This is an upscale district. How can you afford—' The answer quickly occurred to him. 'Your father helps.'

'He never stopped hoping, never stopped paying the rent all the months I was missing.'

As Balenger climbed the eight steps, which felt like eighty, his knees became unsteady. Even though the wooden door was freshly painted brown, it gave the impression of age. Amanda put a key in the lock.

'Wait,' Balenger said.

'Need to catch your breath?'

In fact, he did, but that wasn't his motive for stopping her. 'Are you sure this is a good idea?'

'Do you have another place to go, anyone else to take care of you?'

In both cases, the answer was 'no.' During the previous year, while Balenger searched for his missing wife, he stayed in cheap motel rooms and could afford to eat only once a day, mostly sandwiches from fast-food restaurants. His savings account was drained. He had no one and nothing.

'You barely know me,' he told her.

'You risked your life for me,' Amanda responded. 'Without you, I'd be dead. What else do I need to know?'

Neither commented that at the time Balenger believed the woman he had saved was his wife.

'We'll try it for a few days.' Amanda unlocked the door.

3

The apartment had one bedroom, a living room, and a kitchen. The ceiling was high, with molding around it. The floors were hardwood. Although everything looked bright and well maintained, Balenger again had the sense of age.

'While we were in the hospital, my father stocked the refrigerator and the cupboards,' Amanda said. 'Do you want something to eat?'

Balenger sank on to the leather sofa. Before he could answer, exhaustion overwhelmed him.

When he woke, it was dark outside. A blanket was over him. Amanda helped him to reach the bathroom and return to the sofa.

'I'll heat up some soup,' she told him.

Afterward, she changed his bandages and dressings.

'While you were asleep, I went out and bought some pajamas for you.' She helped him put on the top, frowning at his injuries.

4

A nightmare jerked him awake, memories of shots and screams. Through frightened eyes, he saw Amanda hurry from the bedroom. 'I'm here,' she assured him. In the pale light from a corner lamp, she looked even more like Diane, making him wonder if impossibly Diane's spirit had merged with Amanda's. She held his hand until his heart stopped racing. 'I'm here,' she repeated. He lapsed back into a troubled sleep.

A cry from the bedroom jolted him upright. Wincing, he mustered the strength to rise from the sofa and struggle through the doorway, where he saw Amanda thrash beneath the covers, fighting her own nightmares. He stroked her hair, trying to tell her she was safe from the darkness and violence and fear, safe from the Paragon Hotel. *Clang*. In the back of his haunted memory, a flap of sheet metal slammed against the side of an abandoned building, *clang*, the mournful, rhythmic toll of doom.

He fell asleep next to her, the two of them holding one another. The next night was the same. And the next. They always had a light on. They kept the bedroom door open. Closed rooms gave them the sweats. Two weeks later, they became lovers.

5

He managed increasingly long walks. One gray December afternoon, as he returned from the snow-covered monuments in Grand Army Plaza, two men got out of a car in front of the brownstone. They wore somber overcoats. Their faces had pinched expressions. The cold air made their breath white with frost.

'Frank Balenger?' the taller man asked.

'Who wants to know?'

They pulled out identification: UNITED STATES DEPARTMENT OF THE TREASURY.

'Sign this.' When they reached the apartment, the heavier agent handed Balenger a pen and a document.

'It'd be nice if I could read it first.'

'It says you relinquish any claim to evidence you gave the Asbury Park police.'

'The double eagle,' the taller agent said.

Now Balenger understood. He disliked them even more.

'The Gold Reserve Act of 1933 makes it illegal to use gold coins as currency,' the heavier agent said. 'It does permit citizens to own them as collectibles. But you can't own something if you stole it.'

'I didn't steal it.' Balenger felt heat rise to his face. 'The original owner died in 1939. The coins were hidden in the Paragon Hotel. For all these years, *nobody* owned that coin until I put it in my pocket.'

'The only coin that survived the fire. Did you take a close look?'

Balenger worked to steady his voice. 'I was a little preoccupied, trying to stay alive.'

'It's dated 1933. Before the government made it illegal to use gold as currency, the mint manufactured the double eagles for that year. All the coins needed to be destroyed.' The taller agent paused. 'But some were stolen.'

'Including the one you put in your pocket,' the other agent said. 'Which means it's the property of the US government. They're so rare, the last time we got our hands on one, it was auctioned at Sotheby's.'

The first agent added, 'For almost eight million dollars.'

The number had so much weight that Balenger didn't trust himself to speak.

'Because of legal technicalities, we gave the person we got it from a portion of the money,' the agent continued. 'We're prepared to offer you a similar deal. We'll call it a finder's fee. Something generous enough to get a lot of publicity and encourage collectors to surrender similar illegally acquired coins, no questions asked.'

Balenger tried to sound casual. 'What kind of fee are we talking about?'

'Assuming this coin sells for as much as the previous one? You'll keep two million dollars.'

Balenger needed to remind himself to breathe.

6

A glorious Saturday in May. Sweating after a long jog around Prospect Park, Balenger and Amanda unlocked the brownstone's front door and sorted through the mail the postman had shoved through the slot.

'Anything interesting?' Amanda asked as they climbed the stairs.

'More financial advisors eager to tell me what to do with the money we got from the coin. Pleas from more charities. Bills.'

'At least we can pay them now.'

'Weird,' Balenger said.

'What's wrong?'

'Take a look.'

Outside their apartment, Balenger handed her an envelope. Its old, brittle feel made Amanda frown. She raised it to her nostrils. 'Smells musty.'

'It ought to. Check the stamp.'

'Two cents? That's impossible.'

'Now look at the postmark.'

It was faded with age but readable.

'December thirty-first?'

'Keep reading.'

'*Eighteen ninety-nine?* What the . . .' Amanda shook her head. 'Is this a joke?'

'Maybe an advertising gimmick,' Balenger said.

After they entered the apartment, Amanda tore open the envelope and removed a sheet of paper. 'Feels as brittle as the envelope. Smells as musty.'

The message was handwritten in thick strokes. Like the postmark, the ink was faded with age.

Mr Frank Balenger

Dear Sir,

Forgive the intrusion. Knowing your fascination with the past, I took the liberty of using an old postmark to attract your attention. I invite you and Ms Evert to join me and a group of guests on the first Saturday of June at one p.m. at the Manhattan History Club (address below). After refreshments, I shall deliver a lecture about messages to the future that we open in the present to understand the past. I refer, of course, to those fascinating future-past artifacts known as time capsules.

Yours,
Adrian Murdock

'Time capsules?' Amanda looked bewildered. 'What on earth?'

'The first Saturday of June?' Balenger leaned into the kitchen and glanced at a calendar. 'That's next weekend. The Manhattan History Club?'

'You're right. It's got to be an advertising gimmick.' Amanda examined the paper. 'Sure seems old. It ought to, considering it comes from a history club. They're probably looking for new members. But how did they get our names and address?'

'Last fall, when everything happened, the newspapers indicated you live in Park Slope,' Balenger said.

'The club waited an awfully long time to get in touch with us.'

Balenger thought about it. 'When the coin was auctioned last month, there was more publicity. The media dredged up what happened at the Paragon Hotel. They mentioned my fascination with history. Maybe this guy thinks he can persuade me to give his club a donation.'

'Sure. Just like those financial advisors eager to get commissions from you,' Amanda decided.

'Time capsules.' Balenger's tone was wistful.

'You sound like you're actually tempted to go.'

'When I was a kid . . .' He paused, transported by the memory. 'My father taught high-school history in Buffalo. His school was tearing down an old classroom building to make space for a new one. There was a rumor about a time capsule – that a graduating class from years earlier put one in the foundation when the building was new. After the demolition workers went home each day, a couple of kids and I used to search for the capsule in the wreckage. Of course, we had no idea what something like that would look like. It took me a week, but by God, I finally spotted a big stone block in an excavated corner of the building. The block had a plaque that said CLASS OF 1942. ALWAYS TO BE REMEMBERED. AT THE THRESHOLD OF OUR FUTURE. What happened was, over the years, grime covered the plaque. Shrubs grew in front of it. People forgot.'

Amanda gestured for him to continue.

'Anyway, the block had a hole in it,' Balenger explained. 'I saw a metal box inside. When I ran home and told my father, at first he got angry that I was playing in a demolition area and could have gotten hurt. But when he learned what I'd found, he made me take him there. The next morning, he asked the workers to pry open the block. "For God's sake, don't damage what's inside," I remember him saying. The workers were as fascinated as we were. In fact, a lot of teachers and students heard what was happening and came over too. A worker used a crowbar and finally pulled out a metal box about the size of a big phone book. It was rusted shut. The students urged the worker to break it open, but my father said we should make a ceremony of it and have a fundraiser. People could buy tickets to watch the time capsule get opened. The money would pay for library books. "Great idea," everybody said. So the principal called the newspaper and the radio and TV stations to publicize the event, and the grand opening was scheduled for a Sunday afternoon in the school auditorium. TV cameras were there. A thousand people paid a dollar apiece to watch.'

'What was in it?' Amanda asked.

'Nobody ever found out.'

'What?' Amanda looked surprised.

'The principal had the time capsule locked in a cabinet in his office. The night before the grand opening, someone broke into the office, pried open the cabinet, and stole the box. You can imagine how disappointed everybody was. I always wondered what those students from 1942 thought was important enough for the future to see.'

7

The building was one block south of Gramercy Park, on East 19th Street, in the area's historic preservation district. Saturday traffic was quiet. An overcast sky made the air cool enough for light jackets. Balenger and Amanda stood outside the brick row house and studied a weathered brass plaque that read 1854. Above the entrance, another plaque read MANHATTAN HISTORY CLUB.

They climbed steps and entered a shadowy vestibule that felt as if it hadn't changed in its century and a half. A poster sat on an easel, showing a distinguished-looking, gray-haired man with an equally gray mustache. He was thin, with lines creasing the corners of his eyes. He wore a conservative suit and held a metal cylinder in his hands.

THE MANHATTAN HISTORY CLUB
WELCOMES
ADRIAN MURDOCK
PROFESSOR OF HISTORY,
OGLETHORPE UNIVERSITY, ATLANTA.
'WORLD ENOUGH AND TIME:
THE PSYCHOLOGY OF TIME CAPSULES.'
JUNE 2, 1 P.M.

Balenger heard voices beyond the vestibule.

A matronly, fortyish woman in a plain dark dress entered the corridor from a room on the right. When she noticed Balenger and Amanda, she smiled. 'I'm glad you could join us.'

'Well, the invitation was so clever, we couldn't resist,' Balenger said.

The woman blushed. The rising color in her cheeks was emphasized by her lack of makeup. Her brunette hair was pulled back severely in a bun. 'That was *my* idea, I'm afraid. Our lectures haven't always been well attended, so I thought a little drama was in order. I never dreamed how much work it would take for the committee to deliver the invitations. I'm Karen Bailey, by the way.' She offered her hand.

'Frank Balenger.'

'Amanda Evert.'

'Of course. You're the couple who had the coin. The newspaper article about the auction mentioned your interest in history. I thought this lecture would be perfect for you.'

'You're not by chance having a fundraiser, are you?' Amanda asked.

'Well . . .' Karen looked embarrassed again. 'We always welcome donations. But you needn't feel obligated.'

Balenger ignored Amanda's knowing look. 'Hey, we're glad to contribute,' he said.

'The invitation promised refreshments. What

can I get you? Tea? Coffee? A soft drink?'

'Coffee,' Balenger told her.

'Same here,' Amanda said.

They followed Karen along a corridor that displayed sepia-tinted photographs of Gramercy Park, with cards next to them indicating that the photos were from the 1890s. Faded images showed horse-drawn carriages, men wearing hats, suits, ties, and vests, and women wearing dresses that came down to the ankles of their buttoned shoes.

Old carpeting muffled Balenger's footsteps. The air retained the musty smell of the past. Turning to the right, Karen led them into a long room that had rows of folding chairs. Sepia-tinted photographs decorated these walls, too.

Balenger glanced at a screen. A laptop computer sat on a lectern, linked to a projector. He switched his attention to a half-dozen people who sipped from Styrofoam cups and took bites from quartered sandwiches.

Karen pointed. 'Let me introduce you to Professor Murdock.'

She guided them to a gray-haired, gray-mustached man who was holding a portion of a sandwich and speaking to a man and woman in their thirties. He looked thinner than in his photograph. Although he wore a suit, the couple he spoke to were dressed in jeans, as Balenger and Amanda were.

'. . . term wasn't used until 1939. Before that, they

were called boxes or safes or even caskets. And then, of course, there's the famous—' The man interrupted himself to nod at Balenger and Amanda.

'Professor, I'd like you to meet . . .' Color again rose in Karen's cheeks. She evidently failed to remember their names.

'Frank Balenger.'

'Amanda Evert.'

They shook hands.

'I was just explaining about the Crypt of Civilization,' the professor said.

'The *what*?' Balenger wasn't sure he'd heard correctly.

'That's the name of arguably the most famous time capsule. Of course, I'm biased because it's located at Oglethorpe University where I teach.'

'Did you say the Crypt of Civilization?' Balenger asked.

'Interesting name, don't you agree? The Crypt's the reason the International Time Capsule Society is at Oglethorpe.'

'There's a time capsule society?' Amanda sounded amazed.

More people entered the room.

'Excuse me,' the professor said. 'I need to make sure everything's ready for my presentation.'

As he went to the lectern, Karen Bailey brought their coffee. 'Cream and sweetener are on that table. The sandwiches are catered. Please, try one.' She walked to the front of the room and pulled the draperies shut.

Balenger studied the sandwiches. Their crusts were cut off. He picked one up and bit into it. 'I don't normally like tuna salad, but this isn't bad.'

'It's the lettuce,' Amanda said.

'Lettuce?'

'It's crunchy. The mayonnaise tastes homemade. The bread's still warm.' Amanda took another bite.

So did Balenger. 'I hope he talks about this Crypt of Civilization.'

8

The professor stood in shadows at the lectern and pressed the laptop's keyboard. On the screen, an image appeared, showing a long, shiny metal tube that reminded Balenger of a torpedo. A group of solemn, white-coated men stood next to it.

'Even though the practice dates back to antiquity, this is the first object to be called a time capsule,' Professor Murdock said. 'It was created for the 1939 New York World's Fair. Its sponsor was Westinghouse, an appliance corporation with a reputation for quality. Because the time capsule wasn't due to be opened for five thousand years, the implication was that Westinghouse products were designed to last. Why five thousand years? Because it was assumed that recorded history was five thousand years old. Thus, the World's Fair was midway between the past and the future. The capsule's designers announced, "We choose to believe that men will solve the problems of the world, that the human race will triumph over its limitations, that the future will be glorious." Of course, the horrors of the Second World War would soon make them feel differently.'

When the professor touched the computer, another image appeared on the screen. This one showed a futuristic-looking building, part of what presumably was the 1939 World's Fair. A banner in the background proclaimed THE WORLD OF TOMORROW. People lined up to enter. Balenger was struck that, even though going to the fair would have felt like a holiday, most of the men wore jackets, ties, and dress hats.

'The capsule was made from an extremely hard copper alloy resistant to moisture,' the professor said. 'After being filled, it was lowered into a shaft during the autumnal equinox in what was almost a religious atmosphere, complete with Chinese gongs. The shaft had a cap from which a periscope projected, allowing visitors to see the time capsule interred fifty feet below them. After the fair concluded, the shaft was filled and sealed, then covered with a concrete marker. "May the Time Capsule sleep well," the Westinghouse chairman said. Because more capsules have been lost than have ever been found, Westinghouse prepared *The Book of the Record of the Time Capsule*. Thousands of copies were printed on acid-free paper with fade-resistant ink and dispersed to libraries and monasteries throughout the world, even in Tibet. Among other information, the book contained the latitude and longitude for the capsule's location, a wise precaution because the concrete marker in Flushing Meadows, where the fair took place, has been reduced in size over the years.'

Another image appeared, showing an array of various objects.

'And what did the capsule contain?' Professor Murdock asked. 'What were the precious items that the designers felt would best show a society five thousand years in the future the things that made 1939 significant? An alarm clock. A can opener. A fountain pen. A nail file. A toothbrush. A Mickey Mouse cup.'

Someone in the audience laughed.

'There were numerous other items, but these examples suggest how difficult it is to decide what's important in any society. Will there be can openers in the future? Alarm clocks and nail files? Perhaps the things we take most for granted are what a future world will find most incomprehensible. To echo the title of a novel that was placed in the capsule, all cultures eventually vanish, gone with the wind. The 1939 World's Fair was proud to tell the future what the world was like at that moment in history. But there's a desperation in the thoroughness with which the capsule was prepared, as if the designers were afraid they'd be forgotten.'

A new image showed what appeared to be a sprawling castle.

'This is the campus at Oglethorpe University in Atlanta, where I teach,' Professor Murdock said. 'The idea for the Westinghouse capsule originated there in 1936. Oglethorpe's then president, Thornwell Jacobs, drained an indoor swimming pool and filled it with thousands of items, including microfilmed pages from encyclopedias along with everyday objects such as a toilet brush, a lipstick, a grapefruit corer, a fly swatter, Lincoln Logs, and an ampule of Budweiser beer. The project was so ambitious that Jacobs didn't complete it until 1940, one year after the World's Fair. As a result, Westinghouse received credit for creating the first time capsule, even though the idea was borrowed. Jacobs used a burial metaphor and called his project the Crypt of Civilization.'

Balenger heard a noise behind him. Turning in the shadows, he noted that a man and woman were leaving. At the exit, they whispered to Karen Bailey. The man pointed to his watch. Karen nodded with understanding.

The flash of a new image made Balenger look forward. He saw Nazi soldiers frozen in mid-goosestep. The image became a series that showed the rubble of bombed buildings, tanks marked with swastikas, piles of bodies in death camps, and the mushroom cloud of a nuclear bomb.

'When Jacobs conceived of the Crypt of Civilization, it's possible that the ravages of the Great Depression made him skeptical about the future of civilization. Perhaps his goal wasn't to brag to the future, as the

Westinghouse time capsule did, but rather to preserve something he feared was in danger of being lost. Certainly, by 1940, when the Crypt was sealed, pessimism was rampant as the German army stormed through Europe. In a document Jacobs placed in the Crypt, he said, "The world is engaged in burying our civilization for ever, and here in this crypt we leave it to you." '

Balenger heard other movement behind him. Again turning, he noticed a second couple leaving the shadowy room. He frowned.

'The Crypt survived, but most aren't that fortunate,' Professor Murdock continued. 'Their containers aren't water-resistant, or else their contents include organic substances that rot. Moreover, the accidents of human nature defeat the best intentions. An ambitious town in California deposited a total of seventeen time capsules and lost every one of them. At a high school in Virginia, six graduating students helped prepare a time capsule and buried it somewhere on campus. That was in 1965. The school has now been torn down, and those six former students have a total memory gap about what they put in the capsule and where they buried it. It's as if the event never happened to them. These communities are now engaged in what amounts to a hide-and-hunt scavenger game.'

Balenger tensed as two more people left the room. What's going on? he wondered.

'Of the thousands of time capsules that have been

misplaced,' Professor Murdock said, 'five are considered the most wanted. The first is the Bicentennial Wagon Train Capsule.'

The professor's voice seemed to lessen in volume. Balenger leaned forward to listen.

'On Independence Day, 1976 . . .'

The shadows seemed to thicken.

'. . . a capsule containing twenty-two million signatures was driven to Valley Forge, Pennsylvania, in a caravan of vehicles known as the bicentennial wagon train. President Gerald Ford was to officiate in a ceremony commemorating the US War of Independence.'

The professor's voice became fainter.

'But before the ceremony occurred, someone stole the capsule from an unattended van.'

Balenger's eyelids felt heavy.

'The second most-wanted time capsule is at the Massachusetts Institute of Technology. In 1939, MIT engineers sealed various objects in a container and deposited it under a huge cyclotron they were building. The cyclotron was . . .'

9

Clang.

Balenger drifted toward consciousness. The harsh, persistent tolling seemed to come from a fractured bell.

Clang.

It matched the agonized throbbing in his head.

Clang.

He managed to open his eyes, but darkness surrounded him. A chill breeze made him shiver. He heard waves crash. The breeze carried a hint of burnt wood and ashes.

A light suddenly blazed. Groaning, he raised a hand to shield his eyes. His forearm ached.

'Buddy, you're not supposed to be here,' a gruff voice said. 'On your feet.'

All Balenger could do was groan.

'You heard me. Get moving.'

'Where . . .' Balenger's throat felt raw. He could barely get the word out.

'I won't tell you again. Move!'

'Where am I?' Balenger squinted toward the glare. He suddenly realized that he was lying on sand.

'For God's sake, you screwed yourself up so bad, you don't even know where the hell you are?' a second gruff voice demanded. 'Asbury Park, buddy. The same place you passed out.'

Clang.

Balenger struggled to stand. The stark flashlight beam illuminated the jumbled wreckage of a building. The smell of burnt wood was stronger. 'Asbury Park?'

Clang.

Balanger's mind cleared enough for him to recognize the sound from his nightmares: a flap of sheet metal banging against the side of an abandoned building. A cold shock of fear seized him.

Clang.

'The city's working to rebuild the area. Guys like you aren't welcome here.'

'No,' Balenger said. 'Is that . . .' Frantic, he pointed toward the chaotic stretch of debris. 'Don't tell me that's . . .'

Clang.

'The Paragon Hotel,' the voice explained. 'What's left of it. When all those killings happened and it burned down, we said, "Enough!" We're gonna bring this beach back to life. So scram before we put you in jail!'

Emotion made Balenger shake. The Paragon Hotel? he thought in a panic. How did I get here?

'Hold it a second. Eddie, this guy looks familiar. Hey, aren't you—'

'Balenger,' the other man said. 'Frank Balenger. Yeah, that's who he is. Jesus, man, what're you doing back here? I'd expect this was the last place you'd ever want to see again.'

'Amanda,' Balenger whispered.

'I can barely hear you.'

'Amanda.' Balenger's voice was hoarse.

'Who's Amanda? Somebody's with you?'

'Wait, Eddie. I think I . . . Amanda . . . Last fall when the hotel burned down. What was her last name? Evert. Amanda Evert. Is that who you mean, Frank? The woman you saved?'

Clang.

'Amanda!' Balenger screamed. 'Where are you?' His vocal cords threatened to burst. He staggered through the burned wreckage, searching.

'Frank, talk to us. For heaven's sake, what are you doing here?'

10

'The Manhattan History Club?' Jeff Cochran frowned. A heavy man with red hair and freckles, he was Asbury Park's police chief. Two years earlier, before Balenger quit the department to search for his missing wife, Balenger had worked for him. 'Time capsules?'

'That's the last thing I remember.' Balenger rubbed the back of his neck, working to relieve his headache. 'Look, you've got to keep searching the beach area. Amanda might still be—'

'They're checking for the second time. I promise I'll do everything I can. You went to this history club when?'

'Is today Saturday?' The overhead light was oppressively harsh.

'Not any more. It's past midnight.'

'Saturday was . . .' Balenger fought to concentrate, to get the correct date. His left forearm remained sore. 'June second?'

'That's right. Man, whatever they gave you sure fouled up your memory. Some kind of date-rape amnesia drug maybe.'

'In the coffee and the sandwiches.' Balenger shook his head, aggravating his headache. 'But everybody else drank and ate . . . The woman . . . What was her name? Come on, come on. Karen! That's what she called herself. Karen Bailey. She brought coffee to us. That's when it happened.'

'You said she pulled the drapes shut and turned off the lights.'

'Yes.' Balenger felt sick to his stomach. 'So the professor . . . Murdock. *That* was his name. So Professor Murdock could deliver a lecture and show photographs on a screen. After a while, people started leaving. The room seemed to get darker.'

'Why do you keep massaging your left forearm?' Cochran asked.

'It aches.' Balenger took off his sport coat and rolled up his shirt sleeve. The middle of his forearm was red and swollen. Something had punctured his skin.

'Looks like somebody gave you an injection,' Cochran said. 'More drugs to keep you sedated while they brought you here.'

Hands trembling, Balenger felt in his pockets. 'I've still got my wallet. They didn't take my watch. This wasn't robbery.'

'Your cell phone?'

'I didn't bring it with me. Amanda's just about the only person I talk to on it. Since she was with me, it didn't seem necessary to carry it.'

Cochran shoved the office phone across the desk. 'Does *she* have a cell phone?'

Balenger touched numbers. Palm sweating, he pressed the phone to his ear.

An electronic voice told him, 'The number you are calling is out of service.'

The voice must have been loud enough for Cochran to hear it. 'Try your home,' the police chief said. 'Maybe she's waiting for you, worried about where you are.'

'But it doesn't make sense that someone would drug us, put *me* in Asbury Park, and take Amanda to our apartment.'

'So far, *none* of this makes sense. Try home,' Cochran urged.

Balenger quickly touched more numbers. His hand was now so sweaty that it slicked the phone.

'Hello,' Amanda's voice said.

Thank God, Balenger thought. Abruptly, his spirit sank as he realized what he was hearing.

'At the tone, please leave a message.' Amanda's recorded greeting ended.

Balenger forced himself to speak. 'I don't know what happened,' he said into the phone, alarmed by the unsteadiness of his voice. 'If you get this message, call the Asbury Park Police Department.' He dictated the number on the phone. 'Ask for Chief Cochran.'

'In that case . . .' Cochran motioned for Balenger to slide the phone to him, 'let's see what the Manhattan PD can find out.'

11

Balenger's head throbbed as Cochran steered on to East 19th Street. The Sunday morning light, free of workday traffic exhaust, was so clear that it hurt Balenger's sleep-starved eyes. The dashboard clock showed 8:11.

'The next block,' he told Cochran. 'There. The middle row house.'

Balenger saw a tall, thirtyish, Hispanic man in a tie and sport coat standing in front of the building. Next to him was a severely thin woman in a designer pantsuit. Her hair was platinum. Her excessive lipstick and eyeliner made it difficult to tell how old she was.

Cochran managed to find a parking space at the

end of the block. Balenger hurried toward the row house.

'Chief Cochran?' the Hispanic asked.

'That's me,' Cochran said, catching up to Balenger.

'Detective Ortega.' The man shook hands. 'This is Joan Dandridge.'

'Frank Balenger. That sign wasn't here yesterday.' Apprehension swelling inside him, Balenger indicated the top of the stairs, where a FOR SALE sign was attached to the door. The sign read KNICKERBOCKER REALTY and provided a phone number.

'That's my company,' Joan said. She dropped a cigarette to the pavement and stepped on it.

Balenger stared toward the empty space above the door. 'There was a bronze plaque up there.'

'What?' Her voice became sharp.

'Above the door. With the words MANHATTAN HISTORY CLUB.'

Joan climbed the steps, pulled spectacles from her purse, and stared toward the bricks above the entrance. 'My God, I see holes where the plaque was attached. He promised he wouldn't damage the building.'

'He?' Cochran asked.

'The owner bought this place on spec and wants too much for it,' the realtor complained. 'I keep telling him, the boom's over, the price is too high. So when I got a call from somebody offering to rent the building for a day, I encouraged the owner to accept. I negotiated a very nice rate.'

'Rent the building?' Balenger felt off balance. Amanda, he thought, desperate to get inside.

'For a reception. The man said he lived here until his parents sold it when he was a teenager in the 1980s. He happened to drive by, noticed it was for sale, and decided to have a surprise birthday party for his father, who always regretted selling the place. I kidded him, "Never mind renting it for a day. Convince your father to buy it back." He laughed and told me, "Nostalgia isn't worth four million dollars." '

Balenger quickly asked, 'What did he look like?'

'I never met him.'

'You never . . .?'

'We made all the arrangements over the phone. The contract went through the mail. His check didn't bounce. I got a security deposit and a fee. That's all I cared about. I did find out who owned the property in the 1980s. Victor Evans. The man who signed the rental contract is Philip Evans. The same family name. As far as I was concerned, everything looked legitimate.' She pulled a key from her purse and scowled again at the holes above the door. 'This is a historical district. The damage deposit might not be enough to pay for the repair.'

She unlocked the door.

'Wait here,' Ortega said.

'But I need to find out if anything else is damaged.'

'After we make sure no one's inside.'

Ortega, Balenger and Cochran entered. The vestibule was empty.

'There was an easel here,' Balenger told them. 'A poster with the professor's photograph was on it.'

They followed the corridor. All the old photographs of Gramercy Park were gone.

Balenger gestured to the right. 'The lecture was there.'

They went into the long room. The folding chairs were gone. So were the photographs, the draperies, the lectern, the screen, and the tables for the coffee, tea and sandwiches.

Ortega cautiously opened a door at the back and looked inside a room. 'Empty.'

Balenger listened to the building's silence. 'Amanda!' he shouted.

The echo died. No one answered.

Massaging his forearm, he returned to the corridor and peered up the stairs. Its dark carpet led toward shadows.

'Amanda!'

Still no answer.

The stairs creaked as Balenger hurried up.

'I'm coming with you,' Cochran said.

'You'd better let me go first.' Ortega caught up to them.

'I know how to do this,' Balenger said. 'I used to be a police officer.'

'But are you armed?'

'No.'

'Chief Cochran?'

'I'm out of my jurisdiction. I didn't bring my gun.'

'Then I'll go first,' Ortega emphasized. At the top, he checked a murky room, then proceeded along a corridor.

Balenger went into the room. Its carpet had imprints where a bed, a dresser and a chair once stood. The closet door was open, revealing a couple of hangers on a rod.

The second room contained two empty packing boxes.

On the next floor, all they found were a few more hangers and a strip of bubble wrap.

Ortega opened the final door. 'The attic.'

No one moved for a second. Then they braced themselves and went up a narrow stairway, where the creaking was louder than on the main stairs. Balenger followed Ortega, dust irritating his nostrils. He heard Cochran behind him.

Sunlight struggled through a grimy window. The pitched ceiling was so low that Balenger needed to stoop. He studied an uneven pine floor and an exercise mat, torn at one edge. 'A long time ago, this was probably the servants' quarters.'

'Sort of like a cave,' Ortega said. 'I bet kids would enjoy playing up here.'

Cochran pointed. 'What's that in the corner?'

'Looks like a couple of CD cases,' Balenger said.

Ortega pulled latex gloves from his suit-coat pocket, leaned into the corner, and picked up the cases. 'Not CDs. Video games. I never heard of the first one, but the other is *Grand Theft Auto*. My kids play it. I told them to stop – a cop's kids playing games about stealing cars and beating up prostitutes – but I'm sure they keep playing it behind my back.' Ortega opened the cases. 'No wonder they got left behind. The discs are missing.'

Balenger's forearm continued to ache. The small talk hadn't eased his tension. 'We're not finished searching.'

'I know,' Ortega said. 'There's always the basement.'

12

Descending, Balenger felt his chest cramp so hard that he had trouble breathing. Dankness surrounded him. The basement was a single long area, poorly lit, with old brick walls and cobwebbed pipes. The concrete floor had cracks. The furnace was covered with grit. Rust lay under the water heater.

'Four million dollars for this place?' Cochran murmured. 'It ought to be condemned.'

The attempt at small talk still did nothing to calm Balenger. No matter how thoroughly he looked, there wasn't any sign of Amanda.

'When was the last time you checked your home?' Ortega asked.

'The chief drove me there first. I picked up a photograph.' Balanger pulled it from a jacket pocket. It came from a shoebox Amanda kept on a closet shelf. It showed her playing with her parents' Irish setter in their backyard in Connecticut.

'Ortega studied it. 'How tall is she?'

'Five six. A hundred and twenty pounds.' Balenger's throat tightened. When he rescued her from the Paragon Hotel, she'd been gaunt. It had taken a lot of encouragement to get her to eat enough to regain a healthy weight.

'Eye color? It's hard to tell in the photo.'

'Blue. Soft. Kind of translucent.'

'Hair. Would you call it straw-colored?'

Balenger nodded, overwhelmed with emotion. He gazed longingly at the joyous smile in the image. Shoulder-length hair. Lovely chin and elegant cheekbones. He had an anguished memory of a similar conversation with a detective when his wife disappeared.

'I need to tell you something,' Balenger said.

'Oh?'

'This happened to me once before.'

'I don't understand.'

'My wife disappeared, too.'

The dim lights in the basement didn't hide Ortega's surprise.

'She looked like Amanda.' The dankness penetrated Balenger's core, making him shiver. 'Chief Cochran told you about the Paragon Hotel when he phoned you?'

Ortega nodded somberly.

'I found my wife in that hotel. Dead.' Confronting his memories made Balenger's hands and feet numb. His rapid breathing caused him to feel lightheaded. 'I also found Amanda there.'

Ortega's gaze intensified.

'The physical resemblance isn't coincidental.' Balenger rushed on, unable to control the speed of his words. 'We know who kidnapped my wife. The same man who kidnapped Amanda a year ago. He was fixated on young women with blond hair, blue eyes, and similar features. If I didn't know better, I'd say *he* did this. But I saw Amanda beat him to death with a two-by-four. After it broke, she used it as a stake and rammed it into the bastard's heart. I keep having nightmares about him. But he couldn't have done this.' Balenger felt desperate as he turned toward Cochran, needing reassurance.

'Right. That's all he is – something in nightmares,' Cochran said. 'I saw the corpse on the beach. I saw it in the morgue. I saw it in the autopsy. Later, I spoke to witnesses who saw it cremated.'

Balenger's anguished voice reverberated through the cellar. 'So what other son of a bitch would want to make this happen a second time?'

LEVEL TWO: 'WELCOME TO SCAVENGER'

1

'But before the ceremony occurred, someone stole the capsule from an unattended van,' a voice droned.

Amanda felt as if she was floating upward from a deep pool.

'The second most wanted time capsule is at the Massachusetts Institute of Technology.'

Amanda drifted to the surface.

'In 1939, MIT engineers sealed various objects in a container and deposited it under a huge cyclotron they were building. The cyclotron was eventually deactivated, but the time capsule was forgotten for more than fifty years.'

Her eyes opened.

'It might as well have stayed forgotten. Short of tearing the building apart, no one knows . . .'

Amanda discovered that she was lying on a bed.

'. . . how to remove the capsule from under its eighteen-ton shield.'

She felt groggy and nauseous. Her head throbbed.

But its rhythm didn't match the sudden, frantic pounding of her heart.

'The third is the *M*A*S*H* Capsule.'

Amanda jerked upright. Where's Frank? she thought. Stifling a moan, she scanned the room. Beamed ceiling, stone fireplace, log walls, wooden floor. Sunlight streamed through a window, hurting her eyes. In the distance, she saw jagged mountains capped with snow. She feared she was going insane.

'In 1983, cast members of the popular television program *M*A*S*H* put costumes, props, and other items related to the series into a capsule and buried it on the Twentieth Century Fox film production lot.'

The voice belonged to a man and came from everywhere around her.

'But the studio changed so much in the intervening years that no one can identify the capsule's location. Possibly it lies under a hotel constructed on property the studio once owned.'

Amanda rolled from the bed. She realized that the voice came from audio speakers hidden in the ceiling and walls.

'The fourth is George Washington's Cornerstone. In a Masonic ceremony in 1793, George Washington supervised the placement of a time capsule into the cornerstone of the original Capitol Building.'

Amanda looked down at her clothes. She wore the same jeans, white blouse and gray blazer that she remembered putting on. Straining to focus her jumbled thoughts, she sensed that she'd been unconscious for quite a while. But her bladder didn't ache with the need to relieve it, which meant that the drug she'd been given, like a date-rape drug, allowed her to obey commands. Someone must have carried her to the bathroom, taken her pants off, and coaxed her to urinate.

'The Capitol has grown so much since then that the first cornerstone and its unknown contents have never been recovered.'

Her arms and legs trembled. Her stomach felt heavy. She was as overwhelmed as she'd felt a year earlier when she'd regained consciousness and found herself in the Paragon Hotel. *Again*, she thought. My God, it's happening again.

'The fifth is the Gramophone Company Capsule. In 1907, in Middlesex, England, the Gramophone Company placed audio discs into a time capsule in the cornerstone of its new factory.'

The voice was sonorous. Despite her grogginess, she guessed she was hearing the continuation of the speech Professor Murdock had delivered at the Manhattan History Club. But the voice did not belong to the professor.

'These recordings included music by several then famous opera stars. During demolition sixty years later, the capsule was found. But before the recordings could be played for an audience, they were stolen, the irreplaceable voices on those discs never to be recovered.'

Amanda fought to control her breathing. Frank? she thought. Where *are* you? She started toward a door, only to whimper when the voice returned to an earlier part of the lecture.

'Of the thousands of time capsules that have been misplaced . . .'

Amanda almost screamed.

' . . .five are considered the most wanted.'

Chest contracting, she realized that the voice was on a recorded loop. While she was unconscious, it must have played repeatedly. That explained why the words seemed familiar, even though she had no memory of having heard them.

'The first is the Bicentennial Wagon Train Capsule.'

I'm in hell, Amanda thought. She ran to the door and grabbed the handle, fearful that it wouldn't budge.

'On Independence Day, 1976 . . .'

The handle moved when she pressed down. Heart pounding faster, she yanked at the door.

'. . . a capsule containing twenty-two million signatures was driven to Valley Forge, Pennsylvania . . .'

When she pulled the door open, she found a log-walled corridor. She peered to the left and right, seeing doors and paintings of cowboys.

'President Gerald Ford was scheduled to officiate . . .'

She eased out and shut the door, the only sound a muffled continuation of the recording. A long carpet occupied the middle of the corridor. On her right,

Amanda saw a dead end. She crept silently to the left, hearing the faint voice behind the doors she passed.

'But before the ceremony occurred, someone stole the capsule from an unattended van.'

2

She came to a staircase. Its fresh smell of wood and varnish suggested that the building was new. At the bottom, a large open area led to a door with a window on each side.

She hurried down, reached the door, and grabbed its handle.

Electricity jolted her, knocking her backward. Her mind went blank. The next thing she knew, she landed hard, slamming her head on the floor. Pain shot through her. She groaned and managed to focus her vision.

'Jesus,' someone said.

Turning toward the sound, she saw a man charge down the stairs. Mid-twenties. Short, dark hair. Gaunt, rugged features. Beard stubble.

She raised her hands to defend herself, then realized he wasn't attacking her.

'Are you hurt?' He helped her up.

'Sore.' She wavered, dazed, grateful not to be alone.

'Where *are* we?' he asked.

'I have no idea.' Amanda stared at her tingling hand. 'But I don't recommend touching that door handle.'

'The voice in my room . . . The last thing I remember . . .' The man's haunted eyes scanned the area around them. He struggled to concentrate. 'I was in a bar in St Louis.'

'I was at a lecture in Manhattan,' Amanda told him, baffled. 'About time capsules.'

'Time capsules? The same as the recording in my room. What the hell's going on?'

'I'm afraid to imagine.'

'There's got to be a way out.'

An archway beckoned on the right. They went through it and reached a long dining table flanked by chairs, everything rustic. Windows provided a view of more mountains. Through a further archway, Amanda saw an old-fashioned wood stove, a refrigerator, other windows, and a door.

Her companion hurried toward the latch.

'Don't touch it,' Amanda told him. 'We've got to assume all the doors are electrified.'

'Then we'll break a window.'

A shadow appeared at the entrance to the dining room. Amanda swung around.

3

In the archway, a woman stared at them. She wore camel slacks and a taupe blouse, highlighted by an expensive-looking necklace, watch, bracelet, and several rings. In her thirties, she was taller than Amanda, thin in a manner that suggested she was a compulsive dieter. Her auburn hair was pulled behind her ears. Her tan features were handsome more than beautiful. Her expression was stark.

'What *is* this place?'

Amanda gestured in frustration. 'We don't know.'

'How did I get here? Tell me who you are.'

'Ray Morgan.'

'Amanda Evert.'

'Who drugged us? I was at a cocktail party. A boat show in Newport Beach. Suddenly I was in that bed upstairs.' The woman shook her head. 'I heard that recording. Time capsules? This doesn't . . . Who on earth would do this?'

'I'm getting out of here before I find out,' Ray said. He grabbed a chair and swung it toward a window.

Amanda jerked her arms up to shield her face from flying glass, but all she heard was wood cracking. Twice. Three times. Louder. Ray grunted with effort. When the pounding stopped, Amanda lowered her arms and saw that a leg on the chair had broken off but the window remained intact.

'The glass is reinforced.' Ray studied it. 'Almost as thick as a jet canopy.'

'Jet canopy?' The comparison seemed odd.

'I was a Marine aviator in Iraq.'

His tone suggested he meant to impress her, but all the reference to Iraq did was send a further spasm of fear through her. For Frank. It reminded her of the terror he'd endured there. *Frank.* She was certain that he too had been drugged. Otherwise, if he was conscious, he wouldn't have let anything happen to her. Where *was* he?

'You haven't told us your name,' Ray said to the woman.

'Bethany Lane.' She frowned at her bracelet and watch. 'Whatever this is about, it isn't robbery.'

'That doesn't encourage me,' Amanda said.

Two more figures appeared behind the woman in the archway.

Ray picked up the broken chair leg, holding it as a weapon.

'It's okay,' a man said. He raised his hands to show they were empty. 'I heard what you said. I don't know anything more about this than *you* do.'

A woman was with him. 'And we're just as scared.'

The man was black. In his twenties, he had thick black hair and a lean build. The woman was Anglo, the same age, with cropped brown hair. She too was lean.

They wore khaki pants with numerous extra pockets down the sides. Camping clothes.

'Derrick Montgomery,' the man said.

'Viv Montgomery,' the woman said. She wore a wedding ring. 'The last thing I remember, we were drinking tea next to our tent, getting ready to go to sleep.'

'In Oregon,' Derrick said. 'But that's not Oregon out there. This looks like Colorado or Wyoming.'

'Stand back.' Ray grabbed another chair and stalked past them into the front hall, where he swung the chair at the window to the left of the door. He struck repeatedly. The impacts made the window vibrate but otherwise had no effect.

'Son of a bitch,' Ray said.

Derrick reached for the latch.

'No,' Amanda warned. 'It's electrified.'

Derrick jerked back his hand.

'Find the electrical panel,' Bethany said. 'Shut off the juice.'

'I like the way you think.' Ray went through the dining room toward the kitchen.

'We shouldn't split up,' Amanda told them.

They hurried to follow Ray and found him standing in the kitchen, staring down at a trapdoor handle.

'Maybe it's electrified too,' he said.

Recalling a long-ago high school science class, Amanda said, 'I've got an idea.' She pulled a hair from her head, wetted it with saliva, and eased it toward the handle. When it touched the metal, she felt a tingle and jerked her hand away. 'Yes, it's electrified.'

'Test the handle on the cupboard under the sink,' Viv told Amanda.

Wondering why the cupboard was important, Amanda obeyed. 'I don't feel any current.'

Viv yanked the doors open and groped under the sink. She pushed aside a long-handled brush, a bottle of dish detergent, and a box of scouring pads. 'Yes!' She straightened, holding a pair of long yellow gloves, the kind used for washing dishes.

Rubber gloves, Amanda realized.

Viv put them on and went directly to the kitchen door. She hesitated, then tapped the handle with a gloved hand. Nothing happened. 'We're out of here.' But when she pushed on the handle, it wouldn't move.

'There's no keyhole,' Bethany said. 'It must have an electronic lock.'

'Which takes us back to the trapdoor and trying to find the electrical panel,' Ray said.

With her hand protected, Viv lifted the trapdoor. They stared at the darkness below.

'I don't see a light switch.' Amanda turned toward the counter next to the sink and put the strand of hair against the drawer handles. When she didn't feel a tingle, she yanked at the drawers.

One contained a hammer, a screwdriver, wrenches, and a flashlight.

Derrick aimed the light through the open trapdoor, revealing a short wooden ladder and a dirt floor. 'Not deep enough to be a basement.'

'To move around down there, you need to be on your hands and knees,' Bethany added. 'Any volunteers?'

No one answered.

'Hell, *I'll* do it.' Ray crouched. 'Anything to get out of here. Give me the flashlight.'

'Wait,' Amanda said.

'What's the matter?'

Amanda studied the ladder. 'Shine the light over there.'

It revealed an electrical wire attached to a rung in the steps.

'Change of plan,' Viv said. 'Back to the door. With the gloves protecting me, I can use the hammer and a screwdriver to take the hinge pins off.'

'Excellent.'

But none of them had said that word.

'Who . . .' Derrick peered up.

From the ceiling, the voice continued, 'Really, I'm impressed.'

4

Amanda's heart lurched.

'Jesus,' Ray said.

Everyone jerked toward the side of the kitchen and gaped above them.

'I never expected you to demonstrate your problem-solving talents so quickly.' The voice belonged to a man. It was deep, sonorous, like a TV announcer's. Amanda recognized it from the recording that had wakened her.

'A speaker hidden in the ceiling,' Bethany said.

'But how did he know what we . . .' Ray studied the upper corners of the room. His eyes narrowed. 'Cameras. They're small, but once you know what you're seeing . . .'

Amanda concentrated and saw tiny apertures in each corner, near the ceiling. She went through the archway into the dining room and frowned upward. 'Cameras here also.' Something seemed to turn over in her stomach. 'The house must be lousy with them.'

'Welcome to Scavenger,' the voice announced.

'Scavenger?' Derrick asked. 'What's *that* supposed to mean?'

'Please, go into the dining room and make yourselves comfortable. I'll explain.'

'To hell with *that*.' Viv grabbed the hammer and screwdriver from the drawer. Still protected by the gloves, she rammed the screwdriver under a hinge pin in the kitchen door and whacked the hammer against it. As metal rang, she knocked the pin free.

'Please, go into the dining room,' the voice repeated.

Viv knocked another pin free. She started on the third.

'This isn't productive. You have only forty hours,' the voice said. 'Don't waste time, Vivian.'

'I'm Viv! Nobody calls me Vivian! I hate it!'

'Step away from the door.'

Amanda felt cold. 'I think we'd better do what he wants.'

'Listen to her, Vivian,' the voice suggested.

'Stop calling me Vivian!'

'Leave the door alone,' Amanda said. 'I've got a bad feeling.'

'If you knock that third pin free and attempt to pry the door open . . .' the voice said.

'Yeah? If I do, what'll happen?' Viv demanded.

'The building will explode.'

'I don't believe you.'

The voice became silent.

'You're lying!' Viv shouted.

The silence deepened.

'Yeah, why don't we go into the dining room?' Ray suggested.

Viv kept glaring toward the ceiling.

Derrick went over and touched her shoulder. Her glare softened only a little. 'It won't hurt to let him tell us what this is about,' he said. 'If we think we don't have an alternative, we can always pry open the door later.'

The voice broke its silence. 'Oh, I guarantee you'll have an alternative.'

5

Wary, they entered the dining room and sat at the table, glancing nervously at each other and then at the ceiling.

Ray took a Zippo lighter from a pocket. He fidgeted, opening and closing its chrome lid. 'Anybody got a cigarette?'

Amanda and the others shook their heads.

'Too much to hope for.'

'Let me tell you about Raymond Morgan,' the voice said.

Ray stopped snapping the lighter's cap.

'Former lieutenant. United States Marine Corps aviator. Raymond is a hero.'

'No,' Ray said.

'His story was widely reported in the media,' the voice continued. 'He was flying a reconnaissance mission when a shoulder-launched missile struck his aircraft. This took place in a mountainous area of Iraq with a strong insurgent presence.'

Again, the reference to Iraq made Amanda think of Frank. Where *was* he? What had happened to him? She prayed he wasn't dead.

'The missile strike occurred at dusk. In fading light, Raymond parachuted to the ground. This was both good and bad. Dusk prevented the insurgents from aiming at a clear target. But the poor light made it difficult for Raymond to see where he landed. He struck a rocky slope and rolled, severely bruising himself and spraining his left ankle. Regardless of his pain, he hobbled all night to escape the insurgents. Just before dawn, he covered himself with rocks. Throughout the day, he remained motionless under their weight while the heat of the sun scorched him. Judging from sounds, he estimated that the insurgents came within fifty feet of him. As long as they hunted him, Raymond didn't dare activate a homing device that would have brought rescue helicopters. After all, the signal would have lured the rescuers to the insurgents. Thus began an ordeal of hide-and-hunt in which Raymond hobbled from ridge to ridge each night and buried himself each day. He made the rations in his emergency kit last as long as possible. After that, he ate bugs. When his canteen was emptied, he drank water from stagnant pools. These made him feverish, but he never gave up. Through determination and ingenuity, discipline and self-reliance, he persisted for ten days until he finally outmaneuvered his hunters. US intelligence sources later determined that the insurgents decided he was dead because no one could possibly have survived as long as he did. Only after he reached territory that wasn't dangerous to the rescue helicopters did he activate his location transmitter. He lost thirty pounds and received a Silver Star. That was three years ago. Raymond is now a pilot for a regional air service in Missouri.'

Ray stared down at his lighter and snapped it shut. 'Not a hero,' he said bitterly. 'Friends of mine got shot down and killed. *They* were heroes.'

6

'Bethany Lane,' the voice said.

Bethany squirmed.

'Your story was widely reported too. Bethany sells luxury sailboats. She's based in Newport Beach, where some of her clients are also her friends. A year ago, she was invited to accompany a group sailing to Bali. Her ex-husband encouraged her to enjoy an overdue vacation. Four days into the voyage, a storm capsized the vessel. Bethany and a twelve-year-old girl were the only survivors. Buoyed by life jackets, they managed to cling to a rubber lifeboat until the water calmed enough for them to crawl in. They had a compass and emergency rations stored in the lifeboat. They had their foul-weather clothes in addition to their life jackets. Bethany pulled wreckage from the water and made a primitive lean-to that protected them from the sun. She had no idea of their location, but she knew mostly open water lay to the west, whereas if she headed east, she couldn't fail to miss the coastline of the United States or Mexico. The trick was to get there. So she used her foul-weather coat to rig a sail, and she used more wreckage to make a rudder, and when the wind didn't cooperate, she rowed. Tell your acquaintances about how you handled the emergency rations, Bethany.'

Bethany's cheeks reddened with embarrassment.

'Don't be modest,' the voice said. 'This is the time for everybody to get to know one another. Tell them about the rations.'

'Well, I . . .'

'Do it,' the voice emphasized. 'Tell them.'

'I've never been much of an eater.'

'That's an understatement. You're anorexic, Bethany.'

'Damn you!'

'No secrets,' the voice said.

'All right,' she yelled. 'I'm anorexic. *So what?* I was fat when I was a kid. People mocked me, and my mother never stopped nagging about my weight. Food makes me sick to look at it. In that damned rubber boat, I told myself, "Hey, it's no big deal about the rations. I hardly ever eat anyhow." So I divided the food into daily amounts, and I gave the little girl most of it. I needed to be awfully lightheaded before I allowed myself to eat.'

'Now tell them about the water.'

Bethany stared at her hands.

'Don't be modest.'

Bethany stayed quiet.

'Very well,' the voice said. 'I'll do the honors. When the meager supply of water was gone, they faced a bigger emergency than the dwindling food supply. A person can survive three weeks without food but only three days without water. Bethany and the little girl had plenty of water around them, of course, but the salt content would eventually have killed them. Their only hope was rain, but the sun blazed relentlessly. Bethany deflated her life jacket and tied it over her head as a sunguard while the little girl lay under the shelter Bethany had rigged. At last, Bethany didn't have the strength to row. The meager sail provided their only momentum. They drifted for two weeks before a container ship en route to Los Angeles noticed them. But how did you survive that long, Bethany? How did you solve the water problem?'

'You know so much about this. Why don't *you* tell them?'

'I'm sure they'd rather hear it from you.'

Bethany studied the group and sounded exhausted, as if suffering the ordeal yet again. 'I used the little girl's foul-weather coat to make a soft pail. I put seawater in it. Then I covered the pail with her deflated life jacket. I held the edges tight with my hands. God, it hurt. After doing that all day, my hands ached so bad, I was afraid I wouldn't be able to keep the seal tight.'

'And why was a tight seal important?'

'I don't want to talk about it.'

'Because it gives you nightmares, Bethany? But talking might help. Think of this as therapy.'

'Who the hell *are* you?'

'Someone with the power to let you out of this building. Why was a tight seal important?'

Bethany murmured something.

'Say it so the others can hear you, Bethany. You can see they're interested.'

'Evaporation.'

'Yes.'

Bethany exhaled audibly. 'The heat of the sun on the pail and the life jacket caused vapor to rise from the sea water. The vapor collected on the underside of the life jacket, where it was wrapped over the pail. I waited a long time. Then I eased the jacket away. There were usually about ten drops of water clinging to the underside. I had to be gentle turning it, or else the drops would fall. The point is, the collected vapor didn't have salt in it. The little girl and I took turns licking the drops. I can still feel the rough surface of the jacket on my tongue. I can still taste the bitterness.'

'Who taught you to get water that way?'

'No one.'

'You just figured it out?'

Bethany didn't reply.

The voice marveled. 'And you did it for days and days.'

7

'Derrick and Vivian Montgomery. I beg your pardon. I mean *Viv*. They, too, were featured prominently in the news. The fact that they're a mixed-race couple added a further dimension to the story.'

Derrick's features hardened. He worked to keep his anger under control.

'They're two of the finest mountain climbers in the world. In fact, that's how they met three years ago – on an expedition in the Himalayas. Odd that they went so far before they met – because they both grew up in Washington State. They've been climbing a lot of the same mountains since they were children. Famous climbers can earn a reasonable income by endorsing equipment, teaching at mountaineering schools, and organizing expeditions for wealthy adventurers. Indeed, Derrick and Viv were already well known in the climbing world before an incident last year thrust them into global prominence, no doubt with beneficial effects on their income.'

'Why don't you go to hell?' Derrick said.

'An example of the independence that typifies this group. Good. You'll disappoint me if you don't show spirit. To answer your question, I can't go to hell. I'm already there.'

The dining room became silent.

'Derrick and Viv were hired to lead an expedition to the top of Mount Everest,' the voice resumed. 'The company organizing it set a price of sixty thousand dollars for each person who wanted to join. Eight adventurers were willing to pay. For this particular expedition, they certainly got their money's worth. It takes almost two weeks just to trek to the base camp. After that, progress upward from camp to camp is increasingly slow. The altitude, the wind, the cold. Everest is more than twenty-eight thousand feet high. By the time the expedition reached twenty-five thousand feet, only two of the original adventurers remained. The others surrendered to exhaustion and the elements, returning to base camp. Derrick and Viv stayed with the two remaining climbers. At twenty-six thousand feet, a storm hit – then an avalanche. The amateur climbers were buried. Derrick and Viv managed to dig them out, but the climbers were injured too seriously to be able to move under their own power. The two-way radios were lost in the avalanche. There was no way to send for help. The injured climbers needed medical attention. In a struggle that lasted twelve hours, Derrick and Viv each took charge of one of the casualties, lowering them by rope, climbing down to join them, dragging them along icy ridges, lowering them again. At one point, and at that debilitating altitude, Derrick even found the strength to carry one of the injured climbers for an astonishing twenty feet that must have felt like miles. When they reached a tent in a camp they'd earlier abandoned, Derrick stayed with the casualties while Viv descended to get help. A second storm hit, but Viv managed to guide rescuers back to the tent while Derrick did everything he could to keep the survivors alive. It's an amazing accomplishment, and yet Derrick and Vivian look uncomfortable as I describe it.'

Viv scowled toward the cameras, pursing her lips at the sound of the name she hated.

'Neither they nor Bethany nor Ray are proud of what they achieved. Isn't it interesting that what strikes others as remarkable behavior is minimized by those who lived through it? At the time, they weren't being heroic. They were just desperately trying to stay alive. Fear is an ugly emotion. No one wants to remember it.'

8

'Amanda Evert.'

Throughout, Amanda's heart had pounded increasingly faster. Each time her name wasn't called, she felt relieved, but then her dread increased as the voice ended one account and paused before beginning another.

'No,' Amanda said.

'But yours is the only story I haven't told.'

'Please, don't talk about it.'

'How can I make my point otherwise?'

'Don't talk about the Paragon Hotel.'

But the voice persisted. 'Around ten at night, Amanda got off a train in Brooklyn on her way home from working late at a bookstore in Manhattan.'

'No.' Amanda pressed her hands over her ears. But even then, she dimly heard the voice.

'Amanda's abductor hid in an alley and used a drug-soaked cloth to overpower her. She regained consciousness on a bed in the Paragon Hotel.'

The memory of her terror brought tears to Amanda's eyes. They streamed down her cheeks.

'That Asbury Park landmark was built in 1901, but after a series of disappearances, its doors were sealed in 1971. For five months, Amanda was held prisoner until a group of urban adventurers broke into the hotel to explore its historic corridors. But they soon discovered that some buildings are abandoned for a reason. Only a few survived the wrath of Amanda's abductor.'

Amanda tasted the salt of her tears as the voice spoke of Frank Balenger, her rescuer, and the agony he endured to save her.

Frank, she thought. Where *are* you?

A flame of anger swelled inside her.

'Balenger's heroism was astonishing,' the voice enthused. 'It's difficult to imagine how a man can push himself so long and so hard to overcome so many obstacles and still manage to survive – not just survive but to save Amanda and a companion in the process. Do you see the theme? Determination and ingenuity, discipline and self-reliance. These are the virtues you share. That is why I brought you here.'

'Frank,' Amanda whispered. Her eyes felt raw, blurred from weeping. 'Frank,' she said, stronger. She stood with such force that her chair toppled. Fists clenched, she yelled toward the ceiling, 'What have you done with him, you bastard? Frank was the hero! I didn't do anything, except get rescued!'

'Modesty is an overpraised virtue. You did far more that night than you give yourself credit for.'

'Damn it, where's Frank? Why isn't he here?'

'Would you change places with him?' the voice wondered. 'Would you want him to be here instead of you?'

'He saved my life. I'm proud to take his place. But Frank's the hero! There's just one reason I can think of why you didn't bring him here. You killed him, you son of a bitch!'

The only reply was the sound of breathing.

'Admit it!' Amanda yelled.

'I haven't included this conversation in your forty hours. But the time will soon begin. I suggest you control yourself, or else you'll be worthless to the group.'

Ray snapped his lighter shut. 'Forty hours? He mentioned that before.'

'All of you, reach under the table.'

'Why?' Bethany demanded.

They looked warily at one another. Slowly, they obeyed.

Amanda was the last. Her emotions so ravaged her that everything seemed distant. She felt a wiry object attached to clips. She pulled it free.

'Earphones?' Viv asked.

Each streamlined headset was identical. A thin, curved metal band had a small ear bud at either end. A piece of metal projected from above the left ear bud.

'A microphone,' the voice explained. 'I need to remain in communication with you when you step outside.'

'You're letting us go?' Viv sounded hopeful.

The voice ignored the question. 'The batteries on these units are strong. They'll last the necessary forty hours.'

'Forty hours? Why do you keep talking about—'

'There's something else under the table.'

Puzzled, Derrick sank to his knees and peered under it. Metal scraped as he pulled something free. He showed the group a small object.

Amanda thought it was a cell phone. Emotionally exhausted, she didn't realize she'd said it out loud until Derrick looked at her.

'No.' He frowned. 'It's a global positioning satellite receiver. We use them on climbing expeditions.'

'And for sailing,' Bethany added.

'And flying,' Ray said. 'But the GPS units in jets are considerably more sophisticated.'

'Some new cars have them also,' Viv said. 'But why do we need—'

'There's one for each of you,' the voice told them.

Amanda watched the others reach under the table. Apprehensive, she did the same. The object her fingers unclipped was silver-gray. It had a screen similar to a cell phone, but there wasn't an array of buttons. Instead, just a few buttons protruded on each side. The top had an image of a globe, then the word ETREX. The name of a particular model? Amanda wondered. At the bottom was another word that she guessed identified the manufacturer: GARMIN.

Viv noticed her confusion. 'Never used a GPS receiver?'

'No.'

'It has maps, an altimeter, and a compass. When you turn it on, it orients itself to the signals from global positioning satellites. Then you enter map coordinates to chart a course or find a location. Hey!' Viv yelled at the ceiling. 'What are we supposed to do with these?'

The voice ignored the question. 'Go to your rooms. Each closet has a change of clothes. Return to the front door in ten minutes.'

'And *then* what?'

'The forty hours begin.'

9

'This is what I learned so far,' Detective Ortega said.

Tortured by his emotions, Balenger sat rigidly at a desk in the Missing Persons office of Manhattan's One Police Plaza. The echo of phones and conversations filled the corridor outside.

'First, I called Oglethorpe University in Atlanta,' Ortega said. 'They never heard of a professor named Adrian Murdock. Not in the history department. Not in *any* department. I described the man you spoke to: gray hair, gray mustache, thin. That fits a lot of professors. Oglethorpe agreed to email faculty photographs for you to look at.'

'The man I saw won't match any of them,' Balenger said.

'You know how this works – keep asking questions, keep getting information, even if it eliminates a possibility. I contacted the city clerk's office. Up until 1983, that property was indeed owned by someone named Victor Evans. I checked with the phone company and got the numbers for all the people with that name in the New York City area. One of them turned out to be the man who owned the building back then. But he doesn't know a Philip Evans, and he never had a son.'

Balenger looked dismally at the cardboard cup of tepid coffee in his hand.

Ortega checked his notepad. 'Yesterday afternoon, my partner and I spoke to people who live on that block of Nineteenth Street. They say a truck arrived Saturday morning and unloaded the chairs and tables. Late in the afternoon, the truck came back to take the furniture away.'

'That's when Amanda and I were removed from the building,' Balenger said.

'Probably. If a date-rape drug was used, no one would have needed to carry you. You'd have been marginally conscious and able to walk. True, you'd have been unsteady. But the truck would have blocked the view from the opposite side of the street, and the tables and chairs being carried out would have distracted anybody watching from the buildings on either side. You and your friend would have seemed like just a couple of people being helped into a car.'

'More likely a van. Something without windows.' Balenger's hands felt cold. 'A lot of people were involved. The woman who called herself Karen Bailey.'

Ortega read a description from the notebook. 'Matronly. Fortyish. No makeup. Brown hair pulled back in a bun. Plain navy dress.'

Balenger nodded. 'Plus the people who showed up for the lecture.'

'You said several of them walked out during the presentation?'

'Yes.' Balenger concentrated, remembering. 'A lot of people,' he emphasized, 'too many to keep a secret.

Maybe the audience didn't understand what was really happening. Maybe they were paid to stay only for a limited time. The delivery people. All they needed to be told was a man and woman felt ill and were being helped into a van. It's possible only the professor and Karen Bailey actually knew what was going on.'

'The delivery people.' Ortega indicated a list on his desk. 'My partner and I are contacting all the companies in the city that rent tables and chairs for events. We'll eventually find the company that delivered to that address. Maybe they can give us a description of whoever hired them.'

'Any bets they were hired over the phone and paid with a check in the mail?' Balenger asked.

Ortega studied him with concern.

'And any bets the bank account was established for the sole purpose of paying the realtor and the rental company and maybe some of the people who showed up for the lecture?' Balenger added. 'That bank account won't be used again, and whoever established it no doubt gave a false name, address, and social security number.'

'You know,' Ortega said, 'this is something new for me.'

'What do you mean?'

'I've never had a case in which someone with law-enforcement experience reported a loved one missing. I feel like I'm a magician trying to work with another magician. You're familiar with the procedures. You realize what goes on behind the curtain. While I was making inquiries with Oglethorpe University, the city clerk's office, and the residents of that block on Nineteenth Street, I heard about someone else who made the same inquiries. That wouldn't have been *you* by any chance?'

'I couldn't bear just sitting and waiting.'

'I hope you didn't imply to those people that you're still in law enforcement.'

'I did nothing illegal.'

'Then the best thing you can do right now is make yourself sit and wait a little longer. You're too emotionally involved to go around questioning people. Don't try to do my job.'

'The thing is,' Balenger said, 'I realize how hard this is for you. You and your partner have plenty of cases, and there's only so much time in a day, and speaking of magicians, you and I know magic doesn't exist.'

'Okay, show me how to do my job. If you were me, where would you look to find the people who attended the lecture?'

'I was about to suggest they played their parts with such assurance, maybe that's what they do for a living. Maybe they're actors,' Balenger said.

10

'There's the son of a bitch.' Balenger gestured toward a photograph in a glassed display. 'Minus the mustache and with darker hair.'

He and Ortega were standing outside the Bleecker Street Playhouse in Greenwich Village. They'd spent the previous hour phoning talent agencies and actors' groups, asking about anyone hired for a Saturday afternoon gig on East 19th Street.

Leaving the noise of traffic, they entered a small, dingy lobby, where they paused to assess their surroundings. The box office was behind them. On the left, Balenger saw a coat closet, on the right a counter for refreshments. The stained carpet looked worn, although not much of it was visible because of folded tarpaulins, stacked scaffolding, paint cans, buckets, and brushes. The smell of turpentine hung in the air.

'Definitely needs an overhaul,' Ortega murmured, glancing toward a water stain on the ceiling.

'I hate old buildings,' Balenger said.

Straight ahead, past a double door, muffled voices spoke unintelligible words.

Ortega opened one of the doors and went inside. After a moment, he came back and motioned for Balenger to follow him. The door swung shut behind them. They stood in an aisle that descended past rows of seats toward a bottom area illuminated by overhead lights. On stage, the curtains were parted. Two couples, one middle-aged, the other young, held scripts and recited lines. A tall, thin man stood before the stage, motioning with a pointer to let them know where to stand.

Looking small down there, the young woman glanced toward the back. 'They're here,' she said, her voice echoing.

The tall, thin man turned toward Balenger and Ortega. 'Please, come down and join us.'

Concealing his agitation, Balenger was conscious of the sound of his footsteps in the deserted aisle. The theater exuded a sense of gloom, the old seats unnaturally empty, desperate to be filled with applause.

Ortega introduced himself and showed his badge. 'I believe you're already familiar with Mr Balenger.'

Balenger recognized them. The tall, thin man was Professor Murdock. The four people on the stage had been at the Saturday lecture.

'I certainly remember *you*,' the man with the pointer said, 'and the young woman you were with. Her name was . . .' He glanced up, searching his memory. 'Amanda Evert.'

'And your name was Adrian Murdock, except I'm sure it isn't.'

'Roland Perry. The professor's name was assigned to me.'

'Is something wrong?' the young man on the stage asked.

Ortega addressed Perry. 'On the phone, you said your group was hired to be at that house on East Nineteenth Street.'

'That's right. The event was described as performance art.' Perry's voice sounded vaguely British. 'I was given a speech to deliver. Our playhouse actors received directions about how to behave, plus a description of Mr Balenger and his friend. We were told this would be a practical joke of sorts. Throughout my lecture, the audience would gradually leave. Then I'd stop talking. As the visual demonstration continued, I'd step into the shadows and leave the building. After that, the images would stop, and Mr Balenger and Ms Evert would find themselves alone in the room.'

'Doesn't sound like much of a joke,' Ortega said.

'It was supposed to involve a surprise birthday party. As Mr Balenger and Ms Evert wondered what on earth was going on, friends hiding upstairs would shout "Happy Birthday!" Food and drinks would be carried down. The party would start.'

Ortega looked at Balenger, then asked Perry, 'How much were you paid?'

'For the group, for what amounted to an hour's work, we received two thousand dollars. It was a much-needed contribution to our remodeling efforts.'

'How were you approached?' Balenger asked.

'A woman phoned and arranged to meet me here at the playhouse.'

'Did she give a name?'

'Karen Bailey. The woman you met at the lecture.'

'I had the feeling she was part of your group,' Balenger said.

'Not at all.'

'Do you have a contract?' Ortega asked. 'An address or a signature I can look at?'

'No. It didn't seem necessary. The arrangement was unusual, yes, but the two thousand dollars couldn't have come at a better time. We were thankful for the windfall.'

'But why are you here?' the older woman asked. 'What's the matter?'

'Nothing for you to worry about.' Ortega gave Perry his business card. 'If she contacts you again, let me know.'

'Karen Bailey did leave a photocopy of something,' Perry said. 'She told me to give it to Mr Balenger if he came to the theater.'

'A photocopy?' Balenger frowned. 'Of *what*?'

'I put it in my script bag.' Perry tucked his pointer under an arm, went to a worn canvas bag next to a seat, and searched through it. 'Here.' He offered Balenger a folded piece of paper.

But before Balenger touched it, Ortega said, 'Wait.' He removed the latex gloves from his sport coat. After putting them on, he opened the paper.

Balenger stood next to him and looked down at it. The paper had streaks from a photocopy machine. It showed a book page on which everything was matted out, except one paragraph and an imprint of a stamp: NYPL HUMANITIES & SOCIAL SCIENCES LIBRARY. The stamp was faint.

Ortega read the paragraph out loud.

'It is a wonderful place, the moor,' said he, looking round over the undulating downs, long green rollers, with crests of jagged granite foaming up into fantastic surges. 'You never tire of the moor. You cannot think the wonderful secrets which it contains. It is so vast, and so barren, and so mysterious.'

The passage was so bewildering it made Balenger lightheaded. 'Karen Bailey told you to give this to me if I came to the theater?' he asked Perry.

'Yes.'

'Did she say why?'

'No. I assumed it was part of the practical joke.' Perry tapped his pointer on the floor. 'What's the problem? Why won't you tell us why you—'

'I smell smoke,' Balenger said.

11

Spinning toward the back of the theater, Balenger saw wisps of gray drifting through the seams in the double doors.

'*No*,' Perry moaned.

Balenger heard the four actors scramble down steps from the stage, but all he paid attention to were the strengthening tendrils of gray. He and Ortega ran up the aisle, stopping when they saw light flicker beyond the middle of the doors. Something crackled on the other side.

Perry and the other actors rushed to them.

'The paint supplies.' Drawing a breath, Perry inhaled smoke and stifled a cough. 'Somehow they must have caught fire. Rags in a can. Some kind of spontaneous—'

'Or maybe they had help,' Balenger said.

'Help? What on earth do you—'

Behind them, the stage lights went out. As darkness enveloped them, an actress screamed. At once, battery-powered emergency lights glared from the corners.

'Give me your pointer.' Ortega took it from Perry and used its thick end to push the door open.

Smoke gushed through the opening. Beyond it, orange rippled among the gray clouds, flames licking toward the pointer.

Ortega yanked the pointer away, letting the door

swing shut. As Perry stumbled back, he bumped into one of the actresses, who bent over, coughing.

'Where's the fire exit?' Balenger demanded.

'One's over there.' Perry gestured toward a door halfway down the right aisle. Next to it was a small red fire-alarm box.

Amid thickening smoke, Balenger helped the coughing woman to straighten and guided her along a row of seats. Ahead, the actors banged against arm rests and reached the aisle on the right, where Ortega pushed a bar on the fire door.

The door didn't budge. Ortega rammed his shoulder against it, but it remained firm. 'Who the hell locked this?'

'Nobody! It always works!' Perry insisted. 'It must be jammed on the other side!' The director tugged open the alarm's cover and pulled a lever, groaning when the alarm didn't sound. 'It's supposed to be linked to the fire department, but if we can't hear it, the signal isn't being transmitted.'

In the back of the theater, the smoke was now so thick it obscured the doors. The crackle of flames became a roar. The paint and turpentine were acting as accelerants, Balenger realized. 'Sprinklers? Does the theater have—'

'Yes! I don't understand why they aren't working.'

One of the actors pointed toward the back. 'The fire got through the doors!'

Balenger spun, his skin prickling when he saw

smoke and flames climbing toward a balcony. For a terrible moment, he reeled from déjà vu, as if he were trapped in the inferno of the Paragon Hotel. It's happening again! he thought. 'Is there another emergency door?'

'Backstage!' Perry shouted.

The smoke had a harsh, greasy taste that made Balenger cough. A couple of the actors seemed paralyzed with fear. For a moment, Balenger too felt overcome with terror, his previous nightmares seizing him. 'Move!' he found the strength to yell.

Boards rumbling, they hurried up the steps to the stage. Behind a side curtain, an emergency light glared above another exit. Ortega pushed the bar and crashed against the door, but it didn't open. Balenger joined him, slamming his shoulder against it.

Someone pointed toward the back. 'The fire's on the ceiling!'

Smoke spreading toward him, Ortega noticed circular metal stairs. 'What's on the upper floor?'

'A fire escape off a dressing room!' Perry charged toward the spiral steps. They vibrated as he scurried up. But he suddenly stopped, clinging to the trembling hand rail. When Balenger reached the stairs, he saw what made Perry gape. Smoke obscured the top.

'We couldn't breathe up there,' someone said. 'We couldn't see where we're going.'

The staircase went down through the floor.

'What about the basement?' Balenger asked.

'Three windows!'

'Go!'

As their footsteps clattered on the metal, Balenger stared down toward the gloom and hesitated. A basement, he thought. There's always a basement. Sweat oozed from his forehead, only partly because of the accumulating heat. He saw a flashlight attached to a bracket beside a control panel. Grabbing it, he forced himself down the stairs.

The air became cool. Off-balance from repeated turns, he reached a stone floor. Light struggled through a row of three small windows along the right wall. Close to the basement's ceiling, the dusty panes showed the dirty brick wall of a narrow alley.

The legs of a table screeched as Ortega dragged it toward a window. Balenger switched on the flashlight and aimed it along the length of the basement, revealing painted backdrops of a hill, trees and sky stacked against a wall.

'It won't open!' Ortega tugged at the window. 'It's painted shut!'

'Break the glass!' Perry shouted.

'The opening's too small!' the older, heavyset actor moaned. 'I won't fit through!'

Balenger kept scanning the flashlight, searching for another way out. He saw tables, chairs, and other stage furniture. Costumes hung on poles. Wigs perched on plastic heads. Everything was protected by clear plastic sheets. But not for long, he thought.

He heard glass breaking, Ortega smashing the window with a cane Perry handed him.

'I'm telling you, I can't fit through that narrow opening!' the heavy actor insisted.

'I can't either!' the other actor said.

The flashlight beam reached the wall under the stage. Stacked boxes partly obscured an old door.

Balenger grabbed Perry. 'Where does that door lead? Another building?'

'No! A sub-basement!'

'*Sub-basement?* Why does this building need a—'

'It doesn't! Not now!' Perry trembled from the heat and roar of the approaching flames.

'What do you mean, "not now"? Don't look at the fire! Just tell me about the sub-basement!'

'It's from an earlier building. Way back, there was a stream.'

'What?'

'A long time ago, Greenwich Village had a *lot* of streams.' Perry rushed on. 'Drainage tunnels kept the buildings from sinking. The stream's dry now, but in the old days you could get water from it.'

Balenger ran to the door, shoved the boxes away, and tugged a rusted handle.

'No!' Ortega warned. 'We'd suffocate down there!' Even with air streaming through the broken window, the detective bent over and coughed from the smoke.

Wood scraped against stone as Balenger pulled harder on the door. Rusted hinges protested. He managed to open it far enough to aim his flashlight through. He saw cobwebs across dust-covered stone walls and steps.

'The flames'll absorb all the oxygen down there!' Ortega yelled.

Glancing behind him, Balenger saw Ortega finish smashing the glass in the window. The detective helped the older actress climb on to the table and lifted her toward the opening. She squirmed halfway through and got stuck.

'Squeeze in your stomach!' Ortega shouted.

'I'm cut!'

Ortega pushed her hips, and abruptly the actress moved, struggling the rest of the way through.

As Ortega helped the other actress on to the table, the writhing wall of flames shifted closer.

'I'll never fit!' the older actor insisted.

Nightmarish memories of the Paragon Hotel almost overwhelmed Balenger. He squeezed into the gap he'd made. Aiming the flashlight, his footsteps echoing, he brushed away cobwebs and hurried down the uneven stairs.

He reached a stone chamber. A rat squealed and darted out of sight. Balenger stumbled back. He listened to his hoarse breathing, fought to keep control, and used his flashlight to study his surroundings. The rough, vaulted enclosure was about six feet long, wide, and high. It forced him to stoop. A trough in the stones showed where the stream had gone through. To the right and left, arches of crumbly bricks provided the openings through which the water had come and gone. Even after a century and a half, the air still carried a hint of fetid dampness.

Balenger heard shouting above him. He listened to the fire's roar and felt air rush past, the fire sucking it upward. He put a hand against a stone wall, suddenly realizing how unsteady he felt.

'I'll never get through!' The voice above him sounded more panicked.

Balenger knelt and aimed the trembling flashlight through the arch on the right. Five feet inside, part of the ceiling had collapsed, a pile of dirt and broken bricks impeding the way. Several red eyes reflected the light.

Fear cramped Balenger's chest. He shifted the flashlight through the archway on the left. As far as the light stretched, nothing blocked the way. He came dizzily to his feet, feeling the air rush toward the basement above him.

A man screamed up there.

Balenger mustered his strength and charged up the steps, seeing the rippling reflection of the fire. He no longer needed his flashlight. The approaching blaze showed Ortega's frenzy when he pushed a tall, thin man – Perry – through the broken window. That left two men, along with Ortega and Balenger.

'Can we get through?' Balenger shouted.

'I don't think so!' Sparks swirled over Ortega.

'This way!' Balenger told them. 'There's a chance.'

The heat from the fire roared so near that they didn't hesitate. The three of them squeezed past Balenger. He pushed the door shut, trying to block the outflow of air, and ran down to join them.

'To the left!'

The young actor hesitated. 'You've got to be kidding!'

'Crawl!'

'I just saw a rat!'

'Which means there's a way out! Crawl! I'll come last and aim the flashlight ahead of everybody.'

Smoke drifted down the steps.

'No choice!' Balenger shouted.

'I'll go first!' Ortega drew his pistol.

The heavy actor gaped. 'What do you need the gun for? *How big do those rats get?*'

Ortega dropped to his knees, then his chest. While the detective squirmed through the low archway, Balenger told the others, 'Go, go, go, go, go!' He shoved the men to the ground, urging them forward. 'Move!'

Amid the rush of air, Balenger sank to his chest and squirmed over the stones. Aiming the flashlight forward, he crawled into the archway. The shadows seemed to get heavier. The stones under him changed to dirt. He heard the echo of clothes scraping, of harsh breathing, and the man ahead of him murmuring what might have been a prayer.

Cobwebs clung to Balenger's hair. The brick archway

sank lower. He felt it against his back and pressed his chest against the dirt.

'I don't think I can get through here either,' a man ahead moaned.

'Push the dirt to the side,' Ortega ordered from in front. 'Deepen the channel.'

The line stopped. Air rushed past them toward the fire.

'*What's the matter?*' Balenger called. Dust filled his nostrils. His claustrophobia squeezed his chest so tight he feared he'd pass out.

'I thought I saw . . .'

'Thought you saw *what*?' Balenger leaned to the side and angled the flashlight beam as far forward as he could.

'A shadow moving.'

'If it's a rat, shoot it!' the older actor said.

'No!' the other actor warned. 'The sound might collapse these bricks!'

'Then why don't you stop yelling?'

'Bricks,' Ortega told them. 'I reached some fallen bricks.'

Dirt trickled on to Balenger's neck. He had trouble breathing. After a pause, he heard bricks being stacked to the side.

'Okay, I'm moving forward,' Ortega said.

More dirt fell on to Balenger's neck. Faster, he thought.

The man ahead of Balenger started crawling again. Pulse racing, Balenger followed painfully.

'Hold it!' the man ahead of him blurted.

'What's wrong?'

'The back of my belt's caught against a brick in the ceiling.'

Balenger tensed. In the semi-darkness, he heard strained movement.

'Got it,' the man said. 'I'm free.'

Balenger heard scraping sounds as the man resumed crawling.

'I've reached some old steps!' Ortega called.

Thank God, Balenger thought, unable to catch his breath. Tasting dust, pressing his stomach to the ground, he squirmed forward.

His heart twisted when something held him back. His jacket was caught on a brick above him.

'Keep the flashlight steady!' Ortega called back.

'Yeah, steps!' the man behind Ortega cheered. 'I see them!'

Balenger felt the brick move against his back.

'We'll soon be out of here.' The actor in front of Balenger squirmed ahead.

The brick came loose, weighing on Balenger. More dirt trickled.

'Frank!' Ortega called back. 'What's wrong?'

Balenger didn't dare speak for fear the vibration would dislodge more bricks.

'Why have you stopped?' Ortega's voice echoed.

Another brick weighed on him.

'My God, does it ever feel good to lift my head,' the actor in front of Balenger said. 'I see a door!'

'Frank?' Ortega called.

As panic seized him, Balenger almost shrieked. A third brick shifted. Dust filled his nostrils. He eased forward an inch. Dirt pressed against his shoulder blades.

'Frank?'

The roof squeed down on him. He needed more strength to pull forward. Bricks sank on to him. Abruptly, he couldn't bear the weight any longer. The air was so stale, he feared he'd suffocate. Inwardly wailing, he squirmed faster, and suddenly more dirt fell. He crawled in a frenzy, bricks striking his legs, dirt collapsing, and he was shrieking out loud now, shoving with his knees, pulling, digging with his elbows, lunging, his legs feeling crushed, the noise of the collapse louder than his scream. Hands grabbed him, dragging him upward. The flashlight wavered in his trembling grasp. Dust swirled. He felt smothered.

Moaning, he reached stone steps, charged up, and crashed against a wooden door. It trembled. He crashed into it again. The door was so old it broke off its hinges. But even then it didn't open. Something was blocking it on the other side. Ortega joined him, the two of them slamming against it, and suddenly it tilted, objects clattering behind it.

Amid choking dust, Balenger saw lights beyond the door. When he and Ortega gave the door a final desperate thrust, it toppled, knocking more objects over. Fighting to clear his lungs, Balenger crawled over the door and found himself in a basement filled with old furniture. On wooden steps, a spectacled man in a suit gaped at them.

12

Balenger lurched past him. At the top of the stairs, he encountered more old furniture, a roomful of it, and continued to feel squeezed. Sunlight through a front window prompted him to hurry toward a door. Outside, he almost bumped into someone rushing along the sidewalk. He bent over, coughing. Only after the spasms had passed and he raised his head did he notice a sign on the door: GREENWICH ANTIQUE FURNITURE.

Ortega came out, holding a handkerchief to his mouth. He lowered it and pointed toward the store's interior. 'The owner says he likes to take his customers down to the sub-basement. Evidently, that touch of history makes his furniture seem extra old and valuable.'

Balenger slumped against a light pole. 'Thank God for antiques.'

'Yeah, well, he claims we ruined about thirty thousand dollars' worth of those antiques when we knocked them over breaking down the door.'

'Now we know the price of our lives.' Balenger

glanced at the store's entrance, where the spectacled man frowned. 'Will you take a check?'

'For thirty thousand dollars? I don't think he's the type to appreciate a joke,' Ortega murmured.

'I'm serious. Sometime I'll tell you about a coin I found.' Balenger turned toward the owner. 'Whatever your insurance doesn't cover, I'll pay for.'

Balenger heard sirens. Smoke drifted over the rooftops. People ran along the sidewalk toward the blaze.

'We need to get over there and tell the fire investigators what we know,' Ortega said.

'But it'll take hours before they finish with us! You know as much as I do. Tell them I couldn't stay.'

'Couldn't stay? What are you talking about?'

'There's too much to do. Report for both of us. I'll talk to them later if they still have questions.'

'When you were in law enforcement, is that how you handled things? You let your witnesses tell you to report for them?'

'All right, all right, I hear you.' Balenger struggled to catch his breath. 'Did you manage to keep that piece of paper?'

'In my pocket.'

'Can we use your photocopy machine?' Balenger asked the owner.

The man seemed to think this was the most reasonable question in the world. He nodded.

Balenger swatted dirt from his jeans and sport coat.

They smelled of smoke. 'We've got a piece of paper we need to photocopy so we can read what's on it without leaving fingerprints.'

Ortega studied him. 'You look exhausted. Talking to the fire investigators will at least give you a chance to rest.'

'When I find Amanda, that's when I'll rest.'

It took barely a minute to make photocopies and return to the street, but in that brief time, the crowd increased dramatically. Balenger folded one of the photocopies and stuck it into his jacket pocket. He and Ortega struggled through noisy spectators. Ahead, more sirens wailed.

'Police,' Ortega said. 'Let us through.'

A few onlookers made space, but three steps later, others blocked the way. Balenger felt squeezed. There's no time for this, he thought.

'Police!' Ortega yelled as more people jostled him.

No time, Balenger decided. A determined man shoved in front of him, allowing him to hang back. When three others elbowed past, Balenger used them for cover and ducked away through the crowd.

'Frank, where *are* you?' he heard Ortega shouting.

LEVEL THREE:
HIDE-AND-HUNT

1

Legs unsteady, Amanda obeyed the voice's instructions and climbed the staircase. As Ray, Bethany, Derrick and Viv entered their bedrooms, she went into hers. She'd been told to go to the closet and put on the clothes she found there, but first she went into the bathroom and relieved herself. She didn't care if there were cameras. Urgency cancelled modesty. Suspecting that it would be a long time before she saw another bathroom, she pulled toilet paper off the roll and crammed it into her pocket.

Now that the fog of whatever drug she'd been given was dissipating along with her nausea, Amanda realized how empty her stomach felt. Her mouth was dry. After flushing the toilet, she went to the sink, then paused, frowning toward the toilet. The water swirled down. But the tank didn't make the sound of water refilling it. She had a fearful suspicion of what would happen when she turned the knobs on the sink – or rather what *wouldn't* happen – but she tried it anyhow. No water flowed from the taps.

Amanda's mouth felt even more parched as she went to the closet and opened it. Blue coveralls hung on a hanger, a many-pocketed garment that reminded her of flight suits she'd seen in movies about military pilots. Waffle-soled hiking boots were on the floor. They too were blue, as were the wool socks and baseball cap next to them. Now she did feel modest. Trying to avoid the cameras, she stepped into the closet and hurriedly took off her jeans. In a rush, she stepped into the coveralls and zipped them over her white blouse. The coveralls were sturdy nylon on the outside with an insulating fabric. Briefly, the material chilled her legs. After transferring the toilet paper to the coveralls, she carried the socks and hiking boots to the bed and put them on. Everything fit her.

She glanced around the room, looking for anything she might be able to use to escape.

'Nothing here will help you,' the voice said from the ceiling.

It made her flinch. She heard footsteps in the corridor and left the bedroom, seeing Ray, Bethany, Derrick and Viv come out of their rooms. All wore caps, coveralls, wool socks, and hiking shoes. Ray's were green, Bethany's gray, Derrick's red, and Viv's brown. Because of Ray's pilot background, he was the only one who looked at ease in the jumpsuit.

'Well, at least I can tell the rest of you apart,' Derrick, the only black person in the group, tried to joke.

'I think that's the idea,' Ray said, pointing toward the

ceiling. 'For *him* to tell us apart, especially at a distance.'

Glancing nervously around, they descended the staircase to the large open area in front of the door. Ray pulled out his lighter, opening and snapping it shut. Amanda tried not to let the sound get on her nerves.

'Now what?' Viv asked the voice.

'Go into the dining room,' the voice commanded. 'Put on your radio headsets. Turn them on.'

'Wait a minute.' Bethany's eyes looked fierce. 'The sink in my bathroom didn't work! I'm thirsty!'

'I'm hungry,' Ray said. 'God knows how long it's been since—'

'This is Monday,' the voice said.

'Monday?' Bethany's voice dropped.

'But the last thing I remember . . .' Derrick shook his head. 'My God, I lost . . .'

'Two days.' Viv looked stunned.

'So of course you're hungry and thirsty. The fact that you weren't active during the interval prevented you from expending energy. You still have strength. As I noted when telling you about Bethany's experience on the ocean, you can survive for as long as three weeks without food.'

Amanda felt her lightheadedness return.

'Contrary to popular opinion, going two or three days without food is hardly life-threatening,' the voice assured them. 'People have been known to hike great distances during that time.'

Obeying instructions, Viv went into the dining room. But she kept going into the kitchen.

Understanding, Amanda and the others followed, watching Viv put on the rubber gloves she'd used earlier. She opened the refrigerator. It was empty. She opened all the cupboards, but they too were empty. She tried the tap on the sink. It didn't work.

She moaned.

'Fasting purifies,' the voice said. 'Now go into the dining room and put on the headsets. Otherwise I won't let you outside.'

With no other choice, they did what they were told.

Amanda adjusted the headset, then put her cap back on. As she pulled her blond hair through the back of the hat, the sonorous voice through the ear buds was disturbingly intimate. 'Put your GPS receiver into a pocket. Be careful to protect it. You're going to need it.'

Again the group obeyed.

'Now I'll tell you about Scavenger,' the voice said. 'In 2000, President Clinton signed legislation that allowed global positioning satellite receivers available to the public to receive signals that were accurate within ten feet, almost as accurate as military GPS receivers. Prior to that time, the public could receive GPS signals that were accurate only within twenty-five feet, reserving greater accuracy exclusively for the military. Almost immediately, someone in Oregon posted map coordinates on an Internet site, explaining that anyone who used a GPS receiver to search that area had a chance to find a hidden treasure. The treasure was only a metal box of dime-store novelties. That wasn't the point. The objective wasn't what was in the box but rather the pleasure of the hunt. Even with coordinates as accurate as ten feet, the box was difficult to locate.'

Amanda was so accustomed to hearing the voice come from the ceiling that she felt disoriented now that it sounded inside her head.

'From Oregon, this version of a scavenger hunt spread rapidly around the world. It bore similarities to a similar scavenger hunt called letterboxing, but the GPS version is called "geocaching." Players use an Internet site to learn the coordinates of something hidden – a cache – in an area they want to explore. They program these coordinates into their GPS receiver, then let the receiver guide them to the spot they need to search. Often, within a ten-foot-square area of trees or rocks, the object is so small or so disguised that it's almost impossible to find. A cache might look like an insect, such as a grasshopper, for example. It takes a careful eye to notice that the grasshopper is made of rubber. Or the object might look like a rock, but when examined it turns out to be plastic, containing a cheap ring or some other type of nominal treasure. The player who finds the object leaves something comparable in return, or sometimes just a note, and then reports the victory to a website like geocaching.com. Players gain stature for the number of caches they discover. Only a few years after President Clinton signed that GPS legislation, there were a quarter of a million caches in two hundred and nineteen countries.'

Ray interrupted angrily. 'Grasshoppers? Cheap rings? What the hell do you want with us?'

'No need to shout, Ray. The microphone next to your cheek will supply the proper sound level. What do I want? Step to the front door.'

Amanda tensed as she heard an electronic beep from the door. The lock made a clunking sound, the bolt sliding free.

'You can open it now,' the voice instructed.

'Not until I know I won't get electrocuted.' Viv tapped a rubber glove against the door's handle. Getting no reaction, she pushed down and pulled.

Sunlight streamed in, accompanied by a pleasant breeze.

'Damn, that feels good,' Derrick said. He went outside, as did Viv and Ray.

Hesitant, Amanda and Bethany followed.

2

The sun was warm. The grassy, sagebrush-dotted field was more open space than Amanda had ever seen. All her life she'd lived in cities, where the buildings permitted a view of only a portion of the sky.

The trees in parks created a similar limitation. But here the view was immense. Snow-capped mountains rose in the distance, but they made no impression on the sky. The canopy of blue was vast.

'As you see, you're in a valley surrounded by mountains,' the voice explained in Amanda's ears. She noticed everyone else concentrating to listen. 'On your right, far off, there's a break in the mountains. That's the only exit. I don't advise you to go in that direction.'

Amanda stared at it longingly.

The group walked farther from the building, which reminded Amanda of a log-walled hunting lodge she'd once seen in a magazine. She noticed Viv put the rubber gloves in a pocket of her coveralls. Good, Amanda thought. Save whatever resources we can get our hands on. But the farther she went from the building, the more insignificant she felt in the vastness around her.

'Please, take out your GPS receivers and turn them on,' the voice said.

Everyone complied.

Except Amanda, who was baffled by the unfamiliar object she removed from her pocket. 'Where . . .'

'On the right side,' Derrick said. 'Two buttons. The bottom one. It's got a symbol of a light bulb.'

Amanda pressed the button and heard a beeping sound. The unit's screen glowed, revealing a cartoon of a globe with satellite icons over it.

'Mostly because of the United States and its military requirements, there are a large number of global positioning satellites, twenty-six that the government admits to having,' the voice continued. 'But your receiver needs only to establish a link with three. More is better for accuracy, but three is sufficient. In this valley, the usual number of links is five. The satellites are thirty miles above us, beaming signals at a mere fifty watts, and yet they're amazingly precise.'

Amanda watched vertical bars appear on the bottom of her unit's screen. Five of them darkened.

'These receivers work best in open spaces,' the voice said. 'Buildings and dense forest restrict the signals. But now that you're outdoors, your units have registered your current position. Pay attention to the following coordinates. They indicate your destination. North . . .' The voice dictated a series of numbers. 'West . . .' It dictated other numbers.

Amanda was bewildered as Ray, Bethany, Derrick and Viv pressed buttons on their receivers.

'Not so fast,' Bethany objected, adjusting her microphone. 'Tell me the second set of numbers again.'

The voice repeated them.

'Okay,' Bethany said.

Amanda continued to be baffled.

'It's easy.' Sounding annoyed, Viv took the receiver from her. 'The buttons on each side cycle through the main pages and access the menus on them: a compass, an altimeter, a map.'

'No map on mine,' Ray said.

'Mine neither,' Bethany said.

'Great. So we still don't know where we are.' Viv showed Amanda how each button worked. 'With a little practice, you won't have trouble remembering what they do. Here, I'll enter the coordinates for you.'

Viv showed Amanda how it was done, then handed the receiver back to her.

'Excellent,' the voice said. 'Team spirit.'

'Anything to get out of here,' Viv said.

'That depends on how everyone performs. The forty hours begin . . .' the voice paused, as if double-checking something, '*now*.'

Everyone frowned.

'I advise you not to waste time,' the voice warned.

They continued to remain in place.

'You'll find something you need at the coordinates I gave you.'

'Water?' Bethany asked. 'Food?'

The voice didn't answer.

'Hell, if there's water and food, let's go.' Derrick glanced at his GPS receiver.

Amanda did the same. On the screen, a red needle pointed away from her. Above it, a box was marked DIST TO DEST and indicated one mile.

'In this mode, the arrow doesn't aim north but instead toward the coordinates we entered,' Viv explained. 'Looks like we're supposed to head toward that clump of trees in the distance.'

The trees were opposite the valley's exit, Amanda noticed. She assumed that her thoughts were the same as the others'. The moment she was far enough from the building that she couldn't see it any longer, she'd watch for a chance to escape.

The guarded expression in everyone's eyes told her that the rest of the group had the same plan.

They started walking. Dry grass crunched under Amanda's boots. The sun's glare pained her eyes. Despite its heat, she shivered. Staying behind the others, she couldn't help noticing how unnatural the combination of their blue, green, gray, red and brown jumpsuits looked. When she glanced around, the expanse of the sky seemed overpowering.

A sudden movement attracted her attention. Ahead, something darted from a bush. A rabbit. It zigzagged away from them, racing toward the mountains.

At once, something else appeared, a larger animal bounding from a depression in the ground, chasing the rabbit. For an instant, Amanda thought it was a wolf, but then she realized that its markings didn't match any pictures of wolves she'd seen. It's a German shepherd, she realized. The dog and the panicked rabbit disappeared down a hidden slope.

No one spoke. It struck Amanda as odd that when they were in the building, they hadn't hesitated to talk, but now that they were in the open, a hush fell over them, broken only by the sound of their boot steps.

'Ever see Hitchcock's *North by Northwest*?' Bethany asked unexpectedly.

Her voice came from two places – Bethany herself

and Amanda's earphones. A schizoid effect. Amanda didn't know how long she could bear this. Frank, where *are* you? God, don't let him be dead. I'll go crazy if he's dead.

You're not crazy now? She was terribly aware that she was addressing herself in the second person, something else that was schizoid.

The others, too, looked startled by Bethany's question. It was as incongruous as the way her expensive necklace, rings, bracelet and watch contrasted with her jumpsuit.

Ray answered, self-conscious about being overheard. 'Is that the one with Cary Grant on Mount Rushmore?'

'Yeah, the faces of four presidents are carved into the mountain.' Derrick sounded subdued. 'I saw *North by Northwest* in a course in college. The bad guys chase Cary Grant and, what's her name, Eva Marie Saint, across the faces.'

'In an earlier scene, he gets off a bus at a cornfield,' Viv said.

Amanda sensed a change of tone now, their voices less tentative, as if they hoped that a conversation about something familiar would help them feel normal.

'The cornfield,' Bethany said. 'Yes. Grant gets off a bus in farm country. He's been told to meet somebody and get information about whoever's trying to kill him.'

Two large birds circled above them.

'Vultures,' Derrick said.

As the shadows passed over them, Bethany returned

to the safety of talking about the movie. 'After a long time, a car goes by, and Grant keeps waiting. The situation seems even stranger because he's standing on this deserted farm road wearing a suit.'

Hiking through the brittle grass, Amanda saw a gully ahead.

'Then a truck comes from the side of the cornfield,' Bethany said. 'This is after about a minute of Grant doing nothing but stand there. A woman lets a farmer out. The truck leaves. The farmer and Grant nod to each other. We hear a drone in the background, a crop duster flying over a field. Then another bus shows up, and the farmer climbs aboard, but not before telling Grant how strange it is that the plane's dusting crops where there aren't any. Grant thinks about this. The bus drives away. Grant thinks some more, glances toward the crop duster, which starts flying in his direction, and suddenly Grant races toward the cornfield. The plane sprays machine-gun bullets at him.'

'Right!' Derrick said. 'Grant dives among the corn rows. The pilot drops the fertilizer or herbicide or whatever his plane is carrying, almost suffocating him.'

They neared the gully.

'I read somewhere,' Bethany said, 'that Hitchcock made several movies with a lot of scary enclosed spaces, that spooky old mansion in *Rebecca*, for example, but in *North by Northwest* he wanted to try the reverse – to make open spaces threatening.'

They paused at the top of the gully.

'So quiet.' Ray turned in a circle, surveying the expanse of the valley and the mountains that surrounded them. 'I'm used to the noise of jets and cars and cities. Activity. Lots of things happening.'

'It's like being in that awful rubber boat.' Bethany sounded as if her dry tongue had swelled in her mouth. 'Nothing but sky and ocean around me. So damned quiet.'

'Not for Derrick and me,' Viv told her. 'This sort of place is mostly where we spend our time. Under different circumstances, it would be paradise.'

'Yeah, right, paradise.' Bethany pointed. 'How far do you suppose those mountains are?'

'Hard to tell,' Derrick answered. 'Maybe fifteen miles. Maybe more. When everything's open like this, our eyes play tricks.'

Ray pressed a button on his GPS receiver. 'The altimeter says we're at fifty-five hundred feet.' He looked at Bethany. 'A mile above sea level. If you're not used to it, the altitude would be another reason you're thirsty.'

'No, I'm thirsty because the son of a bitch didn't give us water.'

'Quiet,' Viv cautioned. 'He hears everything we say.'

Bethany adjusted the bill of her cap, shielding her eyes. 'The sun's so bright, my contact lenses feel like they're cooking. Hey, you out there! *Are you listening?*'

No response.

'At least you could have given us sunglasses!'

Still no response.

'Maybe the bastard *isn't* listening.' Bethany looked around. 'Do you suppose there are cameras out here?'

Amanda took for granted there were. But before she could say it, Bethany asked, 'Where? In those trees we're heading toward? Or long lenses watching from the house? Or on posts somewhere, scanning the valley?'

They slid down into the gully. Dust rose under their boots. The gully was about five feet wide, higher than their heads. The shadow at the bottom felt cool.

'I used to love sailing, couldn't wait to get on the water with nothing around me except the horizon.' Bethany shuddered. 'It made me feel like something inside me was reaching out toward God or something. But after two weeks in that rubber boat, all that open space sucked the soul right out of me. I haven't been near the water since. It's hard to get people to buy sailboats when the thought of being on one terrifies me.'

Amanda dug her boots into the slope ahead, raising dust as she climbed. The dust coated her lips and tasted bitter. Emerging into the heat of the sun, she looked back and saw Bethany peering up from the shadow of the gully.

'It's nice and cool down here,' Bethany said.

'This isn't the ocean,' Derrick emphasized. 'At least, it's steady under your feet. It doesn't ripple.'

'Maybe not to you. But my legs haven't felt steady since I woke up. At least in that building I had walls around me.'

'Think of the mountains as walls.'

Bethany looked bleak. 'Mouth's drier.'

'The voice said there was water at the coordinates we were given.'

'No!' Bethany objected. 'The voice said we'd find something we needed. Whatever that means. He didn't say anything about water. We added what we wanted to hear.' She pulled her headset from beneath her cap.

'Climb out of there,' Viv said.

'We're not going to be any stronger than we are now.' Bethany stared at the headset in her hand. With disgust, she dropped it.

'No,' Derrick said.

'What can the bastard do to me?' Bethany spread her arms, making herself a target. 'Shoot me? How? He can't see me down here!'

Amanda looked around and felt a naked spot between her shoulders. Above the gully, everything was a potential sniper site: clumps of sagebrush, the row of trees they were headed toward, the rocks next to it. In the open, we're all easy targets, she realized.

'Take your chance now,' Bethany urged. 'If we all run in a different direction, how's he going to keep track of us all? How's he going to be everywhere at once to stop us? He can't.'

The logic's so tempting, Amanda thought. While we're together, we don't have a chance. She almost told Bethany she was right, almost slid down the dust to join her, but something made her hesitate, a limbic suspicion that things weren't as simple as Bethany believed, that escaping couldn't be as easy as five people fleeing in five different directions.

Then Amanda did slide into the gully, not to join Bethany but to try to stop her. She put a hand on Bethany's shoulder. 'I've got a bad feeling. Don't do this.'

'Hey, the voice said he wanted us to be self-reliant, didn't he?' Bethany tugged Amanda's fingers away, took a deep breath, and walked along the concealing gully. Her pace increased. If the gully maintained its direction, it would lead toward the exit from the valley, Amanda saw.

Running now, raising dust, Bethany disappeared around a curve. Amanda heard the receding noise of her boot steps in the dust, then stared up at Ray, Derrick and Viv, uncertain what to do.

'Are the rest of you going to join her?' the voice abruptly asked.

The intimate sound in Amanda's ears made her flinch.

'There's always a chance that she'll succeed,' the voice said. 'Do you want to take the same chance?'

No one replied.

'What about *you*, Amanda?'

'How the hell does he know what Bethany's doing?' Ray murmured.

'In that case, keep moving,' the voice ordered. 'Don't waste the little time you have.'

Amanda turned toward the curve beyond which Bethany had disappeared.

'It's unfortunate that she took off her headset,' the voice said. 'That prevents me from trying to reason with her.'

'How does he know she took off her headset?' Ray demanded.

With a chill, Amanda picked up the headset and blew dust from it. She brought it close to her eyes, examining the headband, the ear buds, and the microphone stub. 'The microphone.' Her words were filled with despair.

'Very good,' the voice said.

'The microphone?' Derrick asked from the top of the slope. 'What about it?'

Amanda could hardly speak. 'It's not just a . . .'

Viv tore off her headset and stared at the microphone stub. 'My God, it's a camera.' She dropped the headset and stumbled back.

'Derrick, tell your wife to pick it up,' the voice said.

Derrick looked paralyzed.

'Tell your wife to pick it up,' the voice emphasized.

'Viv, he wants you to pick up your headset.'

'No.'

'Everyone step back from her,' the voice said.

Derrick's dark features tightened. 'What are you going to do?'

'Teach you not to make me repeat myself. Step back.'

In a rush, Derrick grabbed the headset from the dirt and made Viv take it. 'Put it on.'

Seeing the fright in Derrick's eyes, Viv trembled and did what he wanted.

'Amanda, climb to the top of the gully,' the voice ordered. 'Join the others. Look toward the east.'

'East?'

'The exit from the valley,' Ray said.

Amanda felt something cold squeeze her heart. 'That's the direction Bethany went.' She scrambled up the side of the gully. Dust crumbled under her hiking boots, but she kneed and clawed and reached the top. She straightened, focusing her gaze toward the continuation of the gully. Amid grass and sagebrush, the gully meandered toward the distant pass. Amanda saw glimpses of Bethany's gray cap and the gray shoulders of her jumpsuit as she hurried.

The voice sounded too resigned, Amanda decided. 'Wait! You said it's unfortunate she took off her headset. You said you wanted to reason with her. If I can catch her . . .' A terrible premonition made Amanda breathe faster. 'If I can stop her . . .'

'Yes?'

'Will you let me bring her back?'

The voice didn't answer.

Before Amanda realized what she was doing, she ran. 'Bethany!' she yelled. 'Stop!' The vast openness swallowed her words.

Amanda charged across the brittle grass. She passed sagebrush, a knee-high boulder, and a stunted pine tree.

'Bethany!'

But Bethany kept racing along the bottom of the gully. Her gray cap and the gray shoulders of her jumpsuit were more visible. She never looked back.

'Stop!'

Amanda increased the speed and length of her stride. 'Listen to me!' she managed to shout between hoarse deep breaths that burned her throat.

Ahead, the gully became less deep. Bethany was visible to her waist now, rushing toward the faraway gap in the mountains.

'Stop!' Amanda yelled. Sweat slicked her skin, making her jumpsuit cling to her. 'He knows!'

Now the gully was so shallow that Bethany's hips showed. The lack of cover increased her frenzy. She charged toward a sandy depression, where water presumably gathered during rainy periods. On the opposite side, another gully began.

'You're not stopping her,' the voice said in Amanda's ears.

'Trying.' Amanda fought to muster strength, to run even faster. A rock dislodged under her, making her stumble. 'Bethany! Stop! Please!'

The urgency in Amanda's words finally had an effect. Halfway across the depression, Bethany seemed to lose energy. She faltered and turned. Chest heaving, she peered back toward Amanda.

'He can get to you!' Amanda yelled. 'I don't know how, but he can!'

Bethany's features glistened with sweat. She looked

ahead toward the opposite side of the depression and the continuation of the gully. Abruptly, she ran toward it.

'Don't!' Amanda's plea was directed to the voice as much as to Bethany.

'She hates open spaces,' the voice said. 'It was only a matter of time.'

Amanda strained to increase speed but found it impossible. Like the gap in the mountains beyond, Bethany seemed to recede.

'Better that it happened soon,' the voice told Amanda. 'This way, the rest of you will learn not to waste time and strength on futile efforts.'

'No!'

'But I'm disappointed that she didn't surprise me.'

The moment Bethany reached the continuation of the gully, Amanda felt a shock wave. Amid a roar, Bethany's gray-covered torso erupted in a spray of red. A hand flew one way while her skull flew another. The vapor of her blood misted the air as parts of her body pelted the ground.

Amanda staggered to a halt, her ears in pain from the explosion. She wavered in shock at the sight of the blood vapor spreading in a sudden breeze. Then the vapor drifted down, speckling the sand.

Amanda felt as if someone kicked the back of her legs from under her. She dropped to her knees. Tears streamed down her face, burning her cheeks.

3

It is a wonderful place, the moor.

Hunched in the back seat of a taxi, Balenger studied the photocopy in his hand, wondering what the hell the paragraph on it meant. The faded imprint of a stamp read NYPL HUMANITIES & SOCIAL SCIENCES LIBRARY. Given the context, he decided that NYPL stood for New York Public Library. He used his cell phone to call information and learned that the Humanities & Social Sciences Library was at 42nd Street and Fifth Avenue.

The Avenue of the Americas was the nearest uptown route from Greenwich Village. Stop-and-go midday traffic slowed the taxi. Frustrated by blaring horns and the lurch of the vehicle, Balenger told the driver to let him out at 40th Street. He paid and ran, relieved to be moving, to find an outlet for his tension.

But impatience wasn't his only reason for leaving the taxi. He continued to feel shocked by the fire. Someone wanted to stop him from finding Amanda, and that person would almost certainly keep trying.

He ran faster. Feeling exposed on the crowded sidewalk, he glanced behind him, wanting to know if anyone got out of another taxi and hurried in his direction. No one did. He looked ahead just in time to avoid crashing into a man with a briefcase. Veering, he charged through the intersection of 41st Street. A truck beeped and passed close enough for Balenger to feel a rush of air.

Ahead, he saw a crowd on benches amid the trees of Bryant Park. He glanced over his shoulder again and still didn't see anyone coming after him. Traffic remained motionless.

Turning right, he sprinted to Fifth Avenue and reached the library, a massive stone building whose wide steps and pillared entrance were guarded by two marble lions.

He hurried through a revolving door and entered a massive hall, where people waited for a guard to examine their purses, knapsacks and briefcases. As he wiped sweat from his forehead, he got curious looks from some of the people in line. He moved forward, glancing over his shoulder. Feeling seconds tick away, he worked to catch his breath. The high ceiling and stone floor had the echo of a church, but he paid little attention. His sole focus was on people coming through the entrance.

The guard waved him through. After asking directions, Balenger climbed two flights of wide stairs. Off another huge hallway, he reached an information desk.

'May I help?' a spectacled woman asked.

'I hope so.' Balenger gave her the photocopy. 'Do you have any idea where this comes from?'

The librarian peered over her glasses, studying the passage.

'It is a wonderful place, the moor,' said he, looking round over the undulating downs, long green rollers, with crests of jagged granite foaming up into fantastic surges. 'You never tire of the moor. You cannot think the wonderful secrets which it contains. It is so vast, and so barren, and so mysterious.'

She sounded puzzled. 'Everything else has been blanked out.'

Trying for a simple explanation, Balenger said, 'It's kind of a game.'

The librarian nodded. 'Yes, we get that on occasion. Last week somebody came here with a list for a scavenger hunt. She needed to find a particular novel, but the only clue she'd been given was "The sun goes down." We finally decided it was Hemingway's *The Sun Also Rises.*'

The thought occurred to Balenger that the paragraph might indeed be part of a game, one of the cruelest anyone could ever imagine.

'The problem is, even though people often call us the main branch of the New York City library system, actually we're a research facility,' the woman said. 'We don't lend books. Patrons can study them only on the premises. I needed to send the game player over to the branch on Fortieth Street.' The librarian continued to study the paragraph. ' "It is a wonderful place, the moor." Interesting.' She debated for a moment, then motioned to a man at a computer next to her.

He approached.

'Brontë or Conan Doyle?' the woman asked.

After reading the passage, the man nodded. 'Those are the two that come to mind.'

'I don't think it's Brontë,' the woman said.

'Exactly. Her style is more emotional.'

Balenger gave the woman a quizzical look.

'Mention a moor as a setting, and two novels stand out. Emily Brontë's *Wuthering Heights* takes place on the Yorkshire moors in northern England. It's very atmospheric, Heathcliff talking to Cathy's ghost as he wanders the moors, that sort of thing. In contrast, the description here is compressed into one sentence: ". . . undulating downs, long green rollers, with crests of jagged granite . . ." It gets the job done, but what the author seems really to care about are "the wonderful secrets" the moor contains, ". . . so mysterious." *That's* the author's focus. I'd be very surprised if this person didn't write mysteries. I think this is Sir Arthur Conan Doyle. *The Hound of the Baskervilles*.'

'*The Hound of the Baskervilles*?'

'Dartmoor, in Devon, England. That's where most of the novel takes place. In fact, it's one of the most famous settings in *any* novel. As I mentioned, we don't allow books to leave the building, but if you go to the reading room' – she pointed behind her – 'someone will bring you a copy.'

Time, Balenger kept thinking. He made himself appear calm when he thanked her. His experience with

Conan Doyle's detective story was only through an old black-and-white film starring Basil Rathbone. He remembered it as dark and moody with plenty of fog over rugged, sometimes swampy terrain.

The spacious reading room had the rich, warm tones of wood that had been polished for many decades. A guard stood at the entrance. Next to him, a sign warned Balenger to turn off his cell phone.

Balenger complied and went to a counter, where he requested a copy of the novel. His nerves calmed only a little when he noticed the reading room's computer area. After receiving an access card, he found an empty computer station. He concentrated to keep his breathing under control and felt a persistent urge to massage the nagging ache in his left forearm. When he pushed up his jacket and shirt sleeves, he saw that the punctured area was more red and swollen. It looked infected.

But that was the least of his troubles. As he stared at the computer keyboard, his fingers trembled. Amanda, he thought. Where did they take you?

He didn't know why Karen Bailey had left the quotation for him or how reading the novel it came from (if it indeed came from *The Hound of the Baskervilles*) would help him find Amanda. He fought to think, to focus on what the quotation was supposed to tell him.

Maybe it's about Sir Arthur Conan Doyle, he thought desperately.

Then why was everything else on the page, including the author's name and the title of the book, removed?

Why single out the quotation? What was special about it?

The moor.

Balenger reached for the computer keyboard. With shaking hands, he accessed Google and typed DARTMOOR. Several items appeared.

DARTMOOR NATIONAL PARK
DISCOVERING DARTMOOR
WALKING DARTMOOR
DARTMOOR RESCUE GROUP

Balenger learned that Dartmoor National Park comprised 250 square miles of low rocky hills that were described variously as bleak, forbidding and primeval. Mist frequently covered the mostly uninhabited area. The frequent moisture collected in boggy mires, which explained the need for a Dartmoor rescue group.

Am I supposed to conclude that somebody took Amanda to Dartmoor? he thought. Why? What would be the point? This isn't getting me anywhere.

Why did Karen Bailey arrange for me to receive the piece of paper?

A thought made Balenger straighten. She could have mailed it to me, but she added a complication. I wouldn't have known about the passage if I hadn't gone to the theater. She told the man who pretended to be the professor to give me the paper only if I showed up.

His temples throbbing, Balenger stared at the other

Google references to Dartmoor. He now realized that he needed to look harder. He couldn't assume anything was irrelevant.

DARTMOOR FALCONRY
DARTMOOR FOLK FESTIVAL
DARTMOOR LETTERBOXING

Preoccupied, he was about to skip to the next item when the subtext of the LETTERBOXING item caught his attention.

History of a hide-and-hunt game begun in 1854 on Dartmoor when a . . .

The description jabbed Balenger's memory. He suddenly remembered the time capsule lecture, during which the fake professor had said that communities who lost time capsules were engaged in a hide-and-hunt scavenger game.

In a rush, Balenger clicked on the item. The text that appeared, with photographs of low hills studded with granite outcroppings, set his brain on fire.

Letterboxing is a hide-and-hunt game invented in 1854 when a Dartmoor guide, James Perrott, decided to challenge hikers to investigate a difficult-to-reach area of the moor known as Cranmere Pool. To make the hikers prove that they had indeed found their way to the remote site, Perrott placed a jar beneath a cairn of rocks on the bank of the pool. Any hiker who managed to reach the jar was instructed to place a message in it. Sometimes, a self-addressed postcard was left inside. A hiker who found it would replace the card with his or her own and then mail the card to its owner.

Over the years, this activity – similar to a treasure hunt – proved so popular that jars were added at other locations on the moor. Later, the jars were changed to metal and then plastic containers, which became known as letterboxes because of the messages left in them. More than a century and a half after James Perrott placed his jar beneath that pile of rocks, there are an estimated 10,000 letterboxes throughout Dartmoor's imposing terrain.

The containers are carefully hidden. Clues guide players to the general location. Sometimes the clues are numbers for map coordinates. Other times they are puzzles and riddles, the answers to which guide the player.

Because of a 1998 article in Smithsonian Magazine, *the popularity of this hide-and-hunt game suddenly spread around the world. In America alone, every state has hidden letterboxes. Not every box is found, of course. Sometimes, on Dartmoor, game players are rewarded by the eerie discovery of a long-lost container that conceals a message left by someone many years earlier.*

Balenger stared at the screen for a long time. The reference to a 'long-lost container that conceals a message left by someone many years earlier' took him back to the time capsule lecture. One of the last things he remembered before lapsing into unconsciousness was the fake professor saying that more time capsules had been lost than had been found.

Balenger's heart seemed to stop, then start again. Coincidence? he wondered. Or did Karen Bailey intend for me to find this article? Why else would she have wanted me to read the paragraph about Dartmoor?

His hands continued to tremble, but now part of the reason for that was a chilling suspicion about why Amanda had been taken from him. He thought of what the librarian had said about clues to a scavenger hunt. A game? he thought. Is this really a damned game?

Breathing faster, he went to the request counter.

'Yes, sir?' asked a woman with streaked hair.

'My name's Frank Balenger. I requested a copy of *The Hound of the Baskervilles*.'

'Of course, sir. Let me see if . . .' She smiled. 'Here it is.'

The book was an old, musty hardback with dented corners. Balenger found an empty chair at one of the numerous tables. He opened the novel and skimmed its pages, concentrating on the first sentence of every paragraph, searching for *It is a wonderful place, the moor*.

Balenger exhaled sharply when he found it. Page forty-six. Two thirds of the way down. But that wasn't all he found. Someone had used a stamp to put words in the margin: THE SEPULCHER OF WORLDLY DESIRES.

The room seemed to tilt. Balenger was eerily reminded of the unusual name for one of the time capsules the professor had lectured about: the Crypt of Civilization. The Sepulcher. The Crypt. Another coincidence? he wondered. He needed to convince himself that he wasn't grasping at imaginary connections. One way to be sure was to look at all the copies of *The Hound of the Baskervilles* the library had. This branch didn't allow books to be taken from the building. Because there was no way for Karen Bailey to control which copy of the novel he was given, the only sure method to guarantee that Balenger got the message was to stamp THE SEPULCHER OF WORLDLY DESIRES in every copy the library owned.

Balenger stood so fast that the screech of his chair made the other readers at his table glare. But when he hurried toward the request area, he had a nervous feeling that someone was staring at him. He turned toward the entrance to the reading room.

Someone was indeed staring at him.

A matronly, fortyish woman in a plain dark dress. Her brunette hair was pulled back in a bun.

Karen Bailey.

4

The moment Balenger noticed her, she ran toward the corridor beyond the reading room's entrance. Balenger's urgent footsteps startled people at the other tables. He charged past the guard, who scowled at the commotion.

In the corridor, Balenger looked in one direction and then the other. No sign of Karen Bailey. Other people scowled as he ran to the stairway. Again, no sign of her.

'Hey,' he said to a man with a nylon book bag, 'did you see a woman in a navy dress? Prim? Around forty? Her hair in a bun?'

The man looked at Balenger's distraught appearance and stepped back, suspecting he was dangerous.

'All of you!' Balenger called to the half-dozen people in the corridor. 'Did anybody see a woman in a navy dress?'

The guard came out of the reading room. 'Keep your voice down.'

Balenger rushed along the corridor, checking various exhibition rooms. He reached a women's room and didn't think twice about shoving at the door, hurrying inside. At a sink, a woman turned and gaped. Balenger peered under the doors to the stalls. Jeans. Slacks. Nobody in a navy dress.

He bolted from the women's room and dodged past the guard, who tried to grab him. 'Karen Bailey!' Balenger yelled. 'Stop!'

Pursued by the guard, Balenger reached the stairs and leapt down two at a time. The next level had closed doors to what looked like offices. Hearing the guard chasing him, Balenger continued to rush downward, only to stop at the sight of Ortega climbing toward him.

'I saw her!' Balenger exclaimed. 'Karen Bailey! She's in the building!'

The guard reached Balenger. 'Sir, I need to ask you to leave.'

Ortega pulled out his police identification. 'He's with me.'

'I saw her at the entrance to the reading room,' Balenger said. 'The same navy dress. Hair in a bun. Then she ran.'

'I didn't see anyone who matches that description when I came into the building.' Ortega turned toward the guard. 'Tell your security staff to block all the exits. Be careful. She might be dangerous.' He pulled out his cell phone. 'I'll call for backup.'

As Balenger and Ortega ran down the stairs, Ortega blurted instructions into his phone. Then he glared at Balenger. 'Ducking away from me in the crowd.

Leaving me to report to the fire team on my own. Maybe you'd like to get arrested for obstructing an investigation.'

'I didn't have a choice. I told you there wasn't time. I couldn't wait.'

'I was forced to lie and claim you'd gone for medical treatment.'

'Thanks. If I can ever repay you—'

'You made me feel like a damned fool. Don't play games with someone who's trying to help.'

'I think that might be what's going on. *A game*.'

'What are you talking about?'

'Karen Bailey leaves a piece of paper for me at the theater, but I need to find the theater before I get to read what's on the paper. A stamp on it leads me to this branch of the library, where I need to pass another test and learn where the paragraph on the paper comes from. It turns out to be from *The Hound of the Baskervilles*. When I get a copy of the novel, I find words stamped next to the paragraph.'

'Words?'

'The Sepulcher of Worldly Desires.'

'The what?'

'I think I'm supposed to find out what it is. This branch of the library doesn't lend books, so she could be sure I'd find the message on the page. Step by step, I'm being led through some kind of game. The moor the paragraph refers to is Dartmoor in England. When I Googled Dartmoor, I learned about a hide-and-hunt game invented there a long time ago, a game called letterboxing that sounds like the game I'm being made to play – hidden messages leading to other hidden messages. Some aspects of letterboxing even sound like time capsules. Everything's related.'

'But why would anybody do this? Do you have enemies? Someone who hates you enough to put you through this?'

'I told you before, the only person I can think of who'd be sick enough to do this is dead.' Balenger hesitated. 'Time capsules.'

'Something occur to you?'

'When I was a kid, I found a time capsule in part of a school that was being torn down. The local newspaper made a big deal about it. My photograph was on the front page. It showed me holding the rusted metal box.'

The skin tightened around Ortega's eyes. 'You're saying someone went to the trouble of researching your past all the way back to when you were a kid? To find the bait that would make you go to the lecture at that house?'

'In the attic, we found two video game cases,' Balenger said. 'One was for *Grand Theft Auto*. You told me you'd never heard of the other one. Do you remember its title?'

Ortega thought for a moment. '*Scavenger*.'

LEVEL FOUR: AVALON

1

As the roar of the explosion echoed off the distant mountains, Amanda stayed kneeling. Her chest was racked with sobs. Before her, the blood mist continued to drift in the breeze. The sandy depression was red with body parts. She smelled something pungent and sickening. 'Bethany,' she murmured. Shock so overwhelmed her that she was hardly aware of the sharp stones under her knees.

'Go back to the others,' the sonorous voice said through Amanda's headset. The words were distorted by a persistent painful ringing that the explosion had caused in her ears.

'Bethany,' Amanda said louder. She mourned not only her lost companion but herself and the others in the group. We're all going to die, she thought.

No, she told herself. I survived the Paragon Hotel, and by God, I'll survive this.

But in the Paragon Hotel you had Frank to help you. She realized that again she had disassociated, referring to herself as 'you.'

She wanted to scream.

'Your friends are waiting for you,' the voice said. 'You don't want to deprive them of your company.' The voice paused. 'As Bethany did.'

Amanda nodded. Responding to the threat, she stood painfully. Frank, she thought. Again she had the premonition that he was dead. She felt the increasing certainty that if, impossibly, she was going to survive this nightmare, she would need to do it alone. Tears clouded her vision. After pawing her eyes, she took one last look at what remained of Bethany and turned away.

A hundred yards from her, past rocks, sagebrush and the stunted pine tree, Ray, Derrick and Viv gaped. Despite the distance, Amanda saw that their faces were drawn and pale. The combination of their green, red and brown coveralls looked even more unnatural.

Amanda plodded toward them. Her throat felt raw from shouting. Hunger contracted her stomach. But mostly what she felt was a thick-tongued, dry-lipped thirst.

All the while she approached them, her three companions fixed their attention solely on the crimson area beyond her. Only when she finally reached them did anybody speak.

'Are you okay?' Derrick managed to ask.

The most Amanda could do was nod.

'How did . . .' Viv sounded stunned. She turned toward Ray. 'You're the military expert. Was it a rocket? How was it possible?'

'No,' Ray said. 'Not a rocket. We'd have seen and heard it coming.'

'Some kind of bomb she was standing on?'

'No. The ground didn't erupt.'

'Then . . .?'

Ray looked down at his jumpsuit. 'Plastic explosive. I think it's in our clothes.'

A moment lengthened as the implication had its impact.

'Our clothes?' Derrick too looked down.

'Jesus,' Viv said.

'Or our shoes,' Ray added. 'Or our headsets.'

'Or maybe it's in these.' Hand unsteady, Amanda withdrew the GPS receiver from her pocket.

Viv lurched back as if struck. 'We're bombs? He can blow us up whenever he feels like it?'

'Whenever you disobey,' the voice said.

The abrupt sound in Amanda's ears startled her.

'Whenever you stop playing by the rules,' the voice continued.

'Rules? What damned rules are you talking about?' Ray shouted. 'I haven't heard anything about—'

'Discovering the nature of the rules as you proceed is the essence of every great game.'

'You think this is a fucking game?'

'Ray, it isn't necessary to use obscenities.'

'*A game?*' Ray looked around as if fearing for his sanity. 'The bastard thinks he's playing a *game*.'

'In which one hour has now elapsed. You have

thirty-nine remaining. Do not waste them.'

'What difference does it make?' Viv spoke so forcefully that the sinews in her neck bulged like ropes. 'You're going to kill us anyhow!'

'I'm aware of only one game in which the winners were killed. It was a ball game played by the ancient Maya. That is not my intention. Winners should be rewarded. What happens to losers is another matter.'

'So how do we win?' Ray demanded.

'That is something you must discover.'

'The map coordinates he gave us.' Amanda wiped away more tears. Her cheeks felt raw. 'We need to reach that area.'

Derrick nodded. 'We're not doing any good standing here. We need to move.'

'And discover the rules,' the voice told them.

Ray studied the screen on his GPS receiver. His whisker stubble made his narrow face look haggard. He seemed all too aware that at any moment the receiver could blow him up. 'This way. Toward the trees.'

Amanda forced herself to put one foot in front of the other. Her legs aching, her lungs still demanding oxygen, she neared the trees.

'Cottonwoods,' Derrick said. 'They need a lot of water.'

Viv looked around. 'There must be an underground stream.'

'And all we need is a backhoe to get to it,' Ray said.

The shadows of the trees provided relief from the

heat. Then Amanda was in the sun again. The ground rose. Sweating, she climbed.

Ray checked his GPS receiver. 'The incline's steeper than it looks. We're at six thousand feet now.' He sounded out of breath.

'Go up on a diagonal,' Derrick said.

'Right. Use a switchback pattern,' Viv told them. 'You expend more energy hiking straight up a slope than you do if you climb back and forth.'

'Very good,' the voice said. 'Use your resources.'

Amanda felt pressure in her knees from trudging up. Slowly, the expanse of the rest of the valley revealed itself.

'Holy . . .' She straightened in awe.

2

A lake. About a hundred yards long, it glistened below them. Amanda thought of light reflecting off a jewel. As the group stared down, she heard their rapt breathing.

'The voice told us we'd find what we needed,' Derrick said.

'I've seen the world from the top of Everest,' Viv murmured. 'But what I'm looking at now is the most beautiful . . .'

'So, what are we waiting for?' Ray started down. 'After the ten days I spent getting chased in Iraq, I promised myself I'd never be thirsty again.'

Derrick and Viv followed Ray down the slope, all of them breaking into a run. Amanda peered around, feeling threatened by the vastness surrounding her. The mountains felt close and yet far, tricking her sense of distance. She was reminded of a psychology course she'd taken in college, an experiment in which natives who lived in a jungle were brought into an immense field. The natives were so accustomed to having their vision blocked by trees that the open space overpowered them. Many developed agoraphobia.

Never having been anywhere in which the horizon wasn't obscured by buildings or trees, Amanda now understood the natives' fear. But in her case, the fear was caused by the realization that everything in the vastness around her was a possible threat. Unlike the Paragon Hotel, where danger was limited to the rooms in the building, here death had what felt like infinite space in which to hide.

'Aren't you going to join them?' the voice asked.

Amanda stifled her surprise. 'I'm just admiring the view.'

'Really? For a moment, it seemed that the view paralyzed you. Take a look at the screen on your GPS receiver. Do the coordinates I gave you correspond with that lake?'

Amanda was still learning to use the device, but even

to her, it was obvious that the red needle indicating their destination was pointed away from the lake and toward a spot on the hill. She glanced to the right and saw a plateau on which lay the ruins of a building. 'Is *that* where we're supposed to go?'

'To play the game, you must learn the rules.'

'Ray,' Amanda spoke into her microphone. 'You passed the coordinates.'

The group kept rushing toward the lake.

'Derrick. Viv. We're not supposed to go to the lake. There's a ruined building up here. That's our destination.'

The group didn't look back.

'Can't you hear me?' Amanda asked louder. 'The lake isn't where we're supposed to go!'

'In fact, they *can't* hear you,' the voice said. 'I isolated our conversation.'

'Why? I don't understand. What are you doing?'

When the voice didn't reply, Amanda felt another premonition. 'Stop!' she yelled to the group.

Either her voice didn't carry, or else they were too fixated on the water to pay attention to anything else.

'No! Stay away from the lake!' Amanda charged down the slope, dodging rocks and sagebrush. 'Wait!'

Viv turned, frowning in Amanda's direction.

'Stop!'

Viv called something to Derrick and Ray, who paused and looked back. Thank God, Amanda thought. The group waited as she ran to them.

'What's wrong?' Derrick asked.

Amanda heard him through her earphones now. The two-way radio was operating normally again. 'He can isolate our conversations. He told me the coordinates he gave us don't correspond with this lake.'

Ray glanced at the needle on his GPS receiver. 'That's true. They match something on the slope.'

'A ruined building,' Amanda explained.

'But why didn't he tell the rest of us?'

'Screwing with our minds,' Derrick said in disgust.

'Fine.' Ray drew his tongue along his dry lips. 'We'll investigate the building. But the water's closer. I'm not walking away without a drink.'

3

A breeze rippled the lake, creating white caps.

'Is it safe?' Ray wondered.

Amanda gazed along the shore. 'I don't see any skeletons or dead animals.'

'Look how clear the water is.' Viv pointed. 'Fish.'

'If it was poisoned, it would kill them,' Ray said.

'Not necessarily,' Derrick objected. 'Think about the mercury and other toxins in some lakes. Fish somehow live in them, but that doesn't mean the water's safe. On

Everest, even melted snow has toxins. We treat everything we drink with iodine tablets.'

'Yeah, well, in case you haven't noticed, we don't have any way to purify the water.' Ray took out his lighter, snapping it open and shut as he debated with himself. 'When I was in Iraq, running from insurgents, I drank some awfully dirty water. It gave me a fever. But I survived.' He put away his lighter and knelt, his reflection rippling in the water. 'My mouth's so dry, my tongue feels swollen.'

He cupped his hands together and lowered them into the lake.

'No,' Amanda said.

Ray splashed water over his face. 'Man, that feels good.' He splashed more water, rubbing his wet hands over his cheeks and the back of his neck. 'Makes me want to soak my feet.' He started to unlace a boot.

'Do not remove your boots,' the voice said.

'Ah,' Ray said. 'Welcome back. I thought you might have fallen asleep.'

'For the forty hours, I do not sleep.'

'Right. You want to share our pain. The boots. Is that where the explosives are?'

The voice did not reply.

'If not, maybe you won't care if I put my feet in the water, even though my boots are on.'

'I don't advise it.'

'Then I'll just rinse my face again.'

Ray lowered his hands toward the water. A snake's

fangs darted from the surface, streaking toward one of Ray's fingers. He screamed and lurched back, falling. 'Mygodmygod,' he blurted, scurrying from the water.

Amanda felt numbness spread through her. Some of the ripples, she saw now, weren't caused by the breeze. Snakes. The lake was infested by snakes. All of a sudden, the water churned with them.

Ray's eyes were wild. He jerked his hands toward his face, staring at them. 'Did it bite me? Did it bite me?'

'Snakes. I can't bear . . .' Viv bent over, retching.

'You son of a bitch,' Derrick shouted toward the sky. 'Those look like water moccasins! They don't belong in the mountains! You put them here!'

'The obstacle race and the scavenger hunt,' the voice said.

'The scavenger hunt?'

'In winter, when the lake froze, the townspeople used to cut blocks of ice and store them in the mine. In summer, the ice kept the town's meat from spoiling.'

'Mine? Townspeople? Ice? What are you talking about?' Ray shouted. 'I nearly got bit by a snake, for God's sake, and you're babbling about *ice*?'

'Wait a minute,' Amanda insisted. 'What town?'

'Avalon. But you'll learn that soon enough.'

Viv wiped bile from her lips. 'The ruined building Amanda mentioned. You want us to go there.'

'As quickly as possible. You wasted time and skipped a step.'

'In the obstacle race and the scavenger hunt.' Amanda stared toward the rippling snakes in the water.

4

They hiked from the lake. Climbing the slope, passing sagebrush and rocks, they conserved energy and followed the zigzag pattern they'd used earlier.

'You need to have a name for me,' the voice said. 'From now on, refer to me as the Game Master.'

To Amanda, the name had the sound of doom.

They reached a plateau halfway up the rise and faced the ruins of a building. Its walls were stone. The left side had collapsed. The roof was made of wood, the beams of which had fallen. The wood was gray with age.

'All by itself up here. Long. Narrow. Feels like it might have been a church,' Amanda said.

'Definitely was.' Viv pointed to the left, where a large wooden cross lay among a chaos of stones.

The group cautiously approached what seemed to have been the entrance.

'Look. The altar's still intact,' Derrick marveled.

Peering deep within the toppled structure, Amanda saw a horizontal slab of rock propped on two vertical ones.

'Where did the slabs come from?' Viv asked. 'These walls of rock . . .'

'The mine,' Ray said. 'The voice referred to . . .' He paused and corrected himself. 'The Game Master referred to a mine.'

'And a town called Avalon.' Derrick turned toward the valley. 'There. Look. Below us. Before the narrow end of the lake.'

Despite the brim of Amanda's cap, her eyes were pained by the stark sun. Squinting down, she saw collapsed buildings partially obscured by sagebrush. The ruins were arranged in rectangular grids. The long spaces between them were once streets, she guessed.

'Avalon. Sounds familiar,' Derrick said.

'I once woke up in a resort in New Jersey called Avalon,' Ray told him. 'I had a terrible hangover and none of the five grand I won playing blackjack in Atlantic City.'

'King Arthur,' Amanda said.

They stared at her.

'The Knights of the Round Table?' Viv sounded baffled. 'What's that Disney movie? *The Sword in the Stone*? *Camelot*?'

'After Arthur was killed in his final battle, a group of women took his body to a place called Avalon. According to legend, he remains alive there, in a trance, waiting to return when the world needs him.'

'Coming back from the dead.' Viv entered the church, stepping on piles of rocks.

'Careful.' Derrick went after her. 'After what happened at the lake, I get the feeling traps are part of the game.'

Amanda studied the rubble, saw nothing that made her suspicious, and followed.

Ahead, a board creaked when Viv cautiously pulled it away. 'What if there are snakes?'

'They wouldn't be water moccasins. They'd be rattlers,' Derrick said. 'They'd be making noise to warn us away.'

'I know that in my head. The trouble is, I need to convince myself to believe it.' Viv climbed behind the stone slab that formed the altar. She peered down at her companions. 'I bet I'm the first woman who ever stood up here.'

'See anything that might help?' Derrick asked.

'There's something engraved on the altar.' Viv blew dust from the slab. 'It's hard to read.' She concentrated. ' "The Sepulcher of Worldly Desires." '

'What's *that* supposed to mean?' Ray asked.

The Sepulcher of Worldly Desires. Amanda felt something stir in her memory, a phrase that reminded her of the words on the altar. But before she could remember, Viv studied the screen on her GPS receiver and distracted her.

'According to this, we're at the coordinates the voice . . .' Like Ray, Viv corrected herself, 'the Game Master gave us. The receiver's accurate to within ten feet. So, what are we supposed to notice?'

Derrick looked around. 'Remember what he said about geocaching. Objects can be disguised until it's almost impossible to find them. He mentioned something that looked like a grasshopper but wasn't.'

'He also mentioned a rock that turned out to have something inside.' Ray's voice rose with excitement. He surveyed the countless rocks around them, then hesitated, asking Derrick, 'No snakes?'

'We're making so much noise, they'd be rattling.'

'You keep saying that. But how many rattlesnakes did you come across on Mount Everest?' Before Derrick could respond to the sarcasm, Ray gingerly picked up a rock and shook it. 'Doesn't feel hollow.' He shook another. 'Not this one, either.'

Amanda stooped, mustered courage, and picked up a rock. No threat was under it. 'This one's real.'

'So are *these*.' Derrick warily picked up one rock after another. 'They're *all* real.'

'Keep searching!' Ray told him.

Their thirst overwhelmed their apprehension. All around Amanda, rocks flew, clattering.

'Too many. This could take all day.' Amanda tried to keep despair from her voice. 'We don't have time. If he hid something in a rock, why would he use that as an example when he described the game? Too obvious. He wanted to mislead us.'

'I'm too thirsty to think straight.' Ray looked around desperately. 'If it isn't a hollow rock, what else would seem ordinary and yet hide something?'

'The wooden beams from the roof,' Viv said quickly.

'Yes!' Ray grabbed a fractured section of a beam. 'Too heavy.' He grabbed another. 'Not hollow.' He grabbed a third one. 'The same bullshit as the rocks. We're not going to . . . Wait.' He raised a fourth chunk from a fallen beam. 'This feels like plastic.'

Amanda watched Ray pull at the two sides of the fake wood. They parted, revealing a plastic bottle of water. Ray howled in victory and twisted the cap from the bottle. He raised the opening to his mouth.

Amanda tried to say 'Stop!' But her dry tongue felt paralyzed. She saw water pouring from the bottle into Ray's mouth. His throat moved rapidly, his Adam's apple bobbing as he swallowed greedily.

Viv did manage to shout 'No!' But the upturned bottle kept pouring water into Ray's mouth, some of it trickling from his lips and down his chin. He made gulping noises. Red-faced from holding his breath, he exhaled and lowered the empty bottle. His chest heaved. He seemed transported with satisfaction until he noticed Amanda, Derrick and Viv watching him in shock.

It took him a moment before he understood their emotions. 'Sorry.'

Amanda felt the start of hopelessness.

'I didn't think. Really, I'm sorry.'

Viv moaned.

'I just wasn't thinking straight.'

Derrick sank on to a pile of rocks, his head on his knees.

'Hey, there must be others. I'll help you look for them.' Ray picked up a chunk of wood. He tried another and another. 'It doesn't make sense that he'd hide only one bottle for all of us.'

'Unless he wanted to see how we'd react,' Amanda said.

Ray hurled the empty bottle against the wall. Its plastic thumped hollowly. 'Well, what did you expect? I told you I'm no damned hero.'

'Okay, okay.' Viv raised her hands. 'Arguing isn't going to help. It's done. We can't change what happened.'

Derrick stood, telling Ray, 'But if we find another bottle, stay the hell away from it.'

'Whatever you say, boss.' Ray took out his lighter, snapping it open and shut.

'Quit making that noise!'

'Right, boss.'

Amanda interrupted, trying to break the tension. 'Let's see if we can find more water.'

5

The bottle was in another fake chunk of wood, this one partially covered by rocks near the altar. Amanda's pulse surged when she found it. Her dry mouth made her want desperately to gulp from it as Ray had. But she merely told the group, 'Here.'

She, Derrick and Viv took turns drinking from it. Like the others, she watched to make sure that no one took a longer swallow than anyone else. Ray frowned in the background.

Amanda was the last to drink. Savoring the moisture on her tongue, she considered the empty bottle. 'Where's the recycling bin?'

No one smiled at the joke.

'On mountains, we always collect our trash and carry it back down,' Derrick said.

'Did anyone ever tell you what a terrific guy you are?' Ray asked.

'I was about to add that worrying about our trash isn't high on my priorities right now.'

'It's a piece of equipment we didn't have before,' Amanda said. 'I'll hang on to it.' She started to lower it toward a pocket in her coveralls, but something caught her attention. 'Numbers.'

'Where?' Viv stepped close.

'On the label. At the bottom. Someone wrote three sets of numbers.'

'Let me see.' Derrick took the bottle. 'The numbers have "LG" in front of them.'

Ray joined them. 'Longitude?'

'They sure seem like longitude numbers. Hours, minutes and seconds.'

'Where's that bottle Ray threw?' Amanda made her

way over the rocks, approaching the wall. She found the bottle next to the remnants of a bench. 'Three sets of numbers. This time the letters ahead of them are "LT." '

'Latitude,' Ray said. 'We'll find out where we're supposed to go next.'

'Wait. Something's wrong.' Amanda tensed.

'Sure. This whole damned game is wrong, but—'

'No. Don't you feel it.' The rocks Amanda stood on were vibrating. The chunks of wood trembled.

Viv stumbled back. 'My God, what's happening?'

'I'm not sure, but I think we'd better . . .' Alarmed by the increasing vibrations, Derrick blurted, 'Get out of here!'

The wall swayed.

'Go! Go!' Viv shouted.

As they scrambled over the rocks, Amanda lost her balance. The wall tilted. With no time to run, she dove to the vibrating rocks, wincing from the impact. Desperate, she pressed herself against the base of the wall and put her arms over her head. With a roar, the wall collapsed, rocks cascading. Impacts made her groan.

The rumble diminished. The vibrations lessened. Soon everything was still, except for the pounding of Amanda's heart. Dust made her choke. Can't breathe, she thought, struggling to clear her nostrils and get air down her throat. The bulk of the rocks had fallen toward the middle of the church. Only the ones immediately above had landed on her, the higher ones following the trajectory of the wall and gaining distance when they plummeted. Even so, she felt crushed.

She heard shouts and charging footsteps, rocks being shoved aside.

'Are you hurt?' Derrick yelled.

'Sore.'

'I bet.'

'But I managed to protect my head.'

Viv and Derrick helped her up.

'And I kept *this*.' Wincing, Amanda gave Viv the empty bottle with the coordinates printed on it.

She couldn't help noticing that Ray stood apart from them. He hadn't made an effort to help dig her out. We can't survive if there's a split in the group, she thought. But then she saw Ray pointing down.

'More water bottles!' he said.

Derrick and Viv spun.

'The impact of the rocks broke open some of these fake timbers.'

As if attracted by a magnet, the group headed in Ray's direction. The bottles glinted in the sun, their contents beckoning.

'There's enough to go around,' Ray said. 'Hey, Derrick, mind if I pick one up?'

Derrick considered him for a long moment. 'Go ahead.'

'Thanks, boss. As long as I have your permission.'

Yeah, a split in the group, Amanda thought. She picked up a bottle, untwisted the cap, and drank, the wonderful liquid clearing the dust in her mouth. She was so thirsty she wanted to guzzle the water as Ray had, to flood it down her throat, but she feared that would make her sick.

Meanwhile, Ray drank from a bottle and continued to look angry.

Viv's stomach growled. 'If we don't get some food soon . . .'

'Always complaining,' Ray told her. 'In Iraq, I lived on bugs.'

'Go easy on her, man,' Derrick said. 'All of us are hungry.'

'Whatever you want.'

'This is more entertaining than I anticipated,' the voice said.

The sound in Amanda's ears made her cringe.

Derrick scowled at the sky. 'Is this part of the game? Hoping we'll fight each other?'

'Gold was found here in 1885.'

'Gold?'

'Thousands of miners flocked to the valley. A town was born almost overnight. An English real-estate speculator bought the land from a rancher who figured that the valley would be overrun no matter what, so why not take the generous payment he was offered and let someone else deal with the chaos he saw coming? As it turned out, the rancher was shrewd.'

'Gold?' Ray scoffed. 'A while ago, you were talking about ice!'

'The Englishman who developed the town had a fondness for King Arthur stories. As you've already guessed, he named the place after the spot where Arthur lies in a death-like slumber, waiting for destiny to summon him. But after eight years, the last of the gold was taken from the valley. Most of the miners drifted on. That was in 1893, the year of a financial depression that spread through America and became known as the Panic. The people in town decided that there wasn't much opportunity anywhere else in the country, so they stayed. The Englishman was forced to sell the valley back to the rancher, whose payroll kept the town in business. But that didn't help the Englishman. Having counted on the boom to last longer, he was so financially overextended that, facing ruin, he trudged into the first blizzard of the winter. Months later, a crew cutting blocks of ice from the lake discovered his frozen body.'

'You keep telling us we've only got forty hours, and now you're wasting our time,' Ray said. 'Make your point.'

'I think that's what he's doing,' Amanda said. 'He's giving us clues to the game. Right?' she asked the voice. 'You told us we're in an obstacle race and a scavenger hunt.'

'You're becoming my favorite player.'

'Swell,' Ray said. 'Now she's got an advantage.'

'I'm right, though, aren't I?' Amanda told the Game Master. 'At each stage you give us a problem to solve and a threat to evade. Then you reward us with information we need to know to win the game. Is that what you meant by learning how to play the game as we go along?'

'You must play the game to learn the rules.'

'*But how do we win?*' Ray yelled.

'Why don't you tell us, Amanda?' the voice asked.

She rubbed one of her bruised arms.

'Amanda, have you figured it out?'

'The words on the altar.'

'Yes?'

'The Sepulcher of Worldly Desires.'

'Yes?' The Game Master sounded eager.

'Nothing's here by accident. That's another clue.'

'But what does it mean?'

'Sepulcher? Sounds like a grave,' Derrick said.

6

Police officers ran up the stairs.

'Do you have any idea how large this building is?' a library administrator asked. 'It'll take hours to search it.'

'I can't wait that long,' Balenger said.

'Is this woman dangerous? She's not a terrorist, is she? You don't suppose she has explosives or weapons.'

'I have no idea if she's armed.' Balenger thought about everything that had happened. 'But yes, she's dangerous.'

More police officers ran across the huge lobby and up the stairs.

Ortega hurried toward Balenger. 'No sign of her.'

'Maybe she left the building before the police arrived,' Balenger said. 'Or else she's hiding on the third floor. That would explain why no one saw her running down the stairs.'

The reading room guard was with them again. 'Hell, I didn't see her either.'

'But she was right there at the entrance to the room,' Balenger insisted.

'My back must have been toward her. When you jumped up and ran from the table, you were the only person I noticed. You made quite a commotion. She could easily have slipped away.'

'But why would she show herself and then run?'

'Good question,' Ortega said.

'Maybe she wanted me to follow her. But if that's the case, why did she hide? Why didn't she give me a glimpse of her so I could keep chasing her?'

'More good questions.'

'Something bothering you?' Balenger asked.

'I don't know yet. I'm still waiting for answers to another part of the investigation.'

'*Another* part?'

'I'll talk to you about it later.'

Puzzled, Balenger glanced at his watch. Almost four o'clock. Time, he thought. He pulled out his cell phone and pressed the numbers for information.

'Who are you calling?' Ortega wanted to know.

Simultaneously, a computerized voice asked Balenger what city he wanted. He stepped back from the noise of the hurrying police officers.

'Atlanta.'

'What listing?' the voice asked.

7

'Oglethorpe University,' the female receptionist said.

'I need to speak to someone in the history department,' Balenger said into his phone.

His heart beat faster as he waited.

'History department.'

Balenger remembered that the fake professor had mentioned something about a time capsule society at Oglethorpe University. He prayed that wasn't a lie. 'I don't know if this is the right place. Does anybody there know anything about time capsules?' It was a measure of how drastically his world had changed that he felt his request made perfect sense.

'I'll transfer you.'

Balenger's hand sweated against his phone.

'International Time Capsule Society,' a male voice said. 'This is Professor Donovan.'

'I'm trying to get information about an object you might have a record of.' To escape the noise in the library, Balenger stepped outside. Instantly, the din of Fifth Avenue made him press the phone closer to his ear. 'Its name reminds me of the Crypt of Civilization.'

'Which is here at Oglethorpe, of course,' the voice responded enthusiastically.

'Just a second. I'm calling from Manhattan, and the traffic noise is awful.' Balenger stepped back into the library's vestibule. 'Have you ever heard of the Sepulcher of Worldly Desires?'

'Certainly.'

'You *have*?'

'Possibly it's a legend. But assuming it's real, it would be on the list of the most wanted time capsules.'

'Tell me everything about it.'

'That'll take a while, I'm afraid. The Sepulcher's a mystery, but there's plenty of historical context. I'll check the files. If you call back tomorrow—'

'I don't have time! I need to find out today!'

'Sir, I'm about to leave the office for an appointment. This'll need to wait until . . . Did you say you're calling from Manhattan? Maybe you *can* find out today. The person who knows the most about the Sepulcher of Worldly Desires teaches at New York University.'

8

Washington Square South. The shadows in the faculty building contrasted with the sunlight on the grass and arch in the park outside. Feeling the increased rush of time, Balenger got off an elevator at the seventh floor and hurried along a corridor until he reached a door with a name plate: PROF. GRAHAM, HISTORY DEPARTMENT.

Beyond it, he heard gunfire. When he knocked, no one replied. Breathing quickly, he knocked again, and this time, a distracted female voice said, 'Come in.'

Opening the door, Balenger heard the gunfire more clearly. He saw a woman in her early sixties, small, with short white hair and a narrow, wrinkled face. She wore a pale blue blouse, the two top buttons of which were open. She sat at her desk, captivated by her glowing computer screen, fiercely working a mouse and keyboard. The shots came from her computer speakers.

'Professor Graham?'

She didn't reply.

'I'm Frank Balenger.'

She nodded, but whether it was in response to his name or what was on her screen, he didn't know. Given her age, she manipulated the mouse and keyboard with amazing speed. The shots were rapid.

'I phoned a half-hour ago,' Balenger continued.

She kept pressing buttons.

'What I need to talk to you about is important.'

The shots abruptly ended.

'Shit,' Professor Graham said. She slammed down the mouse and scowled. 'Broke it. That's the second mouse I've destroyed this week. Why can't they make them stronger? I mean, how much strength can these old fingers have.' She showed the fingers to Balenger. They were bony, with slack skin and arthritic knuckles. 'You said you're a police officer?'

'Used to be. In New Jersey.'

'Ever play video games?'

Balenger was desperate to get the information he needed, but his experience as a detective warned him to establish rapport and not rush the person he was interviewing. He had to work to seem calm. 'They never appealed to me.'

'Because you think they're mindless?'

Balenger shrugged.

'I had the same bias,' Professor Graham said, 'until, several years ago, one of my students made me an enthusiast. Sometimes students are smarter than their professors. That particular student changed my life. Forget the content of video games, many of which are indeed mindless. Concentrate on the skills required to win. These games develop our reflexes. They teach our brains to work quicker and master parallel thinking. Some people claim multitasking is bad, but if I can learn to do a lot of things simultaneously and do them well, what's the harm?'

'The two kids who shot those students at Columbine High School in Colorado were addicted to violent video games.'

'So are a lot of other kids. But out of millions of them—'

'Millions?'

'The video game industry takes in more money than the movie business. Half the people in this country are players. Out of millions of kids who like violent video games, only a few go on shooting sprees. Clearly other factors turn them into killers. You were a police officer in New Jersey? Where?'

'Asbury Park.'

'I ice-skated in competition there when I was a kid.' The white-haired woman seemed to stare at something above Balenger's head. 'A long time ago.' Her gaze refocused on him. 'Anyway, since you were in law enforcement, I'm surprised you don't play video games. The one I was playing just now is called *Doom 3*. It's a version of one of the games the Columbine shooters were addicted to. It's a type called "first-person shooter." Basically, the player sees everything in the game from behind a gun. I'm a space marine on Mars on a base overrun by demons. When a threat jumps out, I blast it. They jump out often, and they're very fast. I feel trapped in a labyrinth. Ceilings collapse. I never know what horrors wait behind locked doors.'

Balenger couldn't help thinking of the Paragon Hotel.

Professor Graham considered him. 'I've heard that police officers play first-person shooter games as a way of maintaining their reflexes when they're not on the shooting range, and they often play them to prime themselves before they go on a raid.'

Balenger's impatience must have showed.

'Sorry. My enthusiasm often gets the better of me. On the phone you said that Professor Donovan suggested I could help you. My specialty's the American frontier, but I'm as fascinated by time capsules as he is. What do you want to know?'

Balenger was conscious of how fast his heart pounded as he told her what had happened during the lecture in the row house on 19th Street.

'The Manhattan History Club,' she said when he finished. 'I never heard of it.'

'Because it doesn't exist.'

'The coffee was drugged?'

'That's right. When I regained consciousness, my friend was gone.'

'Your left forearm. What's the matter? You keep massaging it.'

Balenger peered down. The impulse had become reflexive. 'While I was unconscious, someone injected me with a sedative. The place where the needle went in is red and swollen.'

'Sounds like it's infected. You ought to see a doctor.'

'I don't have time.' Balenger leaned forward. 'Professor Donovan says you know a lot about something called the Sepulcher of Worldly Desires.'

She looked surprised. 'Where on earth did you hear about *that*?'

'Whoever took my friend left those words as some kind of clue. I think it's part of a game, an extremely deadly one.' Balenger couldn't help glancing at the computer.

'The Sepulcher of Worldly Desires.' Professor Graham nodded. 'It's fascinated me for years. On January third 1900, a man named Donald Reich staggered into a town called Cottonwood near the Wind River mountain range in central Wyoming. He was delirious. Not only was the temperature below zero, but snow had been falling for several days. He was taken to the local doctor, who determined that his nose, ears, toes and fingers had frostbite and would need to be amputated before gangrene spread through his body. In Reich's few lucid periods, he told an amazing story about traveling on foot from a town called Avalon. The place, located in a valley within the Wind River range, was once a mining town. But after the mine stopped producing, Avalon fell on hard times. It was a hundred miles from Cottonwood, and Reich claimed to have set out on New Year's Eve, traveling that distance in some of the worst weather in years.'

Balenger listened intently.

'Reich was barely coherent,' Professor Graham

continued, 'but the doctor was able to learn that he was Avalon's minister and that the purpose of his desperate journey wasn't to summon help for the town. He wasn't seeking medicine to fight an epidemic or trying to get food for a starving community. No, his motive was to escape.'

Balenger straightened. 'Escape from what?'

'Reich kept talking about the new century. Recall the date I gave you. January third 1900. Three days earlier, the 1800s had become the 1900s. The start of the new century terrified him. He kept babbling about being a coward, about how he should have stayed and tried to help, about how he'd damned his soul by surrendering to his fear and running away.'

Balenger felt a nervous ripple in his stomach. 'But what on earth so frightened him that he abandoned his congregation and fled a hundred miles in the dead of winter?'

'The Sepulcher of Worldly Desires.'

9

Balenger's fingers tightened on the arms of his chair. Amanda, he thought. I need to find you.

'My book *The American West at the End of the Nineteenth Century* has a chapter devoted to end-of-century hysteria.' Professor Graham went to a bookshelf, pulled out a volume, and flipped through it until she found the section she wanted. 'Take a look at the indented material. It comes from Reich. He had handwritten pages stuffed in his clothing.'

Balenger read what she pointed at.

Dec. 31, 1899
The year hurtles to an end. So does the century. I fear I am losing my mind. I do not mean losing my grasp of reality. I know perfectly well what is happening. But I am powerless to prevent the outcome. Each day, I have less strength of mind to resist.

On this last day, it is supposedly dawn, but outside there is only the darkness of a howling blizzard. The swirl of shrieking snow matches my confusion. I pray that writing these pages will give me clarity. If not, and if the world impossibly survives for another hundred years, you who find this within the Sepulcher will perhaps understand what I cannot.

Balenger lowered the book. 'Sounds insane.'

'The doctor found a dozen scrawled pages in Reich's clothing. What you read comes from the start of the manuscript.'

Balenger indicated the last sentence. 'Reich mentions the Sepulcher.'

'But not its full name. That comes later in the manuscript.'

'What's this about "if the world impossibly survives for another hundred years"?'

The professor spread her aging hands. 'Apocalyptic fears are often part of end-of-century hysteria.'

'So, in a failing town in a valley in the middle of nowhere, this minister let his imagination get the better of him. But why did he run? Surely he didn't think he could escape the end of the world by fleeing to another location.'

'In my research, I sometimes come across apocalyptic fears associated with specific locations: a flood that will destroy a particular area or a hill where the Second Coming will occur,' Professor Graham said. 'But I don't believe Reich was afraid the world would end. As the manuscript continues, what he really seems afraid of is the Sepulcher of Worldly Desires – and a person. Another minister, in fact. A man named Owen Pentecost.'

'Pentecost?'

'In the Bible, when the Holy Spirit descended on Christ's apostles, they had visions. The transcendent experience was called Pentecost.'

'Good name for a minister. Too good to be true, I bet. Sounds like he made it up.'

'Reich's manuscript describes how Reverend Owen Pentecost, who was tall and extremely thin and wore black, who had long hair and a beard that made him look like Abraham Lincoln, walked into Avalon nine months earlier, in April. There was a terrible drought. Winds caused dust storms. Pentecost seemed to materialize from one of the dust clouds. A man looking for a cow that wandered from its pen saw him first, and the first words out of Pentecost's mouth were "The end of the century is coming." '

'Sounds like he had some theatrical training,' Balenger said.

'Or else he was crazy. When he reached Avalon, the first thing he did was march down the main street and up a hill to the church. Reich wasn't there. He was taking care of a sick child. The next people to meet Pentecost were a man and woman who ran the general store and supervised the upkeep of the church. They found Pentecost praying in front of the altar. He had a sack with him. It squirmed.'

'*Squirmed?*'

'We learn why it squirmed in a later section of the manuscript. In the coming weeks and months, Reich spoke to everyone who had contact with Pentecost. He summarizes conversations. When the couple in the church asked Pentecost if they could help him, the newcomer explained that he had come a long way. He could use food and water, but first he needed to know if anyone in town was ill. They told him that a boy was very sick with sharp pains in his lower right abdomen. The boy also had a fever and was vomiting.'

'Sounds like appendicitis,' Balenger said.

'Indeed. At the time, appendicitis was almost a death sentence. Few physicians had the surgical skills to remove the diseased organ. Even if a physician knew how to perform the operation, anesthetic in the form of ether was hard to find on the frontier. An operation without it risked killing the patient because of pain-induced shock. Avalon didn't have any ether.

'When Pentecost reached the sick boy, he found Reich praying with the boy's father. Because Avalon's doctor had left a year earlier, Reich also functioned as a sort of nurse because of medical knowledge he'd acquired in his years of administering to sick members of his church. But appendicitis was far beyond his skills. Basically, Reich and the father were on a death watch. Pentecost asked if there was a forest nearby. In the mountains, Reich told him, but how would that help the boy? Was there anything closer? Yes, there was a grove of aspen by the lake. Reich, who was curious about the newcomer, accompanied Pentecost to the aspens, but there Pentecost told him to wait and entered the trees by himself. A short while later, Pentecost returned with herbs he'd gathered. At the boy's home, he made a tea from the herbs and encouraged the boy to drink it. The boy fell into a stupor. Pentecost then operated on him.'

'Operated?'

'Not only did he operate,' Professor Graham said, 'but the boy survived. Pentecost then asked permission from Reich to conduct a church service and give public thanks to the Lord for saving the boy. During his sermon, he opened the sack and dumped its contents on the floor. You asked what was in it. Snakes. People screamed and charged toward the door, but Pentecost stomped the head of each snake without being bitten and told the congregation that they must be vigilant and stomp out evil just as he had stomped the snakes.'

'The guy definitely had a sense of drama,' Balenger said. 'Those herbs he found. It's awfully convenient that the exact ingredients he needed were in that grove but nobody else knew about them. Any bets that he already had a sedative hidden in his clothes and added it to the tea when no one was looking?'

'As a former police officer, you see the manipulation from the distance of more than a century, but at the time, in that isolated mountain valley, it would have been hard to resist the spell Pentecost was weaving. I can't explain the surgery. Maybe he took a risk and happened to succeed, or maybe he had medical training.'

Balenger felt the seconds speeding by. Amanda, he kept thinking. 'Tell me about the Sepulcher of Worldly Desires.'

'We're not certain what it was, but it sounds like a time capsule. Of course, the term wasn't invented until the New York World's Fair in 1939, but the concept's the same. With each day, Pentecost emphasized that a new century was coming. He warned that their souls would soon be tested, that the Apocalypse was on its way. As autumn approached, he urged everyone to select the physical things they most cared about. In December he ordered them to put these cherished objects into the Sepulcher of Worldly Desires. "Vanity. All is vanity," he told them. "As the new century begins, material things will no longer matter." '

'What did the Sepulcher look like?'

'No one knows.'

Balenger couldn't subdue his frustration. '*What?*'

'Reich's manuscript was hurried. He leapt from topic to topic, trying to compress as much information as he could in the limited time he had before midnight arrived – midnight of what was possibly the last day of the world. The passage you read indicates that he planned to put the pages into the Sepulcher. But then his courage snapped, and he fled, cramming the unfinished pages into his clothes.'

'Okay, the Sepulcher wasn't described in the manuscript,' Balenger said. 'But Reich could have told the doctor what it was.'

'Reich never became fully conscious. The infection from his injuries spread through him like a storm. He lapsed into a coma and died the next day.'

'The Sepulcher was supposed to contain all the treasured objects of the town, so it must have been large,' Balenger said. 'Didn't anybody find it later? The people in Cottonwood must have been curious. Surely, when spring came and the snow melted, they'd have gone to Avalon to learn what was happening there.'

'Indeed they did.'

'Then . . .?'

'They never found anything that they thought might be the Sepulcher.'

'But the people in Avalon could have shown them where the Sepulcher was. A name like that, it was probably buried in the cemetery.'

'The search party from Cottonwood found a deserted town. The buildings were abandoned. There wasn't any sign of violence, of the population having been caught by surprise. No half-eaten meals on tables. No objects on the floor that might have been dropped in a sudden panic. On the contrary, everything was neat and tidy. Beds were made. Clothes were hung up. There were gaps in the rooms where furniture might have been removed or vases or pictures carried away. Even pets were gone. As for the larger animals – pigs, sheep, cows and horses – those were found dead on the grassland, killed by either the freezing weather or starvation.'

'This doesn't make any . . . How many people lived in Avalon?'

'Over two hundred.'

'But that many people can't just disappear and not leave a trace. They must have gone to another town.'

'There's no record of that,' Professor Graham said. 'As word of the mystery spread, someone from Avalon who'd packed up in the middle of winter and moved to another town would have explained what happened. Out of two hundred people, someone would have spoken up.'

'Then where did they go? All those people, for God's sake.'

'Some religious zealots in other towns in the area began to believe that the Second Coming had indeed occurred in Avalon and that everyone there had been transported to heaven.'

'But that's preposterous! Jesus.'

She smiled. 'You see how easy it is to revert to religious terms when a seemingly impossible event occurs?'

Balenger stared dismally at the floor. 'This hasn't helped. I don't know anything more than when I started.' His voice tightened. 'I have no idea how to find Amanda.'

10

Behind him, Balenger heard the elevator open. He turned toward the open door, beyond which footsteps grew louder, heavy, a man's.

Ortega stepped into the doorway. 'I was beginning to think I was in the wrong building.' He didn't look happy.

Balenger introduced him to Professor Graham. 'We've been talking about the Sepulcher of Worldly Desires, but there's not much solid information about it. Did you find Karen Bailey?'

'No.'

Another disappointment. Balenger's shoulders felt

heavier. 'What about the game case? Did you send a patrol car to the row house?'

'We can talk about it later.'

'Look, I understand your reluctance to discuss this in front of a third person, but Professor Graham has a special interest in the topic. She might be able to help us.'

'Still acting like you're in charge?' Ortega asked.

The air in the room felt compressed.

'Acting like someone who's scared,' Balenger said. 'Was the game case still in the attic?'

Ortega hesitated, then reached into his suit coat. He removed a transparent plastic bag that contained the case. '*Scavenger*. The name still doesn't sound familiar.'

Balenger took the case from him. Beneath the game's title, he saw an image of an hourglass in which sand was draining. The sand at the top was white. As it fell through, it changed to the scarlet of blood.

'May I see?' Professor Graham asked. Fatigue lines etched her face.

Balenger handed it over. She examined the cover and turned the case. 'A copyright for this year. But I read all the game blogs on the Internet. I never heard of this one.'

'You read *all* the game blogs?' Ortega asked in surprise.

'People think video games are for teenagers. But the average age for a player is thirty, and plenty of people my age are fans.' She held up her knobby fingers. 'You'd be amazed how it keeps the mind sharp and arthritis at bay.'

'Even so,' Ortega said.

'A professor of history playing video games, many of which are violent?' The white-haired woman forced a smile. 'I suppose I could play a universe-exploring game like *Myst*, which is fairly outmoded now, or a role-playing game like *Anarchy Online*, in which I control a character in another reality. But to tell you the truth, they're too slow for me. The ones with weapons and cars – they're the ones that get my juices flowing, and at this stage of my life, that's not a small thing to accomplish. Believe me, I know every game that's available, and this one never got any publicity, which surprises me, given the money that went into the first-class packaging. I know you're using this plastic bag because you're worried about marring fingerprints, but if there's a way to do it safely, I'd like to take the disk out and play the game.'

'I'd like that too,' Balenger said. 'But when we found the case at the house where the fake professor gave the lecture, the disk wasn't in it.'

'You found this where you heard the lecture?' Professor Graham peered through the plastic bag and read the text on the back of the case. ' "*Scavenger* is the most vivid action game yet created. It has an astonishingly realistic appearance that allows you to identify with characters trapped in a mysterious wilderness, proving that wide-open spaces can be as threatening as any haunted house. The characters engage in a life-and-death obstacle race and scavenger hunt, using high-tech instruments to discover a message to the future to be opened in the present to understand the past." '

Balenger felt cold. 'Part of that was in the invitation Amanda and I received for the lecture. It's what caught my intention and made me go there.'

' "The objective is to find a lost hundred-year-old time capsule," ' Professor Graham continued reading. ' "In the process, both the player and the characters discover that time is the true scavenger, sucking our lives, even as we and the characters spend an irreplaceable forty hours playing the game." '

The professor lowered the case and stared at them. Dark circles under her eyes made Balenger suddenly wonder if she was ill. But before he could ask her about that, Ortega had a question of his own. 'Is that typical of the descriptions you find on the back of video game cases?'

'Hardly. They usually talk about "blood-rushing action," "spectacular graphics," and "battles with Hell." They emphasize effects rather than what the content means. This is so brooding it's almost existential. "Time is the true scavenger, sucking our lives"? You'd think Kierkegaard wrote that on one of his darkest nights.'

'What does the reference to forty hours mean?' Ortega asked.

'That's the length of time most video games take to be played,' Professor Graham answered.

Balenger rubbed his arm. 'Is that how long I've got to find Amanda?' In anguish, he peered at his watch. 'It's after five. Shortly after midnight yesterday, I woke up in Asbury Park. That was more than forty hours ago. God help me, I've lost her.'

LEVEL FIVE: THE MIND OF THE MAKER

1

'Have any of you read Dorothy L. Sayers?' the Game Master asked.

Amanda adjusted her headset, convinced that she couldn't have heard correctly.

'*Who?*' Viv asked.

Amid the ruins of the church, Derrick stared up at the glaring sky. The rocks of the fallen walls radiated heat. 'First you want to know if we can guess what this Sepulcher thing is. Now you ask about—'

'Amanda,' the voice said, 'you ought to be able to tell us about Ms Sayers.'

'Why would *she* know?' Ray demanded. 'You already told us she's your favorite. Are you giving her the advantage, asking questions only *she* can answer?'

'I work in a bookstore,' Amanda told them. She deliberately used the present tense, needing to convince herself that life could be normal again. 'Yes, I know who Dorothy L. Sayers is.'

'Prove it,' the voice said.

'She's a British mystery writer who created an

amateur detective named Lord Peter Wimsey. Her most famous novel is probably *The Nine Tailors*, which is about bells in a church steeple and a body that's found there.'

'This is more bullshit.' Ray wiped his sleeve across his forehead. 'The clock's ticking, and we're wasting time, yacking about a mystery writer.'

His stomach rumbled, the noise so loud that everybody noticed.

'Good heavens, Ray,' the voice said. 'Are you hungry?'

His face turning scarlet, Ray glowered at the others. 'Talk to this guy all you want. Waste your strength as well as your time.'

He yanked the empty water bottles from Viv and Derrick, then programmed the latitude and longitude numbers written on them into his GPS receiver. 'While the rest of you dick around, *I'm* going to find out how to win this game and get away from here.'

He picked up two full bottles that the toppling wall had exposed. After stuffing them into pockets, he rushed down the hill.

'He's right,' Viv said. 'We need to get to the next coordinates.'

Viv stooped toward the rocks and took two bottles. Derrick did the same. When Amanda reached down, she discovered that only one bottle remained.

Furious, she ran after the others. The red needle on her GPS receiver pointed toward the narrow end of the lake, before which lay the remnants of Avalon. Trying not to lose her balance running down the hill, she felt a shadow to her left and looked toward the west. Clouds gathered over the mountains.

'Storm's coming,' Derrick said. 'A couple of hours.'

'Amanda,' the Game Master said, 'you didn't mention that Dorothy L. Sayers translated Dante's *Inferno*.'

'Will you shut up?' Ray yelled below them.

'I'm trying to make things easier for all of you,' the voice said. 'I'm trying to help you understand the game. Sayers wrote *The Mind of the Maker*. Have you ever read it, Amanda?'

'No!' Amanda breathed hard. Reaching the bottom, she chased Derrick, Viv and Ray toward the ghost town.

'That disappoints me.'

'It isn't a huge bookstore, damn it!'

'But you have an MA in English from Columbia University.'

Racing, Viv turned and shot Amanda an angry look.

'We didn't study mystery writers!' Amanda shouted.

The voice sighed with disappointment. 'Sayers was a devout Anglican. But she was troubled by the contradiction between God's omniscience and the free will humans are supposed to have. If God knows everything. He's aware when each of us will sin. But that means our future is locked into place, and we don't have free will.'

'Shut up!' Ray yelled, almost at the ghost town.

'That's why Sayers wrote *The Mind of the Maker*,' the Game Master explained. 'She decided that God is like a novelist. He establishes the time and place for the story. He creates characters and knows generally what they'll do. But as any novelist will tell you, characters often assume a life of their own and refuse to abide by the story. They exist in the novelist's mind, and yet they're independent. They're almost like method actors. "I don't think I should do this," one says. "My character would tell the truth in this scene." Another says, "I think I'm more motivated to turn down the promotion rather than work with someone I dislike." Sayers realized from personal experience that characters in novels have free will. In that same way, she thought, *humans* have free will. The plot's laid out for us, but sometimes we choose not to follow it. Sometimes we surprise even God. That's how we gain salvation, Sayers believed. By showing how resourceful we are and surprising God.'

Ahead, Ray lurched to a stop, working to catch his breath as he studied the screen on his GPS receiver. 'This is it,' he said. 'The coordinates.'

Derrick, Viv and Amanda caught up to him. Sweat clinging to his beard stubble, Derrick pulled a water bottle from a pocket and gulped from it.

'Make it last as long as you can,' Viv said.

They were in the remnant of a street. Sagebrush grew from the dust, straight lines of collapsed buildings on each side. Unlike the church, which was mostly stone, these buildings were made of wood, their walls and roofs lying in heaps from which weeds sprouted. The boards were gray and splintered with age.

'Look around!' Ray ordered. 'These receivers are accurate to within ten feet! Somewhere close, there's something we're supposed to find!'

Ray searched the ruins on the left while Derrick kicked under sagebrush and Viv checked the ruins on the right.

The immense sky made Amanda feel dwarfed. Dizzy, she stared up. 'Are you telling us you think you're God?'

Derrick stopped and frowned.

'I told you I'm the Game Master,' the voice said.

'Are you telling us you think we're characters in your mind?'

Viv, too, stopped and frowned.

'We're not in your mind!' Amanda shouted. Desperate, she remembered Frank telling her that criminals were more inclined to abuse their victims if they considered them objects instead of people. At all costs she had to make the Game Master relate to her as an individual, a personality, a human being.

Frank. The thought of him sent a shudder through her. Grief welled through her with the renewed apprehension that Frank was dead. She knew with all her heart that if he were alive he'd be here, helping her.

'I'm twenty-six! My favorite food is spaghetti and meatballs, even though the carbohydrates put on weight. I like Brad Pitt movies. I like to watch the History Channel. I like to play with my father's Irish setter. I like to jog through Prospect Park. I like to—'

'Stop wasting your breath!' Ray shouted. 'Help find whatever the bastard hid at these coordinates!'

'I imagined Bethany would run,' the Game Master explained. 'That was all right because I needed someone to make an example of. The thing is, it could have turned out another way. She could be there with you right now. Honestly, all she needed to do was surprise me.'

'Like *God* wants to be surprised?'

'Damn it,' Ray said, 'help us search!'

In the ruins on the right, Viv yelled, 'I found something!'

'*What?*' Derrick scrambled toward her.

'Part of a sign.'

'Let me see.' Ray charged over and grabbed the fragment. The letters on it were faint: RAL STOR. 'That could mean anything.'

'General store,' Derrick blurted. 'I bet that's what it means. The store would have sold a little of everything, including food.'

'Food?' Ray looked hopeful only for a moment. 'But after all these years there wouldn't be anything left of it.'

'Those water bottles at the church were put there recently. Maybe food was put *here*.'

Ray pointed at Derrick. 'You're supposed to be such a big-deal outdoor survival expert. Can't you show us how to scrounge for stuff like nuts and berries? I'll eat *anything*.'

'Scrounging expends more energy than you get from

whatever nuts and berries you manage to find. Eventually, you'd starve.'

'Yeah, I figured you'd have an excuse.' Ray yanked up an old board and searched under it. He grabbed another board, which broke in his hands. He hurled the chunks away. 'Come on! Dig!'

Amanda joined him. Splinters stung her hands.

'I found a can!' Derrick yelled. He held it up, showing a label marked PEACHES.

'Another one!' Viv shouted in triumph. The can she held up was marked PEARS.

Amanda and Ray hurled more boards away.

'Where are the others?' Ray dug down to a rotted wooden floor. 'Keep searching! Where are the others?'

Fingers raw, Amanda tossed another board into the street.

'I'll use a sharp rock and bang the tops open,' Derrick said.

'You're not doing anything until we find the other cans!' Ray fumbled through the wreckage.

'I'm afraid there aren't any others,' Amanda said.

Derrick turned toward the street. 'I kicked up a rock over there.' He hurried to it. 'Yes! It doesn't have a sharp end, but we can pound with it!'

'You're not pounding anything,' Ray emphasized, 'until we figure how to guarantee we each get our share.'

'Like you drank the first bottle of water we found?'

'It won't happen again.'

Right, Amanda thought. But everybody took two bottles of water and left me only one.

'You bet it won't happen again,' Derrick said. 'We'll each take a swallow of the juice. Then we'll count how many pieces of fruit there are and share them evenly.'

'Whatever you want. Now that you're running the show, let's find another rock.'

'I'm *not* running the show,' Derrick said. 'All I want is what's fair.'

'Sure. Right. Of course.'

'Over here.' Viv sounded like she hoped to change the subject. She picked up a rock that resembled a wedge. 'We can use this to bang a hole in the top.'

Derrick set the can on a board. He put the wedge-shaped rock on the lid and prepared to slam it with the rock that was flat.

'Stop.' Ray wiped his mouth. 'You'll send juice flying. We don't want to spill a drop.'

'It's impossible to keep that from happening,' Derrick told him angrily.

'No,' Viv said. 'The rubber gloves I took from the building.' She pulled one from a pocket, its yellow bright against her brown coveralls. 'We'll put the can in the glove. If juice sprays, it'll stay inside.'

Viv held the can in the glove's long sleeve while Derrick braced the first rock and slammed it with the second.

The impact made a dull thumping sound. The can's lid pushed inward but remained intact.

'Hit it harder,' Ray said.

'I don't want to crush the fruit.'

'*Hit it*,' Ray said.

Derrick slammed the rock down so hard he grunted. With the sound of metal breaking, juice leapt from a jagged hole but stayed within the glove.

'We'll drink the juice,' Ray said. 'When it's gone, we'll knock the can all the way open and get the fruit.'

'Is that what we'll do?' Derrick handed the can to Viv.

Shaking, she raised it to her lips and took a swallow.

Ray stepped close, watching her. 'How does it taste?'

'Warm.' Viv gave the can to Amanda.

'But not spoiled?'

'Sweeter than I like, but it's fine.'

'Jesus, is that why you didn't complain when I let Viv go first?' Derrick shook his head in amazement. 'You wanted to find out if she'd get sick?'

The thought that the juice might be spoiled made Amanda reluctant to drink. Slowly, she raised the can. The thick, sweet, warm liquid was the most delicious thing she'd ever tasted.

Now Derrick reached for the can.

'No,' Ray said. '*I'm* next.'

'You think so?' Derrick glared.

'Let him,' Viv said. 'Maybe he'll calm down.'

As Ray brought the can to his mouth, Derrick watched carefully. Ray's Adam's apple moved in his long neck.

'That's enough,' Derrick said.

The sun seemed hotter. Ray lowered the can. 'I wasn't going to drink from this after you put *your* lips to it, boss.'

Derrick screamed. In a blur, he surged to his feet, swinging the rock.

The attack took Ray by surprise. Stumbling back, he groaned as the blow meant for his head struck his left shoulder. Wailing, Derrick struck again. Ray jerked up a hand to protect himself, moaning from the impact of the rock against his forearm.

'Stop!' Viv shouted.

Derrick swung again and almost hit Ray's jaw.

'Don't!' Viv screamed.

Ray lost his balance and fell to the dust. Standing over him, Derrick swept back his arm to hurl the rock at his head.

'No!' Viv wailed.

Ray kicked Derrick's legs from under him. As Derrick landed, Ray scuttled toward him. Derrick threw the rock, hitting Ray's chest, but the next moment Ray was upon him, banging his head against the dirt.

Amanda couldn't move. What felt like a minute was only seconds, she knew. At once, it seemed that a powerful spring was released, propelling her into motion. She ran and grabbed Ray from behind, straining to pull him off. She smelled sweat. Ray's breath was vinegary from hyperventilating.

'Stop,' she said.

Viv joined Amanda and struggled to pry Ray's hands

from Derrick's neck. Amanda tugged frantically at Ray's shoulders. Derrick's tongue bulged from his mouth. His face had a blue tint.

'You're killing him!' Viv screamed.

Ray opened his hands.

Thank God, Amanda thought.

Ray took his fingers from Derrick's throat.

'Yes!' Amanda said. 'Let him go!'

Ray moved back.

'Yes!' Viv said.

Then Amanda's heart seemed to slide loose in her chest as she saw Ray pick up the rock Derrick had thrown against his chest.

'Stop!'

Amanda grabbed him again, but Ray swung an arm, striking the side of her head. The blow made her see gray. Feeling weightless, she dropped to the dust. Ray knocked Viv away from him. His hand streaked toward Derrick's head. The rock made a brutal crunching sound. Derrick moaned. The rock came up bloody. It slammed down again, and this time the crunch had a liquid sound.

Amanda hurled herself toward Ray at the same time Viv did. They each grabbed an arm, tugging in a frenzy. Ray squirmed to get free. They pulled him back, and suddenly he went with them, all of them dropping. With a yell he rolled over them, his momentum twisting their arms loose. He dove toward Derrick. His hand still held the rock. He slammed with it. He slammed again. Blood dripped from the rock.

'No black son of a bitch' – he struck – 'is going to tell me' – he struck harder. Hair now clung to the blood on the rock – 'what to do!'

Derrick's crushed face wasn't recognizable. Viv shrieked and ran to him, but Derrick trembled and lay still.

Viv, too, became motionless, kneeling next to her husband. Her features were frozen in shock. Amanda felt as if the metal spring was tightening now, squeezing her.

Ray squinted at the blood-covered rock in his hand and dropped it.

2

A breeze stirred up dust. For a long while, that was the only movement.

On her knees beside Derrick, Viv nudged him. He didn't respond. His cap was blood-soaked. His eyes and nose were bashed in.

'Come on, baby. Wake up,' she sobbed.

Ray stumbled toward the can of peaches. It lay on its side in the dirt, where he'd dropped it when Derrick attacked him. Some of the juice had spilled. Ray picked up the can and wiped grit from the opening. He raised it to his mouth, tipped it all the way up, and drained the remaining liquid down his throat. He put the can into the rubber glove, looked around, picked up another rock, and pounded the can until it split apart.

'Wake up,' Viv murmured to Derrick.

Ray pulled a peach from the can and shoved it into his mouth. He chewed and stared at Amanda, silently challenging her to stop him.

'You'll be okay as soon as you wake up,' Viv murmured.

Ray hooked another peach from the can and crammed it into his mouth, hardly chewing before he swallowed. 'It's not my fault. He attacked me.'

'You provoked him,' Amanda said.

'He shouldn't have given me orders.' Ray took the last peach from the can and ate it. Juice dribbled down his chin.

'Do you remember when Ray kept insisting he wasn't a hero?' the voice asked, startling Amanda. 'That was the truth.'

Slowly, Viv pivoted toward Ray. Her eyes brimmed with tears.

'Oh, his jet was shot down the way I described,' the Game Master said. 'And he survived for ten days on bugs and pools of stagnant water while Iraqi insurgents hunted him. But the reason he didn't use his location transmitter had nothing to do with wanting to stop the rescue helicopters from flying into an ambush. No, the reason he didn't use his location transmitter is that it was broken. The truth is, he'd have done anything and risked anybody's life to survive.'

'That's what I did!' Ray shouted to the sky. 'I survived!'

'Two months after his rescue and return to the United States, Ray got in a fight in a bar. This wasn't the first such incident, but it *was* the first time he'd killed somebody outside his duties as a military pilot. Nasty temper, Ray. However, there was enough evidence to suggest that the victim was drunk and fell and hit his head in what amounted to a mere scuffle. The incident occurred on base. The military chose not to prosecute. Ray was given a medical discharge. His temper became the civilian world's problem.'

Viv's features hardened.

'Not that Amanda and Viv haven't killed also,' the voice said.

'*What?*' Ray looked at them.

'Amanda had to kill to survive the Paragon Hotel,' the Game Master continued. 'As for Viv and Derrick, I told you about their heroism on Mount Everest. I neglected to explain why they were so determined. On a previous expedition, they led climbers across a glacier. Everyone was in a line, connected by a rope. A chasm opened. The climbers at the back fell into it, dragging the others with them. Everything happened so fast, there wasn't time to use ice axes to hook into the side of the chasm. The gap kept spreading. People kept dropping, their weight dragging the next people on the rope. Viv and Derrick slid across the glacier, desperately trying to keep from being pulled into the chasm. They were the last two. At the final moment, Viv . . . or perhaps it was Derrick . . . cut the rope. The climbers attached to it fell a thousand meters. None of them survived. An investigation stopped short of finding fault. After all, were Viv and Derrick supposed to let themselves get sucked into the chasm and die along with the others rather than do anything they could to save themselves? When it comes to survival, difficult choices sometimes need to be made – and made quickly. It has nothing to do with heroism. Isn't that correct, Viv?'

'Yes.' Viv scowled at Ray. 'Nothing to do with heroism.'

Ray picked up the can of pears.

'Get your hands off that,' Viv warned. 'We'll stone you to death if we need to, but you're not eating what's in that can.'

Ray ignored her. He turned the can, examining it. When he looked at its bottom, something attracted his attention. Immediately, he pulled out his GPS receiver and programmed numbers into it. He looked dismissively at Viv and dropped the can. Then he picked up the empty can of peaches and stared at its bottom. Again he programmed numbers into his GPS unit, then headed away down the sagebrush-dotted street.

Amanda hurried to the cans. She upended them and saw a sequence of numbers marked LT on one and LG on the other. 'More latitude and longitude directions.'

Viv glared at Ray, who walked faster along the street.

'Help me,' Amanda said. 'I'm still learning how to

use my receiver. You need to program these numbers for me.'

Viv didn't blink, just kept watching Ray, who studied his receiver and turned to the left, heading down the remnant of another street. When she did blink, tears streamed down her face.

'You need to help me,' Amanda insisted. 'I need to smash this can open, but I can't do that until you program the numbers. Otherwise I might destroy them.'

Viv turned toward Derrick, stroking his arm. 'I'm sorry, baby.'

'Help me!' Amanda said. 'Don't you want to get even?'

With a furious glance toward Ray, Viv came to her feet and stumbled toward Amanda. Revenge was as effective a motive as any to get her moving, Amanda decided, but she herself wanted to punish more than Ray. The Game Master, she thought.

'Okay, they're programmed.' Viv stared at Ray's receding figure.

Amanda put the can of pears into the rubber glove. She picked up two rocks and pounded. Once. Twice. Harder. The lid broke inward.

'You first,' she told Viv.

'Not hungry.'

'Then you won't have the strength to pay him back.'

Eyes raw, Viv nodded with determination and gripped the can, drinking. 'I took two swallows.'

'Okay.' Amanda raised the lid to her mouth and tasted the warm, sweet pear juice.

They went back and forth until they drained the can. Amanda shoved it back into the rubber glove and used the rocks to split it open. Four pears. They each took two.

'Chew them slowly.' Viv sounded weak.

Amanda understood. She might get sick if she ate too fast.

Viv turned toward her dead husband.

The wind blew stronger. The storm clouds obscured the mountains to the west, their shadow entering the valley.

3

'Do you want to tell me what's wrong?' Balenger demanded. He and Ortega were standing outside Professor Graham's faculty building. The trees of Washington Square were across from them.

'Wrong?'

'When you came into the office, we almost had an argument. At the library, you talked about another part of the investigation. You wouldn't be specific, but your tone made it clear I wasn't your favorite person. What on earth's the matter?'

'You mean other than the way you act like you're running the investigation? This morning. I mentioned that my partner and I made some inquiries yesterday. Perhaps you wonder why you haven't met him.'

'I assumed today was his day off.'

'He's been checking your background.'

Balenger was taken by surprise.

'Earlier, you told me this happened to you once before. Your wife was kidnapped. The same man also kidnapped a woman who looks like her.'

'Amanda. So what's your point? Psychopaths often fixate on women who resemble one another. The victims tend to remind the killer of his wife or his mother or another female who so traumatized him, he's been getting even ever since.'

'And what makes you such an expert?'

'If your partner's been checking my background, you already know the answer. When I was in law enforcement, my specialty was investigating sex crimes.'

'Ever been to a psychiatrist?'

Balenger felt heat rise to his face. 'I assume your partner told you what happened to me in Iraq.' A car drove by. Balenger waited for the engine noise to recede, using the time to try to calm himself. 'In the first Gulf War . . . Desert Storm . . . I was a Ranger.'

'Nineteen ninety-one. Check,' Ortega said.

'I got headaches. Muscle pains. Fever.'

'Gulf War syndrome. Check.'

'Some people said it came from a disease spread by sand fleas. Others said it came from the depleted uranium we use in our artillery shells. The army doctors tried various treatments. When those didn't help, they suggested I talk to an army psychiatrist to see if the illness was psychological, a form of post-traumatic stress disorder.'

'That was the *first* psychiatrist,' Ortega said.

Balenger almost walked away, but he kept telling himself that Amanda was all that mattered. I'll do anything to get her back, he thought. 'After the war, I became a police officer in Asbury Park.'

'Where you took psychology courses about sex crimes.'

Balenger worked to keep his voice steady. 'Then my wife disappeared, and after a year, when the authorities couldn't find her, I quit my job so I could look for her. Eventually I needed a lot of quick money so badly that I signed on as a private security operator in the second Iraq war. Twenty-five thousand dollars a month. All I needed was a couple of months guarding convoys and I'd have enough cash to keep searching for my wife. You could have asked me about this.'

'Tell me about your second time in Iraq.'

Balenger sensed the old panic taking control. 'You *know* what happened. Shortly after I got there, the convoy I was guarding came under attack. An explosion knocked me unconscious. When I woke up, I was being held prisoner by a bunch of Iraqis wearing hoods, one of whom threatened to cut off my head if I didn't look into a video camera and denounce the United States. After a Ranger unit attacked the compound where I was tied up,

I managed to escape, but even when I was safe in the States, I didn't *feel* safe. I had nightmares. I couldn't bear being closed in. I broke out in sweat.'

'Post-traumatic stress disorder,' Ortega said.

'Check,' Balenger said, mocking Ortega's earlier expression. 'So, as you know, I went to another psychiatrist.'

'Who had an unusual method of therapy.'

'He advised me to do everything I could to distance myself from the present. Study history. Read novels about the past. Try to do everything possible to imagine I'm somewhere a hundred years ago and more. It was sort of like trying to transport myself back in time.'

'What happened after you went inside the Paragon Hotel and you found your dead wife and rescued Amanda?'

Balenger didn't trust himself to speak.

'Your fists are clenched at your sides,' Ortega said. 'Do you want to hit me?'

'I woke up in a hospital, where a psychiatrist wanted to know why I called Amanda by my dead wife's name.'

'Psychiatrist number three. Did you get that straightened out, by the way? The names?'

Balenger was too furious to answer.

'You and Amanda. In the night, in the shadows, do you ever think you might be seeing a ghost?'

Balenger felt a scalding fury. 'Stop.'

'You said psychopaths often fixate on women who resemble one another. The victims tend to remind the killer of his wife or his mother or whatever.'

'I don't think I'm living with my dead wife! I don't think I'm *sleeping* with my dead wife!'

Ortega didn't reply.

'You believe I'm responsible for Amanda's disappearance?'

'It's a theory,' Ortega said. 'Maybe you freaked out when you understood the implications of your domestic arrangements. Maybe you got so disgusted with yourself that you did something you regretted. You used to be a police officer. You could predict how the investigation would proceed.'

'Be careful,' Balenger warned.

'I told you it's a theory. Everything needs to be considered. You set up a diversion. You rented the row house on Nineteenth Street. You hired a woman to arrange for the actors to be there. You showed up with someone you paid to impersonate Amanda. As instructed, the actors left during the talk. With everybody gone, you thanked the woman who impersonated Amanda. She was puzzled, but you paid her well, so she thought, Another weirdo, and went home. Meanwhile, everybody believed they'd seen the real Amanda and that someone had abducted her.'

'For any of that to work, I'd also need to be responsible for the fire at the theater. But you and I were always together.'

'Except for the time you waited in the lobby while I went into the main part of the theater to look around. You could have started the fire then. I wouldn't have noticed.'

'We almost died. Why would I put myself in danger?'

'To convince me of the threat. Anyway, according to this theory, you were never in danger.'

'What do you mean?' Balenger's forearm felt as if an abscess wanted to burst.

'You should have come with me to talk to the fire investigators you tried so hard to avoid. The conversation was revealing. It seems the woman who hired the actors asked for a tour of the theater. She was very interested when she learned about the sub-basement. She asked to be taken down there so she could have a look. A couple of weeks ago, a woman matching her description also visited businesses along the street. The antique store was one of them. While she pretended to think about buying something, she mentioned that she'd heard about dried-up streams under Greenwich Village and passageways where the water used to flow. As it turns out, the antique store owner was happy to talk about it because that piece of history helps him sell antiques. He has the only other building in the area with a sub-basement that matches the one in the theater.'

'You think I set the fire, hoping I could escape by crawling along a passageway that I couldn't be sure was open? That's crazy!'

'Is it any more crazy than your claim to have seen this same woman in the library this afternoon? A woman who magically disappeared and who hasn't the slightest reason to show herself and whom nobody else saw except you.'

'Why would I lie?'

'To make me continue believing there's a threat. To keep throwing me off track. You took every chance you could to assume control of the investigation.'

Balenger stared past Ortega toward the end of the street where a woman wearing dark slacks and a white blouse waved at him.

'You're wrong,' he told the detective.

'It makes as much sense as your theory that somebody abducted Amanda to force you to play a sicko game.'

'You're wrong, and I can prove it.'

'Believe me, I'd like a little proof about *something*.'

'The woman who showed herself at the library, the woman who hired the actors and introduced herself as Karen Bailey at the lecture.'

'What about her?'

'She's standing down the street, waving at us.'

4

As Ortega spun to look, Balenger was already running. For a moment, Karen Bailey didn't move. Then she ducked around the corner on the right.

Balenger raced. It was almost five thirty. Classes were finished for the day, students having returned to their dormitories or homes elsewhere in the city. Few pedestrians got in Balenger's way. He reached the corner and saw Karen Bailey's white blouse disappearing around another corner.

He avoided a passing car and turned the next corner in time to see her charge into what looked like an apartment building. Her shoes were lace-up, low-heeled, like a man's, giving her mobility.

'Stop!' he yelled.

He heard Ortega's rapid breathing behind him. Then Ortega was next to him, and they rushed toward the building.

'Now do you believe me?'

A wire fence blocked the sidewalk. A Dumpster held broken plaster and boards.

Chest heaving, Balenger reached the fence. No one was around. He studied a gate that seemed to be locked. Then he saw that the lock hung loose. Furious, he shoved the gate open.

Ortega grabbed his shoulder. 'For God's sake, wait till I call for backup. We don't know what's in there.'

'*You* wait.' Balenger raced over bits of debris toward grit-covered steps that led to a sheet of plywood tilted over the entrance as a makeshift door.

'You're not a police officer!' Ortega shouted. 'You don't have authority!'

'Which means I don't have a job to worry about!' Balenger yelled over his shoulder. 'I can do whatever I want!'

He gazed warily through the gap beyond the plywood, then eased inside. The place smelled of dust, mildew and old plaster. As his eyes adjusted to the murky light, he saw exposed floorboards and walls stripped to their joists. A corridor led to doorless entrances to what he assumed were other stripped rooms. On the right, a stairway didn't have a banister. The ceiling had dangling strips of ancient paint.

Another old abandoned building, Balenger thought. Shadows. Narrowing walls. Shrinking rooms. Sweat oozed from his pores, but not because he'd run to get there. With all his being, he wanted to turn and escape.

Amanda, he thought. Footsteps echoed on the next floor. He climbed the stairs, stretching his legs over gaps. A noise behind him made him pause. He turned and saw Ortega enter the building.

'Backup's on the way,' Ortega said.

'You're sure this isn't another diversion I arranged.'

'The only thing I'm sure of is that I want to talk to this woman.'

Ortega joined him. Boards creaked as they climbed. The upper area gradually came into view: more strips of paint dangling from the ceiling, more exposed walls and naked joists, another staircase without a banister. At the top, they listened for footsteps, but all Balenger heard was the muffled sound of distant traffic.

'This seems to be the only stairway. She can't get out,' Ortega said.

'Can't she? Maybe there's a way into the next building.'

A noise to the left made Balenger turn. He stepped across a hole and eased along a dusky corridor. Grit scraped under his shoes. They checked each opening they passed, seeing more gutted rooms.

In the gray light, Ortega examined a jagged edge on each side of the hallway. 'Looks as if a wall was here and the renovators smashed through. It's an awfully long corridor for one building.'

'But not for two,' Balenger said. 'This is a couple of buildings being made into one.'

They came to a corridor on the right. It stretched deeper into the structure.

'Maybe *three* buildings,' Ortega said. 'Maybe the university's combining them into one big classroom complex.'

A creaking sound stopped them. It came from an area farther along. A board lay across two sawhorses. Other boards were stacked against a wall, boxes next to them. On the floor, a tarpaulin was littered with bits of wood and sawdust. A rope dangled from the upper level.

'There's something on that sawhorse,' Ortega said.

The small rectangular object was silver and black, with buttons and a screen.

'A cell phone,' Ortega said. 'One of the workers must have left it.'

'Looks different than a standard phone.'

Ortega took a step closer. 'It's a BlackBerry.'

Although Balenger had never used one, he knew that a BlackBerry could connect to the Internet and manage email. 'Aren't they expensive?'

'Several hundred dollars,' Ortega said.

'Would a construction worker, who managed to afford one, be careless enough to leave it behind?'

They stopped next to the sawhorse. Balenger reached for the BlackBerry.

'Better not,' Ortega cautioned. 'If you're right about somebody playing games, that thing might be a bomb.'

'Or maybe it's like the video game case, and it'll lead me somewhere else.' Balenger picked up the Black-Berry.

'One of these days, you'll listen to me,' Ortega said.

Balenger noted that the BlackBerry was slightly heavier and thicker than his cell phone. It had a bigger screen and many more buttons that included the alphabet as well as numbers.

'I hear voices.' Ortega turned. 'Sounds like they're coming from the entrance. Must be the backup team.' He pulled out his cell phone. 'I'll tell them where we are.'

Sudden movement caught Balenger's attention. On the other side of the work area, a white blouse appeared in the corridor. Flushed from her hiding place, Karen Bailey ran.

Balenger shoved the BlackBerry into a pocket and chased her. He crossed the tarpaulin, and at once, it sank through a hole it disguised. His knees went down. His hips. He grabbed the rope that dangled from the next level. The tarpaulin kept sinking. His chest dropped into the hole. The rope in his hands tightened, suspending him.

Ortega hurried to grab Balenger's hand.

'Be careful,' Balenger warned. 'With the tarp, it's hard to know where the edge of the hole is.'

Holding Balenger's hand, Ortega leaned so far over the tarp that he needed to grip the rope for support.

The rope went slack, whatever it was attached to giving way. Ortega lost his balance. Balenger felt weightless again, groaning when Ortega landed on him, both men dropping with the tarpaulin through the hole. The rope fell with them, and something else, something that Balenger caught only a glimpse of – a wheelbarrow that the rope was tied to on an upper level.

'No!' Balenger screamed.

The tarpaulin scraped against the hole's edge. When Balenger hit the lower floor, the impact knocked the wind from him, as did the jolt of Ortega against him. He heard a crash, looked up, and saw the plummeting wheelbarrow strike the hole's edge. It broke boards and continued falling.

'Look out!'

There wasn't time to react. The wheelbarrow slammed on to Ortega's back. Something snapped inside him. Blood bubbled from his mouth. His face went slack. His eyes lost focus. Balenger struggled to push the wheelbarrow off him, to do something to revive him, but there was no mistaking the stillness of death.

Grieving, he stopped trying to find a pulse. In the distance he heard distraught voices, people running toward the sound of the crash. The backup team, he thought, trying to adjust to the shock of what had happened. They'll question me at the station. It'll take hours to explain. The footsteps sounded closer.

He struggled to his feet. The BlackBerry weighed in his pocket as he staggered along a hallway, turning a corner just before the voices arrived behind him. He crept along another corridor, then another, feeling trapped in a maze. He passed more sawhorses, boxes and boards. He came to a window frame, its glass not yet installed. Breathless, he crawled over the frame, dangled, and dropped to the ground.

His ribs hurt. His legs ached. His left forearm felt biting pressure. For a few steps, he limped. Then he managed to steady his pace. Following the chain-link fence, he headed toward the end of the renovation site. The sun was lower. Traffic was sparse. The few students going by hardly looked at him.

Sirens wailed in the distance. When Balenger reached another gate in the fence, he found that it was locked. As the sirens came nearer, he found a piece of tarpaulin, climbed on to a Dumpster, and draped the tarp over barbed wire at the fence's top. The sirens stopped on the street around the corner. He squirmed over the fence, unhooked the tarpaulin from the barbed wire, threw it into the Dumpster, and climbed down to the street.

He fought the urge to run. Look calm, he told himself. Keep moving.

Students came out of a coffee shop. A young man with a knapsack asked a friend, 'You want to go down and check out what's happening?'

'I stay away from war zones.'

Wise plan, Balenger thought.

More students came from the coffee shop. Hoping they gave him cover, Balenger turned a corner. He saw his reflection in a window, did his best to smooth his hair, and brushed dirt off his jacket.

Hearing other sirens, he knew he couldn't keep walking much longer. When word spread that a detective had been killed, the police would close off the area for blocks in every direction. All the restaurants and bars in the area were student hangouts. If he went into any of them, he'd look conspicuous.

He tried a door to what seemed an office building. It was locked. Need to get off the street, he told himself.

He couldn't stop thinking about Karen Bailey. When she ran from her hiding place, he'd assumed that he'd panicked her. But now it was obvious that she wanted to make him chase her, and step on to the tarpaulin. Another trap. No, another *obstacle*, he corrected himself.

The words on the back of the *Scavenger* game case nagged at him. An obstacle race and a scavenger hunt. I survived the obstacle, and what did I get? he thought. A BlackBerry phone.

But how did Karen Bailey know where to find me?

An answer to that question abruptly occurred to him. It told him where to hide.

5

The corridor seemed longer than the last time. Reaching the office, Balenger again heard gunfire inside. He drew a long breath and knocked. No answer. He opened the door.

Professor Graham sat behind the computer monitor, furiously working the mouse and keyboard. The dark circles under her eyes were more pronounced.

'I thought you broke the mouse,' Balenger said.

'I always keep spares.' The elderly woman jabbed buttons in a blur, then scowled at the screen. 'Damn, they killed me again.'

Balenger heard sirens outside.

'What happened to you?' Professor Graham looked at him. 'Your pants.'

Balenger peered down and noticed dirt he'd missed. He brushed it off. 'I ran into a couple of obstacles.'

'And the detective who was with you?'

Balenger did his best to keep his voice neutral. 'Same obstacles.'

'Do those obstacles have any connection with the commotion outside?'

Balenger nodded. 'And with everything we talked about. I'm glad you're still here.' He didn't add that, if she hadn't remained in the office, he'd have done everything in his power to find where she lived.

'I stayed because my pills wore off.'

'Pills?'

'The ones I swallowed a while ago haven't started to work yet.' The fatigue lines around her eyes seemed to deepen. 'I won't bore you with the specifics.'

Now Balenger understood why she had seemed to age visibly when he spoke to her earlier. His suspicion about an illness was correct. 'I'm sorry.'

She shrugged fatalistically. 'Years ago, the student who taught me that video games prolonged time also made me realize that the reality in *there*' – she pointed toward the monitor – 'is more vivid than the reality *here*. What made you come back? Not to be rude, but I want to restart the game.'

'I had a thought.' Balenger prayed he was right. 'If I'm being given clues, whoever kidnapped Amanda must have known I'd eventually come here and talk to you about the Sepulcher. You're the expert in it. I reminded myself that you're also a video game expert.'

'An enthusiast. My student's the true expert.' Professor Graham's face tensed, then relaxed, as a pain spasm ended.

Balenger hid his desperation. 'Does he keep in touch with you?'

'Emails. Phone calls. He was upset when I told him about my health problem. That's why he sent me this new computer. It has state-of-the-art game capability. The large monitor's the best I ever had.'

'He's very generous.'

'He can afford it. That's why I didn't refuse.'

'What's his name?' Balenger made the question seem off-hand.

'Jonathan Creed. I see you recognize it.'

'No.'

'But you reacted to it.'

'Only because it's distinctive.'

'Even non-game-players sometimes recognize it.'

'Why?' Balenger had trouble concealing his intensity.

'There are a few people who are undisputed legends in the game world, people who design games of such genius that they set an impossibly high standard. Or else they're marketing geniuses. CliffyB, for one. His game's called *Unreal Tournament*.'

'*Unreal?* That's a significant title if I understand what you said earlier about the power of games to take us to an alternate reality.'

'Then there's Shigeru Miyamoto, who created *Super Mario Bros*. He was the first to give character motivation to the game's hero. Mario navigates an underground maze, fighting monsters while he tries to rescue a kidnapped girl.'

'A kidnapped girl?'

'I can imagine why the parallel strikes you.'

'Tell me more about these designers.'

'John Romero and John Carmack developed the first-person shooter games like the one I was playing earlier. In contrast, Will Wright developed God games.'

'God games?'

'Like *SimCity*. It's a cartoon version of a city. With all the problems of a city. Pollution. Deteriorating infrastructure. Slums. Poverty. Labor problems. The goal of the game is to make adjustments to the city in an effort to improve it. But the game player soon realizes that by making well-intended changes, sometimes disastrous things can happen. That's why it's called a God game. Whereas first-person shooter games are viewed from the limited perspective of a weapon's barrel, the player of a God game has an omniscient view of everything – and total control.'

'But unlike God, the player doesn't know how everything's going to turn out, right?' Balenger asked. 'Unlike God, the player can make mistakes.'

'Who says God can't make mistakes?' Professor Graham's face tightened. 'I don't understand why these pills aren't working.'

Balenger repeated her earlier comment. 'An omniscient view of everything.' He gazed at the upper corners of the room.

'What are you doing?'

'Thinking about God.' With a chill, Balenger scanned the bookcases.

'What are you looking for?'

Balenger's pulse raced. 'When did Jonathan Creed send you this computer?'

'Two weeks ago. Why?'

Balenger leaned close and drew his hands over the monitor, examining it in detail. He suddenly felt off-balance, as if he'd entered the alternate reality they'd been discussing. 'I know you want to continue playing *Doom*. But why don't you let me buy you a cup of coffee somewhere?'

'You're right. I *do* want to continue playing.'

'I think we could talk more freely if we went somewhere else.'

Professor Graham looked baffled.

'The monitor's bugged.'

'*What?*'

'Look at the holes in the front and back corners. Miniature cameras. Probably microphones. We're his private TV show! Let's get the hell out of here.'

LEVEL SIX:
AVATAR

1

The clouds thickened, darkening the valley.

'We don't have much time. Do what I tell you.' Viv swung to survey the ruins. Her gaze lingered over her husband's body and his crushed, bloody face. Then she roused herself into motion again. 'There.' She pointed toward a fallen building where the walls and roof had landed in a crisscross pattern that resembled a pyramid.

Amanda hurried with her.

'Help me pull the boards from the middle,' Viv said. 'We need to make a hollow.'

Amanda tugged the boards out, splinters jabbing her fingers.

'Put the boards on top. Overlay them so they cover gaps. We're trying to make a roof.'

A cold wind pushed Amanda. Shivering, she glanced over her shoulder at the angry clouds roiling across the valley.

'Quickly.' Viv layered more boards.

Amanda worked harder. A cavity formed. As the wind nearly blew her cap away, she pulled and stacked.

Grunting with effort, Viv deepened the hollow. 'Do you know what hypothermia is?'

'A drop in body temperature.'

'In the mountains, weather changes rapidly. Feel how cold that wind is.' Viv crisscrossed more boards. 'If we get wet and chilled, we've got three hours before our core temperature drops so low that we'll die. Basically, we'll shiver to death.'

Amanda looked over her shoulder again, but this time not toward the storm, instead toward Ray. She saw him in an open area beyond the ruins, his green jumpsuit vivid against the dark sky. He stared down at something, obviously disturbed by it, but she couldn't see what it was.

Viv whirled toward the wreckage. 'That door. Help me with it.'

The door lay under part of a roof. It looked flimsy, three boards secured by cross boards. When they freed and lifted it, Amanda thought it might fall apart. The wind almost blew it from their hands. Struggling, Amanda glanced toward the open area two blocks away where Ray now faced the storm. He seemed so disturbed by what he'd found that only now was he reacting to the approaching weather.

They reached the shelter. Amanda saw Ray hurry toward the ruins. Then flying dust obscured him. Rain pelted the ground. Chunks of wood sped past her.

Amanda set the door flat. More rain hit the ground. She felt drops strike her back while she and Viv squirmed into the hollow. It smelled of mold and dust. She and Viv reached out and dragged the door in their direction, tilting it sideways against the opening. They left a gap on each end where they clung to the door's edges.

The wind whistled against the gaps. Cold rain struck Amanda's fingers.

'Don't let go!' Viv's shout was amplified by the small enclosure. Even so, the wind was so loud that Amanda barely heard. 'Whatever happens, don't let go!'

A hand grabbed the door and tugged.

'Let me in!' Ray yelled.

'No room!' Viv screamed.

'You've got to let me in!'

'Go to hell!'

Another hand grabbed the door. Ray yanked so furiously that he opened a gap at the top. His face leaned toward them: gaunt, beard-stubbled, eyes filled with rage. Rain streaked at him. Dust and chunks of wood flew past him. His gaze narrowed fiercely, suggesting he intended to drag Amanda and Viv out and take their place.

He seemed to debate with himself. Unexpectedly, he released his hold on the door. As the wind strengthened, almost veiling him in dust, he charged away.

Amanda got a tighter grip on the door an instant before the wind would have hurled it along the street. She and Viv pulled it over the shelter's entrance. Rain struck the door's edge, pelting Amanda's fingers.

'Do you believe in the power of simultaneous prayer?' the voice asked.

'Shut up!' Viv yelled.

'Suppose a woman is seriously ill, and her church prays that she'll get better. Hundreds of believers, all praying at once. What if the church's pastor contacts churches all across the country, and those congregations pray at the same time also. Hundreds of thousands of simultaneous prayers. Do you believe those prayers will have an effect?'

The rain pounded the shelter's roof so loudly that the Game Master's words were faint through Amanda's headset. Her fingers gripped the side of the door.

'Some studies suggest that if the sick person knows about the prayers, the psychological effect is so powerful that healing can occur. Now consider the power of a massively multiplayer online video game.'

'A massively *what*? You're not making sense! Shut up!' Viv pleaded, gripping the door.

'One of the most popular massively multiplayer games is called *Anarchy Online*. A player pays a monthly fee for the right to assume the identity of a character on the alternate reality planet of Rubi-Ka. It's filled with exotic creatures in a spectacular locale with a humanoid culture.'

The rain became icy. When Amanda couldn't move her fingers, she released her right hand from the door and blew on it, trying to warm it.

'No!' Viv told her. 'Don't let go!'

'Amanda,' the voice asked, 'do you know what an avatar is?'

'Leave me alone!' Amanda switched hands, blowing on her left while her right hand gripped the door.

'Surely someone with an MA in literature knows what an avatar is.'

Again, Viv gave her an angry look.

'An avatar is a god in bodily form,' Amanda answered.

'Your education wasn't wasted on you. In massively multiplayer games, the character a player assumes is called an avatar. An alternate identity. Sometimes a player wants to assume another identity because his identity in so-called real life isn't satisfying. Maybe he's overweight and has pimples, and he's thirty years old, but he still lives with his mother while he earns a minimum wage in a fast-food restaurant. But when he functions as his avatar on the planet of Rubi-Ka, none of the other players knows what he looks like or how big a failure he is. On Rubi-Ka, he still needs to get a job in order to have a place to live and buy clothes and eat. But there, his mind is all that matters. He has a chance for a brand new start, nothing holding him back. Using his intelligence, he can improve his avatar's life. Indeed, it's amazing how failures in *this* life become achievers on Rubi-Ka, and it's interesting that half the male players choose to switch genders and portray women.'

Blowing on her numb fingers, Amanda felt sensation

seep back into them. She understood now what hypothermia was and how she could die from it.

'*Anarchy Online* is owned by a company called Funcom, which has an array of computers in Oslo, Norway,' the voice said. 'They need enormous computing power because at any given time perhaps as many as two million people play the game. All around the world. Every country imaginable. Millions of people simultaneously assuming identities in an alternate reality, playing the game all day and all night, because their life here disappoints. A massively multiplayer online game. If studies show that there's validity to the psychological power of massive simultaneous prayer, how much more validity is there to the force of a massively multiplayer game? Which is more appealing? The pimply face, the room next to his mother's, the loneliness of masturbation because no female will go out with him? Or living an alternate reality as a female avatar in a virtual world where everyone has equal opportunities?'

As the wind howled, a few drops of water seeped from the roof and landed on the hip of Amanda's jumpsuit.

'On Rubi-Ka,' the Game Master said, 'avatars accumulate possessions the same as we do in our version of reality. Some are precious objects. Others are valuable tools or expensive dwellings. Players covet these. If their avatars don't manage to gain these objects on Rubi-Ka, a player can sometimes buy them on eBay.

In theory, these are imaginary objects, but they take on their own reality. On eBay, you can even buy and sell avatars, assuming new identities if the old ones no longer suit you. One reality merges with another.'

Shivering, Amanda noticed another drop of water dangling from the ceiling. 'It's seeping through.'

'As long as it doesn't soak us,' Viv said.

Amanda told the Game Master, 'I've got news for you. *This* is reality.'

'So you say. Perhaps this is a good time for me to tell you about Reverend Owen Pentecost.'

'Who?'

'The genius who created the Sepulcher of Worldly Desires. You survived another obstacle. You deserve more information. Ray, can you hear me?'

No answer.

'Ray?'

'I hear you.' Ray sounded bitter.

'How are you getting along out there?'

'Just fine.'

'Not too cold?'

'I've been through worse.'

Ray's anger was palpable through Amanda's headset.

'Well, as long as you're comfortable,' the Game Master said. 'Reverend Owen Pentecost. That wasn't his real name, and he wasn't a minister. His father *was*, though, and after Pentecost was expelled from Harvard medical school, he assumed the mantle of a minister and left Boston, heading toward the frontier to spread the good word. He arrived in Avalon in April of 1899. There was a terrible drought, but Pentecost knew that it couldn't last for ever, so he encouraged the town to pray and keep praying. When the rain didn't come, he told them it was because they hadn't truly repented their sins. They needed to pray harder. Finally, when the rains arrived in June, they couldn't thank him enough for helping to end the drought. But that was the only good news. The first sign of what was to come involved a shopkeeper named Peter Bethune, who was struck and killed by lightning as he ran from his wagon toward his store.'

Something bumped against the door.

Amanda flinched. At first she assumed it was Ray making another effort to get in. But the bump was accompanied by a cluster of quick, guttural breathing. She heard numerous paws splashing through puddles and recalled the German shepherd that had attacked the rabbit. But now it wasn't alone.

A snout appeared to the right of the door.

'If they pull it down . . .' Viv warned.

Amanda heard a snarl. 'We can't use our hands to hold the door. They'll bite off our fingers.'

A snout appeared on the left now, teeth bared.

'They're pressing against the door, holding it in place. But if they start pulling . . .'

'Our belts,' Viv said. 'We'll hook them to it.'

Amanda tugged at hers. 'Mine's sewed to the back of my suit.'

'Tear it loose.'

'No. We don't dare rip the suits. Our boot laces.' Amanda freed one hand and squirmed to reach her boots. Fumbling with her cold fingers, she pulled a lace from one eyelet and then another.

The snarls got angrier. The next bump made the door tremble.

'I've got one free,' Amanda said.

'So have I.' Viv tied the ends, making a circle.

A snout shoved past the door.

Amanda banged it with a chunk of board. 'Get the hell away!'

The dog jerked back.

Viv looped the lace around the door's middle board. As the dog recovered from its surprise and lunged, she tugged on the lace, holding the door in place.

Amanda heard her own hoarse breathing. I sound like one of those dogs, she thought. She tied the ends of her boot lace, eased her fingers past the edge of the door, and looped the lace around the middle board. She yanked her fingers back just in time to avoid getting bitten.

Claws scraped the door. Snouts tried to wedge it free. The lace cut into Amanda's palms. She prayed that it wouldn't break. Then she feared that the *door* would break.

'We're going to be all right for now,' Viv tried to assure her.

'Yeah, we've got them where we want them.' Amanda

laughed strangely, hysteria seizing her. 'Not eating us.'

'God help me,' Viv said. 'What I wouldn't give for something to eat.'

Amanda stopped laughing, suddenly cold sober. 'It's right outside.'

'What?'

'If I need to, I'll kill one of those bitches and make Ray build a fire with his lighter so I can cook it.'

Viv stared at her.

'What's wrong?'

'I never would have thought of that,' Viv said.

The snarling stopped. Paws splashed in puddles. The dogs retreated.

'Where are they going?' Amanda listened closely.

'Maybe they've gone after Ray. Ray? Can you hear me?' Viv asked into the microphone of her headset.

No answer.

'Ray, are you safe?' Viv sounded angry. 'Don't let anything happen to you. We need your damned lighter.'

The only sound was the patter of rain. Suddenly the dogs started yelping insanely. They seemed to be fighting with one another, determined to get their share of the quarry, baying in a frenzy.

'*Ray?*'

One by one, the dogs became silent.

Sickened, Amanda relaxed her hold on the lace. Her palms throbbed for several minutes. Peering warily through the gap in the door, all she saw was the rain.

'Then a child drowned in a flash flood,' the Game

Master said, 'and a farmer fell from a hayloft and impaled himself on a pitchfork, and a family died from . . .'

2

'Hidden cameras?' Professor Graham couldn't get over her shock. 'Jonathan was spying on me?'

'On *us*.' Balenger sat across from her in a coffee shop on Lower Broadway, a few blocks from the university. 'The son of a bitch wanted to monitor my progress in the game.'

'Game?'

'If he had cameras in your office, it's logical to assume he put them in other places as well. The theater. Outside the library. Outside your faculty building. In the building that was being renovated.'

'But someone would have noticed.'

'Not after 9/11. Anybody wearing a uniform marked SECURITY doesn't get questioned. We take video cameras for granted. They're next to traffic lights, above building entrances, inside stores and hotel lobbies – just about everywhere. That doesn't include cell phones with cameras, many of which have video streaming. It's almost impossible to walk down any city block and not get photographed. With careful planning, he could have followed my progress.'

A waitress brought tea, coffee, and a ham sandwich for Balenger. Professor Graham didn't have an appetite. Desperation had destroyed Balenger's, but he warned himself that he was useless to Amanda if he didn't maintain his strength. 'Tell me how you met Jonathan Creed.'

'He showed up one afternoon, standing in the hallway outside the open door to one of my classes. He looked so pitiful, all I wanted to do was help him.'

'Pitiful?' Balenger knew the one thing Jonathan Creed wouldn't get from him was pity.

'Short, thin, geeky. Frail voice. Wispy blond hair. He reminded me of pictures of Truman Capote when he was young. He was thirty-five, I found out, and yet he looked like a boy. "Would you care to join us?" I asked. He nodded, entered, and took a seat at the back. What attracted him to my class was its subject: the Sepulcher of Worldly Desires.'

Hearing the name again, Balenger shivered.

'I eventually learned that he'd suffered a nervous breakdown because of a new game he had in mind. Apparently he'd been catatonic for six months, with his mind trapped in what he called the Bad Place. He never described what it was, except that it was unspeakable. He said that, as he recovered, he decided to find truth in anything except games.'

'He spoke like that?'

'It seemed natural coming from someone with an IQ of one hundred and ninety. He told me he wanted to acquire the education he'd never had the patience or time to pursue.' She stopped, waiting for another spasm of pain to go away.

Balenger glanced down, trying to give her privacy.

She breathed and continued. 'Jonathan went to the philosophy department first, on the assumption, he told me, that truth was most likely to be found there. He studied Heraclitus, Parmenides, Socrates, Plato and Aristotle. Do you know much about philosophy?'

'A little from history books I read.'

'Some philosophers maintain that the buildings, trees and sky around us are as insubstantial as shadows in a cave. Others believe that reality is as solid as the rock a person kicks in bright sunlight. Jonathan thought it was a pointless debate. It seemed obvious to him that those who believe the world is a dream are right. To him, the world of imagination was far more vivid than so-called physical reality, as any game designer and player knows.

'He tried literature next but felt that most literature teachers believe they're adjuncts of the philosophy or political science departments. Nowhere did he hear anything about the hypnotic way in which stories transported him to a reality more vivid than the supposedly solid world around him.

'Then he tried history. Understand, he didn't sign up for courses. He merely wandered the corridors and paused outside any classroom where something interested him. He told me he overheard lectures about the assassination of Julius Caesar and the Norman invasion of England and the murder of the princes in the Tower of London and the Hundred Years War and the almost million casualties of the American Civil War. He regarded none of this as fact. Every first-hand description of an event was biased, the secondary accounts more so. All were merely stories, he told me. Shadows. There was no way to prove they happened. But their plots were fascinating and transported him from his nightmares.

'He was prepared to walk more corridors and hear stories about the assassination of the Archduke Ferdinand and the chlorine gas attacks of the First World War and the death camps of the Second World War when he paused outside my classroom and heard about the Sepulcher of Worldly Desires. His life changed at that moment, he said. He never explained why, but for the next three months, he attended my classes and visited me during office hours. We had breakfast meetings or took afternoon walks through Washington Square.'

Her face looked grayer, emotion making her pause.

'My husband had recently died. I never had children. I felt motherly toward him. Jonathan taught me that the fantasy world within a game could be more real than the grief I wanted to escape. Then I had my first cancer scare, and he taught me that games didn't waste time but rather extended it. The speed of the countless choices they required subdivided each second and filled it to the maximum. In the end, after turning his back on games, he embraced them again. He entered what he called his next evolution and decided that games were the metaphysics that the philosophers failed to grasp. They were the truth.'

Professor Graham took another breath and reached into her purse for a vial of pills. She swallowed two with some tea, then looked at Balenger. 'He and his sister—'

Balenger straightened. 'Wait a minute. He has a *sister*?'

'She's taller, a brunette, while Jonathan is blond.'

Balenger spoke quickly. 'Does she wear her hair pulled back in a bun? Tight features? No makeup?'

'I met her only a few times, but yes, she tries hard to look plain. You know her?'

The memory of meeting her filled Balenger with rage. 'She told me her name was Karen Bailey.'

'Karen *is* her first name. She and Jonathan look different from one another because they had different fathers. Their mother was promiscuous. The man who raised them wasn't their father, but he lived with the mother for a time, and when she left him, she also abandoned the children. He kept them as bait, hoping that the mother would come back to see them and he could persuade her to stay.'

Professor Graham braced herself to continue. 'The stepfather was a drunk. A violent one. Jonathan told me he never took his eyes off the man because he never knew when he'd fly into a rage. The stepfather also had an unnatural interest in Karen, who looked so much like her mother that she wasn't safe alone with him. That's why she tries hard to look plain, even though I suspect she could be attractive. She's determined to avoid attention from men.

'Karen became a surrogate mother to Jonathan, while he in turn protected her by making the stepfather angry and distracting him from her. They hid whenever they could. Out of spite, when he found them – in a closet or the basement, for example – he locked them in. Jonathan said he and his sister once spent three days in a cubbyhole their stepfather nailed shut. No food, no water, no toilet. In the darkness, Jonathan invented fantasy games, the equivalent of *Dungeons & Dragons*. He and Karen escaped into the alternate reality he created.'

Balenger's forearm ached worse. As he listened intently, he couldn't stop rubbing it.

'The single positive thing the stepfather did was buy the children a video game machine. That was in the late 1970s when the only game machines were the kind you connected to your television set. Jonathan was just a child, but he took the machine apart, learned how it worked, and improved it. Eventually, the stepfather died from liver disease, and the children were put into foster care, but they never stayed with any family for more than a half-year. Something about Jonathan and Karen made their various foster parents uneasy. Basically, the children could relate only to one another and the games Jonathan invented.

'By the time Nintendo came out in 1985, he was programming for it, using the computer labs in the numerous high schools he and Karen went to. He took special pleasure in knowing that the bullies who made his life hell in school probably went home to play games he designed, without dreaming who created them. He pioneered many of the important advances in video game technology. For example, the early games could only move up, down, right and left. Jonathan was the first to add front-to-back motion. He was also the first to overlay scenery in the background. Both techniques contributed to the illusion of three dimensions.'

She paused, in pain.

'I know this is hard for you,' Balenger said.

'But I want to help. You need to understand about *Infinity*.'

'What?'

'In previous games, there was always a limit to the number of variations in which a player could move. The action happened within a predictable, closed space. But Jonathan designed a game called *Infinity*, in which two spaceships chase each other throughout the universe. He told me he created it in reaction to the three days he and Karen spent in that cubbyhole. The game gives the impression that the spaceships can keep going for ever in any direction and find constant new marvels. He joked to me that he wanted a player to zoom around a comet and expect to see God.'

'*Infinity*.' The concept gave Balenger vertigo.

'Sounds like a player could disappear into the game.'

'That's what happened to Jonathan.' Professor Graham closed her eyes for a moment. 'Game designers are obsessive. It's not unusual for some of them to work as long as four days and nights without sleeping. They live on Doritos and Jolt cola. For variety, Jonathan told me, he drank strong coffee sweetened with Classic Coke.'

'But that long without sleep can make a person psychotic,' Balenger said.

'His sister watched over him when he was in these four-day visions. That's apparently what they were: visions. Jonathan scribbled computer codes as if they were automatic writing. His royalties and patents earned him over a hundred million dollars. But he never cared about the money. What mattered were the games. In the industry, there's a constant challenge to take designs to the next level and the level after that. Jonathan was determined to create a game so ultimate that no designer could ever outdo it. With Karen mothering him, he went into new visions that lasted even longer without sleep. Five days. Six. Until finally he had the breakdown that Karen always worried about.'

Balenger could no longer tolerate the burning, swelling sensation in his arm. He pushed up his jacket and shirt sleeves. An abscess startled him, angry red surrounding it.

Professor Graham viewed it with alarm. 'You'd better go to a hospital. That looks like blood poisoning.'

'It feels as if something's . . .'

'Something's what?'

Under the skin, he thought in dismay. 'Wait here for a minute.'

He made his way past tables to a door marked MEN'S ROOM. Inside, he saw sneakers under the closed door of a stall. At the sink, he took off his jacket and draped it over his right shoulder. He rolled his left shirt sleeve all the way up, took a breath, and squeezed the swelling.

The fiery pain made him groan. Yellow liquid popped out. He kept squeezing. Now the yellow oozed, followed by red. Good, Balenger thought. I need to get this thing bleeding. I need to find what's festering in there.

He bit his lip from the pain. Something black appeared. Small. Thin. Square. Metallic. He squeezed until it reached the surface. He put it on his index finger and held it up to the overhead light.

Son of a bitch, he thought. He didn't know anything about electronics, but he could imagine only one reason the object had been embedded in him. To track his movements.

Furious, he put it in a handkerchief and shoved it into his jacket. He set to work soaping the hole in his arm. He rinsed. He soaped again. He didn't think he'd ever feel clean.

3

Professor Graham had her head down when Balenger returned to the table. She looked up, her expression weary. 'Your arm?' she asked.

Trying to sound calm, Balenger took the BlackBerry from his pocket. 'I washed it, but that only made the infection look worse. You're right. As soon as we finish, I'll go to a hospital.'

He studied the BlackBerry. It was silver, with a gunmetal-gray front. Its screen was larger than on a conventional cell phone. In addition to the many number and letter keys, it had a button at the top as well as a wheel and a button along the right side. He was certain now that it was equipped with an eavesdropping device. Maybe a tracking device also, he thought, a backup to what the bastard put in my arm.

'How do I turn it on?'

He tried the button on the top. Instantly, the screen glowed. The coffee shop's overhead lights made the icons hard to see, but he discovered that by tilting the BlackBerry away from the glare, the screen was vivid. On the upper right part, a red arrow flashed. A few moments later, a green light pulsed.

'Looks like I can receive calls.'

The BlackBerry rang.

Balenger tensed. Two of its buttons had phone icons,

one red, the other green. Green for go, Balenger thought, and pressed that button.

'Where's Amanda?' he insisted into the phone.

'Do you know what an avatar is?' a man's voice responded, sonorous, like an announcer's.

Balenger's rage almost overpowered him. After so many obstacles, he was finally speaking to the man who had abducted Amanda and was responsible for so much pain and fear. He thought of Ortega, the blood seeping from his dead mouth. He wanted to scream obscenities, to vow to get even in the cruelest way possible. But all his military and police training warned him that everything would be lost if he didn't keep control.

'An avatar?' Balenger repeated bitterly. 'Afraid not.'

'Amanda knows what that is.'

Balenger kept steady. 'Is she hurt?'

The voice paused so long that Balenger worried the phone transmission had failed. 'No.'

'Where *is* she?'

'That's what you need to find out.'

'To win the game? Then you'll set her free?'

'You'll need to do more than find Amanda to win the game.'

Sickened by the rush of his heart, Balenger realized that Professor Graham might be able to identify the voice and confirm that it belonged to Jonathan Creed. He held the phone between them.

'You mentioned an avatar,' Balenger said. 'Tell me what that is.'

'A god in bodily form.'

Professor Graham listened.

'*You* are my avatar,' the voice declared.

'Does that mean you're the god?'

'I'm the Game Master.'

Balenger felt his head throb.

'Scavengerthegame-dot-com,' the Game Master said.

'What about it?'

'You understand that a BlackBerry can access the Internet? Use the wheel on the side to scroll down to the icon shaped like the world. Press the wheel, and you'll have access to the web. Your BlackBerry has high-speed capability. You should be able to enter the website quickly.'

'Internet? Website? What are you talking about? What am I going to see?'

The transmission became silent, the connection broken. Balenger pressed the red phone button to discontinue his end of the call.

'That isn't Jonathan's voice,' Professor Graham said.

'No. It's got to be. Everything points toward—'

'I told you Jonathan has a thin, frail voice. *That* voice sounds like it belongs to someone who reads the evening news on television.'

Balenger couldn't believe he was wrong. 'Maybe it's been distorted. Amplifiers and filters can do a lot to change a voice.'

Balenger followed the directions he'd been given, accessing the Internet. It took him a frustrating couple of minutes to familiarize himself with the controls. The BlackBerry used an hourglass icon to tell him it was processing the information he typed into it. The symbol reminded him of the hourglass half filled with blood on the cover of the game case for *Scavenger*.

That game case now appeared on the screen. Abruptly, its hourglass changed to a series of still photographs that showed Amanda in pursuit of another woman. Pressure made Balenger's veins feel swollen. He'd never stared at anything more intensely.

Amanda wore a blue jumpsuit and baseball cap. The other woman wore gray. They were outdoors, with mountains beyond them. Amanda's mouth was open, as if yelling in desperation.

A red blur filled the screen. Balenger took a startled moment to realize that the photograph showed an explosion. Chunks were suspended in mid-air. Body parts. A hand. A section of skull. Blood. The effect was all the more surreal because there wasn't any sound.

Ice seemed to line his stomach. My God, is that a photograph of Amanda being blown apart? he thought. A new image showed her gaping at the explosion. Relief swept through him, even as the horror on her face became *his* horror.

What am I seeing? he thought.

The screen went blank. A moment later, words appeared, telling him THIS SITE IS NO LONGER AVAILABLE.

Balenger's fingers ached from the force with which he gripped the BlackBerry.

'What's the matter?' Professor Graham asked. 'What did you see?'

'Hell.'

The BlackBerry rang.

He pressed the green button. More than ever, he wanted to express his rage. Instead, he forced himself to be silent.

'Thanks to technology called Surveillance LIVE, you're able to see those webcam photographs. They were taken several hours ago,' the voice said.

Balenger felt breathless. 'Hours? In that case, I have no way of knowing if Amanda is still alive.'

'She is.'

'Suppose you're not telling the truth.'

'Then the game would be flawed. The rules are absolute. One of them is that I do not lie. Here's another rule. It's very important. From now on, no police, do you understand?'

For a moment, Balenger couldn't make himself answer. 'Yes.'

'No FBI, no law enforcement, no military friends, nothing of the kind. At the start, it was natural for you to go to the police. But not any more. We're at another level in the game. You're on your own. Understand? Say it.'

The words felt thick. 'I understand.'

'You are my avatar. Through you, I take part in the action. I cheer for you. I want you to win.'

'Bullshit.'

'But I *do*. I want you to rescue the kidnapped maiden and struggle to the final level where you find the secret.'

'The Sepulcher of Worldly Desires?'

'And everything it represents. I don't exaggerate when I say it's the meaning of life. If you rescue the maiden and find the Sepulcher, you are worthy to know the secret. I already know that secret, but I want to feel its discovery one more time. Through *you*.'

'I thought the game was over. I thought it took forty hours and ended at five this afternoon.'

'No. For you, *Scavenger* began at ten this morning. You have less than thirty-one hours remaining.'

'*Scavenger*.' The word carried the chill of death. 'What happens if I don't rescue Amanda and find the secret within the remaining time?'

The connection was broken.

4

Outside the coffee shop, buildings obscured the setting sun. The sky had an orange tint, but Lower Broadway was sufficiently in shadow that cars had headlights on.

Balenger put the BlackBerry in his pants pocket and tapped his hand against it, preventing the Game Master from hearing what he asked Professor Graham. 'How do I find the valley you mentioned? Where's Avalon? Where's the Sepulcher of Worldly Desires supposed to be? You mentioned Wyoming and the Wind River range.'

Professor Graham looked exhausted. 'Avalon no longer exists. To call it a ghost town gives it too much stature. Cottonwood doesn't exist either. Even with the help of the Wyoming Historical Society, it took me a month to identify the valley Reverend Owen Pentecost visited.'

'Where is it?'

'Lander is the nearest large community. The valley is fifty miles north along the eastern edge of the mountains.'

Balenger kept tapping his hand against his pants pocket and the BlackBerry inside. 'How will I know I've found the right place?'

'In that area, it's the only valley with a lake. Any hiking or hunting store in Lander has terrain maps for the local area. You won't have trouble finding it.'

'Did you go there?'

'Seven years ago. I spent all of July trying to find the Sepulcher. Sometimes, I wonder if it existed only in Donald Reich's fevered brain. Jonathan tried to find it also.'

'And?'

'I'm sure he'd have told me if he'd located it.'

Maybe, Balenger thought.

He put a gentle hand on the professor's shoulder. 'Thank you.'

Her shrug was wistful.

He kissed her cheek.

She might have blushed, it was hard to tell. 'No one's done that in a long time,' she said.

'Then I'm proud I took the liberty.' He waved for a taxi and gave the driver twenty dollars. 'Take care of my friend.'

He watched the taxi disappear into the busy traffic along Lower Broadway. The street had numerous businesses crammed next to each other. He walked to an ATM machine, inserted his card, and got the maximum amount of cash he was allowed: five hundred dollars.

He marched up the street to a phone store. Inside, he again tapped the phone in his pocket so the Game Master couldn't hear what he said. 'Do you sell BlackBerrys?'

'Sure do.' The male clerk had a ponytail and an earring. 'Over there.'

Balenger took one that matched the type the Game Master had left for him.

'Good choice,' the clerk said. 'The latest model. It's three hundred dollars, but we're giving a hundred-dollar mail-in rebate.'

'As long as you activate it right now, I don't care.'

'No problem.'

No problem? In what universe, did *that* apply? Balenger wondered.

'I need to make sure it can handle a webcam program called Surveillance LIVE.'

'That's a special download. Costs extra. You do it through your home computer, then transfer it to the BlackBerry.'

'But I'm going on a trip where I won't have access to a computer,' Balenger said. 'I'll pay you a hundred dollars cash to download it for me right now.'

'Definitely no problem. Why do you keep tapping your pants pocket?'

'A nervous habit.'

Ten minutes later, the clerk presented Balenger with his BlackBerry. 'Fully loaded. You'll need to charge the battery pretty soon. Right out of the box, it'll be low. Here's the charger cord, the carrying case, and the rest of the stuff it comes with.'

'And here's your hundred dollars. It's good to meet someone who knows his business.' Balenger gave him a check for the equipment and went outside. Only then did he stop tapping the BlackBerry in his pocket. He took it out. 'Hey, are you listening? Make a note of this phone number.' He dictated the number for the new BlackBerry.

Then he put the Game Master's BlackBerry into a trash bin, trying not to inhale the smell of old French fries. He took out the handkerchief that contained the location marker chip he'd removed from his arm. He watched a homeless man pushing a cart of bags and old clothes along the sidewalk.

'Here's twenty dollars,' Balenger told him. 'Buy yourself something to eat.'

'I don't need your charity.'

'Yeah, but take it anyhow. Save it for a rainy day.' He tucked the twenty-dollar bill into the homeless man's shirt pocket, along with the miniature tracking device. 'Have a good night.'

'Yeah, I bet they saved me a suite at the Sherry-Netherland.'

Balenger hailed a cab and got in. 'Teterboro Airport,' he said.

'I do not know where that is,' the turbaned driver said.

'I don't, either. It's in New Jersey if that helps.'

The driver muttered.

'I'll pay twice the fare if you get me there quick.'

The driver reached for his two-way radio.

5

Teterboro is a so-called 'reliever' airport, taking pressure off the major commercial airports in the area by providing runways and hangars for corporate and private aircraft. That was all Balenger knew about it, but during the twelve-mile drive from Manhattan, he used the BlackBerry's Internet connection to learn a great deal more.

He suspected that no commercial flights went

directly from JFK, La Guardia or Newark to Lander, Wyoming. The websites of several airlines proved him right. He would need to make a connecting flight in cities like Chicago or Denver, but there wasn't a seat on those flights until the morning. Moreover, Lander didn't have a commercial airstrip. The nearest airport for airlines such as United was in Riverton, about a half-hour drive from Lander. The soonest he'd reach Lander would be early afternoon, and probably much later. Too much time lost. Most of his remaining thirty-one hours – correction: thirty hours now – would be wasted.

There was only one choice. The taxi went through a security checkpoint and let Balenger out at the terminal for Jet Aviation, one of Teterboro's large charter and aircraft storage facilities. The sky was dark when he gave the driver his promised bonus and walked under arclights toward the shiny five-story building.

The glowing interior resembled a first-class lounge at a major airport.

A pleasant-looking man in a suit came over. 'Mr Balenger?'

They shook hands.

'Eric Gray. I charged the flight to the credit card number you gave me on the phone. The jet's being fueled right now. Just to be clear, the cost is three thousand dollars an hour.'

'That's what we agreed.' Balenger had expected questions about why he needed a jet in a hurry and why he didn't have luggage, but now he realized that the people who could afford this kind of luxury weren't accustomed to explaining.

'We ran your name through a security list.' Eric smiled. 'You'll be pleased to learn that you're not considered a terrorist or on any law enforcement wanted list.'

Balenger managed to return the smile. 'Good to know.'

They went through glass doors and faced a tarmac bordered by hangars on every side. Eric pointed to the right. 'That's your jet over there. The Lear 60.' It was small and sleek. 'They're almost ready for you.'

'Thanks.'

The BlackBerry rang. It had rung several times earlier while Balenger drove to the airport, but he'd refused to answer it. Now, in the glare of the tarmac's lights, he removed it from the case on his belt.

Eric stepped into the terminal, allowing him privacy.

'Like that website you sent me to, I can give you only a minute,' Balenger said bitterly into the phone.

'You managed the impossible – to stay in one place and yet keep moving at the same time,' the voice said.

'The rigged BlackBerry you arranged for me to have is in a trash can. The location marker you put in my arm is in the pocket of a homeless man, walking down Broadway.'

'But how can you be my avatar if I can't track your progress? I want to know where you are.'

'And I want to know *this*. Why Amanda? Why us?'

'The Paragon Hotel.'

'We didn't suffer enough? You decided to put us through more?'

'I needed players worthy of the game, people who proved they know how to survive. You and Amanda have amazing strength and resources. The prototype of *Scavenger* can't succeed without you.'

'Prototype? For God's sake, don't tell me you think you can license this thing?'

'In 1976, there was an arcade game called *Death Race*. Players drove to a haunted cemetery. Stick figures appeared on the road. They were supposed to be ghosts, and the object of the game was to win points by hitting them, causing a cross to appear on the screen. A woman caught her son playing it and was so horrified that she started a campaign against violence in video games. *60 Minutes* and other major news programs added to the outcry. Local governments passed laws about where video arcades could be located, all because of some stick figures that turned into crosses. And what was the result? Video games became more popular.

'By 1993, a game called *Mortal Kombat* was so bloody it allowed the winner to reach into the defeated character's throat and yank out its skeleton. Congress investigated the video game industry, insisted on a rating for all games, and tried to impose censorship. Not that it mattered. The uncensored *Mortal Kombat* sold three times the copies that the censored version did. Today's action games are even more graphic. Players can steal cars, hit pedestrians, shoot policemen, and beat up prostitutes. The US Army commissioned two vivid combat games, one for recruiting and the other for training.'

'Your minute is up,' Balenger said.

'Ever see the movie *Network*? In 1976, audiences thought it was a satire with an exaggerated storyline. Peter Finch plays a network news anchor named Howard Beale. His ratings are in the basement. In despair, he threatens to commit suicide during his broadcast, and suddenly everybody wants to watch him. He switches from presenting the news to ranting and raving. His ratings go higher. Meanwhile, the network's entertainment division takes over the news department, and the news gets manipulated to make it more dramatic. Television becomes dominated by loudmouths shouting at each other on talk shows.'

'All right, I get the point. You just described most of the news programs on cable television.'

'Do I think I can license *Scavenger*? Not today or tomorrow. Not next year or the year after that. But I guarantee one day I will. Because the line between reality and alternate reality becomes ever more blurred, and things always get more extreme.'

In the background, a jet roared, taking off.

'What's that noise?' the voice asked.

'Me coming to get you.'

Balenger broke the connection.

6

The surge of the Learjet off the runway made Balenger think he was in a sports car. The noise from the twin jets was muffled. He peered from a window on his right, seeing the lights of New Jersey's Meadowlands. In the middle distance, lights reflected off the Hudson River. Beyond was the brilliance of the Manhattan skyline. Under other circumstances, the sight would have thrilled him, but now it only emphasized how far away Amanda was. When the jet headed west, he plugged his BlackBerry's charger cord into a specially designed receptacle and leaned back in his seat. He felt small and alone.

Not hungry, he forced himself to bite into a turkey sandwich that he'd brought from the terminal. Eat whenever you can, he reminded himself.

And try to rest. The cabin lights were dim. He felt as if he'd been on the run for ever. Allowing himself to admit exhaustion, he removed his shoes and tilted his seat back. He glanced at his watch: 9:14. He'd been told that the flight to Lander was a little under five hours. That would get him to Lander around 2:14 New York time, 12:14 Wyoming time.

Time, he kept thinking, reminded of the text on the back of the game case. Time is the true scavenger. If the game started at ten a.m., as the Game Master suggested

. . . His name is Jonathan Creed! Balenger thought. Use his damned name. But Balenger couldn't resist calling him the Game Master . . . then more than eleven hours had elapsed. Twenty-nine to go. Endgame would be at two a.m. the day after tomorrow.

No, Belanger told himself. The fearful symmetry of the true deadline abruptly occurred to him. He was thinking in New York time. But in Wyoming, with the two-hour time-zone difference, the endgame would be tomorrow at midnight.

He closed his eyes, knowing he needed to sleep. But he couldn't clear his mind of the shocking image he'd seen on the BlackBerry screen – the woman in the gray jumpsuit, the explosion, red mist, flying body parts, Amanda's look of horror.

I'll be there soon, he thought, straining to project his thoughts to her. Don't give up. Keep fighting. I'll get there. I'll help you.

Chilled, he folded his arms across his chest. Unable to do anything now except wait, he couldn't stop trembling.

LEVEL SEVEN: FIRST-PERSON SHOOTER

1

The wind died. Amanda no longer felt it trying to yank the door away. In the night, the rain continued, but it now fell straight down, drumming on the boards above them. She allowed herself to relax, only to become tense again when Viv murmured, 'An MA in English? From Columbia? I hear that's an awfully fancy school.'

Was Viv trying to grasp at small talk and distract herself from what had happened to Derrick? Amanda wondered. Or was the remark confrontational? She remembered the angry look Viv had directed toward her when the Game Master mentioned her education.

'I wanted to go to college, but I couldn't pay the tuition,' Viv said.

Amanda wondered if another fight was about to start. Was that how Viv would handle her grief, by lashing out at whoever was close?

'Hell, I don't know why I got angry at you.' Viv's unexpected comment made Amanda less uneasy. 'I'd probably have flunked. What I really wanted was to climb mountains with Derrick.'

A raindrop fell through the roof.

'Cold,' Viv said. She wearily opened a water bottle. 'We used a lot of energy. Make sure you drink.'

Amanda raised the single bottle she had, savoring each swallow. 'That's the end of it.'

'Leave the cap off, and set it outside. Some of the rain'll collect in it. Meanwhile, we'll share my other bottle. If we're going to get out of this, we need to help each other.'

The thought was encouraging until Amanda remembered Ray. Then she thought of something else, although she hesitated to raise the subject. 'There's another source of water.'

'Where?'

'It's difficult to talk about.'

'Tell me.'

'Derrick has two water bottles.'

'Oh.' The word was faint

'He finished most of one, but he has a full bottle in a pocket of his jumpsuit.'

Viv didn't respond.

'We need it,' Amanda said.

'Yes.' Viv sounded hoarse. 'We need it.' Her throat made a choking sound. 'And the shirt under his jumpsuit. And his socks. And his boot laces. Anything we can use. If another storm hits . . .'

Her voice broke.

'The most ill-fated video game of all time is the first

home version of *ET*,' the Game Master said without warning.

'Shut up!' Amanda yelled.

'The cute little extraterrestrial falls into a pit. The idea was to manipulate the controls so he could climb out. But no matter what players did, they couldn't get him out of that damned pit. Pretty soon, the players felt *they* were in a pit. Millions of copies were returned or remained on shelves. The first home version of *Pac-Man* didn't fare much better. It functioned so poorly that twelve million of those went back to the warehouse. The manufacturer got so disgusted that it dug a huge pit in the New Mexico desert. Ironic, given that the *ET* game's problems involved a pit. The company dumped all those games, packed them down with a steamroller, and poured concrete over them. How's *that* for a time capsule? One day in the future, maybe after a nuclear war or a catastrophic weather change exposes that concrete lid, somebody'll find those millions of video games and wonder what was so important about them that they were saved for posterity. *Pac-Man*. Did you ever stop to consider that the game always ends in Pac-Man's death? The smiley guy gets eaten and shrivels. In fact, a lot of games end in death. But players keep trying again, doing their hardest to postpone the inevitable. The SAVE button allowed a form of immortality. Players work their way through obstacles in a game until a threatening decision is required. They save what they've accomplished. Then they move forward in the game. If their avatar dies, they return to the saved position and try another decision and another. Or else they pay for cheat codes, which allow them to avoid threats and get a new life in the game. Either way, the avatar is capable of constant rebirth. Players achieve in a game what they can't in life. Immortality.'

'You bastard, you think you can hit a SAVE button or use a cheat code to bring my husband back to life?' Viv screamed.

'Or Bethany!' Amanda shouted. 'You think you can bring *her* back?'

'I never allowed cheat codes in my games. *North by Northwest*,' the voice said.

'What?' The sudden change of topic made Amanda's mind spin.

'When you spoke about Mount Rushmore earlier, I meant to tell you about the Hall of Records.'

At once Amanda realized that her mind was spinning not just because the Game Master kept shifting topics. Her breathing was labored. The air in the small enclosure was becoming stale, accumulating carbon dioxide.

'The Rushmore monument was started in the 1930s during the Great Depression,' the Game Master explained. 'The carved faces of the four presidents were intended to represent the solidity of the United States at a time when the country and the world seemed to be falling apart.'

Amanda noticed that Viv's breathing, too, was forced. 'We need to get fresh air in here.'

They tilted the door outward. Amanda took deep breaths of cold, sweet air. Then rain poured in, and they covered the entrance.

'Some Rushmore organizers were so fearful about the nation's survival that they designed a chamber called the Hall of Records. The plan was to build the chamber under the monument and use it to store the Declaration of Independence and other important American documents. If rioting destroyed the nation, those treasures would be protected.'

Amanda lowered her head. Fear, cold and fatigue drained her. She couldn't keep her eyes open.

'But as the economy improved and social unrest waned, the project was abandoned.'

Dozing, Amanda barely noticed that the isolated drops of water had stopped falling through the roof. The sound of the rain became fainter.

'Finally, in 1998, a historical group sealed documents about Mount Rushmore into the small portion of the Hall of Records that was completed a half-century earlier.'

The noise of the rain stopped altogether.

'Another time capsule,' the Game Master whispered.

2

Hunt Field Airport, Lander, Wyoming, ten minutes after midnight. As the Learjet touched down, Balenger stared out a window toward the lights on the runway, which glistened from recent rain. He waited impatiently to get into motion again. Before leaving Teterboro Airport, he'd made several phone calls and now prayed for the results he'd been promised.

The jet's engines slowed, their muffled whine stopping. After the hatch was opened, he went down steps, saw a lighted window, and walked through puddles toward a door.

Inside, he found a mustached man in a cowboy hat sitting behind a counter watching a Second World War movie on a small television. 'You Frank Balenger?' the man asked.

'That's right.'

'Your rental car's outside. The guy who brought it from town said to remind you there's a surcharge for after-hours service.'

'That was the agreement.'

'Sign these papers. Show me your credit card and driver's license.'

Balenger went out the front of the building and found a dark, water-dotted Jeep Cherokee. As promised, maps lay on the passenger seat. He studied them with the help of the overhead light.

'Can you give us a ride into town?' one of the pilots asked.

'It's on my way.'

'You wouldn't think an airport this small would be busy this time of night,' the other pilot said.

Balenger almost let the remark pass. A warning thought made him ask, 'What do you mean?'

'The fellow inside told us a Gulfstream flew in five minutes before we did. Just like you, only one passenger. Funny thing, that flight also came from Teterboro.'

'What?' Balenger dropped the maps on the seat and went back inside the building. 'Someone flew in on a Gulfstream from Teterboro?' he asked the man in the cowboy hat.

'Five minutes ago. A woman. She just drove off.'

'What did she look like?'

'Didn't pay attention.'

'In her forties? Plain? Hair pulled back in a bun?'

'Now that you mention it . . .'

3

On Lander's main street, Balenger let the pilots out at the Wind River Motel, then continued. The Jeep's tires whispered on wet pavement as he studied the sprawl of low buildings. He stopped in a parking lot of a bar, familiarized himself with a map of local businesses, and drove to a sporting goods store. By then, it was after midnight. The windows were dark, the place closed. But at least he knew its location and could find it quickly the next morning. He drove to a truck stop, got a strong cup of coffee to go, returned to the Jeep, set the mileage indicator, and headed north along Highway 287. He passed a sign that warned ELK CROSSING. To his left, snow capped the hulking shadows of the mountains. Only occasional headlights came in his direction. Most belonged to pickup trucks and SUVs. One was a police car.

Fifty miles, Professor Graham had said. When the Jeep's distance indicator reached forty, Balenger started looking for roads that led off the highway toward the mountains. He lowered his speed and studied the first one. It was primitive and blocked by a gate. The lights from the Jeep showed that there weren't any tire tracks in the mud. The next side road didn't have a gate, but there, too, Balenger didn't see any tracks. He drove all the way to mile sixty. Of the remaining four side roads, only two had tire tracks. He checked a map. Neither road was marked on it. The map didn't have topographical features, so he couldn't tell if either road led to a mountain valley. But the road at mile fifty-eight was in line with lights in a building, whereas the road at forty-eight had only dark mountains beyond it.

The time was 1:52 a.m. When Balenger returned to Lander, the dashboard clock showed 2:48. Exhausted, he checked into a motel, lay on the covers of the bed, and might even have slept a little. The motel's desk clerk phoned to wake him at eight as requested. He showered and used a razor and toothbrush that he'd bought from the truck stop the night before. He almost didn't take the time to clean up, but he remembered an old movie, *The Hustler*, in which Paul Newman plays an epic pool game with Jackie Gleason. Newman's character doesn't shave and looks increasingly disheveled while Gleason washes his hands and face, gets his jacket brushed, and puts a fresh flower in his jacket's lapel. Gleason wins.

Balenger drove to a McDonald's and got takeout orange juice, coffee, hash browns, and two Egg McMuffins. He ate them in his car while waiting for the sporting goods store to open, as its sign promised, at nine.

The store sold firearms. He walked alongside a counter on the left and paused at the semiautomatic rifles.

'Anything special you're looking for?' The clerk was hefty, wearing jeans, a denim shirt, and a belt buckle shaped like a saddle.

'Got any Bushmasters.' Balenger referred to a civilian version of the M-16 he'd carried in Iraq.

'Fresh out.'

'Let me look at that Ruger Mini-14.'

'The ranch gun? Sure.'

The clerk took it from a group of rifles in a vertical rack. He pulled out its magazine and tugged back its bolt, showing Balenger that it was empty.

Balenger inspected the weapon. As its name implied, it was a cut-down version of the military's M-14, the precursor to the M-16. But unlike the harsh, distinctly military look of most assault rifles, the Mini-14's blue steel and wooden stock made it resemble a standard hunting rifle. Indeed, its comparatively benign appearance had caused it to be exempted from a 1994–2004 law that made it illegal to sell semiautomatic assault weapons, even though it fired the same .223 caliber and could deliver as much firepower as the civilian version of the M-16. When Balenger was in law enforcement, he'd known police officers who carried Mini-14s in their cars, choosing that model because it was compact.

'Good for varmint hunting,' the clerk said.

'Got any Winchester 55-grain Ballistic Silvertips?'

'Long-range accurate. Nice fragmentation. You know your ammo. How many boxes?'

Balenger knew there were twenty rounds per box. 'Ten.'

'You must have a lot of varmints.'

'New rifle. Need to sight it in. Better make it fifteen.'

'All it comes with is that five-round magazine,' the clerk said apologetically.

'Got any for twenty rounds?'

'A couple.'

'I'll take them. How about a red dot sight?'

'This Bushnell HOLOsight.'

Balenger knew that the battery-powered sight used holographic technology to impose a red dot over its target. But the dot wasn't projected in the manner of a laser beam, thus giving away the shooter's position. Rather, the dot was projected only within the sight. Lining it up with the target was remarkably easy, virtually assuring an accurate shot. 'You'll attach it for me? Good. I'll take that Emerson CQC-7 knife. A sling for the rifle. A knapsack. Tan camping boots and clothes. A first-aid kit. A canteen. Rain gear. Gloves. Wool socks. A flashlight. That wide-brimmed tan hat. Sunglasses. Sunscreen. A box of energy bars. And binoculars that convert to night vision.'

'It's nice to have a customer who knows what he wants.'

Balenger gave him a credit card.

'Sign here for the ammo,' the clerk said.

Recalling his Ranger training, Balenger added, 'I also need a compass and a topographic map of the eastern Wind River range.'

'Which section?'

Balenger went to a map on the wall and pointed.

He put his purchases in the back of the Jeep, then drove to a truck stop on Highway 287, where he filled the canteen and bought a case of water along with a packet of Kleenex. The latter was a substitute for something he'd forgotten in the sporting goods store and was as crucial as the water. He also bought a roll of duct tape from a shelf next to radiator hoses.

Back in the Jeep, he studied the topographic map. The valley wasn't difficult to locate. As Professor Graham had told him, it was the only valley in the area that had a lake. Most of the roads he'd checked the previous night were also indicated on the map, but not the one where he'd seen the unexplained tire tracks, even though he believed *that* road did lead to the valley, just as he believed that Karen Bailey was in the vehicle that had made the tracks. She'd presumably gone to meet her brother. But if Balenger followed that road, the Game Master . . . Why don't I want to call him Jonathan Creed? Balenger wondered . . . the Game Master was virtually certain to notice him. Virtually certain. The words struck Balenger as morbidly apt. The Game Master's world was virtual. Studying the map, he noticed that a little farther north, a road ran in the general direction of the valley but then stopped where the foothills blocked the way.

He drove.

For the first time since flying from Teterboro, he activated the BlackBerry. Almost immediately, it rang. He picked it up.

'You exposed a flaw in the game,' the deep voice said. 'Because I'm testing the prototype, I suppose I ought to be grateful.'

Again Balenger wanted to shout in rage, but he managed to resist the temptation. To hide his emotions, he said nothing.

'You can't be my avatar if I can't follow your progress at all times,' the Game Master said.

'If you identified with me, you'd give Amanda back.'

'Tell me where you are. Maybe you're going in the wrong direction.'

'I doubt it. Think positively. The game just reached a new level.'

'How?'

'You're a player now instead of an observer. Try to anticipate my moves.'

'Do you ever watch *Survivor*?'

'All I watch is the History Channel.'

'Attractive people from different backgrounds are brought together in a hostile environment – a jungle, for example.'

Balenger stared ahead, impatient for the side road to come into view.

'The program attempts to create the illusion that the group is marooned, forced to survive by whatever means possible,' the Game Master continued. 'But any thoughtful viewer sees through the illusion by realizing that the cameras, most of them handheld, need to be controlled by operators and that the hidden microphones are linked to audio technicians, and that behind the scenes there are crew members and producers, who aren't in danger even though the contestants are supposedly struggling to survive.'

A police car went past. For a moment Balenger was tempted to stop it and ask for help, but he kept remembering the BlackBerry image of the woman exploding in a red mist. Even if the police could somehow invade the valley without revealing their presence, it didn't seem possible that they could get organized by midnight, and Balenger had no doubt that if he didn't save Amanda by midnight, she would die.

'What if a show like *Survivor* had a fatal accident?' the Game Master asked. 'What if, despite every precaution, someone fell off a waterfall, for example, and died? Would the producers cut the accident from the broadcast? Would they say, "This is a tragedy, and we can't let you see it?" Or would they say, "We need to include the accident to pay tribute to the brave contestant who risked his life for the program?" Including it would prove that the show is indeed dangerous. Thereafter, viewers would tune in with the understanding that lethal accidents might occur at any time. People wouldn't miss an episode.'

Balenger drove past the road to the valley, the road on which he'd seen tire tracks in the mud the previous night.

'With that precedent established,' the voice said, 'other programs would include similar high-risk contests. It isn't hard to imagine the inevitable evolution and the implied enticement: "Watch tonight's episode. Someone might die." '

'As you said earlier, things always get more extreme.' Balenger could barely conceal his disgust.

Ahead, the side road beckoned.

'Yes, but that's merely a television show, while *Scavenger* is a God game combined with a first-person shooter game. Above the players is the Game Master, who can speak to the competitors, provide clues or withhold them, and observe the life lessons that the players acquire.'

'A God game,' Balenger said acidly. 'But what kind of God doesn't allow the participants to win?'

'Who said anything about not winning? Every superior game needs a worthy goal. To survive, all the participants need to do is find the Sepulcher of Worldly Desires.'

4

Amanda raised her head from the boards she lay on. Light struggled through the gaps on each side of the door. She and Viv were huddled against each other, trying to share body heat. Exhausted despite having slept, she worked to open her heavy eyes. Peering through the gap on the right of the door, she frowned. Everything outside was white.

She pushed the door. As it flopped down, the reflection from the bright sky made her squint.

Viv raised her head, blinking. Grief hollowed her features. She needed several moments to focus on what she saw.

'It snowed,' Amanda said, bewildered. 'In June.'

Viv hesitated, straining to adjust to the renewed shock of Derrick's murder. 'In the Rockies,' she finally said, sounding numb, 'I've seen it snow in July. What time is it?' She had trouble focusing on her watch. 'The carbon dioxide must have drugged us. It's almost nine o'clock.'

Fear overcame Viv's grief. Startled by the time they'd lost, she and Amanda hurried to remove the laces from the door and shove them through the eyelets in their boots.

Amanda picked up the empty bottle she'd set outside. Snow capped the top. A little moisture was inside.

'Stuff snow into it,' Viv said. Another emotion – anger – was in her voice, and the confidence that she knew how to survive in the wilderness. 'It won't hurt us for now. The snow fleas haven't shown up yet.'

Amanda felt her skin itch. 'Snow fleas?'

'In spring, they hatch. They look like dirt on the snow. I don't see any yet.'

The snow wasn't deep – only an inch. Amanda studied it, making sure there weren't specks. Then she skimmed some into a hand and raised it to her mouth.

'No,' Viv warned. 'The heat your body uses to melt snow in your mouth saps your energy.'

Amanda found it strange that her thirst was greater than her hunger. Perhaps the fruit juice and pears she'd eaten the day before were of greater benefit than she'd hoped. Or perhaps my digestive system's shutting down, she thought. Some kind of protective mechanism. She felt lightheaded.

They filled their lungs with the cool morning air – and something else.

'Smoke,' Viv said.

They turned to the right. About fifty yards away, Ray had managed to get a fire going in the street. The flames crackled. Smoke rose. He stared at them, opening and closing his lighter.

'I see the dogs didn't get you,' Viv said angrily into the microphone on her headset.

Ray pointed toward a horizontal open space under a pile of boards. It resembled a coffin on its side. A door lay in front of it. 'Sorry to disappoint you.'

Viv put a hand over her microphone to prevent Ray from hearing what she said next. With a worried look, she turned toward Amanda. 'I haven't felt the need to urinate. We're not getting enough water for our kidneys to work.' She drank half her remaining bottle of water and gave it to Amanda. The motive was clear – they couldn't get revenge if they didn't survive. 'Drink the rest of it. I'm going to try to force my bladder.'

'Here, you'll want this.' Amanda pulled the toilet paper from her jumpsuit and divided it.

Viv touched the paper as if it were something she'd never seen before and she couldn't imagine why Amanda would share it. Boots crushing the snow, they walked in the opposite direction from Ray, then separated, each finding wreckage to crouch behind.

As Amanda unzipped her jumpsuit, she said into the microphone on her headset, 'Game Master, if you're watching, maybe you should be looking at porn movies instead.'

'Sex was never important to me,' the voice responded. 'I'm not looking.'

'Right.'

'Not even Ray is looking.'

Amanda peered over the rubble and saw that Ray was indeed facing another direction, toward the area the GPS coordinates had led him to the day before. Seen in profile, he appeared to be frowning.

Amanda squeezed the muscles in her abdomen. Urine dribbled, orange, with a strong odor. Not good, she thought. After she covered the toilet paper with boards, she went back to Viv. 'We need to get that water bottle from Derrick.'

Pale, Viv nodded. '*You*. I can't.'

Amanda walked up the street. As the sun got warmer, the snow made liquid sounds under her boots. She neared Derrick's body, seeing its contour under the slush.

'Stop,' Ray said.

Amanda thought he was telling her to keep a distance from him. But she didn't give a damn what he wanted. She needed that water bottle. She stepped closer.

'No!' Ray yelled.

Then she did stop, because the contour didn't look the same as the last time she'd seen Derrick's body. It had an odd shape. Melting snow slid off him. If Amanda's stomach hadn't been empty, she might have thrown up.

Hearing Viv walk toward her, she whirled, trying to form a shield. 'Go back!'

'What's wrong?'

'Don't look!'

But Viv did look. What she saw made her eyes widen.

Derrick's corpse – not just his battered face, but his entire body – was unrecognizable. His guts had been torn out. His arms and legs had been chewed to the bone. His hands were missing.

The dogs, Amanda realized. Last night when we heard them fighting, I thought they'd cornered Ray. But now she understood that it was Derrick's corpse they'd been fighting over.

'Hey, where's she going?' Ray asked.

Amanda turned. Viv was plodding away from them.

'Viv?'

She staggered on. Her gaze was fixed on the pass through the mountains at the end of the valley.

Amanda hurried to her.

'Too much,' Viv murmured.

'Stop.' Amanda kept pace with her.

'Enough,' Viv mumbled, staring toward the exit from the valley. 'I can't bear this any longer.'

'Remember what happened to Bethany,' the voice said through Amanda's headset.

How could she not? The roaring explosion, the spreading red mist, and the flying body parts were seared in Amanda's memory.

'Nobody leaves the game,' the voice warned.

Amanda put an arm around Viv. 'You need to stop.'

'No more.' Viv reached the edge of town and trudged across slush-covered grass.

'Step away from her, Amanda,' the voice cautioned.

'Viv, turn around. We're going back.'

'Can't.'

'Final chance,' the voice said.

'Viv, listen to him. *Go back.*'

Hands grabbed Viv, pulling her toward town. They belonged to Ray, who gripped her tightly, forcing her up the street.

'Get away from me!'

'Make me.' Ray tugged her farther up the street. 'Try to hit me. Go ahead. It won't matter. You can't hurt me.'

Viv twisted an arm free and swung, punching his shoulder.

'Is that the best you can do?' Ray mocked.

She swung at his jaw.

He dodged it, moving backward.

She pounded his chest. He shifted deeper into town. She punched him again, striking his mouth, his nose. Blood flew. With each blow, he stepped backward. They reached the middle of town and neared the shelter where Amanda and Viv had survived the night. The next time Viv swung, Ray grabbed her arm. When she swung with the other arm, he grabbed that too. She writhed, trying to get away. Slowly she lost strength and sank to her knees. Her chest heaved. Her sobs seemed to come from the depth of her soul.

'I'm sorry,' Ray said.

Amanda pulled Viv to her feet. 'Come on. You need to lie down.' She helped Viv to the shelter and eased her into it. The snow she'd stuffed into a bottle was now melted. 'Here. Drink some water.'

When Viv didn't respond, Amanda tilted the bottle to her mouth. Water dribbled down Viv's chin, but Amanda was relieved to see that she swallowed most of it.

Need to fill the bottles before the snow's completely gone, Amanda thought. She put a bottle in each hand and held it under boards from which water trickled. Ray was suddenly next to her, doing the same thing.

She was troubled by his changed behavior. Did he feel guilty? Was he trying to make amends for killing Derrick? But somehow, guilt didn't seem part of Ray's nature. The only explanation that made sense to her was that Ray's alpha-male personality compelled him to challenge any man he encountered, but when his only companions were women, he needed to try to make them like him. If I'm right, I can use that, she thought.

With Ray's help, she filled seven bottles. She noticed the rubber gloves in the snow, where Viv had dropped them.

Putting them in her pocket, she told Ray, 'I need to talk to you.' As Viv lay staring at the roof of the shelter, they avoided Derrick's body and walked toward the fire. 'I don't know how we're going to do it, but . . .' She had trouble saying it. 'We need to bury him. If those dogs come back . . .'

'I found just the place for it.' Ray wiped blood from his mouth and indicated the area outside town where he'd gone the day before.

'What's over there?'

'Use your GPS receiver and find out. Maybe that's not the right spot. Check to see if I made a mistake.'

'You know more about these units than I do.'

'Check anyhow.'

She pulled her receiver from her jumpsuit. She turned it on and accessed the coordinates that had been written on the cans of fruit. A red arrow pointed toward the area beyond town.

'It appears to indicate the same place yours does,' Amanda said.

She and Ray walked to a connecting street and headed past more wreckage. As they neared the area, Amanda saw objects the wreckage had concealed.

'They look like . . .'

'Grave markers,' Ray said.

Fifty yards from town, a collapsed wooden fence marked the boundaries of a cemetery. Scrub grass and sagebrush grew among wooden crosses, gray and cracked, some broken.

The names and dates on the crosses were carved into the decaying wood. Amanda went from grave to grave, managing to decipher the words. 'More women and children than men.'

'Because a lot of women died in childbirth back then,' Ray said. 'And a lot of kids died from diseases we now treat easily.'

Amanda heard a clatter and spun. Back in town, Viv was dragging boards from the wreckage and stacking them over Derrick's body.

'She's tough,' Ray said.

'That's why the bastard chose us,' Amanda said. 'Yesterday, when you found this place, something bothered you. What is it?'

'That line of crosses.'

Amanda read what was carved in the wood. 'Peter Bethune. Died June twentieth, 1899.' She moved along the crosses. 'Margaret Logan. June twenty-first, 1899. Edward Baker. June thirtieth, 1899. All in June.'

'Jennifer Morse. July fourth, 1899,' Ray said. 'Arnold Ryan. July twelfth, 1899. There are seventeen in a row. Each of them died between June and October of 1899.'

'Seventeen? Dear God,' Amanda said.

'After that, the ground would have frozen. Maybe there were even more deaths that year, but the earth was so hard that the people in town couldn't dig graves.'

'A place this size. That many deaths so close together. The community must have been in shock.'

'They were indeed,' the voice said through Amanda's headset.

She tensed.

'Ray guessed correctly,' the Game Master continued. 'There were in fact other deaths before the end of the year. Eight. In those days, when people died after the earth was frozen, they were put in coffins and stored in someone's barn. In the spring of 1900, when a search party arrived from a town called Cottonwood about a hundred miles away, they found the coffins and the bodies inside them. But that was the only sign of anyone. Over the winter, perhaps on New Year's Eve, the people of Avalon disappeared.'

'Disappeared?' Ray asked.

'Several later search parties were organized, but they didn't learn anything either. The townspeople had vanished from the face of the earth. Nor did the search parties find the Sepulcher of Worldly Desires. Some religious extremists theorized that on the eve of the new century, the people of Avalon were assumed into heaven.'

'But that's crazy,' Amanda said.

'Not in context. Focus on the cluster of deaths that began in June. Peter Bethune was killed when lightning struck him as he ran from his wagon to his store. The townspeople were stunned. But after the long drought, the rain was so welcome that their emotions were divided. They treated it almost as a price that needed to be paid. That's how Reverend Owen Pentecost spoke of it. But then Margaret Logan, age twelve, drowned in a flash flood. She was playing near a swollen creek. The ground collapsed. She was swept away. Then Edward Baker and his wife and two sons died when their home caught fire. A farmer was trampled by his horse. Another child drowned, this time in the lake. A woman was bitten by a rattlesnake. A family mistakenly ate poisonous mushrooms. The litany of disasters seemed endless. The shadow of death hovered over the valley.'

Amanda scanned the line of graves, awed by the suffering they represented.

'Reverend Pentecost told the townspeople that God blessed those who served Him and punished those who did not. Something in the hearts and souls of the town was turning God against them. They needed to look inward and examine their consciences. They needed to eradicate the stain of whatever secret sins had earned them God's disfavor. With each mounting death, the town prayed harder and longer.'

'The pressure would have been almost unbearable,' Amanda said.

Ray peered toward the sky, the direction in which thcy instinctively addressed the Game Master. 'And they just assumed God was responsible? Didn't it occur to them there might be another explanation?'

'Like what?' the Game Master asked. 'Unrelenting bad luck isn't any better an explanation than God's disfavor.'

'Like maybe this Reverend Pentecost was somehow involved. The town changed when he arrived.'

'You're suggesting Reverend Pentecost killed some of those people?'

'How hard would it be to push someone from a hayloft or substitute poisoned mushrooms for safe ones? All Pentecost needed to do was look for an opportunity.'

'Based on yesterday's events, we know how easily *you* could have done it,' the voice said.

'Derrick attacked me! I was defending myself!'

'Certainly. Why don't we save this conversation for another time? Right now, pay attention to the clues. Reverend Pentecost finally warned the townspeople to rid themselves of all vanity and avarice, to take every object they cherished and place it within something he called the Sepulcher of Worldly Desires. He told them that the Sepulcher would be an example to the future.'

'Example?' Amanda asked.

'Pentecost fixated on the looming new century and concluded that the continuing deaths were a sign of a coming apocalypse. "All is vanity," he told them. "As the new century begins, material things will no longer matter." But those outside the valley might not see the truth. When the Sepulcher was eventually found and opened . . . perhaps in a hundred years, when another apocalypse occurred . . . it would show the path of salvation to those left behind.'

'A time capsule,' Amanda realized. 'A damned time capsule. That's why you drugged Frank and me during the time capsule lecture.' The memory came as a shock. Thinking of Frank, she struggled not to let grief weaken her. I'm going to survive, she thought. I'm going to find a way to get out of here and pay him back for whatever he did to Frank.

In a frenzy, she yanked a board from the fallen fence and plunged it into the mud. 'The logical place to put a sepulcher is a graveyard. We're probably standing on it. The townspeople buried it here.'

'Be careful of your time,' the voice said.

Using the board as a shovel, Amanda hurled wet earth. 'Help me!' she told Ray. Again she drove the board into the mud, but this time the board broke. 'Damn it, help me!'

'Fifteen hours remain,' the voice said.

As Ray picked up a board from the collapsed fence, a grave marker at the end of the row caught his attention.

'Why aren't you helping?' Amanda shouted.

'This cross. The numbers on it are different.'

Amanda took a moment to react to his puzzled tone. She dropped the broken board and joined him at the cross.

'The month isn't spelled.' Ray pointed. 'Instead, there are only numbers.'

'But those numbers aren't for a month, day and year,' Amanda said.

'No. Two sets of them. LT in front of one. LG in front of the other. They're map coordinates.' Ray programmed them into his GPS unit.

'They'll take us to the lake,' an unexpected voice said through Amanda's headset. It belonged to Viv and made Amanda swing in her direction. Viv had finished stacking the boards over Derrick's corpse and now stared across the ruins toward them. 'Whatever this Sepulcher is, they couldn't have buried it, for the same reason they couldn't bury coffins. The ground was frozen. What other place *is* there? The Sepulcher's in the water.'

'But the lake would have been frozen also,' Ray said.

'That's the point.' Amanda suddenly understood. 'The townspeople could have walked on to the lake, stopped in the middle, and cut a hole through the ice. Then maybe they dropped the Sepulcher, whatever it looks like, through the hole.'

'It must have been huge if it contained everything they cherished. A hell of a big hole,' Ray said.

'Maybe the Sepulcher was big enough that more than just it went through the hole.' Viv marched past wreckage toward them. 'Maybe the ice cracked. Maybe the entire town went into the water.'

'But in the spring, the search party would have looked for them in the water, in case somehow they'd all drowned,' Ray objected.

'How would the search party have checked the

water?' Viv came nearer. 'The middle looks deep. It's not like the searchers had scuba divers or grappling hooks.'

'In the spring, the bodies would have bobbed to the surface,' Ray insisted. Immediately, he paused. 'Unless . . .'

'Unless what?' Amanda asked.

'Maybe it wasn't an accident.' He looked disturbed. 'Could it have been a mass suicide? If the bodies were weighted, they wouldn't have risen to the surface after the ice melted. They'd never have been found unless the lake was drained.'

It seemed as if a breeze died. The valley became silent.

'The lake.' Ray frowned at the needle on his GPS unit, then stared toward where it pointed. 'That's where the coordinates seem to be.'

'Yes, the lake.' Amanda felt excitement growing in her. 'That's why the snakes are in it. To keep us from searching there.' She looked at Ray. 'You said "unless the lake was drained." I don't see how it's possible to do that.'

'It's possible when you realize it's not really a lake,' Viv said, reaching them.

'What are you talking about?' Ray demanded.

'When this is over, I'll make you pay for what you did to my husband. I swear to you, I'll get even.'

Ray met her gaze. 'You can try.'

'But I'm not going to die here because I let you

distract me. Right now, all that matters is winning.'

'Sure. Later,' Ray said. 'We need to get out of here alive. Then you can try to get even.'

Amanda felt the latent violence between them. She interrupted. 'Viv, what do you mean it's not a lake?'

'Did you notice its shape?'

'It's got water. That's what *I* noticed,' Ray told her. 'It's rectangular.'

'No. It's shaped like a wedge. The tip points toward the western mountains, where the stream comes from. The blunt end has rocks that slope below it. The shape's symmetrical. *Too* symmetrical. It's not a lake. It's a *reservoir*.'

Ray needed only a moment to think about it. 'Jesus.' He started running.

5

The sun had baked the mud. As Balenger guided the Jeep along the narrow dirt road, he heard the crust braking. On either side were sagebrush and scrub grass. Ahead, foothills rose toward snow-capped mountains. The road showed no sign of recent use. He didn't see any buildings. He permitted himself to hope.

The road descended into a stream. The high chassis on the Jeep allowed him to drive through it, the four-wheel drive gripping the slippery surface on the other side. Bumps jostled him, preventing him from going faster than twenty miles an hour. Time, he kept thinking. Near the foothills, he reached cattle drinking from a water trough next to a windmill.

The road did not continue. He drove past the windmill and steered between bushes, aiming toward whatever open area presented itself. Rocks and holes forced him to zigzag. The ground began to rise. He avoided more rocks and sagebrush. The incline became steeper. When he crested a ridge, he faced a steep drop on the other side, so he followed the ridge, passing aspen trees. Then he reached another slope, too rocky and steep for him to drive farther. He backed the Jeep to the aspens and stopped where they screened the car.

He changed clothes, putting on the tan boots and hunting outfit, which blended with the terrain. Feeling the strength of the sun, he covered his face with sunscreen, put on the sunglasses and the hat, and drank from one of the water bottles he'd purchased at the truck stop. After clipping the Emerson knife inside a pocket, he loaded the magazines and shoved one into the Mini-14. He buttoned the compass and the packet of Kleenex into his shirt pocket, hooked the canteen to his belt, and stuffed the knapsack with the remaining equipment. He had a memory of packing his gear to go to Iraq, an apt comparison, he thought, because he was about to enter a war zone.

When he put on the knapsack, he estimated that it

weighed around forty pounds. I've carried worse, he thought. He pulled the bolt back on the Mini-14, arming it, engaged the safety catch, and slung the rifle over his shoulder. What else do I need to do? he thought. There's always something.

The BlackBerry, he realized. He took it from a pocket and set it to vibrate mode so a noise from it wouldn't give away his position. Then he started up the slope. He was relieved that he didn't feel any of the jitters, sweaty palms, and nervous breathing of the post-traumatic stress disorder he'd suffered for so long. After Amanda disappeared, he'd expected that his weakness would come back to torture him. Instead, his determination to save her so filled him that there wasn't room for conflicting emotions.

He climbed past more aspen trees, but despite their shade, sweat slicked his forehead and stuck his shirt to his skin. Finally he crested a ridge and came to a shelf of rock that protruded from the aspens. After taking off his knapsack and rifle, he sank on to the shelf, did his best to conceal himself, and studied the valley below. Morning sunlight reflected off a lake, making its ripples glisten. The lake was wider at one end, reminding him of a long triangle.

He removed his binoculars from his knapsack. Using his hat as a shield to prevent the sun from reflecting off the lenses, he focused on the water. An embankment of rocks resembled a dam. At once he understood it was a reservoir, not a lake. Movement caught his attention.

Redirecting the binoculars, he saw tiny figures on the embankment and wondered excitedly if Amanda was one of them. They were doing something to the embankment. Throwing rocks away, he realized. That didn't make sense. What were they trying to do, breach the dam? Why?

He put on his hat and shoved the binoculars into the knapsack. After he crawled back into the aspens, he hefted the knapsack on to his back and reslung the rifle over his shoulder. To his left, the ridge descended until it reached the narrow entrance to the valley. That was the obvious route the Game Master would expect him to use. But he couldn't convince himself that the Game Master would rely on the obvious. In Iraq, he remembered, he couldn't take anything for granted. Any street could provide an ambush. Any object along the road might be a bomb.

It's the same here, he thought. Nothing's what it seems.

Making sure that his boots were solidly placed, he started down the uneven slope toward the valley, scanning the trees and rocks for signs of a trap.

6

Amanda threw another rock to the side. It was as big as a football. She ignored the cuts on her hands and grabbed yet another. It seemed she'd been doing this for ever. She, Ray, and Viv were fifteen feet below the top of the spillway. Last night's storm had flooded the reservoir. Water cascaded over the edge, pouring down the rocks, throwing up spray that chilled her face. To see what was in the reservoir, they needed to breach the dam and drain the water.

'Be careful!' Viv yelled amid the water's roar. 'Remember to watch for the snakes!'

Amanda didn't need reminding. Twice already she'd seen water moccasins slide past her, the force of the water carrying them over the rim and down the slope.

'This rock's too heavy!' Ray shouted. 'Help me tug it free!'

Amanda stumbled to him and gripped the rock. The blood on her hands made them slippery, but she squeezed as hard as she could and tugged. The rock came free, throwing her and Ray off-balance while it rumbled to the bottom of the spillway. She fell, banging her right arm.

'Are you all right?' Ray asked.

Amanda ignored the pain and reached for another rock.

'I finally see dirt,' Viv told them. 'Four layers of rocks until I got to it.'

Amanda studied the embankment. 'A lot more to do.' She stooped and pulled and threw. Her chest heaved. 'This is taking too long. We need to reach into the water. If we expose the dirt there, the current'll wash it away and undermine the other rocks.'

'The snakes,' Viv warned.

'No choice.'

Spray washed grit from Amanda's face as she put her hands in the water and pulled at a rock. The force of the current helped tug it free. She yanked at another rock, and it too went with the current. She reached again and suddenly jerked her hands back. Something that looked like a piece of rope sped past her.

For a moment, she couldn't move. She stared at the water, feeling as if the snake was inside her, writhing. When she mustered resolve and reached for another rock, the current pushed at her hands. She needed to brace herself to keep her footing. Then the rock came loose, and the roaring water carried it down.

Ray followed her example, but Viv concentrated on rocks away from the water, too phobic about the snakes.

The cascade sucked dirt from under a rock. It spread in the current.

'Yes!' Ray shouted.

Amanda found the energy to work harder. The icy water numbed her fingers. She pulled another rock. A moment later, another snake sped past.

Ray shouted, 'More dirt's flowing!'

A large plume of earth spread into the current.

'If we can make the hole deeper and wider . . .' Ray tugged.

Amanda helped him, pulling out another rock. And another. The plume of dirt widened. A rock moved on its own. The current became earth-colored, more rocks shifting.

'Get back!' Amanda shouted.

The old embankment hadn't been maintained in more than a hundred years. Amanda realized that she was standing on the site of what amounted to a chain reaction. A half-dozen rocks toppled free. Earth washed away behind them, dropping more rocks, which in turn freed more earth. The force of the current was relentless. The top of the dam settled, opening a channel, more water roaring down the slope, taking away more earth. As the rocks beneath Amanda threatened to give way, she turned and tried to hurry across the uneven surface. But the slope moved as though something alive was under it, and she needed to struggle for balance, working toward the embankment's edge. Ray was ahead of her, Viv behind.

She heard Viv scream. Pivoting, she saw Viv teeter on a section of collapsing rocks. Amanda lunged for her, caught her left hand, felt the jolt of Viv's weight, and started to topple with her.

Ray's arm snared her waist, straining to pull them to safety. The slope kept collapsing, the rush of water sucking at Viv's boots. Viv twisted, the torque of her hand prying Amanda's fingers open. As Amanda lurched back, Viv dropped, vanishing into the current.

'No!' Amanda wailed.

The top of the dam collapsed, a wall of water hurtling toward the bottom. Amanda glimpsed Viv's brown jumpsuit in the plummeting current. A churning pool enveloped her.

'We've got to pull her out!'

Amanda raced toward the side of the spillway and charged toward the bottom. Hearing Ray's urgent steps next to her, she saw Viv struggle to the surface, breathe, and get sucked under again.

'Her boots!' Ray yelled. 'She won't be able to swim!'

But Viv tried. Breaking the surface again, she stretched her arms, clawing at the water. The flood carried her forward.

Amanda and Ray hurried along the water's edge, trying to keep pace with its speed.

'Don't fight the current!' Amanda shouted. 'Let it take you! Where it's slower downstream, we'll grab you!'

She dodged sagebrush and rocks, desperate to stay next to Viv. She rounded a curve, lost sight of the brown jumpsuit, moaned, then saw it, and kept running. Viv got her head above the water, breathing frantically.

The flood rushed over the banks of what, until five minutes ago, had been a stream bed. The water made two sounds, one on top of the other, a hiss and a rumble.

It picked up debris. It dragged Viv under. Her brown jumpsuit was hard to distinguish now in the earth-colored water.

As the flood spread over level grassland, Amanda charged into it, only to find that the current almost knocked her over. Ray pulled her to solid ground.

'Viv!' Amanda screamed.

The water kept widening. Amanda saw Viv struggle to keep her head above the surface while the current swept her along. She struck something – a boulder, Amanda realized – and clung to it.

'Yes!' Amanda shouted. 'Hang on!'

As the torrent spread, it slowed. It dropped to a foot. Six inches. Viv released her hold on the boulder and slumped behind it.

'Keep your head up!' Amanda yelled. She splashed into the water. Even shallow, the current was powerful. She and Ray needed to hang on to each other to keep from falling. Then the water dropped to three inches, and Amanda hurried through it. Glancing upstream, she saw a massive hole in the embankment, emptiness beyond it, only a trickle coming out. She increased speed and came to the boulder.

Viv lay on her back, her face above water. Amanda reached for her. Ray pulled her hand away.

'Let go of me! We need to help her!'

'We can't! She's dead!'

'Like hell! I see her chest moving! Get your damned hands—' The words stuck in Amanda's throat. A snake emerged from Viv's jumpsuit, its black body slithering across her shoulder. The tail of another projected from her left pant leg. The snake made her leg seem to move. A third snake was halfway up her right sleeve.

'The force of the water,' Ray said. 'It tore her boots off. It shoved the snakes into her clothes.'

Snakes writhed everywhere, visible now that the water was only a couple of inches deep.

'We need to get out of here,' Ray said, pulling Amanda away.

'But . . . Viv . . . Maybe we can still help.'

'No. Look at her eyes.'

Despite the sun's glare, they didn't blink.

'Let's go. Those snakes are awfully angry,' Ray said.

One hissed at them.

Ray tugged again, and this time Amanda went with him. Numbed by grief, she kept looking back until the boulder obscured Viv's body.

They reached dry ground. The snakes remained where the earth was wet. Amanda thought of Viv's bulging eyes and trembled.

'When Viv saw how the dogs mutilated Derrick's body, remember what she told us?' Amanda asked.

'She said she couldn't bear this any longer.'

'Exactly.' Overwhelmed, Amanda sank to the ground. '*I* can't bear this any longer.'

7

Balenger worked his way down a slope. His boots almost slipped on wet dead leaves, but he gripped a tree trunk, caught his balance, and continued down. He saw occasional patches of snow where the sun hadn't reached and realized that here the storm the previous night had brought more than rain.

To his right, the foothills rose to mountains. A mile to his left, the foothills shrank, merging with the valley's entrance. Knowing the Game Master's fondness for monitoring devices, he expected that there'd be intrusion detectors. But four deer bounding away from him through the trees made him realize that intrusion detectors would be impractical. Animals would constantly set off alarms triggered by pressure sensors and infrared beams. Under the circumstances, video cameras were more reliable, and for now, the close cover of the aspen trees made this an unlikely area for the Game Master to hide any. The view would be limited. Better to aim cameras at open spaces where a few could accomplish a lot.

Balenger kept descending to the right, wanting to gain more distance from the valley's entrance. He reached the slope's bottom. Still encircled by trees, he took out his compass and terrain map. A mountain visible through the treetops gave him a landmark to orient the map. He calculated that in another mile, he'd be in a north–south line with the reservoir.

After he forced himself to drink some water and bite a piece from an energy bar, he continued through the trees, following the rim of the valley. He scanned everything ahead of him, reminding himself to think as if he were in Iraq, watching for any sign of an ambush or a bomb. He decided that buried explosives connected to trip wires or pressure plates weren't practical in this location. Animals would constantly set them off. More likely, explosives would be radio-controlled, triggered by a visual confirmation of the target. Just like the roadside bombs in Iraq. Although he remained convinced that cameras would be aimed toward open spaces, not into the limited viewpoint of the forest, he took the precaution of avoiding obvious routes through the trees – a game trail, for example, or a clearing.

A rumble made him pause. It sounded like distant thunder. The noise persisted, then faded. An explosion? he wondered. No, it had lasted too long. Maybe the people on the embankment had succeeded in breaching the dam. Although he couldn't imagine why they'd work so hard to do that, he kept hoping Amanda was one of them. Worry for her made him want to hurry, but he restrained himself, knowing that he wouldn't be any use to her if he allowed himself to get careless.

When his compass and map told him he was abreast of the reservoir, he turned left and moved cautiously through the trees. The forest thinned, revealing the extent of the valley and the mountains surrounding it. The passage of time weighed on him. Already it was almost one p.m. Eleven hours until endgame at midnight. He held his gun at the ready and peered from the trees. Nothing on either side aroused his suspicions.

Wary, he stepped into the open. After the protection of the forest, the vastness before him was unnerving.

The BlackBerry vibrated. He took it from his camouflage suit and pressed its green button.

'Welcome to *Scavenger*,' the voice said.

Balenger studied the expanse in front of him. Sagebrush, a few pine trees, occasional boulders. Despite the rain the night before, the ground looked parched.

'After I learned about the Sepulcher of Worldly Desires, I bought this valley,' the Game Master said.

'Nice to be able to afford whatever you want.' Balenger turned to the left, and scanned the line of trees behind him, concentrating on the upper branches.

'I walked the valley until I knew it like an old friend.'

'You have friends?' Balenger turned to the right now, scanning the upper branches of the trees in that direction.

'I used a metal detector to search the cemetery in case the Sepulcher was buried there. But the only metal the detector reacted to came from jewelry that some of the townspeople were buried with.'

'You dug them up to find out?'

'I used the detector to scan the town, a painstaking

process. As you might expect, the device reacted to all sorts of metal, from nails to hinges to rusted knives and forks. But no reaction was strong enough to indicate that the Sepulcher was buried under Avalon.'

'You assumed the Sepulcher was huge?' Balenger kept studying the trees as he pressed the phone to his ear. 'Maybe it's tiny, just room enough for a Bible and some handwritten prayers.'

'No,' the Game Master said. 'It's huge. I hired a plane and equipped it with an infrared camera, the kind that records variations of heat in landscapes. Soil absorbs heat, for example, while stone reflects it. Soil on top of rock has a different-colored image than deep soil or soil with metal under it. Hot spots almost seem to glow on photographs this camera takes.'

Balenger saw what he was looking for and nodded in a minor victory.

'The camera took thousands of photographs. It documented the heat signature of every part of the valley. The photography took days. Studying the results took weeks. A few aberrant images gave me hope, but when I had those areas excavated, I found nothing.'

'So maybe the Sepulcher's a myth. Maybe it never existed. If it can't be found, there's another flaw in the game. Call it off.'

'Oh, the Sepulcher exists all right. I went back to the original documents and finally understood that the clues were there all along. I just hadn't looked at them in the right way.'

'You found the Sepulcher?'

'Indeed.'

'And it's here in the valley?'

'Absolutely.'

'Where?'

'That would be too easy. It's up to you to find it. If you do, you win.'

'And Amanda goes free.'

'Provided she overcomes the remaining obstacles.'

'Then I don't have time to chat.'

Balenger broke the transmission and put the phone away. He removed the packet of Kleenex from his shirt pocket and took out a piece. He tore it in half, wadded the sections, and shoved them into his ears. Then he raised the Mini-14, peered through its site, and lined up its red dot with what he'd discovered in the upper branches of an aspen tree: a video camera. He hadn't fired a rifle since he was in Iraq a year and a half earlier. Shooting was a perishable skill. Accuracy depended on practice. Hoping that the holographic gunsight would compensate, he held his breath and pulled the trigger.

Even with Kleenex wadded in his ears, the sound of the shot was palpable. The rifle bucked, an empty shell flipping away. He looked toward the camera in the branches fifty yards away, twenty feet up in the tree. A dark hole in the bark below the camera warned him that he'd jerked the trigger, lowering the barrel.

He aimed again. This time, he squeezed instead of jerking. *Crack*. The recoil swept through him. Fragments of the camera flew through the air. The rest of it dangled from an electrical wire.

He walked along the trees and saw another camera in the aspens, about fifty yards farther down. The valley was presumably flanked with them. So many cameras, so many corresponding screens. Balenger knew it would be impossible for the Game Master to watch all the monitors. Some kind of motion sensor probably activated individual screens if a human-shaped figure came into view.

Well, here's another image that won't take up his time, Balenger thought. He raised the rifle, lined up the red dot, squeezed the trigger, and blew the camera to pieces. The BlackBerry vibrated in his pocket. He ignored it.

He kept walking, scanning the expanse around him. The extent of the sky reminded him of Iraq. Amanda, he thought. Amanda, he kept repeating. Amanda, he inwardly shouted, the mantra giving him strength.

He saw another camera, this one hidden among rocks. He shot it.

Again the BlackBerry vibrated in his pocket. But he had something more important to occupy his attention – a gully that stopped him from going farther. It was wide and deep. Water from yesterday's rain flowed at the bottom. It was a seemingly natural stream bed, but all Balenger could think of was that it couldn't be avoided. Everything was a possible trap.

LEVEL EIGHT:
THE DOOMSDAY VAULT

1

Amanda remained slumped on the ground, staring toward the boulder beyond which Viv lay dead.

'Let's go,' Ray urged.

'I meant what I said. I can't do this any longer.'

'No one leaves the game,' the voice warned through her headset.

'Who said anything about leaving?' Weariness muffled Amanda's voice. 'I'm just not playing any more.'

'We don't have time for this,' Ray said. 'We need to see what's in the reservoir.'

Amanda looked in that direction, toward the gap in the embankment and the emptiness beyond. 'It doesn't matter.'

'I can't wait.' Ray walked toward the reservoir.

'Inaction is a form of playing,' the Game Master told Amanda. 'It's a choice not to win. What would Frank say?'

'*Frank?*' Amanda looked up. The name was a spark to her nervous system. 'Leave him out of this! Damn it, what did you do with him? What sick way did you think of to kill him?'

'Leave him out of this? I don't want to. In fact, I *can't*.'

'What are you talking about?'

'Frank's coming to play.'

The words didn't make sense. *Frank's coming to play?*

A gunshot startled her. It echoed back and forth across the valley, but as far as she could tell, the initiating sound came from beyond the flooded area, from the mountains to the north. A second shot followed. Yes, from the north.

Coming to play?

With difficulty, Amanda stood. She heard another shot. Frank? Is that you? Coming to play? What's that shooting about? She waited, listening hard, but there wasn't a fourth shot.

Frank?

She looked toward Ray. Near the ruptured embankment, he too had turned, staring across the meager flow of water toward the northern mountains. As the air became still, his lean features toughened. In the harsh sunlight, he resumed climbing the slope toward the emptied reservoir.

Amanda started after him. Her legs ached from crouching to pull at the rocks, but urgency told her that if the Game Master wasn't lying, she needed to do everything possible to help Frank.

She reached the slope and climbed in a zigzag pattern, conserving energy as Viv had taught her. Viv. The shock of her death struck Amanda even harder. Keep moving, Amanda told herself. Get what Viv wanted. Get even.

Near the top, she came to the water bottles that she, Ray and Viv had filled with melting snow. Their frenzy to breach the dam had made them so thirsty that they had drunk nearly all the water. A few swallows remained in one bottle. Amanda emptied it into her mouth, the water unpleasantly warm from the sun, and continued on.

She found Ray studying the reservoir's muddy basin. Despite the force of the escaping flood, some objects remained embedded in the muck. Rotted tree trunks. The remains of a buckboard wagon. The skeleton of a cow. Something that might have once been a rowboat.

The basin was a hundred yards long, ten yards wide at its narrow end, and forty yards wide at the embankment, where she stood. Fish flopped in the puddles. A few snakes followed the meager flow of water across the mud.

'I don't see any human bones,' Ray said.

'They might be under the mud.'

'But that cow skeleton isn't. There's nothing to prove this is where the townspeople disappeared. I don't see anything that looks like a container, either, if that's what we're supposed to find.'

'I bet it's forty feet deep. A lot of area. Whatever we're searching for could be anywhere.' Amanda looked across the mud toward the northern mountains, again wondering what the shots had been about. Frank, are you coming? she wondered, desperately hoping. Then she realized how wrong it was for her to look in that direction. She didn't want the Game Master to think about Frank. She wanted him to concentrate on how she and Ray played the game.

Ray pulled out his GPS receiver and accessed the coordinates they'd found in the graveyard. The red arrow pointed across the basin. 'We need to triangulate. Go along the bank. See where the needle on your receiver points.'

Amanda walked thirty feet and paused, looking at her receiver. The needle aimed beyond the horns of the cow skeleton toward something that protruded a few inches from the mud.

'What is it?' Ray asked.

'Not sure. It looks like it's metal,' Amanda answered. 'A rim of something.'

The object, whatever it was, seemed to be about four feet long by three feet wide.

'Worldly vanities,' Ray said. 'That's what the Sepulcher is supposed to contain. But *that* doesn't look like it can hold much.'

'Reminds me of something, but I can't remember where I saw it.' Nagged by the memory, Amanda stepped on to the reservoir's slope. The ground was spongy but supportive. After she took a half-dozen steps, it became mucky, but its base was solid. A further half-dozen steps, and the mud rose over the toe of her boots.

'I don't know how much farther I can go.'

The object was still thirty feet ahead of her. She waited until a snake wriggled a safe distance away, then took another step down the slope. Her right boot went into the mud.

She kept going. Gasping, she watched as the boot sank completely, mud enveloping the ankle. It sank farther, throwing her off balance. In panic, she planted her left boot to steady herself, but the mud was like a mouth, sucking at her right leg, threatening to tug her forward. It was almost to her knee. She turned, landing on her left elbow. Mud flew. A snake hissed. She tried to crawl sideways, but her hands and elbow went into the muck and she had trouble pulling them out. The mass of her body kept the rest of her from sinking, but she was trapped.

Helpless, she peered at Ray, who watched from the basin's rim. His lean, beard-stubbled face revealed no emotion, making her realize that his earlier effort to pull her and Viv off the collapsing embankment was the limit of his heroics for the day.

The angle at which her imprisoned leg was twisted caused such pain that Amanda worried about dislocating her knee or popping a tendon. Her lungs felt empty. She put weight on her shoulder and used it as a support to try to tug her right hand from the mud. Like a living thing, the mud resisted. She pulled harder, feeling the heat of adrenaline when the hand came free. She took several deep breaths, found herself staring at the cow's skeleton, and understood why the animal hadn't been able to escape the water. Its skull pointed toward her. She stretched her right arm, straining her shoulder. Her fingers grazed a horn. She groped farther, wincing from the pain in her wrist and elbow, managing to clutch the horn. She needed something solid to tug against and pull herself free, but the skull broke loose from the skeleton, and she jerked back.

She moaned. In desperation, she dragged the skull toward her. The horns gave her an idea. She turned the skull upside down and exhaled forcibly as she drove the horns into the mud. With a jolt, they touched something solid. Shoving her right hand against the skull's bottom, she gained the purchase she needed and kept pushing against it, raising her elbow. The mud made a sucking sound as her left hand came free. Instantly, she propped that hand on the bottom of the skull, pushed, and with effort sat up, the mud clinging to her.

The pressure on her right knee became less painful. She used her hands to scoop the mud from around her right leg, throwing handful after handful away. A lot poured back in to the hole she fought to make, but she kept digging. One more tug, and her leg was free. But if she tried to stand, she knew she would sink into the muck again. Turning, she grabbed the bottom of the embedded skull and pulled herself on her stomach across the mud. She tugged the skull free and plunged it into the muck closer to the basin's rim. She dragged her body higher, touched ground that was spongy, and managed to stand.

Ray kept watching. 'There was no point in both of us getting trapped,' he said.

'Sure.'

'If I thought I could help, I would have. But I'm heavier. My boots would have sunk in deeper than yours.'

'Of course.'

'I want you to understand.'

'Believe me, I do.'

'Not that it matters,' Ray said. 'We're as good as dead anyhow. There's no way to reach that thing down there, whatever it is, and learn about the Sepulcher.'

'Wrong.' Amanda hoped that her next statement, combined with her crisis in the muck, would distract the Game Master from Frank. 'I know how to get down there.'

2

Balenger stared at the gully. Water flowed along its bottom. It was five feet deep and ten feet wide – too far for him to jump across.

He glanced to the right and left, noting that the stream bed extended to each end of the valley. He would take too long trying to find a way around it, he decided. But all his instincts warned him not to step into it.

Maybe it's just what it seems, he tried to assure himself.

But he couldn't take the chance. He needed to assume it was a trap. Were explosives hidden in it? If so, they couldn't be pressure-activated. Animals drinking at the stream would set them off. The only alternative was for the Game Master to detonate them electronically when the cameras revealed that Balenger was in the stream bed.

Another good reason to destroy the cameras.

Time, he thought. Forced to make a decision, he concluded that hiding mines all along the stream bed would require an enormous amount of explosives. Not easy to acquire. There was too great a risk that law enforcement agencies would notice the shipments. Would the Game Master take that gamble?

So if not explosives, what's down there? Balenger thought. What else is equally deadly but easily hidden in the gully?

Something about the words 'detonate them electronically' nagged at him. As a suspicion formed, he glanced toward the forest a half-mile behind him. He wondered if it was possible to drag a dead tree to the gully and use it as a bridge, but he decided that, even if he managed to do so, it would exhaust him and take too long. Midnight was rushing toward him.

He noticed rocks on the ground, picked one up, and tossed it into the gully. He did this again and again, building a footbridge across the water. He needed to work quickly because the rocks formed what amounted to a dam, and as the water rose, it spilled over them. He couldn't allow his boots to touch the water because he increasingly believed there was an electrical cable underneath. Most of the time, the Game Master would leave the power off, preventing animals from dying when they came to drink. But as soon as cameras told him that Balenger was in the valley, the electricity would have been activated.

Balenger worked fast, dropping more rocks into the water. But the water kept rising, flowing over the barrier. He wasn't accomplishing anything.

Amanda, he thought.

He saw a much larger rock and shoved it. Not used to the altitude, he grunted with effort. Hurry! he thought. He gave a final push and watched the rock tumble into the gully, where it rolled to a stop in the shallow water below the dam he'd unintentionally built.

But water splashed the top of the rock. If Balenger was right about the electrical cable, he didn't dare step on the wet rock. He needed to wait until it dried. Noting that the stark sun had dried the bank after last's night rain, he eased down the slope, careful to press his weight against it so he wouldn't lose his balance and fall into the water. The rock's top started drying. The water smelled deceptively pleasant.

To occupy the frustrating minutes, he studied the walls of the gully and tensed when he noticed a box built into the wall. About fifty feet away, it was carefully placed so that it wouldn't be noticed from above. In the box was a video camera. No doubt there were others positioned at regular intervals along the gully.

Balenger put the Kleenex back in his ears. He raised his rifle, superimposed the red dot over the target, and blew the camera to hell. In his pants pocket, the BlackBerry vibrated. He didn't bother answering it.

The rock was sufficiently dry now. He slung his rifle over his shoulder, took a long step, and braced his right boot on the rock. He gasped when he felt a shock. Even without water to conduct it, the electricity remained powerful enough to come through the rock. It wasn't enough to kill him, but it was so painful that he almost lost his balance and fell into the water, where he certainly would have died. He jerked his left boot off the bank, stretched that leg over the water, and jumped to the other side. When he pushed from the rock, it shifted beneath his boot, almost dumping him into the water, but he threw his arms forward, the weight of his knapsack giving him momentum, and landed on the bank. He almost rolled back into the water. Chest cramping, he dug his fingers into the earth and stopped.

Carefully he came to his feet, reached for the gully's

top, and pulled himself up, kneeing against the dirt. As he raised his head over the edge, teeth snapped, saliva spraying his face. Gasping, he let go and slid down the bank.

A dog was up there. At once, it leapt.

Balenger rolled to the side, feeling the rush of air when the dog struck his right knee and hurtled down. It landed on the bank, avoided the water, snarled, and charged. On his back, weighed down by the knapsack, Balenger kicked, banging the animal's nose. He didn't have time to unsling his rifle. Even if he'd managed, the fight was too close for him to be able to aim. Kicking again, he grabbed the knife clipped to his right pants pocket, flipped the blade open, and worked to raise himself so he could swing.

Another snarl came from behind him, a second dog stretching its head from the top of the bank, snapping at him. Simultaneously, the first dog lunged past Balenger's boots, teeth aimed toward his groin. Balenger slashed, catching the snout above the nose. As blood flew, the dog lurched back in shock, hit the water, and wailed, its body contorting from the force of the electricity. It jumped from the water, but damage to its nerves took away its strength. Hitting the water again, it thrashed in a death convulsion. Its wail became frenzied grunts that turned to silence, the dog lying still.

The second dog, too, became silent, startled by what had happened. Balenger turned and slashed upward, cutting under its jaw. With a yelp, the dog skittered backward, retreating out of sight beyond the top of the bank.

Balenger surged to his feet and ran to the left along the bank, in the opposite direction from where the dog on top seemed to have gone. Feeling a sharp pain in his right knee, he glanced down and saw blood. The damned thing bit me! he thought. My God, was it rabid?

He reached a spot that looked easy to climb but jerked his hands back when teeth snapped at them. Two dogs lunged into view, foam dripping from their jaws. One had a cut under its muzzle. The other was bigger, the size of a German shepherd.

Balenger dropped his knife, unslung the rifle, and risked a quick look to make sure that dirt wasn't plugging the barrel. Both dogs darted back. He aimed, ready if they showed themselves. Even with the Kleenex in his ears, he heard growling beyond the top of the bank.

He eased to the left along the stream, staring toward the top, hoping to outflank the dogs. A snarl above him warned that they were keeping pace with him.

Maybe I can scare them off, he thought. He fired, hoping the sharp noise would drive them away.

For a moment, there was silence.

Then the growls resumed.

The dogs were big but scrawny. Balenger wondered if they were crazy with hunger. He slipped out of his knapsack. Holding his gun with one hand, he opened the flap and pulled out two energy bars. He hurled them to his left over the bank. When he heard movement, he grabbed his knapsack and ran to the right, picking up his knife and clipping it into his pocket as he hurried. He passed the dead dog in the stream and kept running.

He climbed a gentle part of the slope, peered over the top, didn't see a threat, and scrambled up. The two dogs were a distance away, snarling at each other, fighting over the energy bars. The bigger dog grabbed a bar, swallowed it whole, wrapper and all, and attacked the other dog before it could get to the remaining bar.

The BlackBerry vibrated in Balenger's pocket. Ignoring it, he stalked toward the reservoir.

3

'Stack them on!' Amanda urged. In the ruins, she held out her arms while Ray set board after board on to them.

'Too many!' he said.

'Give me more!' The strain made her wince.

Amanda headed toward the drained reservoir. She heard another gunshot. It, too, came from the north, but it sounded closer. Frank? she thought. Is that really you? What are you shooting? At once, she feared that he was the one being shot at. Don't think that way, she warned herself. Frank's coming. I've got to believe that.

The weight of the boards hurting her arms, she staggered onward, finally reaching the basin. With a clatter, she dropped them. Her mouth felt dry, as if it had been swabbed with cotton.

Ray plodded to her and dropped what he was carrying. He squinted at his watch. 'Twenty to two.'

'The time goes fast when you're having fun,' Amanda said. She grabbed two boards and set them next to each other on the muddy slope.

'Or slower,' the Game Master said through her headset. 'Time is relative in video games. It all depends how it's divided.'

'Go to hell!' Amanda told him. She and Ray hurried to place more boards in the mud.

'Many games have time counters, but in games that deal with the development of virtual civilizations, the counters indicate months and years instead of seconds or minutes. Indeed, a month might last only a minute. Conversely, some games pretend to measure conventional time, but a minute on their timers might actually last two minutes in so-called real time. The player exits the game and discovers that twice as much conventional time has elapsed than the game indicated. The effect can be disorienting.'

Amanda continued making a walkway, trying to shut out the voice.

'Then, too, as you discovered, a game's subjective time can be different from clock time. A friend who's dying from cancer learned that the intense speed of multiple decisions many games require gives a fullness to each instant and makes time appear to go slowly. For some players, the forty hours that the average game takes can be the equivalent of a lifetime.'

Another shot echoed from beyond the drained reservoir. Amanda stared toward the mountains to the north.

'You can bet *Frank* feels it's been a lifetime,' the Game Master said.

'Don't believe him. He's jerking your chain,' Ray said. 'Those shots are probably from hunters. If we're lucky, maybe they'll find us.'

But what could they do to help us? Amanda wondered. We're walking bombs. For that matter, what can *Frank* do to help us?

'I never lie,' the Game Master said. 'If I tell you those shots indicate Frank is coming, you can take my word for it.'

'You never lie? Hard for me to know.' Ray glared toward the sky. 'But sure as sin, you never told the complete truth.'

Don't think that way! Amanda warned herself. Frank's coming. He's got to be. Just keep trying to distract the Game Master. She put the last board into the mud and hurried to get more.

4

Balenger reached a solitary pine tree, the only elevated object around, and discovered, as he had anticipated, a video camera mounted on its trunk. He aimed his rifle, steadied the red dot, and blew the camera to pieces.

Lights out, he thought.

He put a fresh magazine into the gun and reloaded the partially empty one. All the while, he glanced to his right, where the two dogs watched him, maintaining a distance of thirty yards. He resumed walking. So did they. He paused again. They did also.

The pain in his knee made him look down. His camouflaged pant leg was stained with blood. The dog's teeth had torn the fabric. He saw puncture wounds and worried about the saliva he'd seen at the dog's mouth.

What's the time limit for getting anti-rabies shots? he wondered.

He set down his knapsack and leaned his rifle against it, making sure the barrel didn't get fouled with dirt. As the sun intensified, he removed the first-aid kit and the duct tape. He glanced toward the dogs. Their attention was riveted on him.

Shoot them, he thought.

But although his knapsack was heavy with ammunition, he needed to use it sparingly. It was better to blast the cameras apart . . . or kill the Game Master, he thought . . . than shoot two dogs he maybe didn't need to. Later, he might want to give anything to get those two shots back.

Let's see how smart they are.

He lifted the gun and aimed at the bigger dog, the one that looked like a German shepherd.

It raced away, its partner following. He tracked the bigger dog, tempted to squeeze the trigger, but hitting a target that got smaller and lower as it receded in the distance wasn't easy, and he finally set down the gun.

He untwisted the cap on a bottle of water, sipped the unpleasantly warm liquid, and poured some over his knee, wiping away blood and dirt. The puncture wounds were circled with red, probably already infected. He opened his first-aid kit, took out an antiseptic packet, and tore its edge. The sheet inside smelled of alcohol. He rubbed it over the holes and winced from the pain. He tore open a packet of antibiotic cream, smeared it over the holes, and covered them with gauze. Finally, he used his knife to cut strips of duct tape and secured the gauze to his knee, creating a pressure bandage that he hoped would stop the bleeding. Duct tape. He remembered what some of the security operators he'd worked with in Iraq called it. The gunfighter's friend.

He scanned the grassland, looking for more cameras.

When the BlackBerry vibrated again, he pulled the Kleenex wads from his ears and pressed the green button.

'Stop destroying the cameras,' the voice said.

'I thought the idea was for me to be resourceful.'

'Except for the vandalism, you're doing everything the way I imagined I myself would.'

'Then why don't you get down here and play the damned game yourself?'

No reply.

'Come on!' Balenger shouted into the BlackBerry. 'Be a hero!'

'But someone needs to be the Game Master.'

'Why?'

Again, the voice didn't reply.

'Think about it a different way,' Balenger said. 'We talked about a flaw in the game, the fact that you couldn't keep track of me. How about the flaw in the universe?'

'The game and the universe. Both the same. What flaw are you talking about?'

'God became lonely and created other beings, magnificent ones, angels, and that's how evil got started because some of those angels betrayed Him. Then God became lonely again, but He thought He'd learned his lesson and created lesser beings, humans, so insignificant that they couldn't possibly have the pride to betray Him. They betrayed Him nonetheless. Is that your problem?'

'That people betray me?'

'That you're lonely? You want someone to play with?'

In the distance, a hawk cried while the phone became silent.

'We'd be delighted to play with you,' Balenger told the Game Master, 'as long as you don't kill us.'

'Sometimes . . .' the voice said.

'Yes?'

'You confuse me.'

Balenger felt a surge of hope.

'How can I possibly come down and play with you? You're not real.'

The transmission went dead.

'The rounds in this Mini-14 are real,' Balenger murmured. He put the BlackBerry in his pocket, looked for more cameras to destroy, and moved forward.

5

Hands bleeding, Amanda lifted the door at one end, Ray at the other, and helped carry it from the shelter that she and Viv had built the previous night. She recalled Viv sharing water with her and saying that they needed to work together if they were going to survive.

And now Viv was dead.

The shock remained numbing as she worked with Ray to carry the door. Her knees felt limp, her boots heavy. Hunger made her sluggish, but she wouldn't allow herself to give in to weakness. Not long ago, she'd heard yet another shot, still closer, and if Frank was coming, as the Game Master promised, she wouldn't let him see a quitter. She would do everything she could to help. She would work until she dropped.

That almost happened. Her boot struck a rock. She nearly fell with the door, but she regained her footing and plodded on, coming to the walkway she and Ray had constructed in the mud.

'This ought to do it,' Ray said.

He moved backward down the slope, holding his end of the door. Amanda followed, taking short steps that helped her stay upright on the downward-tilted boards.

When they reached the precarious bottom, they lowered the door to the walkway, setting it on its side so that Ray had room to shift along it, moving higher, reaching Amanda. The boards below them wavered on the mud. Around them, the stench of decay was nauseating. They upended the door so that it stood on its bottom. They walked it forward to the end of the boards, shoved it, and let it flop in the mud. Muck flew. Twenty feet away, a snake hissed.

The door landed next to the mysterious object whose rim was the only part that was visible.

The boards beneath them wobbled. Amanda and Ray held out their arms for balance.

'Too much weight.' Amanda bent her knees, trying for

a low center of gravity. 'We can't both be in the same area.' She stepped on to the door, which settled but held. 'I'm lighter. I'm the logical one to do this.'

Ray stepped on to higher boards.

Gradually, what they stood on became steady.

Amanda pivoted toward the rim of the object embedded in the mud. Four feet by three feet. Muck was inside it. 'I still have no idea what this thing is.'

She knelt and peered warily into it, making sure a snake wasn't inside. 'So what am I supposed to do? Scoop out the mud and see if anything's buried?'

She tugged out one of the rubber gloves. She put it on her right hand, hesitated, then sank the glove into the mud. She didn't feel anything and groped deeper. The pressure of the mud rose almost to her elbow, reaching the upper limit of the glove's sleeve.

'Find anything?' Ray asked.

'A lot of goo.' Afraid she might fall in, she knelt farther forward. 'Wait a second.' Her fingers touched something hard. Round. The edges were rough. She closed her gloved fingers around it.

'Careful,' Ray said. 'For all we know, there's a trap inside. Something sharp.'

'No, feels like a . . .'

She strained her arm to pull the object free. The suction almost pulled the glove off.

'A rock,' she said, looking at the object in her hand. 'Just a rock.' But she knew that seemingly insignificant objects often turned out to be important in the game, so she tossed it on to the bank. 'I felt a lot of other rocks in there, also.'

'Maybe something's under them,' Ray suggested.

'But I don't know how to reach under them to find out.'

Ray checked his watch. 'Twenty after two. Less than ten hours to go. We've wasted more time.' He frowned at something below her. 'On the rim in front of you. The mud's drying. Does it look like something's engraved in the metal underneath?'

Amanda looked where he pointed. She rubbed the drying mud. 'Numbers.' Although she tried to sound triumphant, her voice had the tone of the crust she broke away. 'Two sets. LT before one. LG before the other.'

'Map coordinates,' Ray said.

Amanda wiped mud off the rim to the right and left. 'Same thing here. I bet the numbers are on the opposite rim also – to guarantee we saw them, no matter which side we approached from.'

'Read them to me.' Ray programmed them into his GPS receiver. He studied the needle. 'Points west. But I don't know where exactly. The reservoir slope's in the way.'

Amanda staggered up the boards. 'Let's find out.'

scavenger

6

Balenger's earlier suspicion was accurate – the rumble he'd heard was the sound of the dam being breached. As he came to the muddy basin and peered down at the devastation, he was puzzled why the muck seemed to move, until he realized there were snakes. Appalled, he shifted his gaze toward the deepest section and was startled to see two figures across from him. They were on a makeshift walkway that led down to a rectangular metal object in the mud.

One figure was a lanky, beard-stubbled man in a dirty green jumpsuit. The other was a shorter figure in a blue jumpsuit and cap smeared with mud. That figure's back was turned, but with a surge of excitement, Balenger instantly knew who it was.

Overjoyed, he opened his mouth to shout 'Amanda!' But the emotion shooting through him seized his throat shut. The sight of her made him dizzy.

On the opposite slope, the man noticed Balenger and blurted something to Amanda. She whirled. Her face was as muddy as her jumpsuit. But there was no mistaking it. Balenger's heart pounded so fiercely that he thought it might break.

Amanda took a moment, as if she didn't dare hope that the person she saw was actual. Then she stood straighter, and her smile – in the midst of her muddy cheeks – was dazzling.

Balenger managed to get his voice to work and ask the most important question. '*Are you hurt?*'

'Lots of small stuff, but I'm still moving!' She pointed. 'Your leg! It's bleeding!'

'Dog bite!'

'*What?*'

'I've got the bleeding stopped. Your hands!'

'Lost some skin. Broke some nails. My hands were never my best feature anyway!'

Balenger swelled with love for her.

The man shouted, '*Have you got food?*'

'Yes. And water!'

'Thank God!' The man climbed the walkway.

Balenger watched Amanda follow him. Making her way up the boards, she looked repeatedly over her shoulder, determined to keep her eyes on him as much as possible.

For his part, Balenger never took his gaze off her all the while he hurried toward the shallow end of the basin.

'I thought you were dead!' Amanda shouted, moving parallel to him.

'I thought *you* were dead!' Balenger yelled back.

'What happened to you?'

'No time!' Balenger shouted. 'I'll tell you when we've got the chance!'

Getting closer, Balenger saw that both Amanda and her companion wore headsets with microphone stubs. They reached the narrow end of the basin, where an old bridge spanned the creek that fed the reservoir. On the opposite side, Amanda rushed toward the bridge.

'Stop!' Balenger warned, his instincts alarming him. 'Stay off the bridge! It might be a trap!'

Amanda and her companion faltered.

'Food!' the man shouted. 'We're dying over here!'

Balenger took off his knapsack, removed two energy bars, and hurled them over the bridge. He was shocked by the desperation with which Amanda and her companion ran to them. They tore off the wrappers and chewed frantically. He was reminded of the two dogs who'd attacked him and how the energy bars had driven them into a frenzy. He tossed two bottles of water into grass on the other side of the creek.

Amanda and the man lunged to them and twisted off the caps.

'Slowly!' Balenger yelled.

'We know!' The man's eyes flashed a warning, as if he hated being told what to do.

'The last time we ate was yesterday afternoon,' Amanda said. 'A few chunks of canned fruit.'

Knowing cameras were focused on him, Balenger tried not to show how enraged he felt. Jonathan, he thought, for a rare time using the Game Master's name, you're going to pay.

He peered under the bridge. The shadows were thick. He took his flashlight from the knapsack, moved closer to the bridge, and knelt, aiming the light. Strapped to a shelf, a dark, rectangular object had a smaller object attached to it.

'A bomb,' Balenger said.

Amanda and her companion stopped chewing the energy bars. They stepped back.

'The bastard,' the man said. 'I should have thought.'

'Because you're starving,' Balenger said. 'Those energy bars will help.' He went down to the creek and decided that the water couldn't be electrified if the snakes survived in it. He splashed through a shallow section and climbed to the other side.

Amanda hurried to him, holding out her arms. Balenger couldn't wait to embrace her. But she surprised him by abruptly stopping. 'Stay away.'

'What's wrong?' he asked.

'He planted explosives on us.'

'What?'

'We don't know if they're in our boots, our headsets, or these GPS receivers.' She pulled a unit from her pocket and showed it to him.

Now Balenger understood the image he'd seen on his BlackBerry: the woman exploding.

'The microphone on the headset also functions as a video camera,' the man explained.

'Yeah,' Balenger said acidly, 'the Game Master likes cameras.'

The man lowered his bottle of water. 'You *know* about him?'

Balenger nodded. 'I don't think he's going to blow us

up now that he finally got us together.'

Balenger walked to Amanda, touched her muddy face, and grinned. 'I can't tell you how much I missed you.'

When they kissed, it went on and on. He didn't want it to end. Although midnight loomed, he needed to hold her for ever. But abruptly she broke the kiss and pressed her cheek against him, shuddering.

He leaned back, not bothering to wipe away the mud that had brushed from her cheek to his. 'We can do this. We can get out of here.'

Her eyes changed focus, as if she was listening to a distant voice. 'The Game Master says to tell you to put on Derrick's headset. He wants to talk to you.'

'Derrick?' Balenger frowned. 'How many others are there?'

'We started with five.' For a moment, Amanda couldn't bring herself to speak. 'Three are dead.'

'Three?' Balenger felt stunned. 'Where's the headset?'

'I'm not sure,' Amanda said. 'It must be over where . . .' She looked at her companion, who in turn looked away. 'It must be there.' She pointed behind her, toward the ruins of a town.

'Show me.'

As they walked, the man said, 'I'm Ray Morgan.'

'Frank Balenger.'

They shook hands.

'Yeah, the Game Master talked about you,' Ray said.

'I'm sure it was flattering.'

'I don't suppose you've got any cigarettes.'

'Afraid not.'

'It figures.' Ray had an edge in his voice. 'I ate the energy bar slowly, like you said. Got any more?'

Balenger opened his knapsack and pulled out two more bars and two more bottles of water.

This time, Amanda and Ray weren't frenzied when they tore open the bars.

'I was surc wc'd lost so much strength from hunger and thirst that we couldn't win the game,' Ray said.

'*Scavenger.*'

'You know about that too?' Amanda asked in surprise.

'The Game Master and I had some heart-to-heart chats,' Balenger said.

'When I saw you, I wondered if I was hallucinating.' Ray gestured toward Balenger's tan camouflage suit. 'You look like you stepped out of Iraq.'

Something about Ray's bearing made Balenger ask, 'You've been there?'

'Marine aviator.'

'I was a Ranger in the first Iraq war. Proud to know you, Marine, although I wish to God it was under other circumstances.'

'Roger to that.'

Amanda pressed a hand to her headset. She sounded puzzled when she turned toward Balenger. 'The Game Master wants to know if you've heard of the Doomsday Vault.'

'No, but I bet he's going to tell me.'

They entered the ruins of the town. Balenger saw a pile of boards in the middle of the weed-studded street. The smell from it told him something dead was under there.

When he glanced at Amanda, expecting an explanation, she gave him a warning look. Ray appeared uneasy. Balenger didn't raise the subject.

'Where's the headset?' he asked.

Amanda listened to her ear buds. 'The Game Master says . . .' She pointed. 'There.'

Balenger walked to the edge of a collapsed building and found the headset among more boards. He picked it up and examined it. Specks of dried blood were on it. Remembering the cautionary look Amanda had given him, he didn't ask about the blood. The sturdy headband was thin. The ear buds and microphone-camera were compact. He opened a small battery case on the left side of the headband.

'I don't see any space for a detonator,' he said. 'There doesn't seem room inside the headband or the ear buds for plastic explosive. Maybe in the microphone. But I think the more likely place for a bomb is in your boots or your GPS receivers.' He glanced down at Amanda's mud-covered boots. 'Did they get wet?'

'Soaked.'

'The detonator would need to be awfully watertight not to short out. I could be wrong, but I think the GPS units are the bombs.'

Amanda listened to her ear buds. 'The Game Master says, put on the headset.'

Balenger took off his hat. Under the weight of the sun, he adjusted the headset to his ears, then replaced the hat. 'So what's the Doomsday Vault?' he asked the Game Master. He scanned the wreckage, looking for a camera.

'You're supposed to be suffering from post-traumatic stress disorder,' the voice said.

'I am. I've got a fan club of psychiatrists to prove it.'

'But you don't show weakness.'

'I'm goal-oriented. Give me a task, and I focus on it so hard I forget I'm a psychological mess.' Balenger continued to survey the wreckage. 'And believe me, I'm a mess. Can't sleep without a light. Can't stand closed doors. I have nightmares about a guy who wants to cut off my head. I tremble for no reason. I wake up screaming. The bed sheets are soaked with sweat. After this is over, after we win, I guarantee I'll fall apart.'

'You're confident you'll win?'

'Anybody who plays a game and doesn't intend to win has already lost. I have a question for you. How did you know where the headset was?'

Noticing what he searched for, Balenger pulled out his ear buds and inserted the wads of Kleenex. He raised his rifle.

'What are you doing?' Ray asked in alarm. He and Amanda stepped quickly to the side.

The camera was concealed in a jumble of boards. Balenger imposed the holographic red dot on the camera's lens and squeezed the trigger. *Crack.* Absorbing the recoil, he was vaguely aware of the empty shell flipping through the air. Amid the smell of burned gunpowder, he lowered the rifle and regarded with satisfaction the catastrophic damage that his bullet had inflicted on the camera.

He took the wads of Kleenex from his ears. 'That's another Peeping Tom we don't need to worry about.'

'Now listen to me carefully,' the Game Master said. 'That's the last time you destroy an essential part of the game.'

'Oh?'

'If you do it again, I'll detonate the explosive in Miss Evert's GPS receiver.'

I'm right, Balenger thought. That's where the bombs are. 'Even at the expense of ending the game?'

'Without the cameras, there *isn't* a game. Do you believe I'll do it?'

Balenger turned toward Amanda, who looked terrified. 'Yes.'

'Then leave the cameras alone and play the damned game.'

'Okay, we'll play the damned game.'

The tension in Amanda's body subsided.

'Any other restrictions?' Balenger asked. 'You claim you want us to be resourceful, but when we are, you complain. If we don't have a chance, tell us now, and save us a lot of trouble.'

'*Scavenger* can be won. I don't create unfair games.'

'Right,' Balenger said. 'I'm late to this level. Somebody bring me up to speed.'

'We found map coordinates engraved on whatever that thing is buried in the reservoir.' Ray indicated his GPS receiver, which he handled with considerable misgiving. 'The needle points *that* way. West.'

'Toward those mountains,' Balenger said.

'Or whatever's between the mountains and us,' Amanda said. 'I also found rocks in that thing in the mud.'

'Rocks?'

'I threw one on to the bank.'

Balenger touched her shoulder in a way that he hoped communicated reassurance. 'Show me where.'

7

They passed the pile of boards from which the smell of death rose in the afternoon sun. Amanda stared at Ray. Again, Balenger didn't comment.

'The Doomsday Vault,' he said to the microphone. 'You still haven't told me about it.'

'The ultimate time capsule,' the Game Master replied. 'It's a chamber in a mountain on an island in the Arctic Circle. The island is called Spitsbergen. Norway owns it.'

They reached the outskirts of the wreckage of Avalon, from which King Arthur would never rise, Balenger thought, recalling the myth.

'What makes it the ultimate time capsule?' Ahead, Balenger saw the rim of the breached reservoir.

'Because it literally contains a form of time. The chamber is immense: the size of half a football field.'

'A form of time? What's inside: an atomic clock? Whatever it is, it must be gigantic.'

'Actually, the reverse. Most of the objects are very small.'

Balenger paused on the rim of the drained reservoir. 'Small?'

'Millions of them.'

Balenger peered toward the metal rim of the rectangular object hidden in the mud. 'What makes them a form of time?'

'They're seeds.'

'I don't understand.' Balenger felt a rising apprehension.

'For every type of edible plant on Earth,' the Game Master said. 'Those seeds contain ten thousand years of experimental breeding. When humans started practicing agriculture, the process was trial and error. They took wild plants and tried to domesticate them. Many of the grains and vegetables were small and didn't hold anywhere near the nutrition we now take for granted. Maize, for example – what we call corn – was a wild grass with ears only a couple of inches long and just a few rows of kernels. Several millennia of careful breeding resulted in the large plants we have today.'

'Why are these seeds being put in a chamber in a mountain in the Arctic Circle?'

'Because a number of scientists and countries are worried about the ability of human beings to survive,' the Game Master answered. 'It's not only global warming that frightens them. A nuclear holocaust poses an increasing risk. Or suppose a virus makes unprotected seeds sterile? Or what if an asteroid strikes the earth? There are near hits that we've never been told about. These days, though, it's not nature but ourselves that we need to fear. If clusters of humans manage to survive global devastation, the Doomsday Vault will provide them with the seeds necessary to grow food.'

'First, people would need to know where it is,' Balenger said. 'This vault isn't exactly common knowledge.'

'Its location needs to be kept secret to protect it. Barriers and vacuum-locked doors prevent its contents from being stolen.'

'So even if I knew where to find this thing, I couldn't get in.'

'Those in authority know where it is and how to unseal the doors.'

'Suppose they're killed in the disaster they're afraid of.'

'You'd better hope they aren't. Without the Doomsday Vault, a global catastrophe would force humans to regress ten thousand years to the dawn of agriculture and begin the process of selectively breeding seeds all over again. That's why it's a time capsule. Preserved in the cold sleep of the Arctic, it sends ten thousand years to an uncertain future.'

'Cold sleep?' Balenger frowned. 'If global warming's a fact, the Arctic Circle will melt, the temperature in the vault will rise, and the seeds won't be preserved.'

'If global warming's a fact? *Nothing's* a fact.'

'This game is a fact. The dog bite on my knee is a fact. Amanda's cut hands are a fact.' Balenger looked at her. 'Where's the rock you took from whatever that thing is in the reservoir? Where did you throw it?'

'Over here.' Amanda picked it up. Caked with dried mud, the rock was the size of a fist, its surface uneven.

Balenger felt its heaviness. He returned to the stream and rinsed it. The rock was gray.

'There's another color,' Amanda said.

'Worldly desires, worldly vanities.' Balenger's voice was hushed.

'My God, is that . . .' Ray took the rock from him and turned it over. 'Gold! Holy . . . A vein of gold straight through it.'

The gold's yellow was pale and dirty. But it had a primordial allure, all the same. Balenger's gaze lingered on it. Then he looked across the valley, in the direction that Ray's GPS needle had pointed, toward the mountains to the north.

'The mine,' Ray said.

Amanda indicated the object buried in the reservoir's

mud. 'Finally I think I know what that thing is. It's a mining car.'

'With ore in it,' Balenger added.

Ray murmured. 'The Hall of Records.'

'What?' Balenger was troubled by the sudden change of topic.

'The Game Master gave us the clue, but we didn't recognize what it was. Mount Rushmore. The Hall of Records.'

'I still don't get it.'

Amanda explained, 'The Game Master told us that when they started to carve the presidents on Mount Rushmore, the Great Depression was at its worst. The monument's designers got so worried that riots would destroy the country, they built a chamber under the monument. The idea was that crucial documents such as the Declaration of Independence would be protected there. But then the Depression ended, the risk of social chaos disappeared, and the only documents eventually sealed there described the history of the monument.'

'Under the mountain.' Ray's voice strengthened. 'Damn it, he gave us the answer, but we didn't know it. The Sepulcher's in one of those mountains! In the mine!' He looked frantically at his watch. 'It's almost three thirty.' He studied the needle on his GPS receiver, splashed across the stream, and hurried through the scrub grass toward the mountains.

Balenger waited until Ray was out of earshot. Then

he took off his cap, wiped his brow, and removed the headset. He took off Amanda's headset as well and tapped the microphones against his leg so Ray wouldn't hear their conversation.

'What didn't you want to tell me?'

'That pile of boards,' Amanda answered.

'What about it?'

'There's a body underneath.'

'I smelled it.'

'I mentioned a man named Derrick. Ray beat him to death.'

'Beat him to . . .?' Balenger felt choked by the unstated word.

The BlackBerry vibrated in his pocket. Emotions swirling, he answered it.

'Put the headsets back on, or I'll set off the detonator,' the voice ordered.

Balenger directed his answer toward the sky. 'Jonathan, did you enjoy that part of the game?'

'Don't call me Jonathan. I'm the Game Master.'

Amanda looked amazed that Balenger knew the Game Master's name.

'Did you enjoy watching someone get beaten to death?' Balenger asked.

'Nothing in the game is planned. No one could have predicted that the beating would occur.'

Balenger pressed the BlackBerry to his ear. 'But did you enjoy watching it happen?'

Silence lengthened.

'Yes,' the Game Master said. 'I enjoyed it. Put on the headsets.'

'I'm standing so close to Amanda, you'll kill both of us if you detonate the explosives. You're cheering for me, remember. I'm your avatar. It'd be like killing yourself.'

'Killing myself? Are you an analyst now? Because you went to all those psychiatrists, do you think that qualifies you as one?'

'You have an interesting concept of human character. I wonder if *you* ever went to an analyst.'

'One last time. Put on the headsets.' The voice was tight with anger.

Balenger quit tapping the microphones against his pants. He gave Amanda her headset, then put on his own.

Ray's voice instantly intruded. 'What were you talking about that you didn't want me to hear?' He stood a hundred yards away in the grassland, staring at them.

'We were just discussing some finer points of the game,' Balenger said.

'Like what?'

'Actually, it was private, some guy–girl stuff we didn't want to embarrass you with.'

'Bull. She told you what was under that stack of boards.'

'Hey, we're all in this together. There's no point in keeping secrets,' Balenger said.

Ray didn't reply. Even from a distance, his anger was

obvious. He turned and continued to the west in the direction that the needle on his GPS receiver indicated.

8

As they followed Ray, Amanda ate another energy bar. She told Balenger what had happened since she'd wakened in the bedroom. The concern Balenger felt was matched by hers when he described what had happened since he'd wakened in the ruins of the Paragon Hotel. Throughout, he kept glancing to his right, where the two dogs, having returned, moved parallel to him about fifty yards away. He raised his rifle. They scurried off.

Ahead, Ray peered down at something in the grass. Whatever he found excited him enough to make him walk faster toward the mountains. When Balenger reached that area, he stepped into the deep furrows of an old wagon road.

'For the mine,' Amanda said.

They started along it, noting how the furrows stretched toward the mountains. Balenger could almost hear the rattle of wheels and plod of hooves from the countless wagons that came and went, bringing supplies to the mine and carrying away gold. The road seemed to lead toward a middle mountain. After an hour's walking, the peak loomed. The dogs came back but kept a wary distance.

Ray stopped and waited for them. He pulled his lighter from his jumpsuit, clicking it open and shut. 'Why are you staying back? Does your knee hurt?'

'Nothing I can't deal with.'

'If it's giving you trouble, I need to know. I can't waste time waiting for you to catch up.'

'I can manage.'

'I mean if you can't keep pace with me, maybe I should take the rifle so it doesn't weigh you down.'

'The rifle's not heavy.'

'I could use more water.'

Balenger gave him a bottle. 'Only five left.'

'Not enough.'

'We can make it last till midnight. The main thing is, keep a positive attitude.'

'I heard enough about a positive attitude when I was in the Marines.' Ray opened and shut the lighter again. 'Amanda gave you the wrong idea.'

'Wrong idea?'

'What happened back there was self-defense.'

'I wouldn't know. I didn't see it.'

'He came at me with a rock.'

Ray didn't give the corpse a name, Balenger noted. 'A man needs to defend himself.'

'Damned straight.' Ray put the lighter away.

They followed the old wagon road toward the mountains. Balenger felt a premonition, wondering why the town hadn't been built close to its principal customers.

Amanda pointed. 'I think I see the mine.'

While the slopes on either side were grassy, the one straight ahead was denuded. Only chunks of rock covered the incline. Balenger saw what appeared to be railroad tracks at the bottom, in a line with the road, emerging from the rocks.

Ruins came into view, a chaos of boards where several large buildings had collapsed. A breeze blew dust.

'No grass. Not even weeds,' Balenger said.

'The gold made a wasteland.' After a long absence, the voice was startling. 'The ore was sledgehammered, drilled and blasted from the tunnels. Exhausted men filled mining cars and pushed them along tracks. Emerging into sunlight, they used the brakes on the cars to keep them from running down the slope. In what was once a building on your left, steam-powered grinders reduced the ore to bits. The result was mixed with liquid poison, a solution of sodium cyanide that separated the gold from the pulverized rock. But cyanide isn't the only reason for the sterility around you. Sulphuric acid was another ingredient used to separate the gold from the rock.'

'Is that why the town's a distance from the mine?' Balenger asked.

'The fumes from the acid could be smelled for miles,' the Game Master replied. 'A lot of the miners died from lung diseases.'

The sun descended beyond the mountain. A shadow brought a chill.

'Where's the entrance?' Amanda wondered. 'It's got to be in a line with the railroad tracks.'

They walked to where the tracks angled uphill. A landslide had buried the upper part of the tracks.

With Amanda and Ray on either side of him, Balenger climbed the slope, his boots dislodging rocks. He stopped on a level area and faced a wall of rock.

'This is where the entrance probably was,' Ray said. 'Where we're standing.'

'The tunnel must have collapsed,' Balenger said. A suspicion made him add, 'Or else it was buried for the game.'

Amanda peered down at her scraped fingers. 'There's no way we can clear it by hand.'

The shadow they stood in lengthened, becoming cooler.

Balenger thought about the possibilities. 'The Game Master wouldn't give us an obstacle unless there's a way to get around it.'

'Explosives would do it,' Amanda replied.

'But where the hell are we going to find them?' Ray gestured in exasperation. 'If Mr Positive Attitude here was thinking, he'd have brought the explosives from under the bridge. But now it's too late to go back for them.'

'Would you have risked carrying them?' Balenger asked. Ray avoided his gaze. 'Anyway, we don't have a radio or know the frequency that would set off the detonator.'

Amanda studied him. 'You can't set off explosives without a detonator?'

'Nitroglycerine's so unstable you can blow it up simply by dropping it. But explosives that are safe to handle need a jumpstart.'

'And only a radio signal can set off a detonator?'

'Or a pressure switch or a fuse attached to a blasting cap. There are several ways, but the Game Master seems to prefer a radio signal. What are you getting at?'

'What about an impact?' Amanda asked.

'Impact?'

'A bullet. Would *that* set off the detonator?'

'Yes.' Ray sounded like he was talking to a child. 'A bullet would set off a detonator. In Iraq, sometimes unexploded bombs blew up if something banged against them while they were being dug out. But that doesn't change the fact that the explosives and the detonator are miles behind us, back in town.'

'I wasn't thinking of those,' Amanda said.

'Then for God's sake, what are you talking about?'

Amanda showed them her GPS receiver.

They stared at it.

'He'd never let us try it,' Ray said.

'If we *don't* try it, we'll still be on this slope at midnight, and this is probably what the Game Master will use to destroy us,' Amanda told them.

They didn't move. They didn't even seem to breathe.

Balenger asked Ray, 'Can you think of an alternative?'

'No.'

'Game Master, do you truly want us to be resourceful?'

The Game Master didn't answer.

Balenger set down his rifle and started lifting rocks.

'But we don't have time to dig our way in!' Ray said.

'I'm making a hole for the GPS unit. The deeper it is, the more force the explosion will have.'

Immediately, Amanda and Ray helped him.

'Angle the hole so it points down the slope,' Balenger said. 'I need to see the receiver from down there.'

Amanda and Ray made the hole a couple of feet deep. Balenger noticed that Amanda's hands had started bleeding again. He saw too that nervousness made her tremble when she set her GPS unit into the hole.

Once more Balenger peered toward the sky. 'Game Master, if you've got a problem with this, tell us now.'

The voice remained silent.

'This could be the last moment we know we're alive,' Ray said.

'I prefer my positive attitude.' To the sky, Balenger said, 'It's awfully lonely being God if you have no one to talk to. You enjoy your conversations with us. Why end the entertainment when there's more to the game?'

The voice continued to remain silent.

Balenger picked up his rifle. 'Then let's do it.'

Rocks clattered as they descended. Needing cover, they went to the largest pile of wreckage.

Balenger waited until Amanda and Ray lay flat. 'Put your hands over your ears,' he told her. 'Open your mouth to relieve the pressure.'

He shoved the Kleenex wads in his ears, then knelt on his good knee and aimed the rifle. The gun's stock was solid against his shoulder. But the GPS receiver was difficult to see, gray against the rocks. The shadow of the mountains didn't help.

'Problems?' Ray asked.

'Just making sure.'

'Let *me* try.'

Balenger squeezed the trigger.

The roar of the blast jolted him, its concussion shoving him back. He dropped to the ground, landing on his right side, holding the rifle off the ground. Debris pelted around him. He felt the impact of a rock landing near his head. Despite the Kleenex wads in his ears, he heard ringing. Dust blew over him, acrid with the smell of detonated explosives.

The echoing rumble lessened. He looked toward Amanda, relieved to see that she wasn't injured. She rose to a crouch and peered toward the slope. Ray came to his feet. So did Balenger, who surveyed the slope, pleased to see a huge opening. He took the Kleenex from his ears and stepped from the wreckage.

Amanda hurried toward the slope. 'I see a door!'

They scrambled up the rocks and reached the

opening. A barrier of old gray wood was visible at the end, jagged from flying rocks.

Balenger saw hinges, a handle. 'Yes, a door.'

The force of the explosion had knocked it askew. They stepped over rubble and pushed, toppling it inward. Dust made them cough.

Amanda and Ray leaned inside.

'Can't see much,' Ray said. 'Let's widen this opening.' He shoved boards away.

Daylight probed twenty feet into the tunnel. Railroad tracks went down the middle. Posts held up roof supports.

'Looks solid,' Amanda said.

Balenger aimed his flashlight, revealing more of the tunnel. But deeper inside, darkness confronted him. Closed spaces, he thought with a shiver.

Ray hesitated. 'Do you think it's safe to go in?'

'Do we have a choice?' Amanda asked.

Balenger studied the walls and saw a small video camera attached to a roof beam. 'We're in the right place. The tunnel's monitored.'

'I don't see any container, anything that might be a time capsule,' Ray said.

Balenger gave Amanda the flashlight. 'Stay just behind me and point the light. I'll take the lead.'

He ejected the magazine from his rifle, pulled a box of ammunition from his knapsack, and reloaded.

LEVEL NINE: THE SEPULCHER OF WORLDLY DESIRES

1

The temperature cooled. The air smelled stale. Balenger's boots made scraping sounds on the rock floor as he shifted forward through shadows.

'When I was a kid,' Ray said, 'a couple of friends and I explored a cave.' He sounded like he was trying to distract himself.

'Find anything interesting?' Amanda asked.

'I got stuck.'

'What?'

'My friends bicycled for help. I was in there ten hours before an emergency crew got me out.'

'I'm not sure that helps me keep my positive attitude,' Balenger said.

'Hey, I got out, didn't I? Can't get more positive than that. Quit complaining. Wait. Stop. Shine the light to the left. There. On the floor.'

Amanda pointed the light in that direction and revealed two dusty rounded objects.

Ray hurried to them and picked one up. 'Lanterns!' He blew dust away, then rubbed the curved glass with his sleeve. When he shook the lantern, something splashed inside.

'My God, it still has fuel in it.'

Balenger frowned. 'The fuel didn't evaporate after more than a hundred years?'

'How could it evaporate? The cap to the fuel tank is tight,' Ray answered.

'It could evaporate through the wick.'

Ray pulled up the glass sheath and studied the wick. 'Maybe the wick acted as a plug so the air couldn't get at the fuel. What difference does it make? The point is, we can use this thing.' He pulled out his lighter.

'No,' Balenger said.

Ray put his thumb on the lighter's wheel.

'Don't!' Balenger grabbed Ray's hand.

In the flashlight's glare, Ray's eyes darkened. 'Let go.'

'Put away the lighter.'

'I'm warning you.' Ray's voice was hoarse. 'Let go.'

Balenger took his hand away. 'Just listen.'

Ray put the lighter in his pocket.

'The Game Master didn't object when we used the GPS receiver to blow our way in here. That's not like him,' Balenger said.

Ray set down the lantern.

'Are we supposed to believe that we impressed him with how resourceful we are? I don't think so,' Balenger continued.

With a scream of fury, Ray grabbed the stock and

barrel of the rifle. Balenger felt a jolt when Ray shoved it across his chest and rammed him toward a wall. Balenger's boot caught on a railway track. As he fell, Ray dropped with him, landing on him, squeezing the rifle across his chest. Balenger's hands were pinned under the gun. He struggled to push back, but the pressure of the rifle made it difficult to breathe.

'Keep your fucking hands off me!' Ray shouted.

Balenger strained harder.

'Don't tell me what to do!' Ray's face was twisted with rage. He was surprisingly strong, his movements a frenzy, pressing the air from Balenger's lungs.

'Stop!' Amanda screamed.

Squirming on the tunnel's cold floor, Balenger couldn't free his hands. He tried to knee Ray in the groin, but Ray's legs pinned him down. Abruptly, Ray slammed his forehead down on Balenger's nose.

Balenger felt an excruciating crack. Blood spurted from his nose. His mind dimmed.

'Damn you, stop!' Amanda yelled.

Peering up through double vision, Balenger saw Amanda charge into view and tug at Ray.

'Get off him! Don't you understand what he's trying to tell you?'

Again Ray slammed his forehead on to Balenger's nose. Balenger groaned, seeing gray. He fought to breathe.

'The lanterns are a trap!' Amanda shouted. 'The GPS unit! Why didn't the Game Master complain?'

Ray's eyes were slits of rage. He pressed all his weight on the rifle across Balenger's chest. Amanda pulled at his shoulders.

'He wanted us to get into the tunnel! He wants us to feel confident and let our guard down!'

Amanda put an arm around Ray's throat. He jabbed his head back, smashing her face. She staggered away.

'The lanterns might explode!' Amanda shrieked. 'Or a flame might set off gas in the tunnel!'

Balenger felt lightheaded, his nose filling with blood, his lungs unable to draw air.

A shadow rose behind Ray. Balenger's gray vision made him think he was hallucinating. The shadow held a rock with both hands. The shadow slammed the rock down so hard that Balenger felt the shock go through him. Ray's head sprayed blood. The shadow struck again. The crunch of bone was accompanied by a liquid sound.

Balenger saw Ray's dark eyes widen. They rolled up. The shadow struck a third time, and now the sound was hollow.

Ray trembled, wheezing. It was as if the strings on a puppet had been snipped. At once he dropped on to Balenger, his dead weight adding to the pressure on Balenger's chest.

Balenger's mind sank. Blood clogging his swollen nostrils, he felt as if something heavy was forcing him deep into water. The weight suddenly left his chest. Hands pushed Ray's body away and turned Balenger face down in the tunnel. Blood drained from his nose.

'Breathe!' Amanda shouted.

He coughed and managed to get his lungs working. Air moved along his raw throat. On the cold floor, he heard the echo of Amanda's own raspy breathing. Slowly, he managed to sit up. Dim light from the tunnel's entrance showed her standing over him, her back against a wall. She slid down next to the flashlight on the floor. Its glare made her face look stark.

'Is he . . .' She couldn't finish thc question.

'Yes.'

'The son of a bitch,' she said.

'Yes.'

'I feel sick.'

'Violence will do that.'

For a while, the only sound was the continuing echo of their breathing.

'He didn't give me a choice.'

'That's right,' Balenger agreed. 'Keep telling yourself that. He didn't give you a choice. If you hadn't stopped him, he'd probably have killed me.' But he knew that no matter how much he tried to assure her, it wouldn't matter. She had something else to add to her nightmares. 'How bad are you hurt?'

'My cheek's swelling where he banged his head against it. You?'

'My nose is broken.'

Balenger pulled off his knapsack. His back hurt from the indentations the ammunition boxes had made when he fell on them. He poured a palmful of water from his canteen and wiped it across his face, trying to clear the blood. Then he got his first-aid kit and tore open an antiseptic wipe.

'Let me.' Amanda crawled toward him and gently wiped his face.

Balenger tried not to react to the pain. 'I hope you don't mind rugged features.'

'I always wanted to live with a man who looks like a boxer.'

In the flashlight's glare, Balenger studied the bruise on her left cheek.

They held each other.

'Thank you,' Balenger whispered.

He didn't want to let go. But then he looked over her shoulder toward Ray's body. 'The tunnel. The Sepulcher. Midnight.'

Amanda nodded. 'If we don't meet the deadline, all the Game Master needs to do is blast the tunnel and bury us. We'll never get out.'

Balenger turned toward a camera on a post. 'Game Master, did you enjoy seeing Ray die?'

He listened for a response, then realized that the headset and his hat had fallen off during the struggle. He put them back on, waiting for the Game Master to speak.

'Maybe the radio signal can't penetrate the tunnel,' Amanda said.

'Oh, it penetrates,' the voice said abruptly. 'Don't worry about that.'

Balenger gave three aspirins to Amanda and three to himself. They swallowed the pills with water. Balenger's nose continued to bleed. He put cotton batting into it, ignoring the pain.

'Ready?' he asked Amanda.

'Ready.'

She picked up the flashlight.

He put on his knapsack and reached for the rifle.

They continued along the tunnel. Abruptly, Balenger went back through the shadows. He grabbed one of the lanterns by its handle and gave it to Amanda.

'Why?' She studied it with suspicion.

'Not sure.' He overcame his revulsion and groped in a pocket of Ray's jumpsuit, pulling out the lighter. 'We never know what we might need.'

Again they proceeded along the tunnel, the flashlight partially dispelling the darkness.

'It's colder,' Amanda said.

They turned a corner.

'My favorite quotation comes from Kierkegaard. It's appropriate for a time capsule,' the voice said through Balenger's headset.

They approached a small chamber.

'What's the quote?' Keep him talking, Balenger thought. Keep him relating to us.

' "The most painful state of being is remembering the future, in particular one you can never have." '

'I don't understand.'

'It refers to someone who's dying and what it feels

like to imagine future events that he or she will never experience.'

The air got even colder. Amanda's hand trembled as she scanned the flashlight across the chamber. 'Looks like we found it,' she murmured.

2

In the shadows, a man faced them. He was tall and gangly with a beard that made him resemble Abraham Lincoln. His dark hair hung past his shoulders. He wore a black suit, the coat old-fashioned, its hem reaching down to his knees.

Balenger almost fired, but the man's posture didn't pose a threat, and Balenger's police training took control. As his instructor at the academy had said, 'You'd better have a damned good reason for pulling that trigger.'

The man stood straight, holding something close to his chest.

'Put up your hands! Who *are* you?' Balenger shouted.

The man didn't comply.

'Damn it, put up your hands!'

The only sound was the echo of Balenger's command.

'He isn't moving,' Amanda said.

They stepped warily forward, the flashlight providing details.

'Oh my God,' Amanda said.

The man had no eyes. His cheeks were shrunken. The fingers that clutched the object to his chest were bones covered with shriveled skin. Dust filmed him.

'Dead,' Amanda murmured.

'A long time,' Balenger said. 'But why didn't he rot?'

'I read somewhere that caves have hardly any insects or microbes.' Amanda's voice was hushed. 'And this tunnel's deep in the mountain. The ice.'

'What do you mean?'

'Another clue the Game Master gave us, but we didn't realize what it was. He said that in the winter the town harvested ice from the lake and stored it in the mine. The tunnel was cold enough to preserve the ice through the summer. The town used it to keep food from spoiling.'

'The cold mummified him,' Balenger said in awe.

'The object he's pressing against his chest looks like a book. But what's holding him up?' Amanda stepped closer.

Now it was clear that the corpse was tilted slightly back against a board supported by rocks at its base. Ropes at the knees, the stomach, the chest and the neck secured the mummy to the board.

'Who tied the ropes?' Balenger shivered, and not just from the cold.

'The knots are in front. Maybe he did it himself.' Amanda moved the flashlight up and down. 'He could have kept his hands free until he tied the final rope around his chest. Then he could have shoved his right hand up under the rope to press the book to his chest. Next to him, we see how the illusion works, but at the entrance to the chamber, he looked like he was greeting us.'

'Meet Reverend Owen Pentecost,' the Game Master said. But this time, the voice didn't come from Balenger's headset. Instead, it came from speakers in the walls. The echoing effect was unnerving.

'The bastard had a sense of drama,' Balenger said.

'You have no idea,' the Game Master replied.

'I suppose the book in his hand is a Bible.' Amanda tilted her head to try to read the title on the spine. When that didn't work, she set down the lantern, hesitated, then directed a finger toward the book, reluctantly intending to nudge it and expose the title.

Balenger grabbed her hand. 'It might be booby-trapped.'

In the flashlight's beam, the bruise on Amanda's cheek contrasted with her sudden pallor.

'Iraqi insurgents loved to hide pressure-sensitive bombs under US corpses,' Balenger explained. 'As soon as the bodies were lifted or turned, the explosives would detonate.'

Amanda pulled her hand back.

'It's not a Bible,' the Game Master said. 'It's called

The Gospel of the Sepulcher of Worldly Desires.'

'Not exactly catchy,' Balenger said.

'Pentecost wrote it in longhand. It predicts the evils of the coming century and the need for people to understand the truth.'

'So, what is the truth?'

'See for yourself.'

Amanda aimed the flashlight toward an opening in the wall behind Pentecost. Ready with his gun, Balenger stepped forward while she guided him with the flashlight. They went through the opening and entered a much larger area.

Amanda gasped.

Balenger tasted something bitter. 'Yeah, it's a sepulcher all right. Worldly desires.'

3

A cavern loomed. Stalactites and stalagmites partially blocked what Balenger and Amanda were staring at. Because of the limitations of the flashlight, it was impossible to see everything at once. Amanda needed to move the light from object to object, place to place, tableau to tableau.

Corpse to corpse.

The citizens of Avalon awaited them. They wore what

might have been their Sunday go-to-church clothes, now dusty and drab after more than a century. Like Pentecost's, their faces were sunken, cheekbones made prominent by withered flesh. Mummified in the tunnel's preserving cold, they looked tiny. Their clothes hung on their bodies like shrouds.

The group nearest Balenger and Amanda consisted of four men, who sat at a table, playing cards.

'Remember not to touch anything,' Balenger warned her.

The men were tied to the chairs, but unlike the ropes that secured Pentecost, these were concealed. The cards were glued to their hands. Their bent arms were nailed to the table. A pile of money lay before them.

At another table, men sat before a whiskey bottle and glasses covered with dust. Ropes and nails held the corpses in place.

'Sins,' Balenger murmured.

At a further table, this one long, he saw men, women and children seated before plates that might once have held mountains of food. Indistinguishable desiccated masses were all that remained. Bones from what looked like pork ribs and chicken drumsticks crammed their mouths.

On a bed, two naked female mummies lay beneath a naked man. In another bed, a man touched two naked children, male and female. Elsewhere, a naked man lay face down over a table while another naked man lay over him. Further on, a man had congress with a dog.

'It seems Reverend Pentecost had sexual hang-ups,' Amanda said.

A woman sat before a dusty mirror, a hairbrush and containers of dried makeup before her. A man lay face down on a table, a hole in his temple, a revolver in his hand. A mummy played a fiddle while a man and a woman danced in a close embrace that seemed impossible until Balenger realized that they were nailed to a board positioned between them and held up by a base of rocks.

Everywhere Amanda turned the flashlight, similar tableaux came into view.

'Music and dancing? Pentecost considered a lot of things to be sins,' Balenger said. The flashlight revealed a camera attached to a wall. Taking angry steps toward it, he asked the Game Master, 'Aside from the man with the bullet hole in his head, how did all these people die? What *was* this, a mass suicide like what happened when Jim Jones made his people drink poisoned Kool-Aid?'

'Flavor Aid,' the Game Master corrected him. 'The poison Jones used was cyanide. His church was the People's Temple. More than nine hundred of his followers committed suicide. At Jones's urging, they claimed to be protesting "the conditions of an inhumane world." In recent times, it's only one of many mass suicides motivated by religion. In the late 1990s, the members of the Order of the Solar Temple Movement killed themselves to escape the evils of this world and find refuge in a heavenly place named after the star

Sirius. The Heaven's Gate cult drank poisoned vodka so they could go to paradise by being transported to a spaceship concealed behind the approaching comet Hale–Bopp. But my personal favorite is the Movement for the Restoration of the Ten Commandments of God. They had visions of the Virgin Mary and believed that the world was going to end on December thirty-first, 1999, the eve of the recent millennium. When the apocalypse didn't arrive, they recalculated and decided that March seventeenth was the true date for the end of the world. More than eight hundred people died in anticipation of what they believed would be the end of worldly time.'

'So I'm right,' Balenger said. 'This *was* a mass suicide.'

'No. Not even the man with the bullet hole in his head is a suicide. The shot was delivered after he died.'

'Then . . .?'

'A mass murder,' the Game Master said. 'Pentecost killed all two hundred and seventeen townspeople, eighty-five of them children. For good measure, he included family pets.'

'So many people against one man.' Balenger could barely speak. 'Surely they could have stopped him.'

'They didn't know it was happening. Pentecost convinced them to come here on New Year's Eve of 1899 because they believed they were going to be transported to heaven. They believed it so strongly that they braved a storm to get here. The mine, Pentecost assured them, was the appointed place. He needed this cavern. It was the only way he could kill everyone at once.'

'How?' Amanda insisted. 'Poison? Was there enough food or water for him to poison all two hundred and seventeen of them? How could he have poisoned it without them noticing?'

'Not in food or water.'

'If he didn't shoot them, I don't see how he could have killed so many people at once.'

'Arsenic is an interesting substance. When heated, it doesn't liquefy but instead transforms directly into a gas.'

'Pentecost *gassed* them?'

'It smells like garlic. It came from a sealed chamber with hidden air vents, so they couldn't stop it from filling the mine. After Pentecost started the fire that heated the arsenic and released the gas, he went outside and locked the entrance to the mine. Back then, the buildings at the bottom of the slope were intact. He waited out the storm in one of them. Then he opened the door to the mine and let a ventilation shaft dissipate the gas. Later, he arranged the tableaux. He wanted the Sepulcher of Worldly Desires to be a lesson to the future. When he fulfilled his mission, he arranged his own tableau, then poisoned himself, and went to what he believed was heaven. As you noted earlier, mines and caves don't have many insects and microbes. Along with the cold, that's one reason the bodies were mummified. But this mine did have *some* insects. The reason those few insects couldn't do their work is that the arsenic on the bodies killed them.'

Balenger surveyed the tableaux in disgust. 'While I was on my way here, you told me the Sepulcher would show me the meaning of life. I don't see what that is, unless the truth is that everyone dies.'

'But not us,' Amanda emphasized. 'At least, not this evening. We found the Sepulcher before midnight. We won! We get to leave!'

The Game Master didn't respond to her statement but instead told Balenger, 'The meaning of life, the hell of it, is that people believe the ideas in their minds. Worse, they act on those ideas. Consider the great mass murderers of the previous century. Hitler. Stalin. Pol Pot. Millions and millions of people died because of them. Did those men consider themselves insane? Hardly. They believed that the agony they caused was worth the result of implementing their visions. The ancients thought that the sky was a dome with holes through which celestial light glowed. That was their reality. Later, people believed that the sun revolved around the earth, which they thought was the center of the universe. *That* was considered reality. Then Copernicus argued that the earth revolved around the sun and that the sun was the center of the universe. *That* became reality. Reality is in our minds. How else can anyone explain what happened in this cavern? Reverend Pentecost and Jim Jones and the Order of the Solar Temple and the Heaven's Gate group and the Movement for the Restoration of the Ten

Commandments of God. Their thoughts controlled their perceptions. A spaceship hiding behind the comet Hale–Bopp? Hey, if you can think it, it's real. Poison two hundred and seventeen people so they can be a lesson to the future? For Pentecost, that was the most obvious idea imaginable. "We create our own reality," an aide to the second President Bush once said. The truth of the Sepulcher of Worldly Desires is that ideas control everything, and all of it is virtual.'

'Which means that *your* idea isn't any better than anyone else's!' Balenger's voice rose in outrage. '*Your* thinking is as flawed as Pentecost's. So is your game. But now it's over! We won! We're leaving!'

The Game Master didn't reply.

Balenger motioned for Amanda to turn the light toward the exit. They stepped toward the other chamber, in which Reverend Pentecost had stood for more than a hundred years, waiting to greet the future.

Balenger felt the punch of a shock wave. His muscles compacted as the rumble of an explosion reached him. The walls trembled. Rocks fell. He almost lost his balance.

'No!' he shouted as the reverberation lessened. He and Amanda ran to the tunnel, but thick dust blocked their way. Coughing, they staggered back.

Amanda spun, looking for a camera. 'You son of a bitch, you told us you didn't lie! You swore you never created a dishonest game! You promised we could leave if we won!'

The Game Master remained silent.

Gradually, the dust settled. Balenger and Amanda went cautiously forward, aiming the flashlight toward the continuation of the tunnel. They came to where they'd left Ray's body. A barrier of fallen rocks now covered him.

'Jonathan must have detonated Ray's GPS receiver,' Balenger said.

'Don't call me Jonathan,' the voice ordered.

'Why not? You're not playing by the rules any more. Why the hell should we call you the Game Master?'

'Who said the game is over?'

Balenger and Amanda studied each other in the flashlight's glare.

'I don't know how long the batteries will last. Did you bring others?' Amanda asked.

'No.'

After a long, desperate silence, Amanda said, 'Maybe we can make torches from the clothes in the Sepulcher.' She tried to sound optimistic, but her voice dropped. 'Bad idea. The flames might ignite combustible gas.'

Balenger grasped at a possibility. 'If there was gas, wouldn't it have overpowered us by now? Wouldn't the explosion have set it off?'

'Maybe. But now that I think of it, the flames from the torches would use the oxygen in here. We'd suffocate faster than if we waited in the dark.'

Her voice became still.

A growl replaced it. As Balenger and Amanda

whirled, the flashlight revealed the two dogs that had stalked Balenger from the creek. They seemed larger. The light made their eyes red. Saliva dripped from their teeth. My God, they followed us inside, Balenger thought.

Snarling, the dogs came forward. Balenger raised the gun, but immediately, they reacted to it. Before he could shoot, they turned and raced into the darkness.

'They're trapped in here with us. They don't have anything else to eat. When this flashlight goes out . . .' Amanda couldn't finish her sentence.

'Yeah, it's getting harder to keep a positive attitude.' Balenger kept aiming toward the darkness.

'The lantern,' Amanda said.

'What about it?'

'If it's a bomb, we could use it to try and blow these rocks out of the way.' The flashlight in Amanda's hand wavered.

'Maybe. Or else the blast might collapse the tunnel.'

'What about the ventilation shaft the Game Master mentioned?'

'Yeah.' Balenger felt the start of hope. The dust in the flashlight beam seemed to drift, as if responding to a subtle draft.

They inched forward. Amanda shifted the flashlight from one side of the tunnel to the other. Balenger listened for sounds from the dogs. His mouth was dry. He and Amanda made a wide turn at the corner and faced the continuation of the tunnel. It was empty.

'The dogs must have gone into the Sepulcher,' Amanda said.

Aiming, Balenger neared the entrance to the first chamber. Amanda pointed the flashlight. Reverend Pentecost greeted them with his hand on the book on his chest.

Balenger approached the entrance to the Sepulcher. Amanda followed, leaving Pentecost in darkness. At once, a blur leapt from the cavern. Coming under the rifle, the dog struck Balenger's chest. As the rifle jerked up, Balenger's finger squeezed the trigger. The sounds of the shot and the ricochet were amplified by the closed space. Chunks of stone flew. The dog's weight shoved Balenger backward. They struck Pentecost, knocking over the board that supported him. Balenger landed on the mummy, feeling the crack of dry bones.

The dog clawed at Balenger's jumpsuit while its teeth snapped toward his throat. Balenger let go of the rifle and strained to push the dog away, but it clawed harder. He tried to squeeze its throat, but the dog snapped at his hands, saliva flying. Desperate, Balenger yanked out the knife clipped to his pocket. He pressed his thumb against a knob on the blade that allowed him to open it one-handed. He rammed it into the dog's side but hit a rib. The dog kept snapping at Balenger's throat. Striking again, Balenger plunged the knife under the ribs and sliced. Blood cascaded. The blade must have cut something vital. The dog shuddered against him, dying.

Balenger hurled it away and surged to his feet,

aiming toward the Sepulcher's entrance. His racing heart made him nauseous. He shouted, 'Watch out for the other dog!' Amanda spun, redirecting the flashlight.

The only sound was Balenger's frenzied breathing. He glanced down at Pentecost's corpse, the mummy crushed into fragments. A fetid odor invaded his nostrils.

'Did the dog bite you?' Amanda asked.

'I'd be surprised if it didn't.' The front of Balenger's jumpsuit was torn open. The clawed skin throbbed. Blood covered the cuts, some of it from the dog.

'Even if it didn't bite you, it dripped saliva. You'll need rabies shots,' Amanda told him.

'Which implies we'll get out of here. I like your optimism.' Balenger noticed that the dust the fight had raised was drifting away. 'Does it seem like air is coming from the Sepulcher?'

'Now that you mention it.'

'The ventilation shaft.'

They entered the Sepulcher.

The dog in here is bigger than the other, Balenger thought. If it attacks, it'll be harder to fight off.

He must have said it out loud, because Amanda responded, 'Well, if it's bigger, it'll be easier to see. That gives us an advantage.'

'Yeah, a tremendous advantage. The odds are in our favor. I don't know why I didn't realize that.' Balenger was amazed by her determination.

She waved the light back and forth, casting shadows

from the grotesque tableaux, searching for the dog. When Balenger grabbed dust from the floor and hurled it, the light showed that a subtle draft nudged it past him. They went forward, trying to locate the origin of the draft. All the while, Balenger listened for a snarl or a scrape of claws. He and Amanda passed a mummified man who leaned back in a chair, his hand on his groin.

They came to a wall and searched along it, finding a barrier of rubble.

'Looks like a cave-in,' Balenger said.

Amanda illuminated a hole at the top of the rubble. 'That's where the air's coming from.'

Uneasy, Balenger turned his back on the cavern and the dog. He set down the rifle and tried to climb the rubble to see what was beyond the hole, but the angle was too steep, and rocks slipped under him. The abrupt movement aggravated the pain of the claw marks on his chest.

'Do you think we can clear this by hand?' he asked.

'Before the batteries on the flashlight die?' Amanda shook her head. 'My hands are awfully raw. I'll work as hard as I can, but it won't be quick.'

'If we build a platform of rocks, we can stand on it and widen the hole at the top.' Wary of the dog, Balenger picked up a rock to start making the platform. Immediately, he paused. 'Do you smell something?'

'Like what?' Amanda stared toward the gap at the top of the rubble. 'Now I do. It smells like . . .'

'Garlic.' Balenger stepped back.

'Arsenic.' Amanda's voice shook.

As the smell of the gas intensified, Balenger coughed, sick to his stomach. They hurried across the cavern, scanning the tableaux, on guard against the dog. They reached the chamber where Reverend Pentecost no longer greeted his visitors.

Amanda stopped, forced to take a breath

Balenger tested the air. 'I don't smell the garlic here.'

'That'll change soon.' Amanda pointed the flashlight toward an area beyond Pentecost's shattered remains. It showed the lantern, where she'd set it earlier. 'If that thing's a bomb, maybe we can use it to blow away the rubble and get to the chamber. Then we can put out whatever's heating the arsenic.'

'The same problem as before. The explosion might bring down the roof,' Balenger said.

'I'd sooner die that way. At least we'll go out trying.'

Balenger stared at her with admiration. Mustering strength, he used his knife to cut a strip from Pentecost's coat.

'A fuse?' Amanda asked.

Balenger nodded. He unscrewed the cap to the lantern's fuel reservoir and shoved the strip of cloth into the opening. 'We'll need to cover this with rocks,' he said. 'How long can you hold your breath?'

'As long as it takes to do the job.'

Balenger gave the lantern to Amanda. He inhaled, exhaled, and inhaled again, drawing air deep into his lungs. Breath held, he raced into the cavern, ready to shoot if the dog attacked. Amanda charged behind him. They passed the tableaux and reached the wall of rubble. Balenger set down the gun and grabbed rock after rock, making a hole. His chest urged him to breathe. While Amanda directed the flashlight, he cleared more rocks. His lungs cramped, demanding air, but he kept working. When the hole was deep enough to hold the lantern, he set it inside and piled rocks over it, leaving a space for the fuse. Then he pulled out Ray's lighter and flicked its wheel.

Earlier, he and Amanda had worried that a flame would ignite combustible gas in the tunnel, but the explosion that sealed the mine would probably have set off that kind of gas, Balenger decided. Although 'probably' didn't fill him with confidence, there wasn't another choice – he was forced to take the risk. When the lighter flamed, he winced, anticipating an explosion. It didn't happen. He lit the strip of cloth, grabbed the rifle, and hurried with Amanda toward the adjacent chamber.

Pain in his lungs compelled him to breathe before he got there. The smell of garlic made his stomach turn. Sensing the flicker of flame on the cloth behind him, he reached the adjacent chamber, heard Amanda gasp, and pulled her to him, taking shelter around the corner.

'Put your hands over your ears!' he reminded her. 'Open your mouth!'

He held his breath again, desperate not to inhale the arsenic. *One, two, three.* Despite the pounding of his heart, time seemed to go slowly, like a video game in which the minute that elapsed was really two minutes in conventional time. *Four, five, six*.

Did the fuse go out? he wondered in a panic. Did the flame get smothered in the rocks? I don't know if I can hold my breath long enough to relight it.

Maybe the lantern isn't a bomb at all.

He was about to risk peering into the Sepulcher when a blast sent a concussion that felt like a punch. Dust and rocks fell from the roof. Despite Balenger's precautions, the roar caused an agonized ringing in his ears. A rumble shook the chamber. It's going to collapse, he thought, pulling Amanda closer. The rumble persisted, threatening to throw him to the floor. He held Amanda tight, leaning over her, determined to shelter her. Slowly, the vibration died. Rocks stopped falling. Forced to breathe, he tasted dust and garlic. Amanda turned the corner and scanned the flashlight into the Sepulcher.

A haze filled the cavern. Despite it, Balenger saw that the tableaux had been blown apart. A chaos of rags and wood chunks littered the floor. Mummies had turned into scattered bones. He and Amanda ran over them, again holding their breath, as the flashlight revealed an opening beyond the rubble. Balenger expected to see a sophisticated device heating the poison, but it was only a charcoal grill that was now overturned, remnants of glowing coals scattered across the floor. A yellow chunk of what Balenger assumed was arsenic lay next to them. He kicked it out of the way.

Reeling from the garlic smell, he found a door that the rubble had hidden. The explosion had blown it open, exposing a tunnel. A light glowed at its end. Taking Amanda's arm, he lurched along it, desperate to get away from the nauseating, lethal smell.

They reached a door, above which a light bulb shone. But the door wasn't wooden and gray with age. It was shiny metal.

Balenger reached for the knob, only to find that now it was Amanda who grabbed *his* hand.

'Don't,' she said.

She pulled a rubber glove from her jumpsuit, explaining, 'Where I woke up yesterday, the doors were electrified.'

She put on the glove and turned the knob, which moved freely. After pushing the door open, she dodged to the side so that Balenger could aim the rifle.

What they saw made them gape.

4

A huge, glowing area extended before them, giving off an electrical hum. The roof was vaulted stone, while to the left, numerous levels of metal shelves supported long rows of computer monitors. Every screen was illuminated. They showed the valley, the drained reservoir, the mine entrance, the tunnel, the demolished Sepulcher, and the glowing area in which Balenger and Amanda stood. As Balenger walked along the monitors, he saw one that displayed the viewpoint of the camera on his headset. Another monitor displayed the viewpoint from Amanda's headset, an image of Balenger standing in profile twenty feet away from her. The multiple levels of perception made him dizzy.

But what shocked him more than the expanse of the monitors and the ambitious scope of the surveillance was that none of the images on any of the countless screens had a conventional appearance. The valley, the reservoir, the mine entrance, the tunnel, the Sepulcher, the glowing control room, Balenger and Amanda – nothing was depicted in a so-called realistic way. Everything resembled a brightly colored cartoon.

'My God, we look like we're in a video game,' Amanda said.

'Welcome to *Scavenger*.' The voice's deep resonance filled their earphones.

Balenger turned to the right. There, numerous shelves supported a complex array of computer equipment that stretched for what might have been fifty yards. Above them, a glass wall provided a view of the monitors.

'You survived the final test,' the Game Master said. 'You proved yourself worthy.'

'For what, you lying piece of shit?' Balenger shouted. Bathed in the glow of the cartoon colors, he had a partial view of the area behind the glass wall above him. A raised chair was near the glass. Its arms were equipped with numerous buttons and levers. Its occupant was short and slight with wispy yellow hair and a tiny, wrinkled face that made Balenger think of a boy who had suddenly aged. Goggles reinforced the impression that he was a child.

'Frank!' Amanda yelled. 'This monitor! Look how he sees us!'

Balenger turned toward where she pointed. On a screen, he saw the image that the Game Master received through his goggles. It was from a high angle, from the glassed-in observation area. It showed Balenger and Amanda staring toward the monitor, on which was an image of them staring toward the monitor. Again Balenger's mind reeled. His lightheadedness was intensified because on this monitor too, he and Amanda were cartoons. It wasn't just the surveillance cameras that depicted everything as a graphic. The goggles the Game Master wore turned everything he saw into a scene from a video game. Worse, Amanda's swollen purple cheek and Balenger's broken nose looked inconsequential in the cartoon. The blood on his clawed chest and duct-taped knee appeared merely colorful.

'We're not cartoons!' Balenger screamed toward the boy-man in the control chair behind the glass wall.

He raised the Mini-14 and centered the holographic red dot on the tiny wrinkled face. When he fired, feeling the shock of the noise in the cavern, the bullet whacked against the glass but sent only a few specks flying. Balenger knew that most bullet-resistant glass could be defeated by placing five bullets in a five-inch circle. Again and again he pulled the trigger, shell cases arcing, bullets fragmenting against the glass, but except for minor starring, the shots had no effect.

Furious, he spun toward the monitors showing cartoon graphics of him and Amanda. He shot those monitors, destroying the video game images that depicted him shooting the monitors. Sparks flew, chunks of plastic erupting.

His rifle stopped firing. 'Amanda, there's another magazine in the outside flap of my knapsack!' Amanda handed it to him. He shoved it into place, released the bolt that slid a round into the firing chamber, and blew five more screens into pieces.

Monitors can be easily replaced, Balenger thought. He swung toward the shelves of computer equipment to inflict greater damage. As bullet after bullet blasted them apart, sparks turned into smoke and flames. In a cascading reaction, numerous monitors stopped glowing.

He stalked toward metal stairs that led up to the observation room.

'Stop!' a voice pleaded.

But it didn't belong to the Game Master. The voice was a woman's. Balenger stopped in surprise. *Karen Bailey.*

She appeared at the bottom of the stairs. Cartoon

colors still radiated from some of the monitors. They contrasted with her drab clothes, similar to those Balenger had seen at the time capsule lecture. Her face looked plainer, her hair pulled back more severely.

'You won! Now get out of here! Leave!' she yelled.

'After everything you did to us?' Amanda shouted back. 'You expect us just to walk away?'

'I'm begging you, take your chance! Go! Through there!' Karen pointed urgently toward a metal door behind her. 'It'll lead you out!'

'Another trap!'

'No! You'll find an SUV!' Karen hurled car keys toward the door. They clattered on the stone floor.

'The vehicle's rigged with a bomb, is that it?' Balenger demanded.

'I'll prove it isn't! I'll get in first! I'll start it for you!'

'When we finish, we might let you do that!' Amanda yelled. 'At the moment, we've got business to take care of!'

'Leave *now*! Let him be!'

'Let him be? Hell, I'm going to kill him!' Balenger stepped forward.

'No!' Karen blocked the stairs. 'This is wrong! You weren't supposed to win!'

'We got that impression. Sorry to ruin your fun.'

'I never dreamed he'd allow anybody in here.'

'He didn't allow anything!' Amanda shouted. 'We got here on our own!'

The Game Master's booming voice filled the cavern.

'That's true. Their survival skills are better than I expected. They honestly surprised me. At the start, I told Amanda that that was all it took for salvation – to surprise me.'

'You want a surprise?' Balenger asked. 'Wait till I get up there.'

'If you kill him, he'll win!' Karen sounded desperate.

'What?'

'He'll *win*. How can it satisfy you to give him what he wants? He tricked *you* the same as he tricked *me*.'

'Tricked you?'

'If I'd known the truth about the game, I'd never have helped him! I only discovered its real purpose a while ago!'

'The truth about the game? That he's God and we exist only in his mind? That's not the truth! *This* is the truth!' Balenger fired three rounds. They blasted through several consoles, throwing up sparks and smoke.

He stormed in her direction.

'Stop!' Karen shouted, blocking the stairs.

'It's okay if he kills people, but it's not okay if he gets punished?'

'Not *this* way! He's insane! He belongs in a hospital!'

'Then why didn't you put him there earlier? You could have stopped this, but instead you helped! People died! I don't care what your stepfather did to the two of you! I don't care about the cubbyhole he sealed you in for three days!'

'You know about that?' Karen asked in shock.

'And how your mother abandoned you to a drunken pervert. That doesn't give you the right to—'

'His mother didn't abandon him.'

'What?'

'*I'm* his mother. I never abandoned him! I won't do it now!' Karen shouted.

The depth of her delusion almost made Balenger pity her. But what he and Amanda had endured shut out every emotion except rage.

'The cubbyhole was so small that we couldn't stretch out,' Karen said. 'In the dark, we heard him hammering nails, sealing the hatch. We shoved at the hatch, but it wouldn't move. We pounded our fists against it, but that didn't work either. There wasn't enough room for us to kick. The only air came from holes around the hatch's edge. We begged him to let us out, but he wouldn't do it. Three days without water or food. We sat in our shit and piss. The smell made me vomit. I was sure we were going to die, but I couldn't allow Jonathan to know how afraid I was. He started hyperventilating, and I warned him there was only enough air coming in for us to breathe slowly and calmly. I stroked his head. I told him how much I loved him. I put his hand on my chest so he could feel how slowly I was breathing. He whispered stories to me in the dark – about an imaginary world called Peregrine, where birds could think and talk and perform magic. We put ourselves in the minds of falcons and flew toward the clouds. We swooped and soared and glided over waterfalls. The cubbyhole disappeared. Later, I realized how delirious I must have been. The first game Jonathan created was about that world.'

Karen's eyes changed focus, as if she came back from another place. 'I took care of him from when he was born. The woman who abandoned him wasn't his mother. *I'm* the only mother he ever knew, the only person he ever loved. *He's* the only person *I* ever loved.'

'Get out of my way.'

Karen reached for something behind her. 'I won't let you hurt him. I won't let you hurt my son.'

'He's your *brother*.'

'No!' Karen screamed.

'Frank!' Amanda warned behind him.

Karen raised a weapon. Despite the failing light, Balenger recognized the shape of an assault rifle. He and Amanda dove to the side as bullets tore stones from the wall next to the door they'd come through. Karen wasn't able to control the weapon. Its barrel tugged upward, shooting above the door. Balenger stood, lined up the dot on his rifle's sight, and put two bullets into her head. She collapsed, the rifle clattering.

Balenger hurried along the smoking consoles. He reached the stairs, stepped over Karen's body, and charged up. A metal door was partially open, light glowing behind it. He kicked the door all the way open and faced the observation room, where the tiny Game Master sat in his spaceship-like chair, surrounded by controls. His goggles hid the expression in his eyes, but his wrinkled, child-sized face made him look pathetic.

'Well, what do you know? It's the damned Wizard of Oz,' Balenger said. 'The guy behind the curtain.'

'Does that mean you identify with Dorothy?' After the damage Balenger had inflicted on the computer array downstairs, the Game Master's voice-strengthening devices no longer functioned. He didn't sound like a news announcer any more. His voice was now a puny squeak. 'Perhaps that indicates sexual confusion. In games set on virtual worlds, half the male players choose roles that are female.'

Balenger raised the Mini-14.

'Dorothy's a disappointment,' the frail figure said. 'After the countless colorful wonders she finds in Oz, she can't wait to go back to her drab home in Kansas. She rejects the splendors of alternate reality. What a fool.'

Thinking of the blood that burst from Ortega's mouth after the wheelbarrow crushed him, Balenger aimed. 'Is that where you want me to send you – Oz? Or how about Sirius, where the Solar Temple bunch thought it was going? Or maybe you want to reach a flying saucer on the other side of a comet?'

'Any place is better than this. "The most painful state of being is remembering the future," ' the squeaky voice said.

Balenger paraphrased the rest of the quotation. 'Especially *your* future, which you're never going to have. Who's the guy who said Plato was wrong about everything being an illusion?'

'Aristotle.'

'Well, say hello to Aristotle.' Balenger put his finger on the rifle's trigger.

'It won't mean anything unless you know what you won.'

Thinking of how grievously Amanda had suffered and how near he'd come to losing her, Balenger yelled, 'We won our lives!'

'Not merely that,' the Game Master told him. 'After all the obstacles you overcame, you proved yourself worthy.'

'For what?'

'The right to kill God.'

'Kill God? What are you talking about?'

'Kill *me*.'

Balenger was stunned by the enormity of the concept.

'This is the only way it can happen,' the Game Master explained. 'With massive effort, a character needs to take control of the game when, in theory, only the creator has the power to control it. The character becomes so heroic, he defeats God.'

'You *want* me to kill you?' Balenger asked in disgust. 'Is that what your sister meant when she said she finally understood the real purpose of the game?'

'I need someone worthy,' the frail figure repeated. 'The Doomsday Vault.'

'What about it?'

'If conventional reality exists, the threats that make

the Doomsday Vault necessary show how badly the universe was conceived. Nuclear annihilation. Global warming. All the other possible nightmares. Better that the creator never invented anything. Even God despairs.'

'A suicide game,' Balenger said, appalled.

'Now I'll swoop and soar through infinity.'

Balenger remembered that Karen Bailey had used similar words. 'Like a falcon?'

The boy-man nodded. 'I heard Karen tell you about the cubbyhole.' He shuddered. 'Is she dead?'

'Yes.'

The Game Master was silent for a moment. When he resumed speaking, his puny voice shook. 'It was inevitable. When she learned how the game was designed to end, she refused to allow it. You needed to stop her. But she still exists in my mind. Now she too can soar and swoop through infinity.' Tears trickled from beneath the Game Master's goggles. 'She stayed with me during my entire six months in the hospital.'

Balenger remembered Professor Graham telling him about Jonathan Creed's breakdown.

'I was so determined to take games to their ultimate perfection, I concentrated so hard, that I went longer and longer without sleep, four days, five days, six days, and on the seventh day, my mind took me somewhere else.' He cringed. 'For half a year, I was catatonic. I didn't know it, but Karen sat next to me all that time, whispering my name, trying to bring me back. I never told her where I went.'

'Professor Graham said you called it the Bad Place.'

The puny figure nodded. 'It was unspeakable. For those six months, my mind was trapped in the cubbyhole.'

Balenger realized that he was holding his breath. The nightmare implied in the reference to the cubbyhole struck him dumb.

'I sat scrunched in the dark, terrified, no food or water, the stench of my shit suffocating me. But this time, I was alone. I didn't have Karen to stroke my head and tell me she loved me. I tried to convince myself that the cubbyhole wasn't real. But how could I know the difference? My cramped body and the darkness and the hunger and thirst felt real. My fear was real. The shit was real. I told myself that I could concentrate on anything I wanted, and if I did it hard enough, that would become real. So I concentrated on Karen. I imagined her whispering my name. Soon, far away in the darkness, I heard her faint voice pleading "Jonathan." I yelled. Her voice got stronger, calling my name, and my mind went to her. I woke up in the hospital with her holding me.' More tears trickled under his goggles. 'But of course, that wasn't real either. I never left that cubbyhole. All this is another game in my mind. I never left that cubbyhole the first time. I'm still a boy sealed in that cubbyhole, trapped in my mind in that cubbyhole. Pull the trigger.'

The anguish in what Balenger had just heard overwhelmed him.

'Think of how much Amanda suffered because of me,' the Game Master said. 'Punish me. Punish God. "I'd strike the sun if it insulted me." Where's that quotation from, Amanda?'

'*Moby Dick*,' she answered. 'Ahab chases the white whale around the world. But Ahab thinks everything's an illusion created by God. Basically, he's chasing God Himself.'

'You don't disappoint me. Go ahead,' the frail figure told Balenger. 'You have my permission. Destroy your creator. Strike the sun.'

Balenger couldn't move.

'What are you waiting for?'

Balenger became conscious of his paralyzed finger on the trigger.

' "Myself am hell." Where's *that* from, Amanda?' the Game Master asked, his features impossible to read because of his goggles.

'*Paradise Lost*. Lucifer describes what it feels like to be banished from God.'

'Suppose God's in His own hell. Do it!' he ordered Balenger.

'And reward you?'

'Kill me!'

'You identified with me in the game. You told me I'm your substitute. Your avatar. I'm you.'

'Tall and strong. God in bodily form.'

'If I shoot you, it'll be like you're shooting yourself. I won't do it.'

The Game Master tried to sit straighter, to seem larger. 'You defy me?'

'If you want to commit suicide, have the guts to do it yourself. Otherwise I'll get an ambulance up here. They'll take you to an asylum.'

'You *betray* me?'

'They'll put you in a padded room, a different version of the cubbyhole, and give you a *real* taste of hell.'

'No,' Amanda told Balenger. 'He needs to pay. But he also needs help.'

'The only help I need is what you're holding in your hands,' the boy-man told Balenger.

'No.' Balenger lowered the rifle.

'Like Lucifer and Adam, you disobey me.' The Game Master considered Balenger. Although goggles hid his eyes, Balenger felt the pain behind them. 'You have one last chance to change your mind.'

Balenger didn't reply.

'In that case,' the tiny figure said at last.

He reached for a button.

'Hey.' Instinct made Balenger try to stop him. 'What are you doing?'

'We'll *all* go to hell.' The tiny figure pressed the button.

Balenger felt a spark of apprehension speed along his nerves. '*What's that button?*'

'You proved you're not worthy.'

'What do you mean, we'll *all* go to hell? What did you just do?'

'Have the courage to end it myself? Very well. If you won't accept your destiny, I'll finish the game for you.'

With mounting terror, Balenger stared at the button.

'In a minute,' the Game Master said, 'the world ends the way it started.'

Almost every remaining light went out. The only illumination was on a console before the Game Master's chair: a digital timer whose red numbers counted down from sixty.

'With a bang,' the Game Master said.

'You son of a bitch, you're going to blow this place up?'

'The game failed. So did the universe,' the puny voice said in the darkness.

Amanda turned on the flashlight, but its illumination was weak, its batteries failing. Balenger groped in his knapsack and raised the night-vision binoculars. He saw a green-tinted version of the boy-man sitting in his game chair, staring through goggles toward the timer. Toward infinity. The spectral green made him look like something in a video game.

'Fifty seconds,' the Game Master said.

It seemed impossible that only ten seconds had elapsed, but Balenger didn't have a chance to think about that. Turning to Amanda's green-tinted figure, he yelled, 'Grab my arm!'

His wounds were in agony as he led her down the stairs. At the bottom, they stepped over Karen Bailey's corpse, the green tint of the binoculars making her blood seem unreal. They raced toward the metal door beyond her.

'Forty seconds!' the squeaky voice yelled from the observation room.

Again, the countdown didn't seem right. Balenger felt that it took longer than ten seconds for them to get down the stairs and reach the door.

Amanda used the rubber glove to turn the knob.

The door wouldn't open.

Something growled behind Balenger. Startled, he realized that the remaining dog had entered through the open door on the opposite side of the cavern. Ten feet away, its eyes – now tinted green – blazed at him.

'Thirty-five seconds!'

Impossible, Balenger thought. So much couldn't have happened in so little time.

'Game Master!' Amanda yelled. 'God keeps His word!'

Balenger understood what she was trying. 'Yes, prove your game's honest!' he shouted.

'Thirty-four seconds!'

'Open the door!' Amanda insisted. 'We found the Sepulcher. You swore that's all we'd need to win. But now you changed the rules!'

Silence lengthened, moments passing.

'Show us God isn't a liar!'

The dog snarled.

Abruptly, the door buzzed, the lock thumping, the Game Master freeing it.

Frantic, Amanda twisted the knob. As she opened the door, the dog attacked. Or seemed to. Guessing that the panicked animal's motive was to escape, Balenger pushed Amanda down. He felt the dog leap over them and race into darkness. Then he and Amanda charged through.

They found themselves in another tunnel. Hurrying along, Balenger felt that surely the remaining time had elapsed. The tunnel seemed to extend for ever. Running, he silently counted *seven, six, five, four* and waited for the explosion's impact. *Three, two, one*. But nothing happened. His night-vision binoculars showed a lighter shade of green in the area ahead as the darkness of the tunnel changed to the darkness of the valley. He ignored the pain in his knee and forced himself to run harder.

The clatter of their footsteps no longer echoed. Leaving the tunnel, feeling open air around him, Balenger heard Amanda next to him and suddenly was weightless. The roar of an explosion lifted him off his feet. He landed heavily and rolled down an incline. Unlike the blighted area in front of the mine, the slope here was covered with grass. His breath was knocked out of him. He kept tumbling and suddenly jolted to a stop. Amanda hit beside him, moaning. Rocks pelted the grass. One struck Balenger's shoulder. Agonized, he crawled toward Amanda.

'Are you hurt?' he managed to ask.

'Everywhere,' she answered weakly. 'But I think I'm going to live.'

He'd lost the rifle and the binoculars. In the glow of a three-quarter moon, he turned and saw dust and smoke spewing from the tunnel above him.

'Server down. Game over,' he murmured.

'But *is* it?' Amanda's voice was plaintive. 'How will we ever know if the game truly ended?'

Balenger didn't have an answer. Motion attracted his attention, the dog racing along a moonlit ridge.

Amanda collapsed next to him. 'The Game Master kept his word. He let us go. He proved he wasn't a liar.'

'God tried to redeem Himself,' Balenger agreed.

He trembled.

So did Amanda. 'What's supposed to happen next? Do you think Karen Bailey was telling the truth when she said there was a car?'

'Would you trust it?' he asked.

'No. An exploding car is one way to end a video game.'

'The alternative is to shrivel like Pac-Man.' Balenger thought of something. 'Or like the townspeople in the cave. One thing the Game Master taught me is that a lot of video games can never be won. The player always dies.'

'Yes, everyone dies. But not tonight,' Amanda said. 'Tonight, we won. In the cave, when he counted down, the minute seemed to take longer than usual.'

Balenger realized what must have happened. 'The countdown was in video game time. One minute in *his* reality took two minutes in ours.'

The thought made them silent. In the distance, the dog howled.

'Why did he give us that chance?' Amanda wondered.

'Maybe he didn't intend to give us a chance,' Balenger said. 'Maybe the only time he knew was virtual.'

'Or maybe he knew the difference, and the countdown was the final level of the game. "Time is the true scavenger," he told us. At the end of the obstacle race and the scavenger hunt, he gave us something precious: an extra minute of time.'

'Our bonus round.' Balenger had the feeling that, from now on, this would be the way he thought, as if he had never escaped, as if he were still in the game.

Amanda tried to sit up. 'We've got some walking to do.'

'After we rest a while.' Balenger hugged his chest, trying to subdue his tremors.

Amanda fell back. 'Yeah, a little rest is a good idea,' she admitted.

'It gives us a chance to plan our future.'

'No,' Amanda told him. 'Not the future.'

'I don't understand.'

'A time capsule's a message to the future that we open in the present to learn about the past, right?' she asked.

'That's what he said.'

'Well, the game made me realize that the future and the past aren't important. What matters is now.'

Balenger was reminded of Professor Graham. 'There's an elderly woman I met who learned the same thing from video games. I'll take you to see her. You'll like her. She's dying, but she says that the countless decisions and actions she makes in a video game cram each second and keep her in an eternal moment.'

'Yes,' Amanda said, 'I'd like to meet her.'

Balenger managed to smile. He peered up at the dazzling stars. 'They were right.'

'Who?'

'The ancients. The sky does look like a dome with holes poked into it. That's a celestial light glowing through.'

'Everything exists in God's imagination,' Amanda said.

Balenger touched her arm. '*You're* not imaginary.'

'You're not, either.' Amanda reached for his hand. 'Thank God.'

AUTHOR'S NOTE: WORLD ENOUGH AND TIME

When it comes to ideas for novels, I'm a packrat. My office shelves are crammed with file folders dating back several decades. Scribbled summaries of radio reports and TV interviews are bundled with yellowing pages ripped from magazines and newspapers. Stacks of them. Any time something grabs my interest, a part of my imagination wonders why. The theory is that if a topic catches my attention, maybe it will catch the attention of my readers. Over the years, I put together so many files that I never had time to organize them into categories, let alone develop their contents into novels.

On occasion, curiosity makes me explore them. With great expectation, I put some on the floor, blow away dust, and read them. But nearly always, the brittle pages in my hands refer to issues and events that seemed important at the time but now are lifeless. The narrative themes and situations they suggest no longer speak to my imagination. Musty artifacts of the mind, they show me the gap of years between the person who put those fragments into file folders and the changed person who now reads them.

In rare instances, however, a topic clings to my imagination so insistently that I keep returning to it, trying to find a way to dramatize the emotions it arouses in me. For example, my previous novel, *Creepers*, was inspired by a *Los Angeles Times* article about urban explorers: history and architecture enthusiasts who infiltrate old buildings that have been sealed and abandoned for decades. The page sat under accumulating file folders, but it kept rising to the top of my imagination, and I couldn't help wondering why it insisted. The breakthrough came when I suddenly remembered an abandoned apartment building I explored when I was a child. I used it as an escape from unrelenting arguments between my mother and stepfather that left me afraid to remain at home. The memory of my fear and the need to retreat into the past made me want to write a novel in which urban explorers obsessed with the past discover that it no longer soothes but instead terrifies them.

A similar article that kept nagging at my subconscious led me to write *Scavenger*. In fact, it sat under accumulating file folders for eight years, silently shouting, until I finally surrendered. This time, the newspaper was the *New York Times*. The date was April

8, 1998, the place West New York, New Jersey. I love the off-balancing idea that a town called West New York is so far west that it's in the neighboring state of New Jersey. But for me, the contents of the article were far more unbalancing. 'From Time Capsule to Buried Treasure,' the title announced. 'Somewhere in West New York may be a slice of town life in 1948.'

I learned that as West New York planned celebrations for its hundredth anniversary, someone suggested burying a time capsule. 'Great idea,' everyone agreed. Then a retiree remembered that the same thing had been done for the town's fiftieth anniversary. Whatever happened to it? they wondered. Where was it buried? Searchers spread through the town. They pored through cobwebbed community ledgers and tracked down people old enough to have witnessed the 1948 semi-centennial. At last they found a possible answer in the town's library, where an out-of-print volume by a local historian referred to 'a copper box containing documents and souvenirs.'

That box supposedly was deposited under a bronze fire bell outside the town hall, but there the search ended in frustration, for the bell honored community firefighters who died while protecting West New York, and no one would sanction tampering with it. Moreover, the bell was attached to several tons of granite. Moving it would be costly and difficult, and what if, after desecrating the monument, the time capsule wasn't under it? In the end, nothing was done.

That must have been frustrating because, as the *New York Times* reporter indicated, the town had a powerful need to be inspired by a message from the glory days of fifty years earlier. Back in 1948, the area was prosperous, largely because of the New York Central Railroad and the products it transported from the local embroidery factories. But by 1998, the railroad and the factories were gone, and the streets were silent and bleak. In the context of a story about a misplaced past, I couldn't help noting that the reporter didn't receive a byline.

Moved in ways that I didn't understand, I added this article to my chaotic collection. I forgot it, remembered it, and forgot it again, but never for long. Finally, after eight years, I dug through a stack of files, took yet another look, and made a commitment to try to understand the article's hold on me by writing a novel that involves a time capsule. That the time capsule would be a hundred years old and that the hunt for the past would involve modern instruments such as global positioning satellite receivers, BlackBerry Internet capability, and holographic rifle sights hadn't yet occurred to me. I needed to do my customary research and learn everything I could about the subject.

My first step was to go to the World Wide Web. When researching my previous novel, *Creepers*, I typed 'urban explorers' into Google and was amazed to find over three hundred thousand hits. Now I did the same with 'time capsules.' Imagine my astonishment when I got over eighteen *million* hits. Clearly, this was a topic that obsessed a lot of other people, and with each discovery, my fascination intensified. I learned (as Professor Murdock explains in *Scavenger*) that although what we call time capsules are as old as history, the actual expression didn't exist until 1939, when the Westinghouse Corporation created a torpedo-shaped container and filled it with contemporary objects that its designers believed would be fascinating to the future. As gongs were struck, the capsule was buried in Flushing Meadows, New York, where a World's Fair was taking place. Intended to be opened five thousand years in the future, the capsule is still fifty feet underground but largely forgotten. If you have a GPS receiver like those used in *Scavenger*, you can insert the capsule's map coordinates and let a red needle guide you to the capsule's marker. But to learn those map coordinates, you need to find a copy of *The Book of the Record of the Time Capsule*. In 1939, copies were sent to every major library in the world, including that of the Dalai Lama. These days, however, locating that book requires a scavenger hunt of its own.

I learned that the Westinghouse time capsule was inspired by the eerily titled Crypt of Civilization, begun in 1936 at Oglethorpe University in Atlanta. Disturbed by the increasing Nazi domination of Europe, Oglethorpe's president believed that civilization was on the verge of collapse. To preserve what he could, he drained an indoor swimming pool and filled it with objects that he believed were essential to an understanding of 1930s culture. Among these is a copy of *Gone with the Wind*, an apt title inasmuch as the Crypt, which isn't scheduled to be opened for almost six thousand years, was nearly as forgotten as the Westinghouse capsule. If not for a student, Paul Hudson, who explored the basement of a campus building in 1970, the Crypt would have faded from memory. After his flashlight reflected off a stainless-steel door, the student asked questions that eventually led to the basement being turned into a public area, where a bookstore was established and people could pass the Crypt's sealed entrance every day. Eventually, Paul Hudson became Oglethorpe's registrar and the president of the International Time Capsulc Society.

I found this lore so fascinating that I couldn't stop telling friends about it. Usually, at this point, they said, 'The Crypt of Civilization? The International Time Capsule Society? You're making this up!' But I'm not. The Doomsday Vault in the Arctic Circle is real also, as is the Hall of Records under Mount Rushmore and the millions of copies of the ill-fated *ET* video game buried under concrete in the New Mexico desert. The weirdness wouldn't end. I learned about the town that buried seventeen time capsules and forgot all of them . . . and the college students who buried a capsule and then suffered a group memory blackout as if the event never occurred . . . and the town committee that buried a time capsule in honor of the community's centennial, only to die before any of them thought to make a record of where they had put it.

Who would have thought that there was a list of the most wanted time capsules, or that thousands of capsules have been misplaced, many more than have ever been found? Even if located, they often create a further mystery, for the containers frequently fail to keep out moisture and insects, with the result that these messages to the future that we open in the present to learn about the past are nothing but indecipherable scraps.

As I tried to understand my fascination with time capsules, I thought of the pride that motivates people to create them, the assumption that a particular moment is important enough to be frozen in time for the eyes of the future. Against the background of the Doomsday Vault, in which millions of agricultural seeds are supposedly protected from a global catastrophe, the optimism of time capsules astonishes me. But it's not just pride or optimism. As a character in *Scavenger* says, the obsessive thoroughness with which some capsules are prepared implies that the designers are afraid they'll be forgotten.

'World Enough And Time.' That's the title of the time capsule lecture Professor Murdock delivers in *Scavenger*. It's a quotation from Andrew Marvell's seventeenth-century poem, 'To His Coy Mistress.' The poem expresses the emotions of a young man who feels time speeding by and wants to persuade a lady friend to help him embrace life fully while they can. If we cut some lines and juxtapose others, the poem applies to one motivation for preserving time capsules.

Had we but world enough, and time . . .
But at my back I always hear
Time's winged chariot hurrying near;
And yonder all before us lie
Deserts of vast eternity.

Maybe it's not the future that prompts us to create time capsules. Maybe it's the pressure of time itself, the speed with which it passes, the awareness of our mortality. Prior to 1939, time capsules were called boxes and caskets: funereal metaphors. That same metaphor is in the title of the Crypt of Civilization. Could it be that the emotion implied in time capsules isn't hope, optimism, or even fear, but rather sorrow that everyone dies? Again, I'm reminded of Marvell's poem.

The grave's a fine and private place,
But none, I think, do there embrace.

A community buries what it sees as the ingredients for a golden moment, a distillation of their world. Many years later, another community digs up the capsule, if the capsule can be located. People gather eagerly around. 'What's the secret?' they want to know. 'What important message did the past want to send us?' They open the casket or the crypt or, if you prefer, the capsule, and find that the contents have decayed or that the objects are so quaint that they're meaningless. 'It's hard to believe they thought this stuff was important,' someone murmurs. In the end, that might be the message of every time capsule. From the long-dead past, they warn us that the here-and-now doesn't endure, that the objects around us aren't as important as we think, that what matters isn't the promise of the future but the value of each passing moment. As the Game Master notes in this novel, 'Time is the true scavenger.'

My stacks of file folders are time capsules, I suppose, representing the interests of the person I no longer am. So are my novels, preserving how I felt and thought in the past, just as novels by my favorite authors are time capsules, taking me back to Dickens's fog-enshrouded London or Edith Wharton's old New York or Ernest Hemingway's Paris in the 1920s. Those books not only transport me to the past that those authors experienced but also to *my* past and what it was like to experience those books for the first time.

Researching *Scavenger*, I walked through its Manhattan locations to verify physical details. When I reached Washington Square, I was certain I'd come to the wrong place. The last time I visited there was the mid-1980s. In those days, Washington Square's arch was covered with graffiti, while junkies bought drugs in a park so treeless that the buildings on the neighboring streets were clearly visible. But now those buildings are obscured by massive, sheltering trees beneath which parents play with their children while, in a park of their own, dogs scamper with their owners. Impressed by the gleam of the spotless arch, I was suddenly reminded that twenty whole years had passed, that I'd gotten older. But instead of depressing me, the moment felt alive with the fullness of my memories. Nothing passes as long as we remember it. Each of us is a time capsule.

RESOURCES

Except for the Sepulcher of Worldly Desires, every time capsule reference in *Scavenger* is factual. The most thoughtful essay on the subject is 'Capsule History,' by Lester A. Reingold (November, 1999). It can be found at *www.americanheritage.com*. Type the essay's title into the browser section and click on the link.

Another important source of time-capsule information is 'Tales of Future Past,' by David S. Zondy. Click the link to this essay at *www.davidszondy.com*, where you'll find photographs of the Westinghouse time capsule along with a list of its contents. But there's so much more at this site that you'll be dazzled by this trip to the future past.

As I indicate in my author's note, the Crypt of Civilization is real. Go to *www.oglethorpe.edu/about_us/crypt_of_civilization*. You'll find links to photographs of the Crypt and its contents. You'll also find information about the International Time Capsule

Society, the most wanted time capsules (including the *M*A*S*H* capsule), time capsule secrets, and other eye-opening topics.

The hidden chamber under Mount Rushmore is also real. Go to 'Black Hills Secrets' at *www.rosyinn.com/5100b19.htm*. Click the MORE link to see a photograph.

For information about geocaching and letterboxing, go to *www.geocaching.com* and *www.letterboxing.org*. These activities have become so popular that many resorts specializing in outdoor recreation now emphasize geocaching and letterboxing as much as they do horseback riding and swimming. The sites devoted to these games have information about caches in your neighborhood. I was amused to learn about a cache hidden a mile from my home in Santa Fe, New Mexico.

Scavenger is also about virtual reality and the metaphysics of video games. In *The Medium of the Video Game*, Mark J. P. Wolf's essays about space, time and narrative in video games were especially helpful. Steven L. Kent, Rochelle Slovin, Charles Bernstein, Rebecca R. Tews, and Ralph H. Baer (designer of the 1972 Magnavox Odyssey home video game system) also contributed fascinating essays. In addition, Kent wrote *The Ultimate History of Video Games*, the title of which says everything about it.

Smartbomb, by Heather Chaplin and Aaron Ruby, is a groundbreaking insider's look at the video gaming world. Among other things, it provides a fascinating analysis of God games and first-person shooter games. I thank my friend Janet Elder for telling me about that book and Steven Johnson's *Everything Bad Is Good for You*. Johnson's analysis of video games makes me believe the book's subtitle: *How Today's Popular Culture Is Actually Making Us Smarter*.

While many video games have pointless violent content that possibly desensitizes players to violence in their lives, there have been few violent events with proven links to video games. The best-documented example occurred in 1999 at Colorado's Columbine High School, where two students shot a teacher and twelve fellow students dead, then wounded twenty-four others before committing suicide. The shooters were obsessed with the violent video game *Doom*. But they were also reportedly the victims of relentless bullying that resulted in uncontrolled fury. Did the game fuel the rage, or was the game an outlet for the rage and a postponement of the violence? Because the boys shot themselves, there aren't any answers, but the issue is not as simple as some social commentators make it appear.

In *Scavenger*, Professor Graham notes that half the people in the world play video games. Although not all those games are violent, many are, and yet we haven't seen massive outbreaks of violence that seem caused by those games. Rather than fixate on the topic of violence, I think it's worth considering games from another perspective – in terms of their form instead of their content. The levels of difficulty along with the countless decisions and movements that cram each second of an action game arguably make a player's mind more agile and reflexes more responsive. The mental focus a game requires is a survival skill in a complex society. But it's a special kind of focus because it means concentrating on a lot of things in such rapid succession that they seem almost to occur simultaneously. A parallel with multitasking comes to mind. Some social critics disparage this as a form of channel surfing that leads to shallow understanding and limited attention span. But I agree with Steven Johnson's *Everything Bad Is Good for You* that it's possible for games to train our minds to concentrate on many things at once and perform multiple tasks well. In short, video games might help us experience a new way for our brains to function. If time capsules teach us that things are never what they used to be, video games show us that we keep changing, often in ways that we don't realize.

ABOUT THE AUTHOR

David Morrell is the award-winning author of *First Blood*, the novel in which Rambo was created. He was born in 1943 in Kitchener, Ontario, Canada. In 1960, at the age of seventeen, he became a fan of the classic television series *Route 66*, about two young men in a Corvette traveling the United States in search of America and themselves. The scripts by Stirling Silliphant so impressed Morrell that he decided to become a writer.

In 1966, the work of another writer (Hemingway scholar Philip Young) prompted Morrell to move to the United States, where he studied with Young at the Pennsylvania State University and received his MA and PhD in American literature. There, he also met the esteemed science-fiction writer William Tenn (real name Philip Klass), who taught Morrell the basics of fiction writing. The result was *First Blood*, a novel about a returned Vietnam veteran suffering from post-traumatic stress disorder who comes into conflict with a small-town police chief and fights his own version of the Vietnam War.

That 'father' of all modern action novels was published in 1972 while Morrell was a professor in the English department at the University of Iowa. He taught there from 1970 to 1986, simultaneously writing other novels, many of them international bestsellers, such as *The Brotherhood of the Rose* (the basis for a top-rated NBC miniseries). Eventually wearying of two professions, he gave up his tenure in order to write full time.

Shortly afterward, his fifteen-year-old son Matthew was diagnosed with a rare form of bone cancer and died in 1987, a loss that haunts not only Morrell's life but his work, as in his memoir about Matthew, *Fireflies*, and his novel *Desperate Measures*, whose main character has lost a son.

'The mild-mannered professor with the bloody-minded visions,' as one reviewer called him, Morrell is the author of twenty-nine books, including such high-action thrillers as *The Fifth Profession, Assumed Identity*, and *Extreme Denial* (set in Santa Fe, New Mexico, where he now lives with his wife, Donna). His *Lessons from a Lifetime of Writing* analyzes what he has learned during his more than thirty years as a writer. His previous novel, *Creepers*, appeared on several year's-best lists and received the distinguished Bram Stoker Award.

Morrell is the co-founder of the International Thriller Writers organization. Noted for his research, he is a graduate of the National Outdoor Leadership School for wilderness survival as well as the G. Gordon Liddy Academy of Corporate Security. He is also an honorary lifetime member of the Special Operations Association and the Association of Former Intelligence Officers. He has been trained in firearms, hostage negotiation, assuming identities, executive protection, and offensive-defensive driving, among numerous other action skills that he describes in his novels. With eighteen million copies in print, his work has been translated into twenty-six languages. Visit his website *www.davidmorrell.net.*